Praise for the work of Anne Kelleher . . .

The Ghost and Katie Coyle

"A lighthearted, tightly paced story with entertaining characters. Thoroughly enjoyable." —*Rendezvous*

"A spirited, otherworldly romance that . . . fans will find very entertaining. . . . Ms. Kelleher is rapidly ascending to the pinnacle of the supernatural romance field."
—*Under the Covers*

A Once and Future Love

"This is a wonderful, tender, poignant, and chivalrous tale that will captivate medieval fans everywhere."
—*Romantic Times*

"Anne Kelleher has written a beautiful story of timeless love. For a fascinating time-travel trip of your own, pick up *A Once and Future Love* and enmesh yourself in [an] engaging love story." —*Romance Industry Newsletter*

"A spectacular medieval romance with a time-traveling twist." —*Under the Covers*

The Highwayman

Anne Kelleher

JOVE BOOKS, NEW YORK

THE HIGHWAYMAN

A Jove Book / published by arrangement with
the author

PRINTING HISTORY
Jove edition / August 2001

All rights reserved.
Copyright © 2001 by Anne Kelleher.
This book, or parts thereof, may not be reproduced in any form
without permission.
For information address: The Berkley Publishing Group,
a division of Penguin Putnam Inc.,
375 Hudson Street, New York, New York 10014.

The Penguin Putnam Inc. World Wide Web site address is
www.penguinputnam.com

ISBN: 0-515-13114-8

A JOVE BOOK®
Jove Books are published by The Berkley Publishing Group,
a division of Penguin Putnam Inc.,
375 Hudson Street, New York, New York 10014.
JOVE and the "J" design
are trademarks belonging to Penguin Putnam Inc.

PRINTED IN THE UNITED STATES OF AMERICA

10 9 8 7 6 5 4 3 2 1

For my little Libby Jo, the littlest girl I know,
because she loves Ireland and will live there someday,
with love forever and ever . . . Mommy

Prologue

"*Just a moment,* for the love of Mary!" Lady Moira Fitzgerald struggled to her feet from her comfortable chair beside her cozy hearth, spilling the cat curled in her lap to the floor with a loud mrow of protest. The frantic knocking did not cease. She pulled her red shawl more snugly around her nightrobe and bustled across the smooth floor of her snug cottage. Her lone servant, Emma, peered around the doorway that led into the kitchen.

"Who could that be at this hour, my lady?" Emma asked, her round face pale beneath her frilled white nightcap. Her brown eyes were wide with alarm as Moira reached the door. "Don't open that until you know who it is."

Moira paused with her hand on the iron latch. "Who's there?"

"'Tis I, Mother," came the muffled response. "Let us in!"

"Dear Mother of God," Moira muttered as she fumbled with the latch. At last the door swung wide, and she stepped back from the blast of frigid night air to allow the two black-cloaked men to carry a third into the room. All three wore lengths of black silk wrapped around the upper halves of their faces, but she recognized her son and his agent at once beneath the disguise. "What's happened now, Neville?" Moira asked as she breathed a prayer of thanksgiving that

Neville was not the one slumped, eyes closed and mouth slack and bluish, in the other men's arms.

Her son did not immediately reply. He gestured with his head to the door as a bitter gust of autumn air swirled into the room. "Close that—Harrington, are the horses well out of sight?"

"Yes, my lord." The second man nodded in Moira's direction. "Beg your pardon for the disturbance, my lady."

"I knew there'd be trouble sooner or later," Moira said, eyeing her son's masked face. "What happened?"

"We were shot at, Mother. Merely a miscalculation in timing, nothing more," Neville said. "Where can we put Seamus?"

Moira's eyes narrowed and she bit back the retort that rose to her lips; instead she looked down once more at the slack face of the injured man. His threadbare clothing and stubbled cheek told her he was most likely one of the farmers who worked part of Neville's estates. But now was not the time to confront her son. "Upstairs," she answered as, at the front door, she peered out into the windy night. Gray clouds scudded across the sky and the fitful wind gusted through the trees. But beyond the stone wall that bordered the small cottage, nothing moved except the leaves swirling in the cold drafts. She shut the heavy door, picked up a brass candlestick, and gathered her nightrobe. "Carry him to the extra bedroom under the eaves." She glanced down at the ashen-faced man, who was still unconscious. "Emma, bring water and bandages. He looks as if he's lost a fair amount of blood."

With a few grunts and a muttered curse or two, the men managed to carry the wounded man up the narrow staircase to the small room beneath the eaves. They placed him on the bed. Neville straightened, rolling his cramped shoulders back in a stretch. "The bullet's in his shoulder. We knew he was hit, but he seemed all right until a few minutes ago. Then he just keeled over in the saddle."

"Well, no wonder," Moira said as she bent over the still figure. Deftly, she untied the black silk mask. Beneath it, the man lay like the dead, eyes closed, black stubble stark against bloodless cheeks, She forced the ragged and much-patched jacket back. It was dark with blood, and the linen shirt was soaked through with a spreading red stain. With gentle fingers, she made a quick examination and drew a deep breath. "This is bad, Neville. What's his name?"

"Seamus Malley. He's one of the farmers on Clonmore."

Moira tightened her lips and pushed her gray braid over her shoulder. "This is more than I can manage. The bullet's lodged somewhere in his shoulder—I've not the skill to remove it. He should have a doctor, but we can't risk that." She met Neville's eyes through the slits in the black fabric. There was only one thing to do. Turlough O'Donal, the local hedgemaster, was as skilled in healing as he was in Latin and Gaelic and the old Irish ways. He taught the children in secrecy by night, and tended to the ills of the farmers and their livestock by day. His pay was as often in squares of peat as it was in a bit of cheese or a bowl of milk. If he were ever caught teaching, the penalty could well be death. But dangerous as it was, Moira knew there was no choice but to summon him. "Someone will have to fetch the hedgemaster."

"I'll go," said Harrington. At a quick nod from Neville, he left the room, his booted feet skipping down the steps. The front door opened and shut once more with a bang.

"I'll make sure that door's latched," said Neville, as Emma entered the tiny room with a basket of clean linen rags and a bucket of steaming water.

"You do that," replied Moira. "I'll be down directly as soon as we see what's what here." Without another word, she turned her attention back to the man on the patchwork quilt. Presently she straightened and nodded at Emma. "That's as much as we dare do for now, Emma. Will you sit with him? I need to speak to my son."

"Of course, my lady." Emma met her mistress's eyes in a dark look but said nothing more. The relationship between the two women had long since passed the point of mistress and maid, and Moira knew Emma understood exactly why she needed to speak with her son.

With a deep sigh and bones that creaked nearly as loudly

as the steps, Moira went downstairs. Neville sat in the chair she'd abandoned, the cat curled at his feet, staring into the fire. He had removed his cloak, but not his mask, and the part of his face visible beneath it was as unreadable as a stone. His eyes flicked over to his mother as she paused at the base of the steps, but he did not move his position. "Will he live?"

"I can't say. He's lost a great deal of blood. The bullet's lodged deep—thank God he's still unconscious. When Turlough comes, we'll see what he can do." She crossed her arms and took a few steps closer. "What happened tonight?"

Neville shrugged. "Bad timing. They were waiting for us at the bridge. Harrington and I made it across, but Seamus was in the rear."

"Did anyone see you come here?"

Neville shook his head. "We circled up and around and came back down through the western hills." He looked over his shoulder at the door. "And I think it's safe to say no. Otherwise they'd be knocking on the door by this time."

Moira shook her head and sank down into the high-backed chair opposite Neville's on the other side of the fire. "When is this going to end, Neville?"

"How can it end, Mother, when times are so hard?" He reached inside his black coat and tossed a small leather pouch onto her lap. It fell with a jingle of coins, and a single gold guinea spilled out. "That's a fortune to these people, Mother, and you know it. There's enough money in there to keep Seamus's family for a year."

"And who's to keep them the next year when Seamus is dead and gone?" She picked up the guinea, put it back in the pouch, and tossed it back. He caught it deftly in midair. "This isn't a game you're playing at, Neville, Lives are at stake here—yours and all who follow you. When are you going to give up this masquerade? Surely you can see it's getting too dangerous—they were waiting for you, you said. By the bridge. And can't you see that it's only a matter of time before someone suspects that the outlaw Gentleman Niall and the young Earl of Clonmore are one and the same? What then?"

He drew a deep breath and stared into the fire, the flickering light of the orange flames playing across his chiseled mouth, his straight nose. In the shadowy light, he had the look of a young god. The thought of what lay hidden beneath the mask twisted at Moira's heart. "The people count on what we bring them, Mother. I couldn't help them any other way. Nor could you."

"Men like Seamus would be better off at home at night with their families than risking their necks pretending to be outlaws."

"Begging your pardon, Mother, but we're not pretending. The price on our heads is real enough." Neville chuckled softly.

"How can you joke about this? That man will likely die up there. And then who will provide for his family? Who will provide for anyone when you're swinging at the end of a hangman's rope?"

"Oh, they won't hang me, Mother. I'm a peer of the realm. They'll send me to the block."

Moira rose to her feet, her mouth pressed tightly together, arms folded across her chest. "What if it were you who'd been shot tonight? What physician could I call to come and treat you? Or are you content to leave your own life in the hands of a hedgemaster? Knowledgeable though he may be, he's no doctor, and you know it. It's time you stopped this charade before it gets any more dangerous."

Neville shrugged. "Perhaps. Or perhaps it's simply a matter of gaining control of a certain piece of property. Things have gotten especially difficult since Sir Oliver Wentworth took up residence in Kilmara. He's become great friends with the sheriff and the lieutenant governor."

"And what do you intend to do about that? How long do you think you can get away with leading this double life?"

Neville shook his head and stretched out his long legs. The firelight gleamed on the polished boots that fitted his legs to his thighs. He folded his hands together and tucked them under his chin. "Harrington's made a few inquiries on my behalf. I think there's a way to remove the thorn that is Sir Oliver once and for all."

"And what's that? Surely you don't possess enough to buy the property from him? Kilmara's one of the biggest estates in this part of the country."

"Sir Oliver's weakness is gambling. He's in debt to nearly everyone between here and Dublin. Harrington learned that he's just requested a transfer of funds from his bank in London—apparently he suffered heavy losses at the races."

"And what does that have to do with you?" asked Moira, narrowing her eyes as a dreadful suspicion began to fester.

"Sir William and Lady St. Denys request the honor of my presence—well, the presence of Edmund Neville Fitzgerald, third Earl of Clonmore—at a reception next Saturday evening. Would you care to accompany me? Sir Oliver's sure to be there in search of a rousing game of cards where he might recoup some of his losses."

Moira felt the blood drain from her face. "You can't be serious."

"I'd be delighted to have your company, Mother. You know that,"

"That's not what I mean and you know it. I washed my hands of the gentry long ago, and I have no intention of ever setting foot at another one of their soirees. You can't be serious about gambling for Kilmara."

"Never more so, Mother."

"Your father gambled away almost everything we had." Moira stared at her son in disbelief.

"It's essential I gain control of the Kilmara property, Mother. The Dublin road, not to mention the river, goes right through it."

"Nothing comes without a price, Neville. What will you risk on this game of chance? Surely it's not possible you've forgotten all we suffered—all you've suffered." Moira clutched the thick shawl closer about her shoulders as the flames snapped viciously in a sudden downdraft. A sharp, earthy scent hung heavy in the air of the snug cottage. The cat stretched and licked its paws before it settled down on the hearth rug once more. "What on earth gave you this idea?"

"Ever since Wentworth moved into Kilmara, it's become increasingly difficult for us. We've lost the access to the caves above the house and it's getting too dangerous to stable the horses at Clonmore." He ran a gloved hand across his chin. At thirty, he was tall and lean of body, his black hair combed straight back and held in a queue tied with a piece of thin black ribbon. It curled close about the nape of his neck, visible below the silk scarf that totally obscured the top half of his face. Restlessly, he rose to his feet and paced to the window, but his slight limp and the droop of his shoulders told Moira that he was exhausted. "What's the alternative? We can't burn him out of his house. That will only bring more soldiers. There's already too many soldiers scouring the countryside, asking questions, making life difficult for the people. I've heard Sir Oliver boast that he'll be the one to catch Gentleman Niall and his gang."

"All your work—all you've accomplished in the last two years with so little . . . Isn't there some other way?"

With a sudden movement, Neville turned on his heel and faced her. "What other way, Mother? Wentworth's robbing the tenants blind with his exorbitant rents. He's raised his rents to finance his gambling. And in the next month or two the Bishop will send the tithe money to London. That's a vast sum, Mother, and all of it collected on the backs of the people who work the land. The one thing you took care to teach me that I've never been able to forget was my responsibility to the land and the people who work it. Since Wentworth took up residence in Kilmara, we've lost our ready access not only to the Dublin road, but to the river as well. It's that as much as anything that's made everything so . . ." Here he hesitated. "So dangerous."

"This I understand. But your idea sounds like madness to me. Stop for a while. Let them think Gentleman Niall is retired. Or dead."

The word hung in the air, nearly tangible. Neville shrugged and parted the wooden shutters closed over the windows. He peered outside into the dark night before answering. "You're right, of course, Mother. There's always a risk."

At that, Moira sniffed. "What have you ever proposed that isn't? I think you should just let everything quiet down."

Neville smiled grimly. Outside, in the still night, an owl hooted. "I do intend to lie low, Mother, at least for a while. But you have to try and understand. There's more at stake here than Seamus's life."

Moira opened her mouth, then shut it without speaking.

"Wentworth's not popular anywhere with anyone," Neville continued. "You know that Kilmara came to him through his wife, who died early last year. From what I could discover, it was the dowager Lady Wentworth who sent him packing to the wilds of Ireland. I think she thought to keep him out of trouble. He has a daughter, about nineteen or twenty or so. Apparently his antics were becoming an embarrassment in London—interfering with the old lady's plans to find a suitable match for her granddaughter. So she sent him over here. From everything I could gather, Lady Wentworth may be getting on in years, but she's a most formidable woman."

"And now you think you can induce him to wager the property? And win it?" Moira looked up at her son. "Didn't your father's gambling bring us to the very edge of ruin?"

"Listen to me, Mother. The past is done and there's nothing we can do to change it. I'm not about to wager everything on a hand of cards. But I know Sir Oliver, and I know his weaknesses. And next month the Bishop of Clare will send the tithe money overland as far as Ennis and then ship it downriver to the sea. The hills above Kilmara House are riddled with caves—perfect to stable our horses and hide our supplies. It's getting far too risky to leave them stabled at Clonmore Castle. And there's another cave—one just above the river, near the bridge that leads into town. It would be the perfect place to lie in wait in order to—ah, intercept, shall we say?—the bishop's money train?"

"But, to gamble—what if you simply offered to buy the property—?"

Neville laughed softly. "Mother, I inherited a title. There wasn't much of a fortune attached to it, remember? And Kilmara's a grand house—much better than Clonmore Castle. Have you no wish to live your remaining days in comfort?"

"I'm quite comfortable enough right here, thank you. Of all your mad schemes, Neville, this is truly—"

Neville reached out and took his mother's hand. "Listen to me. If I didn't think it was necessary in the long run, I wouldn't do it. But it's better than burning the roof over Sir Oliver's head, which is what poor Seamus up there suggested we do. If I win, I will control all the property around Kilmara House. And once the road and the river and the bridge are ours, we'll be able to move far more freely than we ever have before. Surely you see that, Mother. And besides, what's one less Englishman in Ireland?"

"And what if you lose?"

A grin spread across Neville's face by slow degrees. "Ah, Mother. Ye of little faith. How can you doubt me so?"

Moira turned away, shaking her head, clutching the shawl closer about her throat. "It's not you I doubt, Neville, and that's the truth of it, as well you know. But there's always a risk, and you better than anyone should know what that can be. It's not a matter of simply losing money. And you know it."

"Then let's hope I've inherited my father's skill with the cards, and not his luck."

Moira raised her chin and stared at her tall son, her mouth a thin, disapproving line. "When you started this, you said it was a game. But it's not a game anymore, is it? It's taking over your life, Neville, and I want more for you than to see you shot down like a dog on a highway."

Before he could respond, there was a quick rap on the door. In two long strides, he crossed the room, lifted the latch, and opened the door. Harrington ushered in a short, burly man with white whiskers, who was wrapped against the weather in a shabby cloak. The man tugged his gray forelock to both Neville and Moira. "My lord, my lady."

"Master Turlough," said Neville. "Thank you for coming at this hour."

"Not much to do but come, my lord," Turlough replied with a grim-faced shrug. He slung the cloak off his shoulders as Moira stepped forward to take it. She handed it to Neville, and beckoned to the hedgemaster.

"This way, Master Turlough. Your patient's upstairs."

"Pray God I have the skill to save him," Turlough answered.

Moira stood back, allowing the hedgemaster to precede her up the steps. In the middle of the stairway she paused and leaned over the rail. Her forehead was creased with concern, but her eyes were soft. "Promise me you'll think long and hard before you do anything you might regret, Neville."

"Of course, Mother."

Moira paused, looking as though she'd like to say more, but only shook her head before following the hedgemaster up the steps.

Neville reached for a fresh sod from the neat stack beside the fire and placed it on the hearth. The earthy smell of the burning peat filled the cottage. He straightened slowly, faced Harrington, and spoke softly when his mother had disappeared. "I told her."

"Could that be a mistake, my lord?"

Neville shrugged. "I only told her about my intention to gamble for Kilmara. I didn't tell her that the men who shot poor Seamus weren't soldiers." He flexed his gloved hands. "Someone else has decided to set up shop in the district, Harrington. We've got to find out who it is, and eliminate them, because my mother's right. The situation is already far too dangerous. If I can acquire Kilmara, it'll give us a refuge. But if we must deal with rival outlaws—" He broke off abruptly as footsteps creaked on the floor above.

"I understand, my lord." Harrington spoke softly beneath the hiss of the flames. "We need not discuss it now."

Neville raised his hands and removed the black scarf he wore around his head. In the firelight, the scars across the right side of his face were softened, but his disfigurement was obvious. He looked at Harrington. "My father left me two things in addition to this face—a title, and the way around a deck of cards. My face is a liability, and the title's worth not much more than the parchment which granted it. Let's hope his third gift may be of some real use at last."

One

The light of a thousand beeswax candles reflected off the long mirrors lining the reception hall of Sir William and Lady St. Denys, where nearly a hundred people, many from as far away as Dublin, gathered. Ladies, gorgeously gowned in silks and satins of every hue, clustered along the walls, and, on the raised dais, musicians played sweetly while dancing couples bowed and swayed in the complicated steps of the minuet.

On a couch beside the hearth at the far end of the room, Susannah, Lady St. Denys, leaned away from the stentorious voice of her companion, Lady Jane Fitzbarth, the widow of Sir Roland Fitzbarth, who'd held the office of Sheriff before Sir William. "It's high time something was done about these outlaws," Lady Jane continued. A fine sheen of sweat beaded in tiny droplets across the widow's ample brow from the effort of making her point yet again. "If I didn't have a fine team and a brave coachman and two stout footmen, why, Susannah, m'dear, you know I love you as a daughter, but I would have given some deep thought to coming this evening. And I'm only speaking the truth." She raised her fan with a little flourish.

Beside her, Lady Susannah forced another sympathetic smile and managed to catch the eye of her husband, who was standing in the middle of a group of men not far from her couch. He paused in midsentence to acknowledge with a raised eyebrow his wife's infinitesimal gesture.

"Well, what I'd like to know," put in Mrs. Addison Hayes, the wife of Sir William's agent, "is what's to be done. Why, Mr. Hayes has told me the most shocking things—gentlemen robbed, ladies set upon, and—and dishonored."

"Raped, you mean," said Lady Jane, fanning herself vigorously. "No reason to beat about the bush, Mrs. Hayes. I've heard equally terrible things. Why, when I received Louisa's note today, I was quite beside myself. She's taken to her bed ever since they were set upon yesterday, and not that I blame her. But she was so looking forward to this evening, Susannah. Something simply must be done."

"And something will be done," said Sir William, who had correctly interpreted his wife's discreet signals and come to join her. He towered over the small group of ladies, resplendent in their burgundy satin and cream-colored lace. He was accompanied by a short, stout little man in bright red military dress, who unfortunately had reminded Lady Susannah of a bantam cock at their first introduction. It was an image she now found impossible to shake from her mind. She bit back a giggle as her husband put his hand on her shoulder, squeezed it briefly, then bowed to Lady Fitzbarth. "Lady Fitzbarth, may I present Colonel Jonathan Melville of Her Majesty's First Highland Guard? He's but just yesterday arrived from Dublin. I'm confident he's the man to rid us of our outlaw."

"William, you admit it's outrageous." Lady Susannah looked up at her husband gratefully, as he walked around the couch to take Lady Jane's hand.

"Now, now, my dear. Of course it's outrageous, but there's no reason to dwell on it. It was an unfortunate incident yesterday, nothing more. No real harm came to anyone, you know that. Now that Colonel Melville's here, the garrison will be reinforced. Isn't that so, Colonel?"

"Indeed, Sir William," replied Colonel Melville. He bowed from the waist with stiff precision. "It's an honor to meet you, ma'am," he said to Lady Jane. "Put your fears to rest. The highways of this district will be ours again quite soon. I give you my word on that."

"Colonel Melville," said Lady Jane, looking him up and down with a cocked head, clearly assessing the man, "we've heard of your successes in the south—was it not you who captured that notorious outlaw in Cork? Black Mike Gallagher?"

Colonel Melville's chest puffed noticeably. "I was instrumental in his apprehension, my lady. "

"Come, come, sir, you're too modest." Sir William clapped a firm hand on the other man's shoulder. "If that blackguard's head is on a pike in Dublin, 'twas you who put it there."

Colonel Melville stood up even straighter and Lady Susannah wondered if the buttons on his jacket might not burst. "I was extremely fortunate to outwit the outlaw on his own terms, Sir William."

"And you'll do the same for us, won't you, Colonel?" Mrs. Hayes asked breathlessly.

"Of course, ma'am. That's why I'm here."

"We'll be taking strict measures of reprisal against these ruffians," put in Sir William. "We'll see how these upstarts handle their homes being burnt to the ground. We'll go after them one by one—they won't be so difficult to manage once they see their families starving."

"Forgive me, Sir William," said a soft voice behind him. "But it would seem to me that the very reason the outlaws have taken to the highways is because their families are starving. Desperate men are willing to try desperate measures."

Sir William turned with a start, clearly taken aback. "Now, see here, sir—" He broke off when he recognized the tall speaker clad in severe dark blue, the only relief the snowy lace of his stock and cuffs and the white silk of the mask he wore around the upper half of his face. "Why, Clonmore, it's you."

"My lord of Clonmore!" Lady Susannah rose to her feet in an audible rustle of pink silk. She extended her hand to the tall man standing just behind her chair. "Forgive me—I didn't see you come in. Why were you not announced?" She craned her neck to see if the footman had abandoned his post by the door, but Neville took her hand and swiftly brought it to his lips as he bowed.

"The apology should be mine, my lady. Don't fret about your footman—he didn't announce me because I asked him not to."

Lady Susannah stared blankly for a moment, while Sir William indicated Colonel Melville. "Clonmore, may I present Colonel Jonathan Melville, our new garrison commander?"

Melville bowed, but his gaze was riveted on the white silk mask Neville wore around the upper part of his face, which left only his eyes visible. The white mask matched the frothy cascade of the stock he wore at his throat, but his costume of dark blue silk was relatively plain and unadorned. It was also impeccably tailored in order to hide the fact that one shoulder was just slightly higher than the other. "My lord. An honor, sir. But am I to infer from your remark that you harbor a certain sympathy for the renegades who plague our highways?"

Neville inclined his head toward the Colonel. The little man reminded him of a rooster. He watched his host and hostess out of the comer of his eye, but beneath the mask he wore, his face was unreadable. "Colonel Melville, the honor is mine. And no, sir, my sympathies are not at all with the outlaws. Something must be done to discourage the depredations. It's only my observation that honest men can easily enough turn to lives of thievery when deprived of an honest means of making a living." He bent his mouth in a bland smile, even as Melville's expression hardened.

"By God, sir, do you mean to imply that our policy to civilize the Irish savages is wrong?" Colonel Melville thrust his chin toward Neville belligerently, and the tension between the two men was palpable. From her place on the sofa, Lady Jane sniffed, and Mistress Hayes made a little sound.

Neville opened his mouth to reply, when Lady Susannah turned to the Colonel with a worried smile. "Now, Colonel, you must forgive my lord of Clonmore. Surely he doesn't mean that. He's a relative newcomer to our land—weren't you raised in London, my lord?"

Neville smiled down at Lady Susannah. It was foolish to express his views in any way at a gathering such as this. He should've known better than to bait this smug little bantam. He spread his hands and bowed once more. "I'm sure you know far more about the situation than I do, Colonel. As Lady Susannah says, I was raised in London, sir."

"I see," Melville replied shortly.

"And I'm most gratified to think that soon our roads will be safe for all of us to travel, now that you've arrived and our safety will be in your obviously most capable hands."

"Indeed, sir," replied Melville, looking taken aback by Neville's flowery speech. But Lady Jane declared, "Hear, hear," and Mrs. Hayes simpered, and the Colonel bowed to both ladies.

Neville looked down at the two women and bowed to each lady in turn. "Lady Fitzbarth," he murmured. "Mistress Hayes."

He was aware that more than a few of the other ladies within earshot glanced in his direction, and just as quickly turned away, to whisper behind raised fans. He ignored the stares and turned to address Sir William. "I received your invitation to the meeting of the landowners for Thursday next, Sir William. Will you inform us then of Colonel Melville's plans to apprehend our friend?"

Sir William spread his hands and turned to Colonel Melville. "Well, Melville?"

"The meeting is intended more to enlighten me, my lord," answered the Colonel. "In order to formulate a strategy to stop him, I must know as much about this outlaw—what does he call himself— Gentleman Niall?"

"Gentleman, indeed," interrupted Lady Jane. "The very idea. I'd wager his father was a mountebank and his mother was a whore."

Neville dropped his eyes to Lady Jane, as Mrs. Hayes tittered in agreement. "Doubtless, my lady," he murmured. "Do continue, Colonel."

"I intend to begin by gathering as much information as possible. Once I've determined a strategy, I shall more than likely call for another meeting, and at that point share as much information regarding my plans as I reasonably can. I may, after all, require your help. Have you been attacked, sir?" he asked, once again pinning Neville with his steely gaze.

"No," answered Neville quietly. "But then I seldom leave Clonmore Castle. I—I find it difficult at times to travel easily." He dropped his eyes.

Colonel Melville raised one eyebrow just a bit and ran his gaze over Neville from head to toe, clearly wanting to ask more, but said only, "Of course, my lord. I understand."

Suddenly Neville wanted nothing more than to escape the stuffy confines of the gathering. He thought about the crystalline air in the hills above Clonmore. The sooner he got this business over with, the better. He turned to Sir William. "If you would be so kind, Sir William, I've a mind for a hand of cards this evening. Is there a game to be had?"

"But, of course, man." Sir William clapped him on the shoulder. "Come right this way with me, sir. I'll set you up in a trice. Ladies, will you excuse us? Would you care to join us, Melville?"

"I would prefer, I think, to find some refreshment, Sir William. If you would excuse me?" The colonel bowed to the group and slipped away, as Sir William led Neville across the dance floor.

They had gone perhaps twenty paces when Mrs. Hayes leaned in close to her companions. "Such a shame he must wear that mask—he seems a fine figure of a man otherwise. What happened to him?"

Lady Susannah pursed her lips as she watched her husband lead Lord Clonmore to the withdrawing room off the reception hall, where a group of men were already deep into their games. "'Tis a bit of a mystery, really. He never speaks of it, of course—at least, not that I've ever heard. Jane, do you know the story?"

"He was burned," Lady Jane said. She spoke with the authority of one who knew. "Happened to him very young—

but Susannah's right. There is some mystery about what happened. And why it happened at all, I don't know, although his father, the late Earl, had a most vicious temper. Still, the idea that a man would burn his own son and heir seems quite preposterous. His mother took him off to London, and they weren't heard of for quite a long time."

"And he never set foot on Irish soil until his father was dead? How long has the father been dead?" Mrs. Hayes puckered her brow.

"A little over three years, actually," put in Lady Susannah. "But the Earl—the present Earl, I mean—was here before, you know, for a few years, when he was a young man of no more than sixteen or seventeen. The father was initially pleased to see him but then there was some falling out between father and son and the young lord packed his bags and went back to England, I believe. That's the story I got from Sir William, who says the young Earl joined the Navy after that. That limp of his is the result of a war injury of some sort—he was wounded at sea—at least that's the tale Sir William told me."

"And do you think it's true?" asked Mrs. Hayes.

"Well, some of it I know firsthand, Mrs. Hayes," replied Lady Jane. "The old Earl was a difficult man, to say the least—quite wild, really. And I met young Neville myself when he first came—he was seventeen, now that I recall, and he walked as well as any man. I remember the scandal in the neighborhood, for he took one of the tenants' daughters with him—" Lady Jane broke off and stared into the distance. "It was quite a surprise to everyone, really, because he was never one for the lassies. His face, I suppose. As unlike his father as one could imagine. They locked up their daughters when the old Earl rode through, let me tell you. Oh, he was one for the lassies then."

"Well, what happened to the girl?" asked Mrs. Hayes, clearly titillated.

Lady Jane shrugged. "I never heard. Have you, Susannah?"

"Nor I," said Lady Susannah. She cast a glance over the company with the eye of a practiced hostess. Everything seemed to be going quite well. This bit of gossip was a welcome respite after the rush of the preparations and the initial hour or two when most of the guests arrived. A few more minutes here by the hearth wouldn't hurt. Everyone seemed to be enjoying themselves. She turned back to her gossip with a clear conscience. "And then of course, you've heard about his mother, Mrs. Hayes?"

"That would be the dowager countess?" Mrs. Hayes raised her fan to her lips and puckered her brow. "I don't believe I've ever heard anyone speak of her? Is she still alive?"

"Oh, aye, she's alive. And well, as far as I've heard, which was quite a while ago, for as you say, Mrs. Hayes, no one ever speaks of her, although once they did—and plenty there was to say, I assure you. She turned her back on the likes of us years ago." Lady Jane spoke with a little sniff. "Oh, yes, there's a story there, all right."

"Then, pray, tell, tell." Mrs. Hayes leaned forward, fan fluttering. "Was there another man involved?"

At that, Lady Jane laughed heartily. "Far from it. It was shortly after the accident that nearly killed the young Earl. Lady Moira was a strong-minded young woman, and she'd had enough of her husband and his antics, I suppose. She sued for a divorce."

"Divorce!" Mrs. Hayes sat straight up.

Lady Jane nodded sagely. "Indeed, Mrs. Hayes. A divorce. I never heard the like of it, myself, nor did anyone else, but Lady Moira packed up young Neville and took him off to London as soon as he was able to travel. And never came back—until the old Earl died and young Neville came home to claim his title."

Mrs. Hayes slumped against the back of the chair, shaking her head. "My, my. Fancy that. A divorce. Was it granted?"

Lady Jane shook her head. "Not that I ever heard tell. She stayed in London with the boy. . . ." She trailed off and, pursing her mouth, looked out over the dancers with a disapproving stare. It must've killed her when he decided to come here and meet his father. But she had the last laugh, after all, for they had a falling out of their own, as you know."

"But why do you suppose she'll have nothing to do with polite society?"

Lady Jane gave a soft snort. "It's more a matter of polite society wanting nothing to do with her. The father never sent them any money. Lady Moira was forced to earn her keep—" Here she paused and raised one eyebrow significantly. "I've heard it said that she had quite a few protectors. She was really a beautiful woman in her day."

"Is that true," Lady Susannah demanded, "or only rumors?"

Lady Jane shrugged. "The only one who'd have a reason to know for sure is Lord Clonmore."

"And what does he say?" persisted Mistress Hayes.

Lady Susannah glanced over her shoulder at her guests once more and turned back to the women with a wry smile. "Lord Clonmore says very little about anything, my dear Mrs. Hayes. According to Sir William, he's raising excellent horses at Clonmore. But he attends very few functions such as this—you're more likely to meet him at a horse auction or at market day than at a house party or ball. And I've never thought it wise to pry too much. Lord Clonmore looks—" She paused and shook her head, for the idea that had occurred to her was preposterous, given his physical deformities.

"What?" asked Mrs. Hayes. "What on earth are you talking about?"

"I've spoken not twenty times to him," answered Lady Susannah. "And he's always been a perfect gentleman to me. But there's something about the way he looks at me from behind that mask he wears . . . something ferocious. I would not like to ask him anything I didn't think he'd want to tell me."

"Aye," added Lady Jane, once more raising her fan. "There's the look of a pirate about that one, that's for certain. He'll have no trouble finding himself a wife—though he may be a less than coveted prize on the marriage block. Mark my words, there're more than a few here who'd be delighted to pass off a younger daughter, perhaps, or an older one not quite so well dowered as she might be."

"Why, I could never think to see my daughter married to someone who can't even show his face in public," countered Mrs. Hayes.

"Humph," sniffed Lady Jane. "There'll be a wedding at Clonmore Castle by Easter—I'll wager on it."

"Now, really," responded Lady Susannah laughing, "who would take that wager? You're absolutely right. Someone is sure to offer a daughter—perhaps not the most attractive, but I'm sure my lord Neville will have no difficulty at all finding himself a wife. After all, it's not every day a landed earl is on the marriage market."

"Well, I'll take the wager," said Mrs. Hayes. "I don't think any miss here would go willingly with our lord Neville—landed earl or no. Who knows what that mask hides?"

"Ah," said Lady Jane, with the dismissive air of one safely widowed and well provided for. "All dogs—like cats—are gray at night."

"My lady!" said Mrs. Hayes, as Lady Susannah laughed and beckoned to one of the footmen who circulated through the crowd bearing tiny pastries on a tray.

"Well, we'll see, won't we, my dear?" Lady Jane smiled up at the young man who bent over her to offer her the tray. "Ah, I see that new cook you got from France is earning his keep." She popped a pastry into her mouth and took another. "Excellent," she said through a mouth full of sweetened cream. "Have one of these, Mrs. Hayes. It will sweeten the loss when you lose the wager."

The three ladies chuckled between themselves, and the conversation soon took another turn, but Lady Susannah sat in quiet bemusement, reconsidering the subject and assessing each of the young unmarried women who passed by in turn. Really, now that she thought of it, landed earl or not, Lord Neville was not likely to be considered a prize on the marriage market at all. In addition to his injuries, if such they truly were, his estate at Clonmore Castle was known to be a crumbling wreck of a place that had come to him heavily mortgaged by his father. The old Earl had been well known as a dissolute rake who'd kept his tenants in a state of terror and demanded the highest rents possible in order to feed his obsessions. It was known throughout the county that the dowager countess, Lady Moira, daughter of an ancient Irish house, had refused to return there upon her estranged husband's death. Now she lived somewhere on the estate, tucked away in a dower house that everyone whispered was not much bigger than a farmer's cottage. And she was never seen in polite society. What a pity, Lady Susannah thought, as she watched her husband stand aside to allow the Earl to precede him into the adjacent room. Neville Fitzgerald was still in many ways a fine figure of a man.

Neville knew they watched him as he limped away after Sir William. The boots he wore were specially made to exaggerate his slight impairment, ordered from as far away as London to prevent inquiries. It was one sure way to further his disguise. He told himself that he was used to the scrutiny, the stares, the whispers behind hands and fans, but each time he ventured into society, he was inevitably the object of speculation. His mother advised him to avoid such gatherings, but Neville refused to bow to social pressure. He had learned long ago that the only real way to cope with the scars left by his injuries, both from childhood and from his years at sea, was to meet the stares and the whispers with a stony nonchalance. And he had spent years and years learning to compensate—to fence and ride and shoot so well that anyone who might face him in a bout or on a horse quickly forgot that he wore a mask or limped.

On the contrary, he thought as he made his way through the crowd, smiling tightly and bowing here and there, if he had any reason to avoid the social crush it was because the profligate waste sickened him. The candles alone that lit the room cost more than the average tenant farmer's family had to live on in a year, he thought. And the gowns the women wore, fantastic creations embellished with pearls and lace and lavish needlework— matched only by the gorgeously embroidered coats and vests of the men—were probably worth more than a farmer would ever see in an entire lifetime.

"Take care what you say, Clonmore," said Sir William once they were safely out of earshot of the ladies. "The ladies are all in a tizzy over this outlaw. And to tell you the truth, although Colonel Melville has the highest of reputations, I'm half-tempted to call in a bounty hunter. This has gone on far too long—why it's nearly two years since Gentleman Niall first appeared."

"A bounty hunter?" Neville asked, careful not to allow any emotion to show on his face or in his voice.

"Aye. Sir Anthony Addams—you've heard of him, sir?"

"Indeed," Neville replied faintly as Sir William launched into a litany of Sir Anthony's successes. He thought of Seamus Malley and his wife, Maeve, who typified the hard-working people who worked long hours for little reward, only to hand over the fruits of most of their labors to the landlords. And now Sir William was about to call in a bounty hunter, a man with the reputation of apprehending outlaws and the clear resolve to carry through with it based on the size of the reward. He remembered meeting Sir Anthony once in Dublin. The man had seemed cordial enough, but the look in his pale gray eyes had chilled him to the marrow.

It was now doubly important that he win Kilmara, if there were to be any way at all that he could continue his fight to help the people. He tightened his shoulders as Sir William led him into the withdrawing room, where, predictably, Sir Oliver Wentworth sat at a table with three other men, his peacock-blue satin coat straining at the shoulders.

The men looked up as they approached, and Neville recognized with some surprise the round countenance and bald head of Hugh O'Neill, the Duke of Desmond, the one man among the peerage he regarded as a friend. The duke nodded a greeting. "Clonmore," he said, putting down his cards. "It's good to see you out and about."

"I'm glad to see you, as well, Desmond." He nodded at

Sir Oliver and the soberly dressed Addison Hayes, who rose to his feet.

"Will you take my place, my lord?" asked Hayes. "I promised my wife a dance, and I fear she will be out of sorts if I forget."

Sir Oliver laughed heartily. "Lost as much as you can bear, have you, Hayes?"

The other man spread his hands with a good-natured shrug. "As you say, Sir Oliver. The cards have not been lucky for me tonight."

"Will you join us, Clonmore?" asked the duke.

"What's the game?" asked Neville, as he nodded a greeting to the third man at the table, a man he recognized as a member of the Bishop's household but whose name he did not recall. The man glanced up at Neville, nodded, and murmured, "My lord of Clonmore."

"We were playing whist till we lost our fourth," replied Wentworth.

"Shall we try a hand or two of loo?" Neville suggested.

At that the Bishop's man raised his eyebrow and pushed away from the table. "Too rich a game for my blood, sirs."

"Forgive me," said Neville. "I did not mean to suggest—"

"Not at all, my lord," the bishop's man replied. "'Tis time I took some air—the hour grows late. I wish you all much luck." He rose to his feet and bowed.

"Well, Clonmore, loo it is, then." Wentworth shuffled the cards and nodded at the two vacant seats. "Have a chair."

"Good luck to you all, gentlemen," Sir William said as he followed the others out of the room.

Neville removed his coat and placed it carefully over the back of one of the vacant chairs. "Good luck to us all, gentlemen. Wentworth, will you deal?"

"With pleasure, my lord," said Sir Oliver with a chuckle. "Ante up, gentlemen."

The evening wore on. Neville played carefully with a quiet determination, watching as the small pile of coins before him grew and the one in front of Sir Oliver diminished. After an hour, the Duke folded his cards on the table and rose to his feet. "I think I've lost enough to you this evening, Clonmore. You've the devil's own luck tonight."

"Indeed," said Wentworth with a surly look.

"What about you, Wentworth?" asked Neville, knowing full well what Sir Oliver would say. "Are we done?"

"Oh, no, Clonmore, not yet." The knight raised his punch glass to his mouth and took a long drink. He set the glass down and wiped the back of his hand across his forehead. "I want the chance to win back some of that."

Neville sat back, his face set and bland. "If you're quite sure, Wentworth."

Desmond leaned across the table and touched Sir Oliver's shoulder. "Are you sure, sir? It might be better to cut your losses, now, Wentworth—you've already lost a mort of money."

Sir Oliver stared up at Desmond, his face working. He slapped the table with an open palm. "Let the Earl give me a chance to win."

Neville exchanged a long look with the Duke, who shrugged. "As you will, Wentworth. But I'm out." Desmond clapped a hand on Neville's shoulder. "Good seeing you again, Clonmore. Ride over and see me someday. I have a mare I'd like you to see." With a bow, he left the room, slipping through the cluster of men crowding the doorway.

Sir Oliver's forehead gleamed in the candlelight. "So, sir. I see your father taught you all his tricks, eh? You play like the son of the very devil himself." He chuckled darkly and leaned over the table, smiling belligerently. "Deal, if you will."

Neville pushed away from the table, feeling a pang of guilt. He had to give Sir Oliver the opportunity to end it. "Perhaps it would be better to stop now, Wentworth. My man of business will call on yours tomorrow, and—

"You mean you're not going to give me the opportunity to win it back, sir? That's hardly gentlemanly of you."

Neville glanced up. The three or four men who hung around the doorway shifted their positions, their interest clearly piqued, although their faces remained bland. Sir Oliver had suffered serious losses. He hesitated, thinking that in the long run it was more gentlemanly to withdraw. But honor and his need for Kilmara both demanded that he stay. "Sir Oliver—"

"Well, sir?" The knight's florid face flushed even darker. "This is between you and me, sir. What do you say?"

Neville drew a deep breath. He glanced over his shoulder. More men had gathered and the tension was growing palpable. An attack on his honor would leave him little choice but to duel. He noticed Harrington standing in the doorway. With a low sigh, he shrugged again. "As you will, Sir Oliver."

With a satisfied humph, Sir Oliver shuffled the cards. "One more hand, Clonmore. Your whole take against—" The knight paused.

"That's agreeable to me, sir, but against what?" asked Neville.

Sir Oliver looked at him with a cunning grin, which puzzled Neville. "Kilmara. I'll wager the property against your pot there—if I win, I've recouped my losses, and if you win, I'll be rid of a noose that's hung around my neck since my wife died."

Neville glanced at Harrington. He swallowed hard. Everything depended on his luck—and his skill. The knight's face was red with sweat, and trickles stained his cravat.

"Then deal, Sir Oliver."

The room was silent but for the slap of the cards as Sir Oliver laid each one on the felt-covered table. Neville picked up his cards, assessing his hand with an expressionless face. *It's how you play the hand you're dealt that matters, boy.* His father's voice seemed to echo through his mind. He glanced at Sir Oliver. Sir Oliver was staring down at his hand with a puckered frown. He looked up and met Neville's eyes. "Well, sir?"

Neville placed a single coin in the center. "Another, if you will, sir."

The game continued. Neville felt the eyes of the men who crowded the doorway boring into his back. Finally Neville looked up. "Call."

Sir Oliver laid the cards down on the table. The silence in the room was profound.

"I believe the game is mine, Sir Oliver."

The knight put his head back and began to laugh. "So it is, my lord, so it is."

Neville cocked his head, more than a little puzzled by the knight's reaction as Sir Oliver continued to laugh. Sir Oliver slammed his hand down on the table. "Damn me, Fitzgerald, but that's a fine one. You've won Kilmara, all right—a monstrous mass of a place if ever there were one—as well as a wife, sir."

At that Neville leaned forward over the gaming table. "I beg your pardon, Sir Oliver?"

"The house is entailed, man." Gales of laughter burst from Sir Oliver. "The house is entailed. It's m'daughter's dowry from her mother—a headstrong devil of a woman if ever there were one—and m'daughter's just like her. So you've not only won yourself a piece of land, Fitzgerald— you've won yourself a wife as well."

Harrington had come up behind them and now stood just to the side of Neville's chair. But Neville could only stare, speechless, first at the laughing knight, then at Harrington's stunned face.

An orange moon hung low in the midnight sky as the coach bounced and swayed over the rough road, the horses' hooves echoing in the stillness. The coachman pulled at the reins, and the coach slowed to a stop. Inside the coach, he could hear his passenger's heavy snores abruptly cease.

Sir Oliver peered out the window. "Is there a problem, driver?"

"Nay, m'lord. Just checking to make sure all's secure before we make a dash through the wood ahead."

The passenger's eyes followed the coachman's pointing whip. Ahead, the road disappeared beneath a dark stand of trees. "Why're we stopping?"

"'Tis Gentleman Niall's wood, m'lord. And it's always best to ride through either during the day or at a gallop so he can't overtake you."

"Me da' says 'tis not possible to outrun Gentleman Niall and his black demon of a horse," muttered the young footman. Despite his designation, he was just past his fourteenth birthday.

"Hush, Jem!"

"Gentleman Niall? Bah," scoffed Sir Oliver. "Let us away. I'd be in my bed by daybreak—I have a terrible pounding head."

With a gulp the coachman flapped the reins and the horses leapt forward, the coach swaying behind. A heavy thud inside told him that his passenger had tumbled to the floor, most likely passed out, as they rumbled along beneath the grasping branches forked out like fingers. The coachman bent low in his seat, cursing softly under his breath. Jem held on for dear life, clutching with white-knuckled fingers the narrow rail which encircled the pillion on three sides, as the horses pounded over the dark road.

"Look there," Jem muttered, and swallowed hard. Twin globes of light shone up ahead, casting an eerie glow in which dark shapes loomed.

The coachman raised his head. At least six riders waited for them in a row. The twin globes of light were made by the lanterns held aloft by the rider on each end. The coachman raised his whip to lash the horses harder, when a dark shape plummeted out of a tree like a huge crow, catching him around the neck. A second fell on Jem with a heavy thump. Jem cried out as the outlaw pushed him aside and he nearly tumbled from the coach. He managed to cling to the side for dear life as the rest of the dark riders closed around them.

The coach rumbled to a sudden, lurching stop, the horses pawing at the ground nervously.

"Beggin' yer pardon, me lord." The outlaw who'd shoved Jem aside gave him another push, and this time he fell back and landed on his side on the relatively soft forest floor. He lay stunned into stillness, trying to catch his breath. The coachman was pushed from the coach with a cry and landed on his shoulder next to Jem. Jem heard a loud crack as the coachman landed.

"Sweet Jesus, I think me shoulder's broke," he muttered

between clenched teeth. In the dim light, Jem could see a bloody wound at his temple and a shiny red swelling on his cheek. Jem made to move, but the coachman raised his hand and pressed his finger to his lips. He shook his head despite a grimace of pain. "Lie still, boy," he whispered.

The riders ignored them, clustering instead around the door of the coach. One yanked open the door. From inside the coach, the sound of snoring issued. There were loud guffaws from all the outlaws.

"Stand aside, lads." One of the riders, presumably the leader, dismounted. He walked over to the coach, where Sir Oliver lay snoring in blissful oblivion. He reached inside, dragged out the sleeping knight, and threw him on the ground, where he landed in a heap with a grunt. Sir Oliver struggled to sit up as the outlaws gathered around. "Where's yer purse, yer lordship?"

Sir Oliver looked around, groggy and bleary-eyed, squinting in the lantern light. "Huh? What? My purse? Don't carry a purse—have nothing left to put in it, anyway." He slumped back down on the ground. He fell flat on his back and lay face up to the heavens. He began to snore. Jem bit back a nervous guffaw, immediately feeling guilty. The situation would be funny if the outlaws didn't look so dangerous. The knight had lost every shred of dignity he'd ever possessed. Jem raised his head and squinted in the dark, trying to get a better look at the man who narrowed his eyes over the knight, stroking his chin. The two lanterns threw off barely adequate light, but it was enough for Jem to see that this man did not match the description of Gentleman Niall which was on every tongue. Where was the outlaw's famous mask? And he surely didn't sound like a gentleman. His brogue was thicker than Jem's own and the slightly different intonation told him the outlaw was not a native of these parts, as Gentleman Niall was rumored to be.

Finally, the leader drew back and his next words confused Jem even more. "No purse? Hm. Well. Look at those clothes, will ye? They should fetch us a fine price—have at him, boys.

A cold chill of fear swept down Jem's spine as the out-

laws bent to their task, snarling like a pack of dogs. There
was no way he could believe that this was Gentleman Niall's
famed band of polite outlaws, who'd never laid a hand on
anyone they'd ever stopped. He glanced at the coachman,
who was lying as still as death beside him. Pale pearls of
sweat laced his forehead and upper lip, and his breathing
was shallow and uneven. Jem made a slight move, and instantly the coachman opened his eyes. He shook his head
slightly at Jem.

Jem turned back in time to see that Sir Oliver had been
systematically stripped of his finery. The clothes were bundled into a heap and stuffed into a sack.

"Now, now, be careful with that," said the leader. He
aimed a kick at Sir Oliver's white gut, but the knight only
grunted in his stupor. He took the sack and swung up into
the saddle. Jem cowered beside the coachman, silently
screaming every prayer he'd ever learned as the outlaw's
gaze swept the scene.

"Take the horses?" one of the other outlaws asked.

The leader nodded. "Aye. Then let's be off."

The outlaws whooped once or twice and galloped away,
leaving Sir Oliver lying naked but for his linen. The coachman moaned softly in the cold dark. Jem lay gasping, his
heart pounding, the chill damp of the ground seeping
through his clothes. "I don't care what anyone says," he
muttered as the sound of hooves faded into the darkness.
"That was no gentleman."

Two

"*Depending upon the* property of the herb, it may be better to harvest it under a waxing or a waning moon. For example, this agrimony . . ." The older woman indicated the slender spikes of yellow flowers which clung to the high stalks of the plant. "As you know, it's very useful when treating coughs, or to poultice inflamed sores, and, being ruled by the planet Jupiter and the sign of Cancer, would be best harvested under the waxing moon. The flux of the force within the herb is at its highest then, and it will be most effective. But of course, if there's the need for it, don't wait, but gather it as ye may." The older woman paused in her lecture and looked at Elizabeth. "Do you understand, m'lady?"

Twenty-one-year-old Lady Elizabeth Wentworth nodded as she leaned forward to inspect the herb, unconsciously fingering the emerald locket she wore around her neck. At times she had to strain to understand what her grandmother's housekeeper was saying, for her Somerset accent was thick. But even her mother, an accomplished herbalist, had not had the breadth of knowledge that Mistress Maddy, as she was affectionately known, possessed. Elizabeth rubbed the agrimony leaf between her fingers. Soft and downy to the touch, it felt far more pleasant than its taste suggested. More times than she cared to remember, her mother had brewed her a tea of agrimony to stave off a troublesome cough.

"Here, miss, smell." Maddy broke off a leaf or two and crushed them between her fingers. She handed them to Elizabeth. "Smell."

Elizabeth raised the dark green mass to her nose and breathed deeply. The woodsy tang, green and spicy, filled her nostrils. How she loved the quiet hours spent among the herbs. The long afternoons spent weeding and clipping and pruning, gently nurturing each plant, while her mother taught her all she knew about their various uses, were her most cherished memories. How many times had her mother done the same, crushing a leaf between her long fingers, holding it to Elizabeth's nose, with the same soft admonition. She opened her eyes and smiled at Maddy.

How lucky that here, at her grandmother's Somerset retreat, there were the same sun-drenched beds of herbs, as well as someone who could teach her even more than her mother. She touched the locket once more. It had been a gift from her mother when she was twelve, and Elizabeth always associated it with her. Since her mother's death, she wore it always, for it made her feel as if her mother were still very close. Working among the herbs gave her the same feeling of connection with her mother, and fortunately, so long as Elizabeth wore gloves and carefully covered her neck and shoulders, her grandmother made no objection.

She took one more sniff, then let the crushed leaves fall to the ground. "But if one gathers the herb by day—"

"My lady! My lady!" The voice of her maid made Elizabeth look up in surprise. "There's a letter, my lady!" Molly, her maid since she was fourteen, burst into the garden, her cheeks flushed, her housecap askew.

"A letter for me, Molly?" Elizabeth brushed off her hands and removed her gloves. Who would write to her besides a few school friends, and the few notes she'd received from them had not roused this reaction in her maid. "From whom?"

Even Maddy stared in avid interest.

"Well, not exactly for you, my lady," Molly answered.

"But it's from your father, and your grandmother told me to fetch you at once."

"At once?" Elizabeth frowned and glanced at Maddy. "There's nothing wrong, I hope." Her parents' life together had been troubled by her father's profligate indulgences. He was fond of gaming, and periodically he won and lost tremendous sums. Her grandmother—his mother—disapproved of her son's activities and had done all she possibly could to control him while his wife lived. As soon as his wife died, her grandmother had packed him off to Ireland and immediately assumed care of Elizabeth.

She brushed off her fingers on the full-length smock she wore over her gown and, slipping it off, handed it to Maddy. "Oh, I hope there's no more trouble," she said as she started off with Molly. She automatically smoothed her simple day dress of blue-sprigged muslin, and hastily patted her honey-blonde hair into place, which was forever escaping its pins. She stood on tiptoe as they reached the house and peered anxiously at her reflection in the window. "Do I look all right, Molly? Grandmother hates it when my hair won't behave." She patted a stray curl into place. Her reflection stared back at her, a pale smudge in the dark glass, her features shadowy and indistinct. But the emerald locket glittered green at her throat, and she remembered how her mother had gazed so fondly at her when first she'd fastened it around her neck, and said, "It's just the same shade as your eyes, Elizabeth. See how green!" And her mother had held up her own looking glass. "See how green!"

Elizabeth sighed heavily and forced the thought of her mother from her mind. It seemed that random thoughts of her were always popping up whenever she least expected it. But now, it was some scrape of her father's she would have to hear about. She only hoped that whatever he'd done this time wouldn't prove too costly. She suppressed a little smile. Her father might well be everything her grandmother said he was, but life with him was never dull. She remembered how he'd taught her to shoot when she was twelve. She'd enjoyed the fuss her mother and grandmother had made, but once in a while, in the intervening years, he'd snuck away with her for a few hours and practiced firing at targets with her. "You never know when you'll be called upon to protect your honor, Lizzie," he'd say, with a twinkle in his eyes.

"You look fine, my lady," Molly said, tugging at her arm gently. "Now come. Your grandmother said to fetch you right away!" Molly led her through the house to her grandmother's sitting room.

Just outside the closed door Elizabeth paused to smooth her skirts once more. "Let's hope my father hasn't got himself into real trouble this time."

She found her grandmother seated in her favorite chair before a crackling fire, a small table placed to one side of her, her lap dog nestled at her feet. A folded letter was in her hands, which were folded on her black silk gown. She looked up as Elizabeth approached. Nearing seventy, her face still bore vestiges of the fabled beauty she had been. Her white hair was smoothed back from a face so finely boned even age could not diminish its inherent grace. Elizabeth had been flattered to hear how much she resembled the portrait of her grandmother as a young girl which hung in the dining room of the great house. Now, however, her grandmother's cheeks were pale, even beneath the light touch of rouge, and her mouth was compressed into a pinched line which told Elizabeth immediately that her grandmother was not pleased by whatever news the letter brought.

"Molly told me there was a letter from Father, Grandmother," said Elizabeth with a little curtsey.

Her grandmother heaved an audible sigh. "Indeed, child. Sit here with me for a moment."

A cold chill went down Elizabeth's back. Her father's relationship with his formidable mother was troubled, to say the least, for her father's profligate ways and his penchant for gambling, drink, horses, and women offended her grandmother's deeply ingrained sense of duty.

"What's wrong?" she asked as she sank down on the low stool her grandmother indicated. The little dog leapt to its feet, wagging its tail, and Elizabeth stroked its long silky ears with a trembling hand. "Father's—Father's not dead, is he?"

Her grandmother let out another long sigh. "No, child. Your father is as hale and hearty as ever. And I think you need have no fear on that score, for it's only the good who die young." She looked down at the letter in her lap and flicked it with what could only be characterized as contempt.

"Has he—has he lost more money?" Elizabeth tried to ask as delicately as possible. It had been an enormous row following a particularly spectacular loss on a horse race that had sent Sir Oliver packing off to Ireland, ostensibly to inspect the estate there left by her mother.

Her grandmother cleared her throat. "Not exactly."

"What is it, then, Grandmother? There must be some sort of trouble—you look very upset."

"I scarcely know what to feel, child. Let alone what to think. Your father writes the most extraordinary tale—and it concerns you." Her grandmother's dark eyes, so different from Elizabeth's, met hers with what could only be sympathy.

"Me?" A stronger chill went down her back, this one tinged with dark foreboding. Up to this point, he'd ignored her very existence since her mother's death, and the only other member of her immediate family, her brother, David, preferred to spend his time at Oxford trying to ignore her father's existence as well. Her father dismissed his son as "that parson."

"You understand, child, that a woman's duty is to marry." Her grandmother obviously chose her words with great care, and suddenly Elizabeth understood something of the nature of her father's letter.

"Of course, Grandmother." She leaned forward, her fingers twined in the dog's silky coat. "Has—has my father found someone he wishes me to marry?" She stared up at her grandmother, thinking furiously. One of the reasons her grandmother had insisted Sir Oliver absent himself from England was so that her grandmother would be free to arrange a suitable marriage for Elizabeth, since all her father's cronies were characterized by her grandmother as rogues and worse. Her brother, in fact, called her father by a few phrases Elizabeth herself was not permitted to use.

"Your father has found someone you must marry." Her grandmother sniffed and stared into the distance, her mouth so drawn her lips completely disappeared. "You have no choice. This—this person has won Kilmara."

"What?" Elizabeth rocked back on the stool, and the little dog whined, nuzzling closer as though it sensed her shock. Her fingers shook as she stroked its ears.

"It's quite extraordinary, really. I have already sent for Master Beauchamp, my solicitor. However, I am not certain that there is anything which can be done."

Elizabeth stared up at her grandmother helplessly, her mind churning. The fleeting fondness she'd felt for her father vanished like spring snow. He might as well have shot her, she thought, so carelessly had he altered her life with one stroke. "Surely—surely there must be some way—can't he offer money instead of the property?"

Her grandmother shrugged. "I have been thinking of that. But Kilmara is a very valuable property. It is worth far more in capital than I—or your father, for that matter—have resources. The value of an estate is not calculated in cash alone, my dear. It is the worth over time that determines its value. The rents alone from Kilmara—" Lady Frances broke off and shook her head.

Elizabeth swallowed hard. "Who—who is this person, Grandmother? Is he . . . someone you would consider suitable?"

Her grandmother opened the letter and scanned it quickly, one eyebrow raised. "He's an earl. The Earl of Clonmore, your father says, and very little else. I shall have Beauchamp make inquiries. Certainly I've never heard of him—most likely one of those wild Irish ruffians who aren't much better than—" She broke off at the stricken look on Elizabeth's face. "I'm sorry, child. Forgive me. I'm so distressed that your father would do such a thing as to gamble off your dowry—"

"You mean my father lost Kilmara in a game of chance?"

Lady Frances nodded her head. "That is exactly what I

mean. He wagered Kilmara—and when he lost it, you went with it."

Elizabeth rose to her feet, shaking. "He can't do this. I won't go. I won't be married off like a—like a piece of chattel—like something you can win or lose on the turn of a game—what does my father think I am?"

Lady Frances gazed at her granddaughter, her face soft with sympathy. "Your father says he's about thirty, set up well enough for a man of his age—whatever that means."

"Likely it means he has teeth, and hair growing out of his nose and his ears." Elizabeth blinked back tears. "I won't go, Grandmother. I absolutely refuse."

"Ah, child." Her grandmother shook her head with another heavy sigh. "Would that it were that easy, child. Would that it were that easy."

"My lady." James, the butler, stood in the doorway, hesitating, clearly stricken by the domestic upheaval.

Of course, thought Elizabeth, of course he knew. Distress was written all over her grandmother's face. If he didn't know the exact cause of it, he would soon enough.

"Yes, James?"

"Master Beauchamp, madam. He's just arrived."

"Well, send him in here, James. Bring some refreshment if you would. Would you like a cup of tea, my dear? It might settle you a bit."

Elizabeth threw her grandmother a sulky look and bit back the retort that rose to her lips. There was no point in antagonizing her grandmother. So far, she appeared to be on Elizabeth's side, but there was no doubt in Elizabeth's mind that Lady Frances would come down heavily on the side of duty and filial obedience if it were determined that nothing could be done to change matters. "Tea would be fine, Grandmother."

Her grandmother smiled. "Come, sit, my dear. There's nothing to be gained by fretting. We'll see what Beauchamp has to say. Surely if there's something that can be done, he'll know what to do."

Elizabeth sank down on the stool, the little dog nestling close. She wrapped an arm around it, more to reassure herself than to comfort it. James bowed and turned on his heel, and in only a few moments, the black-clad figure of Master Henry Beauchamp, her grandmother's solicitor, came striding into the room. He was dressed in black from head to toe, and his gray hair was clipped about his head as closely as a soldier's. There was something of the dandy in the cut of his garments, and Elizabeth noted that not only was his linen startlingly white, but the intricate embroidery at the cuffs and on the lapels of his jacket was of the finest quality.

"I came as quickly as I could, my lady," he said as he bent over Lady Frances's hand. "There's more trouble involving Sir Oliver?"

"No one knows better than you, Master Beauchamp, what a trial my son is to me," replied her grandmother. "Sit down, and read this letter if you will."

Master Beauchamp sat with a nod of greeting to Elizabeth, who huddled miserably with the dog at her grandmother's feet. How could this have happened? Had her father so little regard for her wishes that he would marry her off, sight unseen, to some person she'd never in her life laid eyes on? With a suppressed sigh, she watched Master Beauchamp read the letter.

He glanced up at her once, his eyebrows raised in surprise. Finally he folded the letter and handed it back to her grandmother. "A most unusual situation, my lady."

"Well, what do you think, Beauchamp?" Lady Frances demanded. "Is there a way out of it?"

Master Beauchamp drew a deep breath, looking visibly discomfited. "An earl is a suitable partner for the young lady, don't you think?"

"That's neither here nor there at the moment," snapped Lady Frances. "Is she legally obligated to marry him?"

Again, he hesitated. "It is not just a matter of law, my lady. There is a question of honor here as well. This is more than simply a dynastic arrangement, concerning the property as well as the young lady, of course. By wagering Kilmara, and losing it, Sir Oliver has incurred a debt of honor. A very significant debt, when one considers all the ramifications."

"But—but—but why must I marry anyone?" burst out Elizabeth. "I'm not responsible for my father's gambling."

"Well, no, my lady," answered Beauchamp, his face grim. "You aren't, and herein we see one of the reasons why gentlemen normally don't wager such things. Kilmara, as I am to understand it—and remember, I did handle your mother's will when it was probated to the court—is quite clearly your dowry, and it's entailed. In other words, Kilmara goes with you upon your marriage, and, well, whoever wishes to take possession of Kilmara must marry you."

"So that's it?" Elizabeth looked up at her grandmother while she cradled the lap dog, as if it could protect her from this unexpected twist of fate. "That's the final answer? I'm to be handed over part and parcel because of a gambling debt? I think I'd sooner be sold into slavery."

Both Beauchamp and Lady Frances looked shocked, and Elizabeth noticed the glance the two exchanged.

"Now, now, Elizabeth. Come, you're distraught. We know you don't mean—"

"Don't mean it?" Elizabeth stood up as the lap dog squirmed away, "I certainly do mean it. How can Father—"

Beauchamp spread his hands. "I would be willing to do all in my power, my lady. It's certainly worth a letter, with your permission, of course, Lady Wentworth."

Lady Frances nodded. "Indeed, Beauchamp. And . . ." She paused and gazed at Elizabeth with a thoughtful expression. "It may be worthwhile to find something out about this earl, as Oliver claims him to be. Certainly I've never heard of him. I can't have Elizabeth married off to some ruffian beneath her station, but if it should happen that his title is legitimate—"

"Grandmother, you can't mean—"

"Hush, child." Lady Frances turned and looked at her appraisingly. "You must, after all, marry someone. An earl is certainly far more than even I had hoped, given your father's reputation. But an Irish earl—given the fact that your dowry is, after all, in Ireland—" She broke off as Elizabeth leapt to her feet and ran out of the room. Lady Frances gazed after her with a sigh, then looked at Beauchamp.

Beauchamp raised one eyebrow. "Skittish, isn't she?"

Lady Wentworth sighed. "Well, she's had a shock. First a letter from my son, which we never anticipate without dread, and then this rather startling news . . . quite understandable really, although her manner just now was deplorable."

"Shall I see what I can discover, my lady?"

Lady Wentworth nodded, lips pursed. "Indeed, Beauchamp. But make sure you find out something about this Earl of Clonmore, or whatever he styles himself. My goal has been to make sure that young Elizabeth finds a suitable match. It may not be a terrible thing, if this should work itself out to both their advantage."

Beauchamp stood up and bowed. "As my lady wishes. I am your most humble servant, madam. I shall send a messenger to London immediately. It shouldn't be difficult at all to ascertain if this man is what he claims."

"And"—Lady Wentworth snapped her fingers and the dog bounded into her lap—"Beauchamp, don't write to my son regarding the wager, until we know more about Clonmore."

"As you wish, my lady. But what about—?"

"Elizabeth? Oh, she'll come round. She's been raised to be obedient. I can manage that."

Beauchamp stared down at the determined look on Lady Wentworth's face and tried to suppress a chuckle. "Truly, my lady, of that, I have no doubt."

Elizabeth fled up the stairs, her face burning. She'd just committed a practically unredeemable social slight, but she was fairly sure that her grandmother would understand. She'd have to understand, thought Elizabeth. How could she even think to entertain the idea that such a marriage would be suitable, let alone acceptable? Why, in the last six months, Lady Wentworth had allowed her to reject several proposals from prospective grooms Elizabeth found lacking in one way or another. One not interesting enough, one not kind enough, one the son of a well-known roué? But, whispered a small voice in her mind, weren't there other reasons, as well?

Elizabeth raced to her room and flung herself on the bed. How could it be possible that her father had wagered her dowry—and her very life—on a game of chance? She clutched her pillow tight and buried her face in the snowy linen, too upset to cry, the locket clenched in one hand.

She looked up as someone tapped gently on the door.

"My lady?" Molly's soft voice spoke from the doorway, and Elizabeth turned. The maid stood in the doorway, holding a mug steaming with spices. "Lady Wentworth—she had me make a posset for you—are you quite all right, my lady?"

Elizabeth shook her head. "No. I don't want a posset—I feel sick."

At that Molly looked alarmed and, stepping into the room, closed the door. "What ails you, my lady? You look flushed—shall I call the physician? Perhaps you should be bled—"

"No." Elizabeth sat up. "That's not what I meant. I'm too upset to drink anything, Molly. Just take it away."

"But—but, my lady, what's wrong? You were quite happy until—" Molly broke off. "The letter. There was something in the letter that upset you. What was it? Is your father all right?"

"Oh, indeed," sniffed Elizabeth. "Quite all right, I'm sure. Didn't Grandmother tell you? He lost my mother's property in Ireland that's to be my dowry on a wager. And now, it appears that I must marry the winner. And what's worse, I think Grandmother agrees."

"Agrees?" Molly came closer, a puzzled expression on her face. "Now, surely, child—"

"No, you don't understand, Molly. This person is an earl—or claims to be. And Beauchamp is to make inquiries, but I have the dreadful feeling that if this person is all he's said to be, Grandmother will make me marry him."

"Oh, my lady, surely not."

"Don't you see, Molly? He's an earl—even Grandmother

said it, just now. That's much better than she'd hoped for me—she will make me marry him, I tell you she will."

Molly looked dubious. "Well, I suppose it's true you must marry someone,"

"That's what she said!" cried Elizabeth, and then the tears did come as she realized that not only did her father and her grandmother possess every right to marry her off to whomever they believed to be suitable, but her grandmother would allow her father to get away with such a despicable act if she believed the marriage to be advantageous.

"There, there," murmured Molly. She set the posset down on the table beside the bed and gathered Elizabeth in her arms. "There, there, child. It will all work itself out, you'll see."

Yes, thought Elizabeth, as she rested her head on Molly's soft shoulder and wept without restraint, it would indeed work itself out. Whether or not she liked the outcome clearly made little or no difference to anyone at all. She gripped the locket, as though clutching at her mother's hand. Kilmara was her mother's home. How could her father have so callously, carelessly, gambled it away? She remembered how often her mother had spoken of it with such nostalgia.

From the time she was a tiny child, she'd envisioned Kilmara as a golden faerie land of green hills and soft blue skies, the air scented with the tang of sun-drenched herbs. The smooth sides of the locket warmed in her hand and she drew a deep breath, wiping away her tears. Fate, it seemed, was taking her to Kilmara. She raised her head from Molly's accommodating shoulder and gazed, unseeing, into the distance. Whatever else, somehow, it almost felt as though she were going home.

"Neville, you've done what?" Lady Moira stared at her son over a basket of clean linen fresh from the line. She brushed a wayward strand of hair out of her eyes and looked around, as though she didn't quite believe what she'd just heard. "Come into the house." She thrust the basket at Neville, gathered her skirts, and marched into the house.

Neville followed silently. He had learned long ago that

some battles weren't worth fighting. Moira nodded at the table beneath the open window. "Just put that there. Now"—she folded her arms—"sit down and explain this again."

Neville complied with a suppressed sigh. "I told you, Mother. It turns out Kilmara's entailed. It's Sir Oliver's daughter's dowry. In order to take possession of it, I must marry the girl."

Moira took a deep breath. "Well. I suppose you must marry someone sooner or later. Do you know anything about this girl?"

Neville shrugged. "Not a thing. I don't think it matters much, anyway."

At that, Moira's face softened. "Ah, Neville, have you grown so jaded? I never wanted that for you. I wanted you to find someone you could live with in peace—perhaps even grow to love someday—"

"That's a pleasant fantasy, Mother, but I've never thought that was likely. You know what I think of women like that—"

"I was a woman like that," Moira said gently.

"You're different, Mother, and always were." He sighed audibly. "But as you say, I must marry someone, and the daughter of Sir Oliver is not likely to be any worse than any other, I suppose. And if it's the only way to acquire Kilmara, so be it. Right now, there's far more important matters to worry about than some empty-headed chit who's not likely to look beyond her next gown."

"Neville, how do you think you'll manage your disguise with a wife? You've been able to live with the barest of staff at Clonmore, but a wife will require—"

"Who says I mean to have her at Clonmore? Let her stay at Kilmara."

"So you don't mean to live with her? As man and wife?"

Neville's eyes darkened and his smile hardened. "That would hardly be fair, would it, Mother? To bring some un-suspecting girl to Ireland and inflict myself upon her, so to speak? I should give her some time to get used to the idea, don't you think? After all, I am nothing if not a gentleman."

He made a mocking little bow, and Moira shook her head in disbelief.

"And that, of course, will buy you all the time you need to complete all the schemes you've planned. When will you meet her?"

"Only one last raid, Mother, and then I will retire, at least for a while. Sir Oliver has written to his mother, who's the girl's guardian, and asked that the girl be sent over as soon as possible. I'll marry her as soon as she arrives. I can't lay claim to Kilmara until I do, and Sir Oliver's hot to leave Ireland—after what happened to him after the reception the other night, I can't say I blame him."

"What happened?" Moira leaned forward, a concerned look on her face.

"You didn't hear?"

She looked around and shrugged. "I seldom hear anything that concerns the gentry anymore, Neville, unless I hear it from one of the farmers. What happened?"

"He was attacked on his way home—stripped nearly naked, his servants badly beaten when they tried to defend themselves."

"What?" Moira got to her feet. "You didn't—"

Neville waved his hand. "Of course I didn't, Mother. What do you take me for? I'd never do anything like that— win away a man's property and then rob him to boot?" Beneath the edge of the mask, his mouth grew grim. "I didn't want to tell you, because I don't want you to worry any more than you already do. But in the last month or two, it's become obvious that there's another group of outlaws operating in the area. Outlaws who aren't quite so choosy about their victims as we are, and who don't much care what they do to them. You may as well know that's why I was so set on winning this property—it'll allow me to control the area and find a way to limit the activities of these other outlaws as well."

For a long moment, Moira said nothing. Then she spoke, and her words tumbled out in a rush. "The other night— when Seamus was shot—was that—"

"How is he? I've not had a chance to stop by his cottage."

Moira shrugged. "He lives. He clings to life, but the wound's infected. Turlough's a hedgemaster, not a doctor, and while he's skilled enough with herbs and such, and got the bullet out, still—" She broke off and paused. "There's still a good chance he'll die. And even if he lives, it's likely he'll lose the use of that arm. But you interrupted me. Who shot Seamus? Soldiers or these other outlaws?"

Neville looked down at his hands, then rose to his feet and paced restlessly to the door. The autumn sunlight spilled through the open window, and the soft breeze ruffled his hair above the white silk mask. "It was the other outlaws." He muttered a curse, but didn't answer her question directly. "Poor Seamus."

"This was bound to happen, don't you think?" Moira asked quietly.

Neville turned back to face his mother. "Seamus isn't the first to spill his blood for justice in this land, and he won't be the last. As long as there are landlords like St. Denys and Wentworth and—" He broke off. "There's a new commander at the garrison. Colonel Melville, He's got blood in his eye, I can tell."

"When did you meet him?"

"At the reception. I saw Desmond there, too, but his hands are tied. He's only one man."

"But you've always said that the Duke of Desmond thinks as you do—isn't it possible that together—"

Neville shook his head. "Maybe someday, Mother. But not right now. Desmond's in a difficult position. He's one of the few Catholic nobles left. His voice isn't heard by those in power, and you know it."

Moira drew another deep breath and let it out in a long sigh. He hadn't wanted to tell her who shot Seamus, that much was clear, and she had a very strong feeling that her son had had a closer brush with the outlaws than he wanted her to know. "You will be careful, won't you, Neville?"

"I'm always careful, Mother." In two long strides, he crossed the space between them, bent, and kissed her cheek. "I'm off now."

Moira looked up at him with forced merriment in her eyes. "Congratulations, my son."

For a moment, he looked confused. "Congratulations?"

"On your impending marriage, my dear. Don't forget to bring your bride to see me."

At that Neville rolled his eyes before stepping out the front door of the cottage. "Many thanks, Mother. Am I not the picture of a happy bridegroom?"

"Neville!" Moira shook her head in mock exasperation, but there was a touch of real sadness in her face.

At that, Neville's eyes softened, even as his mouth turned down in a bitter twist. "You really are a romantic at heart, aren't you, Mother? Even after everything—you know what this mask hides, Mother. Happiness in marriage is not something that I expect to find."

Three

The day of her departure dawned bright and fair. Elizabeth saw only a few pink clouds massed above the Somerset hills when she raised her head from the pillow and glanced out the window. For a moment she wondered why Molly had wakened her so early, and then she glanced at the trunk set up before the hearth, her traveling costume laid out across it. She'd been dreaming of Kilmara. She sat up with a lighter heart than she'd expected.

"Time to rise, my lady!" chirped Molly, all false cheeriness. For a moment, Elizabeth clenched her eyes shut against a sudden sinking feeling in her chest, as the anticipation of seeing Kilmara was replaced by the awareness of the circumstances which were bringing her there. As her grandmother had said only yesterday, in her gentle but firm way, it was inevitable that she be married to someone. Beauchamp's inquiries had only yielded the information that the Earl of Clonmore was, in fact, descended through both his mother and his father from generations of Anglo-Irish nobility all the way back to the days of Good Queen Bess. If his estates were now somewhat impoverished—well, her marriage to him and the wealthy Kilmara estate would help restore his family's fortunes. All in all, Master Beauchamp had concluded with her grandmother, a suitable match, all things considered—certainly one where there were significant advantages for both sides. So her fate had been sealed, and every seamstress within ten miles had been brought in to complete a frenzy of sewing that occurred around the clock for a week, as her grandmother made sure that her trousseau was as complete as possible. Now most of it was already packed and on its way to Bristol, where it would go by sea to Dublin.

She was to leave at eight o'clock with Molly and Master Beauchamp.

"My lady?" Molly spoke gently from the window as she threw aside the curtains to let in the gray morning light. "It's time." She pointed to a large tray which held a steaming teapot and several covered dishes of various sizes. "Your breakfast's right here beside the fire." She added coal to the fire, stirring up the blaze with a poker, and turned back to Elizabeth as the flames leapt higher.

Elizabeth reached for the robe on the edge of the bed. "Thank you, Molly. Hadn't you better see to your own packing?"

Molly shook her head with a smile. "Lord love you, miss, there's not so much for old Molly to pack. I've but to put on my cloak and bonnet to be ready." She indicated the sweep of her skirts with a broad hand. "Her ladyship was generous to have a traveling gown made for me. What do you think of it?"

Elizabeth smiled as she sank into the chair, grateful for Molly's attempt to distract her. "It's lovely," she answered sincerely, noting the fine quality of the blue wool fabric. The trim was plain black ribbon, but the gown had been well fitted to Molly's ample frame, and the linen beneath it was clearly of the same serviceable quality.

"Are you all right, my lady?" Molly asked, peering closely at her young mistress in the light of the fire. The pale light of the October dawn filtered through the white curtains, making Elizabeth appear drawn.

Elizabeth twisted her hands together in her lap then smiled bravely at Molly. "I know both Grandmother and Master Beauchamp believe this to be best. I just wish—"

She turned her head so Molly wouldn't see the tears that flooded her eyes. How different this was to be from the way she had always envisioned it. "I just wish things were different."

"Oh, lamb." Molly threw her arms around Elizabeth and hugged her. "I know." She patted her back and then withdrew with a little squeeze. "But, by all accounts, the earl is a young man . . . of a good family . . . with an ancient title . . ."

"Oh, I'm not sad to see Kilmara, Molly. Really, it makes me feel as though it will bring me closer to Mother. But what if this Earl is as much a gambler as Father? After all, he won Kilmara in a game of cards."

"What did Master Beauchamp say?"

"He said Lord Clonmore has no outstanding debts or history of gaming—not that Master Beauchamp could ascertain. But that could mean nothing—Master Beauchamp also says he raises horses—and who's to say he doesn't bet on racing?" Elizabeth broke off and shook her head. "I wish I could at least have met the man—" She shook her head again. "Oh, what's the use? I'm to be married to him and that's that." She picked up the napkin and spread it on her lap. "I'm no worse off than poor Katherine Gascoyne—do you remember her, Molly? She was the daughter of my mother's friend, Lady Leighton? She was married just a year ago to a man older than her father. He had the most dreadful reputation—and he was ugly to boot." She poured the tea as Molly began to tidy the room and ate while Molly supervised the procession of scullery maids who carried up buckets of hot water for her bath.

At last, she was fed and bathed and dressed. She stood before the long mirror and regarded herself for the last time in her grandmother's house. The dark green wool brought out the green in her eyes, but her cheeks, normally so rosy, were pale in the bluish light. She brought her hand to her throat and touched the locket she wore hidden beneath the high collar. *You're going to Mother's house,* she reminded herself She remembered all the stories her mother had told her of her girlhood spent there. Ireland had sounded like a lovely place then, almost an enchanted land where the little people hid beneath the hedgerows and faeries danced at midnight on the lush green hills. Surely there were worse places than her mother's much-loved home.

Molly gave a last-minute tweak to the set of her bonnet. "Perfect, my lady." She smiled at Elizabeth's reflection.

Elizabeth drew a deep breath. "All right, Molly. I'm ready." With another quick glance, she squared her shoulders and marched from the room.

At the bottom of the steps, Lady Frances sat waiting in a high-backed chair, her lap dog cradled in her lap, Master Beauchamp by her side. Outside, Elizabeth heard the stamp and whicker of the horses and the muffled commands of the footmen as they struggled to load her final trunk in back of the coach.

Still holding the little dog, Lady Frances rose to her feet as Elizabeth descended the stairs. "Let me look at you, girl." The old woman's regal expression softened as her gaze swept over Elizabeth from head to toe. "Very nice. Very nice indeed. You'll do your father proud—not that he deserves it." She raised Elizabeth's chin and her faded green eyes met Elizabeth's. "And you're to remember your duty, do you understand? You've been raised well, despite your father's best efforts to the contrary. See that you're a tribute to the memory of your mother."

"I will, Grandmother." Elizabeth touched the locket once more automatically.

"Write to me the moment you arrive, child."

Elizabeth looked up, surprised to hear a catch in her grandmother's throat. "Of course, Grandmother."

"And send it back with Beauchamp."

"Yes, Grandmother."

With a satisfied sniff, Lady Frances stepped forward and embraced Elizabeth awkwardly. She drew back. "Remember your duty, child—to your husband and to your family— and you won't go wrong."

Elizabeth met her grandmother's eyes with a smile that was far braver than she felt. "I'll remember, Grandmother."

The old lady held out a shaking hand. She caught Elizabeth's hand in hers and pressed a round, gold coin into her palm. Elizabeth's eyes widened when she realized she held a gold sovereign.

"Buy yourself a trinket, my dear." Her grandmother's voice was harsh. She looked up and saw tears welling in her grandmother's eyes. Elizabeth moved to embrace her once more, but the formidable old lady turned away, waving her hand. "Well, now, off with you, then. The tide won't wait in Bristol or anywhere else. Beauchamp, you'll see my grand-daughter safe, won't you?"

"Of course, Lady Wentworth." Beauchamp bowed.

Elizabeth felt her own tears threaten to spill down her cheeks. She drew a deep breath, and her grandmother gave her a quick wag of a finger. "Now, now, child. None of that. Tuck that sovereign away and show me you're made of better stuff than your father."

With a quick sniff, and a last glance all around, Elizabeth found herself bundled into the waiting coach, Molly beside her, Master Beauchamp opposite. A gold sun had risen over the soft yellow beeches, and with the coachman's loud cry and the crack of his whip, the coach took off down the tree-lined avenue. Elizabeth felt for the locket beneath the high neck of her traveling costume and squeezed it through the fabric. *Well, Mama,* she thought, *I'm on my way to Kilmara. At last.*

The next three days were a blur of discomfort such as Elizabeth had never experienced. The haste with which they traveled meant that scant attention was given to luxury. The first night was spent at an inn in Bristol, the second on board the ship which bore them to Ireland, and the third at an inn in Dublin frequented, so Master Beauchamp had assured Lady Wentworth, only by the gentry.

Elizabeth craned her head all around, staring in wide-eyed fascination as they marched through the streets of Dublin behind the boy who trundled a small cart containing their luggage over the uneven cobblestones. The further they went from the busy quay, the more dark and winding and narrow the streets became, and the buildings seemed to lean in menacingly. Even though it had been close to noon by the time they'd disembarked, the streets were blue wells of shadow. Dark-eyed children stared from black pools within the doorways, and women, lean as alley cats, stopped their scrubbing or mending and gazed at them as they passed.

Master Beauchamp drew closer to Elizabeth and cleared his throat. "Boy!" he said firmly, and then a little louder, "I say, boy!"

"Aye, me lord?" The boy glanced over his shoulder with sullen nonchalance. Elizabeth shivered in disgust as, in her high boots of stout leather, she stepped around a dark mass which oozed a yellowish slime, then she noticed that the boy's feet were bare on the cold cobbles.

"Isn't there another way to the inn?"

The boy shrugged. "Not one that I would know, me lord." He gave the cart a little jerk and it bounced over an uneven stone. Elizabeth wondered how he could stand the feel of the cold and the filth against his skin.

At last the dingy street spilled out into a broad market square. The narrow tenements opened to a light, airy space graced by the filigreed spires of churches and the columned porticos of imposing brick buildings. Up and down the street, as far as Elizabeth could see, shops offered wares of all kinds to the numerous passersby who were dressed as smartly as any she'd seen in either Bristol or London. Fruit sellers bawled out the excellence of the harvest's apples, while others hawked books, chickens, and fresh-caught fish. She gathered her skirts above the churned muck and picked her way as carefully as the boy's pace would allow. He seemed to have forgotten that they followed. "Hurry along now, my lady," said Beauchamp, struggling to keep his own highly polished boots out of the mire. "Take my arm, Mistress Molly."

Together the three of them stumbled past a church with an open door. Elizabeth glanced inside and caught a glimpse of a crucified figure on a cross, bright red paint dripping across its face. She shuddered involuntarily at the graphic depiction. "Papistry, you know, my lady," murmured Beauchamp. "Papistry." He shook his head disapprovingly, even as Molly craned her neck to see more.

They passed the church, and the street opened up to a wide green, where red-coated soldiers drilled in precise formation.

"So many soldiers, Master Beauchamp," murmured Molly.

"Such are needed to keep the queen's peace, Mistress," answered Beauchamp with a lofty air. "The Irish race is, regrettably, among the least civilized in Europe. They've proven most intractable, unfortunately."

Elizabeth glanced up to see if the boy might have heard Beauchamp, but he stalked on with stolid efficiency. Past the drill grounds, they came to a knot of people clustered around the base of a low platform. A half-naked man was tied to a pole, and a uniformed soldier stood to one side, with a lash in his hand. "What's this, Master Beauchamp?" Elizabeth breathed. Never once had she ever been permitted to attend anything which even hinted at public punishment.

Before Beauchamp could reply, another soldier stepped forward, and Elizabeth saw that his uniform was bright with gold braid. "Hear ye, hear ye! By order of His Grace the lord lieutenant of Ireland! To teach the Irish tongue is treason! To teach the papist cant is treason! But His Grace has ordered mercy. Instead of death, the sentence of Magnus Muldoon, convicted of teaching treason to the innocent, is commuted to twenty lashes." The soldier glanced at the one who held the whip. "Begin."

A shocked gasp and a few ragged cheers went up through the crowd, but Beauchamp took both Elizabeth and Molly firmly by the elbows and led them on, just as the first lash whistled through the clear air. It fell with a hideous slap on the naked white back. Elizabeth shut her eyes as if that could stop the scream that was sure to follow, and felt for the locket at her throat. Had her mother ever witnessed such cruelty? A low, animal moan escaped the prisoner, and he sagged in his bonds even as his shoulders braced for the next blow.

"But—but, why?" Elizabeth asked Beauchamp as he hurried them down the street. The boy had paused at last, below a brightly painted hanging sign, and was looking at them expectantly.

Beauchamp paused and read the sign, then nodded with a satisfied air. He withdrew several coins from the pouch he carried within his waistcoat. "Here you are, boy. Our thanks."

The boy pulled his forelock but instead of scampering off immediately, he paused and looked at Elizabeth. Their eyes met and Elizabeth saw that his were an amazingly clear shade of blue, and that his face, though dirty, was as fine-boned as a prince's. "That man was a hedgemaster, miss. That's why he's bein' whipped."

"That will be all, boy," interrupted Beauchamp, clearly horrified at the boy's impertinence in speaking to Elizabeth.

"What's a hedgemaster—?" she began, but the boy only gave her an apologetic grin and, turning on his heel, melted into the crowded street. Elizabeth looked up at Beauchamp. "Why did you chase him off, Master Beauchamp? I was only asking—"

"And hardly seemly for you to be seen talking in the street with a common urchin, my lady," Master Beauchamp replied with a sniff. "Come, let's go inside and see if our rooms are ready. If I wash the stink of that ship off before dinner, 'twill be none too soon for me."

Elizabeth followed Molly and Beauchamp into the inn, glancing once more down the street. So much was at once familiar and strange about this country, There was much that reminded her of England—the shops, the busy streets, even the inn, which clearly was as well appointed as she'd been told. But the garish statues in the church, the redcoats drilling on the common, and the public whipping— She shuddered at the thought of what that poor man endured. And for what? Teaching a language?

She was quiet all that evening, until Molly began to fuss over her. "No, I'm not feeling poorly, Molly," she replied to her maid's repeated queries. "I'm fine. It's just—" She got to her feet and crossed the narrow space between the four-poster bed and the small gabled window of the room they were to share. She peered out the window, but could see little beyond the rooftops of the nearby buildings. "It's very different here than I'd imagined."

"Ah, lamb, you're just upset by the journey." Molly regarded her with sympathy. "Come to bed now, and soon we'll be safe at Kilmara."

Kilmara, thought Elizabeth as she climbed into the high bed. What if that were as different from everything she'd imagined as the rest of Ireland was turning out to be?

The next morning, they boarded the Ennis stage. Elizabeth peered out the coach window, wide-eyed, as they left the city. Beyond the city limits, the landscape opened up into gently rolling hills of endless green. For a long time she was content to sit and drink in the sights. The low hedgerows bounded lush fields where peasants toiled, bringing in the harvest, and here and there, grazing sheep and cattle dotted the landscape. Then the country grew barer, the fields stripped and empty. The road was bordered on either side by bogs, which stretched out flat in all directions except for the weird-shaped rocks which rose out of the mire like monsters out of nightmares. Elizabeth drew back inside the carriage with a shudder. Beside her, Molly had fallen asleep, and on the seat opposite, Beauchamp drowsed. Beside Beauchamp, a white-wigged stranger smiled at her kindly.

"The landscape not to your liking, miss?" asked the stranger.

"I scarcely know what to think of it, sir," Elizabeth replied. "Before it was so lovely, and here—this part—" She wrinkled her nose as the acrid stench of the peat-tainted water reached their nostrils.

"Ireland is a land of contrasts, I'll give you that." The stranger smiled. He was dressed like a gentleman in a serviceable traveling suit of brown wool, and his linen was as crisp and immaculate as Master Beauchamp's. He bowed first to Elizabeth, then to Molly and Master Beauchamp. "I've spent enough time here to know." He spoke with a bitter twist to his mouth. "Sir Anthony Addams, at your service, miss."

"May I present the Lady Elizabeth Wentworth, daughter of

Sir Oliver Wentworth of Kilmara," said Beauchamp, rousing himself from his drowse. "I'm Henry Beauchamp, solicitor to her ladyship Lady Frances Wentworth of Bruton, Somerset."

"Ah," said Sir Anthony, smiling at Elizabeth. "I know your father slightly, my lady. I had the pleasure of meeting him some months ago at the Dublin races. He struck me as a man most energetic in the pursuit of relaxation. I gather that this is your first visit to Ireland, my lady?"

"Indeed, sir." Elizabeth dropped her eyes and gazed at her lap. He was of middle years, she thought, and his scrutiny was intense in the close confines of the carriage. And what was she to tell him? *Yes, Sir Anthony, this is my first—and my last—visit to Ireland, for I don't expect to leave any time soon.* She imagined how mortified she'd feel if he knew the story. "But you say you've seen much of the country?"

The tall, taciturn man made her curious. There was something about him that reminded her of a cat, something in the way he lounged against the seat, his body adjusting to every sudden bump as if he could somehow anticipate it, that made her wonder exactly what was bringing him to the same destination as hers.

He fastened his gaze on Elizabeth, and she saw that his eyes were gray, a flat, pale shade that held no hint of color. Inexplicably, his eyes made her feel cold. She suppressed a shiver as he answered in a quiet voice, "I have, my lady." He gazed out the window and smiled distantly. "My work takes me far and wide."

"If you know the country well, then can you tell me, sir, what's a hedgemaster?" Elizabeth leaned forward eagerly.

At that Sir Anthony raised his eyebrow. "You've only just arrived, my lady, and already you've found a hedgemaster?"

"We saw one being punished when we arrived in Dublin yesterday, Sir Anthony," said Beauchamp quietly. "And my lady was quite curious—perhaps you could enlighten all of us?"

"'Twill be my pleasure, Master Beauchamp." Sir Anthony turned to Elizabeth with a thin smile and a cold glint in his pale eyes that sent a chill all the way down her back.

"A hedgemaster, my lady, is the bearer of the seeds of sedition that blow through this island like a weed—an accursed weed that will not be rooted out. Let the hedgemasters spread their papist cant throughout the breadth of Ireland, and before a year is out, there will be a Catholic army in Ireland to match the Catholic army in France, and England will find itself squeezed tight between them."

"Oh, I see," murmured Elizabeth, taken aback by the concise explanation. She understood little of the difference between the faith of England and that which was sneeringly, dismissed as "papistry" by everyone she knew, but she'd known since birth that Catholicism was in some way a threat to the very foundation of the English way of life. At least that's how everyone talked. Except her brother, David, and his explanations were so long-winded and full of digressions that she'd never been sure exactly what he was trying to explain.

"So you see, my lady, the true duty of every Englishman in Ireland who would be loyal to our queen is to ensure that this most savage race, who are wholly incapable of recognizing the ways of a civilized life, resistant to all lawful rule, and who are led as easily as wayward children into all manner of disorder by their priests, achieves some measure of order and civility, some shred of prudence and foresight. It has proven to be a most difficult task." Sir Anthony finished with a long sigh and a slight headshake. He squared his shoulders and turned to Beauchamp. "Well, sir? Has my explanation been sufficiently enlightening to the young lady?"

Beauchamp smiled. "My lady Elizabeth has always shown herself to me to be most perceptive, Sir Anthony. Your explanation was as informative as it was succinct."

"Thank you, Sir Anthony," murmured Elizabeth. The intensity of his gaze made her uncomfortable. She dropped her eyes and glanced again outside the window. They had passed the bogs, and now the road wound up a gentle slope. The hedgerows lining the road were planted on top of stone and sod banks which divided the fields. The hedges themselves were so old and thick they were impenetrable, and Elizabeth could see nothing of what lay behind. Movement on the side of the road caught her eye, and she glanced down. The horses galloped past, but Elizabeth was shocked to see a family huddled beneath the hedges, a man and a woman and at least four or five children. The children were round-eyed, dirty, and nearly naked, with stick-thin arms and rounded bellies. A scrawny cow was tethered to a short stick, around which seemed to be clustered a small pile of household goods. Elizabeth glimpsed an iron kettle as they dashed past. She glanced at the woman. For a brief moment, their eyes locked, and Elizabeth saw that the woman's face was lined and drawn with care, and that her eyes were ringed with shadows. Startled, Elizabeth turned back to her companions. "There's a family out there," she blurted. "Under the hedgerows."

"Ah," said Sir Anthony with an airy wave of his hand. "I told you they were savages, did I not?" He folded his hands comfortably across his chest, leaned carefully against the back of the coach lest his wig be disturbed, closed his eyes, and soon his snores joined with Molly's soft breathing. Beside Sir Anthony, Beauchamp, too, drowsed.

But Elizabeth could not be lulled. She stared out the window as the road curved up a hill and the hedgerows thinned so that she could see more verdant green hills, rolling gently to the horizon. But the haunted eyes of that woman beneath the hedges, the scrawny limbs of the children as they crowded together against the chilly air, insisted on rising up before her closed lids, even as she tried unsuccessfully to push the memory from her mind. It was nearly winter—surely, without better shelter, the little family would freeze. Even savages kept themselves warm, didn't they? It seemed that her mother's golden faerie land had a dark side to it, after all, a side far darker than anything Elizabeth had ever witnessed in England. What kind of place possessed such contrasts in ugliness and beauty?

Plagued by an uneasiness she could not shake off, Elizabeth watched the sky change from blue to gray as a soft rain began to fall.

Four

They stopped twice more—once to dine at an inn which served a hearty stew and stouter ale than Elizabeth had ever drunk before, but that both Molly and Master Beauchamp drank with relish—and again at a small village just as an afternoon sun peeped out behind the clouds which had followed them all the rest of the day.

A newcomer boarded the coach with a quick look around, and Beauchamp crowded next to Molly. The man settled down beside Sir Anthony, spread his rough woolen coat as grandly as though he were a gentleman, and nodded to each passenger in turn. "Sir Anthony Addams, as I live and breathe," he said with a knowing air. "So they've broken down and called in the hounds, have they?"

"Tush, man, you speak nonsense." But despite his words of protest, Sir Anthony smiled.

"Do I?" The other man grinned. Elizabeth stared in fascination at his rough clothes, his stubbled cheeks, and hair that was neither powdered nor wigged, and only held back from his face by a long leather cord. "That's not how I hear it. I hear you brought in Black Mike Gallagher single-handed and hauled his arse all the way to Dub—"

"Watch your language, man!" interrupted Beauchamp. "There is a young lady present."

"Ah." At that the man looked at Elizabeth. He ran his eyes over her face and down to her bosom and, to her horror, she felt herself flush. How dare he look at her so boldly? He met her eyes again and winked. He gave a gap-toothed grin and his brown eyes danced in his weathered face. There was something about him that reminded her of her father at his best. Suddenly she had to fight the urge to laugh. "Jack Whittaker, at your service, ma'am. And yours, too, ma'am," he added to Molly, who had placed an arm around Elizabeth. "Have no fear for your chick, mistress—I like a woman with a bit more meat on her bones than that one. Like yours." His smile widened, even as Molly gave a horrified squeak. "But begging yer pardon, ma'am"—he turned back to Elizabeth—"if I may say, you are an uncommonly pretty one."

Horrified, Elizabeth blushed again. She stared down at her laced fingers in her lap while Beauchamp cleared his throat.

"This is Lady Elizabeth Wentworth, daughter of Sir Oliver Wentworth, of Kil—" Beauchamp began, but Jack leaned forward, eyes alight.

"You're Sir Oliver's daughter? The one that's coming to marry his lordship of Clonmore? Well, well." Jack slapped his thigh. "This calls for a drink." He fumbled in his coat and withdrew a leather flask. "Care for a nip, anyone? No?" He sipped from the flask, closed his eyes, and sighed as he smacked his lips. "That's good. Well, my lady. It's honored I am to make your acquaintance. The tale's been told 'twixt here and Dublin how the Earl won himself a wife in a hand of cards."

"Has it?" said Elizabeth faintly. So she was to be a public spectacle as well. Bitter resentment against her father bubbled into anger. No wonder David distanced himself from the family.

"No, my lady, you mustn't fret," put in Sir Anthony. He met Beauchamp's eyes and continued. "You must understand that the county is far removed from the diversions of a city even so large as Dublin. There's little to occupy people but gossip. The whole county shall be abuzz, my lady.

Everyone will be most anxious to meet you." Sir Anthony smiled.

Elizabeth looked down at her hands. "As you say, sir. I wish I could say the same."

"Are you acquainted with the Earl of Clonmore, sir?" asked Mr. Beauchamp.

"I've met him, yes." Sir Anthony hesitated.

"And what sort of a person would you say he is?"

Sir Anthony glanced at Elizabeth and Molly and then at Mr. Beauchamp. "He is . . . a somewhat unusual person, sir."

"Unusual in what way?"

"He keeps very much to himself, as I recall. Only occasionally participates in the county functions. Raises excellent horses—he's making a name for himself as far away as Paris, I've heard. And only last month, a German count was here to purchase a mare."

"Is he—is he—what sort of a man is he, though?" asked Elizabeth. "Is he—well set up?"

Sir Anthony did not answer her. He glanced at Mr. Beauchamp. "That's a difficult question to answer, ma'am. His lordship has certain—distinguishing characteristics, let's say."

"And what are they?" asked Elizabeth, leaning forward, her heart beginning to beat faster in trepidation.

"Oh, tell her," put in Jack. "His lordship isn't at all like other men, and well you know it." He looked at Elizabeth. "He's not had an easy life for one born so high, and he bears the scars of it for all the world to see. He goes about masked so he doesn't frighten little children and women, and he limps. He's got a hump on his back, and one arm's longer than the other—"

"Be still, man," Sir Anthony said with a grimace of disgust. "You're frightening the young lady. Lord Clonmore is a man like any other, my lady, although Master Jack here does speak the truth in some respects. According to gossip, he was the victim in childhood of some unfortunate occurrence. He does indeed wear a mask. But he doesn't have a hump."

Elizabeth gripped the seat, feeling slightly faint. Molly tutted beneath her breath. "I'll thank you to keep your mouth shut, Master Whittaker," she said, her chin thrust forward, a hen defending her chick. "My lady's young and impressionable—it's not for the likes of you to go about upsetting her. A hump indeed!" She put her arm around Elizabeth. "There, lamb, don't look so upset. I'm sure Lord Neville is made as other men. This—this creature is just saying nonsense to upset you." She hugged Elizabeth and glared at Jack.

But Jack only winked and raised his flask. "But if you're the one he won, miss"—he took another long drink and shook his head—"that's enough to make a man think of turning to a life of cards and chance." He guffawed and belched.

"Enough of that talk, man!" said Sir Anthony. "There's little but gossip to occupy the time of most"—here he glanced at Jack with a slight sneer—"but I think you will find that once you are settled there, there will be other topics to occupy the idle tongues."

"And you'll supply it, will you not?" said Jack, chuckling.

"What's so funny?" asked Elizabeth. "Why does this man address you so, Sir Anthony?"

Sir Anthony spread his hands and gave a self-deprecating shrug. "Well, my lady, the outlaw he mentioned before, Black Mike Gallagher, it's true I had a hand in his capture—"

"Oh, tell her the truth plain," interrupted Jack. "You were quick enough to tell her all about his lordship, weren't you? This one here's a bounty hunter. They call him in when they've done all they can to capture a murderer, or a thief, or in this case the canniest outlaw in three counties—Gentleman Niall. Sir Anthony here is known throughout Ireland as the best there is at what he does, and what he does is haul 'em in and see 'em strung up—for a price, of course." He winked at Sir Anthony over his flask.

"Who has called you in, sir?" asked Elizabeth as Sir Anthony shot Jack an angry look. "Your destination is the same as ours—do you mean to tell me that there are outlaws near Kilmara?"

"You've not heard yet of Gentleman Niall and his band?" Jack stared at her. He raised the flask to his lips once more. "You will. Might even meet him tonight—but I took care to tell the bishop I'd be coming on the morning coach. No one will expect the Knockamurra rent money tonight—" He broke off as Sir Anthony seized him by the waistcoat.

"You've got rent money on you?" demanded Sir Anthony.

"Aye—what of it?" Jack struggled back. "You've got no cause—"

"Damn and blast you, man. This road's a picking-ground for those blasted outlaws as it is. If they've any idea there's rent money on this coach, they'll be down upon us like flies on a dead dog's carcass."

Elizabeth glanced at Molly, who drew her closer with a muttered prayer. "Are we safe, Master Beauchamp?" she asked.

"Now, Mistress Molly, I'm sure that the coachman will take all precautions—" Beauchamp broke off as thumps above their heads told them that someone was moving about on top of the moving vehicle.

"What's that?" whispered Molly, clutching Elizabeth closer.

"Now, now, ma'am." Sir Anthony released Jack with an ugly look and settled down on his side of the narrow seat. "That's just the coachman's boy." He shot Jack another look, this one full of meaning, but spoke reassuringly to Elizabeth. "They'll do all they can to keep us safe."

"Besides," Jack said, taking another swig from his flask, "Gentleman Niall's a gentleman—there's never been a tale told of a lady attacked, or even of anyone seriously hurt. He takes your money and your valuables and then he leaves you in peace."

"Peace!" cried Molly. "To take the possessions of honest people is hardly leaving anyone in peace!"

Sir Anthony sighed. "I quite agree with you, ma'am. But

rest assured, the sheriff at Ennis—one Sir William St. Denys—has brought me here to apprehend this fellow. And believe me, just as in the Black Mike affair, I anticipate a speedy resolution to the problem." He paused and smiled first at Molly, and then at Elizabeth. "No need to worry."

Elizabeth settled back with a sigh, and just in that moment, the coach leapt forward. The coachman shouted something indistinguishable, and the rickety coach rattled over the rutted road. Her head slammed back. "Ow!" she cried. She gripped the edge of the frayed seat lest she be bounced against the roof. Were it not for the fact that she was wedged tightly between Molly and the side of the coach, she would have fallen to the floor. The coach jounced over a particularly large pothole. "Oh!" she cried when the coach took what felt like a flying leap over a chasm and her head hit the roof again.

"Are you all right, my lady?" Beauchamp asked through gritted teeth. "This is ridiculous—this coachman must be possessed."

"Aye," answered Jack. He winked at Beauchamp with a wide, gap-toothed grin. "He's possessed all right—possessed with the fear of the devil himself. Long Jim up there's decided to make a run for it."

"This is quite unacceptable," Mr. Beauchamp said, gripping for purchase on the side of the coach. "What ails the man?" He struggled to open the window, but the second passenger reached out and touched his arm. "This can't continue."

"'Twill do you no good, sir," said Sir Anthony. "From here through to Ennis, there'll be no stopping or slowing, if the coachman can help it."

"We can't ride all the way there like this!" said Elizabeth, as another bounce threw her into Molly's lap and the serving woman cried out as her head slammed against the back of the coach.

"If the outlaws can't catch us, they can't stop us, miss." Jack patted the side of his much-patched jacket of brown worsted wool and nodded toward the window. "The last person I want to meet today is Gentleman Niall with his gang."

"What more can you tell us about this so-called gentleman?" asked Beauchamp over the clatter of the wheels.

"He's a particularly daring outlaw," answered Sir Anthony. "A rapparee, the peasants call him. He's earned a reputation which is as audacious as he is polite. Hence, the appellation 'gentleman,' although I can assure you, miss, he's anything but." He paused to brace himself against the back of the seat. "Twilight is his preferred time to rob the innocent traveler. And he's made his reputation robbing rent money." He glared at Jack.

"Aye, he might be a gentleman," put in Jack, "but he's the devil himself when it comes to taking the money and jewelry off the gentry. Why, it was just two weeks ago that a solicitor from Dublin was on his way to visit the bishop and met Gentleman Niall and his men. They stripped him of all his money and tied him backwards to his horse when he gave them some mouth, and the poor man had to ride into Ennis like that—oh, they're still talking about it." Jack chuckled, reached inside his coat, and removed his leather flask. He glanced at the others, and held it out. "Sure you don't want a bit now? No?"

Beauchamp shook his head with an aggrieved little sniff. Sir Anthony smiled thinly.

"Is he—has he ever killed anyone?" asked Elizabeth.

"All these outlaws are murderers, miss," replied Sir Anthony. "The roads of Ireland are plagued by lawless gangs which rob and pillage and take from honest men what they're too lazy to earn for themselves."

Jack Whittaker laughed. "And that's where you came in, right, Sir Anthony? Tell the little lady the truth, m'lord. Ye're here to wipe this county clean of the likes of Gentleman Niall and his ilk and make yerself a fine penny in the bargain. Invited, my arse! Begged is how I had it told to me in every tavern 'twixt here and Knockamurra. And I heard you held out for a very pretty sum." He took another deep swallow from his flask and wiped his mouth with the back of his hand, while Mr. Beauchamp glared, Molly gasped an outraged "Well, I never—and in front of a young lady, too!" and Elizabeth tried not to giggle.

Then her head slammed against the back of the seat, and pain flared once more from the back of her head to her temples. Suddenly she wanted nothing more than to wake up in her bedroom in her grandmother's house in Somerset, safe and warm, and unbruised. "Please tell me, Sir Anthony," began Elizabeth as another violent jerk nearly threw her to the floor. She clung to Molly as the older woman tried to brace them both.

The coach came to a sudden halt.

Jack peered outside and, draining his flask to the dregs, replaced the stopper and looked back at the others. Whiskey spilled down his chin, and his face was white. "It's them." He crossed himself hastily.

"Hush, man," Sir Anthony admonished him, frowning. "You'll frighten the ladies." He reached inside his coat and spoke quietly. "Are you armed, by any chance, Beauchamp?"

Mr. Beauchamp looked startled and shook his head. "No—"

Sir Anthony raised his finger to his lips. "I didn't think so. Throw out the rent money, Whittaker."

"What?" exclaimed Jack. "I'll do no such thing—"

Elizabeth strained to hear what was happening outside the coach, but all she heard was men's voices, rough and indistinct. Suddenly, the coach rocked violently from side to side, and there was a single gunshot. One of the horses screamed. Then she heard the clamor of feet above and realized that the coachman and the boy riding pillion must have been dragged off the coach.

Mr. Beauchamp leaned forward to peer out the window, when Sir Anthony gently reached across the seat and pushed him back. "Be still, man!" He gestured to Whittaker. "Throw out the rent money—now!"

"But the bishop—"

"The bishop be damned—do as I say!" hissed Sir Anthony.

Jack reached into his coat and withdrew a fat leather

pouch, but before he could do anything with it, the door was yanked open and a hairy arm, roped with muscle, reached in, caught Jack by the throat, and dragged him, struggling, out of the coach. Elizabeth gasped and stifled a scream as a rough voice shouted, "Outside, all of ye! Move quick, now—hands up above ye're heads! Now!"

The coach rocked as the door was yanked on its hinges again. Beauchamp glanced at Sir Anthony. "Now what?" he mouthed.

Sir Anthony shrugged. "Get out. You and the women. While you've distracted them, I'll sneak out and shoot. Try to get the leader as close to the door as possible, and for God's sake, stay out of the line of fire."

"But how—" began Elizabeth, but the voice roared again.

"If we have to come in and get ye, we will!"

Molly gripped Elizabeth's hand. "You first, Mister Beauchamp." She nodded, wide-eyed.

Beauchamp gulped visibly, then clambered from the coach. He turned to help first Molly and then Elizabeth emerge onto the road. The road was a pool of gathering shadows as the red sun began to sink toward the low hills. The hedgerows rose black and menacing all around them, and as Elizabeth looked around, she noticed a narrow opening, which gave a glimpse of the harvested field on the other side. Two men on horseback milled around the coach. Four others looked up as Elizabeth emerged. One stood over Jack, who lay moaning on the road, blood running from his head.

Elizabeth bit her lip hard. The coachman and the boy were being tied together by another pair of outlaws. And one more stood by the coach, his black beard rough on his pale face. All the outlaws were roughly dressed in much-patched rags of clothing, and their horses were shaggy and lean. The one who stood near the coach looked at Elizabeth and swore. "Ah, look here, me lads. Look what we've captured here." He swaggered closer, dagger drawn in one hand, pistol in another. "Let me look at you, m'beauty." He grinned a jagged, gap-toothed smile and snarled at Beauchamp and Molly. "Step away from her."

Molly and Beauchamp clung closer to Elizabeth. "I will not—" began Molly, but the outlaw jerked his head at two of the horsemen who circled close. They leapt from their mounts with practiced ease and advanced. Elizabeth quivered. What did these men mean to do? She gripped Molly's hand, even as the men gripped both Molly and Beauchamp and held them away. Beauchamp struggled, and the outlaw swung a huge fist and hit him in the jaw. Beauchamp went down with a gurgle.

Elizabeth looked at the outlaw. He was grinning at her. She asked, "Are you—are you the one they call Gentleman Niall?"

At that the outlaw laughed, and the others guffawed. Molly bit the hand of the one holding her and he cuffed her across the head so hard the older woman fell to her knees, moaning. Elizabeth rushed to her side, and the outlaws gathered closer. Elizabeth glanced over her shoulder at the coach. Where was Sir Anthony?

She knelt beside Molly, even as the leader and another outlaw dragged her away from the older woman. She struggled as one pinned her arms behind her back. Her hair tumbled from its pins, and the outlaw who appeared to be the leader grinned once more. He reached out and touched the heavy honey-colored mass. "Ah," he breathed. "You are a beauty."

His eyes roamed over her face, to her throat, and lit on the emerald locket. "Hm. What's this?" He twined his thick fingers in the thin gold chain and as Elizabeth screamed an anguished "No!" ripped it off her neck as easily as he might a flower from a stem. He held it up, and in the dim light, the bright green heart dangled, gleaming green fire. Then he pocketed it while Elizabeth felt the breath stop in her throat. Her mother's locket was gone. But the outlaw was speaking. "I'd wager a king's ransom that whoever lays claim to you will pay dear to have you back, beauty." He swung her roughly around again, so that her back was held tight to him, her arms pinned behind her. The rank odor of his body made her gag. "Sean! Help me tie her."

Elizabeth struggled, throwing her weight as hard as she could against the outlaw's restraining arm. He tightened his grip and she reached down and tried to bite his arm. "Ah, so you're one of that kind, are you?" He raised his hand and casually hit her with a heavy fist. Her head jerked from the force of the blow, and her chin flared with pain. "No more, I said." A dirty rag was shoved into her mouth, and her arms were bound to her sides. Her ankles were laced together and she was flung over the back of one of the horses. Her nose was buried in its thick, dusty coat, and she struggled to breathe.

She managed to turn her head in time to see Beauchamp struggle to his knees and an outlaw knock him down again. His assailant rustled through his clothes as the barely conscious man moaned in pain. Another was systematically patting down Whittaker. Another two held a struggling Molly down on the ground. Her skirts were above her waist and, to Elizabeth's horror, they were fumbling with her underlinen. "No!" Molly screamed. "Sir Anthony, help us!"

Just at that moment, Sir Anthony emerged from the coach. He pointed the pistol at the leader and shot once. The bullet went harmlessly over the man's head. The leader turned from Elizabeth, and the two on the ground with Molly rushed at Sir Anthony, who aimed again and this time shot one square in the face. The outlaw toppled over as part of his face exploded in a fountain of red flesh. Sir Anthony smiled grimly, just as another shot rang out, and he fell over, groaning, clutching at his thigh. He lay on his side, struggling to reload his pistol.

Elizabeth tried to struggle, but the outlaw jumped into the saddle. "Parraig, Ronan, away," he cried. The horse danced impatiently, as though eager to be off. The outlaw held the reins in one hand, his other hand flat on Elizabeth's back, pressing her down. She struggled, and he slammed his hand down on her backside. "None of that, darlin'," he muttered, as she gasped in pain. "Away, now!" He dug his knees into the horse's sides, and the beast leapt away into the falling twilight, carrying Elizabeth away into the wood.

Molly struggled to sit up, screaming, as Elizabeth was carried off. The other outlaws were scattering to mount their horses when another series of shots, this time quick and clean and very fast, rang out. Two, then three, then four of the outlaws toppled over with hardly a whimper. The remaining two or three rode away in the direction of the leader.

Three more men galloped out from between the hedgerows, all clothed in black, all wearing masks. "Drop the pistol, sir." Two of the black riders aimed at Sir Anthony. "Drop the pistol!" The command was repeated and this time accompanied by a shot which landed in the wooden frame of the coach. At that, Sir Anthony obeyed; he slowly placed the pistol on the ground, his teeth clenched in a grimace.

Molly rose to her knees, pulling down her skirts, her face swollen and flushed. "My lady!" she cried with a sob.

"Looks as though the other gang got away with everything worth taking, Niall," one man said to another.

"My lady," Molly cried. "They took my lady." She pointed after the outlaws.

The two men exchanged glances. The taller glanced over his shoulder to the third man. "See to these people. We'll be back to take care of the bodies." The two touched their spurs to their horses and galloped away across the fields.

Riding hard across the fresh-turned earth, on a pair of the horses he'd bred especially for speed, Neville and Harrington quickly gained ground on the outlaws. They drew their pistols, aimed as carefully as possible, and fired. One outlaw toppled over, another galloped away, but the third, the one with the girl, struggled to bring his horse under control as it wheeled and reared. The girl rolled off the animal and fell, beneath the flailing hooves, rolling in the soft dirt down a low mound.

Neville drew his rapier and attacked, while Harrington paused to reload. The outlaw, teeth bared in his black beard, snarled what could only be a curse, gathered the reins, and dug his spurs into his horse's sides. The animal wheeled and leapt away as Harrington's bullet screamed harmlessly over his head.

Neville reined his own horse and jumped out of the saddle. He ran to the girl. She was lying on her side, body curled protectively. Her eyes were closed. Neville gently rolled her onto her back. In the purple light of the fading twilight, he gasped. She was beautiful—no wonder the outlaws had kidnapped her. Her pale brown brows arched over rosy eyelids and dark lashes; her nose was delicate, smudged with dirt. He saw one cheek was swollen and bruised. She opened her eyes. For a moment, she stared at him blankly, and then her eyes focused and she gasped.

"It's all right," Neville replied, in the deep brogue he adopted for his disguise. He pulled the gag out of her mouth and helped her to sit up. "I'm not going to hurt you." He untied the bonds around her wrists. "Are you all right?"

She touched her throat in a gesture that appeared nearly automatic, and then drew her fingers away as if stung. A shadow crossed her face momentarily and she looked down. "I'm—as well as can be expected under the circumstances," she managed. She looked up, met his eyes through the slits of the mask, and smiled fleetingly, a tremulous expression that flitted across her face and was gone.

Neville faltered. Her eyes were dark green, the lashes long and curling. He'd had plenty of women kiss his hands in gratitude, and gaze at him with near worshipful devotion, since he'd taken on his new role, but never one who looked like this. And certainly never one who roused this instant need. He felt as though his breath had been knocked out of him, even as his pulse began to throb. He swallowed hard and dropped his eyes, staring at the ground. He was behaving like a moonstruck fifteen-year-old boy.

Behind him, he heard Harrington lead both horses forward. "Are you all right, miss? What about you, Niall?"

"I'm fine, Shane," Neville answered, using Harrington's outlaw name. He pushed the girl's skirts above her ankles and untied the leather cord, his hands moving as rapidly as if he handled hot coals. He rose to his feet and extended a hand to the girl. "Can you stand, do you think?"

"I can try," she replied with a little toss of her head and that same flicker of a brave smile. She took his hand and, clinging to it, got to her feet. Their eyes met once more, and this time, a hint of a flush stained her pale cheeks. "Thank you, sir."

Neville felt the heat surge in his blood, and he dropped her hand abruptly. "We'll take you back to the coach, miss. You should have that cheek attended to as soon as possible. Come."

"Who—who are you?" she asked.

Neville smiled. "Why, miss, I thought you'd guessed." He swept her a low bow, exaggerating the motion, diving as deeply as he could into the masquerade. "Gentleman Niall, at your service, miss." He straightened. "This is not the first time these ruffians have invaded my territory. My apologies."

"Will someone find them? Capture them?"

Neville shrugged. "There's a garrison in Ennis, miss. And as for whether they'll be captured—well, if the same soldiers that've been after us are to be responsible, it's not likely it'll be any time soon." He tried to speak lightly, but he saw that a shadow crossed her face. "What's wrong?" he said gently. "Did they take something of yours?"

Her hand went to her throat again. "My locket—my mother's locket. She gave it to me when I was twelve—it was hers, you see. It—it always made me feel close to her." The girl looked up, and once more their eyes met.

Neville drew a quick breath. Suddenly he wanted nothing more than to hunt down the rival gang and find the locket. But even though he was sure he would indeed find the outlaws, he knew that the locket most likely would have been long sold. "I'll do what I can to find it for you, miss." He heard the words leave his mouth and looked up to see Harrington regarding him with an amused expression. To cover his confusion, he motioned to Harrington. "This man is my right hand."

Harrington smiled and bowed. "Shane, at your service, miss. May we have the honor of your name, miss?"

The girl gave a little laugh at their clumsy courtesy. She put her hand in front of her face as if to hide her smile. "My name is Elizabeth Wentworth. I'm the daughter of—"

"Sir Oliver Wentworth?" Harrington looked at Neville. "You're his daughter?"

"Yes," she answered.

Neville felt as though the air had been punched from his lungs. This was the woman he was bound to marry? For a moment, an image of her white body naked on his wide bed in Clonmore Castle flashed against his eyes. Then the realization of the demands of the life he'd chosen to lead, the need for absolute trust in all who were close to him, the unlikelihood that the daughter of a baronet whose loyalties were staunchly English, no matter what his luck was with the cards, would ever understand what drove him to this masquerade smashed upon him like a wave on a driftwood raft. Then he thought of his face, of the deep ridges of scars which marred the top right half of his face, and the horrified reaction she would have to it. Suddenly he knew anything even approaching a real marriage was a foolish hope. He doubted she'd stare at him so appealingly if she knew what lay beneath the black silk. He met Harrington's eyes with a steely glint that immediately confused his friend. "Come," he said again, this time gruffly. "Shane, take the lass. See that they get on their way, then meet me at the gathering place."

His heart twisted as the girl looked up at him, her expression one of faint disappointment. How transparent she was. And how innocent. She knew nothing of the reality of the harsh side of Ireland, and he told himself she wouldn't care if she did. He turned away with a cold expression. Harrington threw him a questioning glance, but did as he was told. He helped the girl into the saddle, then gathered the reins in his hands and swung up behind her. "Aye, Niall. At the gathering place."

With a nod, Neville watched as Harrington walked the horse across the field toward the road. They disappeared against the hedgerow in the falling dark. He breathed a hard sigh and gazed up at the sky. The early clouds had disappeared, and the full moon stared down at him, the face as merry as if it harbored secrets never guessed at. Sir Oliver Wentworth's daughter. The heiress of Kilmara was not just a cosseted chit of a girl. She was beautiful and possessed a certain spirit besides. Despite his resolve, he knew it would not be as easy to keep his distance as he'd supposed. He gathered up the reins as the horse whickered in the night. "You're right, boy. Time to get home and think about what to do next." He swung into the saddle and cantered off across the fields, a dark figure against the black landscape.

Five

Elizabeth opened her eyes. She lay still, staring up at the white silk lining of the canopy above her head, and for a moment, she felt as though she were back in her grandmother's house in Somerset even as her cheek throbbed with a dull ache. Then she touched her throat and felt the locket's absence. Yesterday evening came crashing back in all its awful reality. She shut her eyes and forced the images of the crude outlaws from her mind. It was over. She was safe, thanks to Gentleman Niall and his men. The image of the tall, masked outlaw rose before her, and she smiled to herself as an unfamiliar wave of warmth spread across her body. What was the word Sir Anthony said the Irish used— a rapparee? It had a wild lilt to it that described Gentleman Niall perfectly. His eyes had smiled so kindly at her, his voice had been so gentle as he promised to find her locket, his hands so careful not to further upset her in any way when he removed the bonds from her wrists and ankles. But she remembered how cold he'd turned when he'd heard her name, and she was rudely reminded that in his eyes, she was one of the enemy.

She turned her head on the lace-trimmed pillow and gazed across the unfamiliar room to the wide windows which were covered in pale blue drapes over white lace curtains. The sheets smelled of lavender. Sunlight streamed in through gaps in the drapery, and for a moment, the terrors of the night before receded as though they only existed in some far distant past. This had been her mother's girlhood room. She was here at Kilmara at last.

She sat up in bed and stared across the room at her reflection in the wide mirror above the clothespress. Her long blonde hair curled down over her shoulders, hiding the purplish swelling on her cheek. She turned her head a little, and pushed the wavy locks behind her ear, as she frowned at her reflection. At least a week or more, the housekeeper had said, before it would be gone completely. She was lucky the ruffian hadn't hit her any harder. She hoped she would at least be presentable by the wedding, which her grandmother had told her would take place in a week. She vaguely remembered being handed out of the coach, and folded in the housekeeper's—what was her name? Mistress Gallagher?— —capable embrace.

Somehow they'd gotten her up the steps and into a hot bath steeped in sweet-smelling herbs. She remembered being fed a warm, buttery porridge and being put to bed wrapped in a clean white nightgown that smelled of fresh air and sunshine, cool compresses steeped in herbs placed against her cheek, and a grassy-smelling balm applied to the bruise. She breathed a deep sigh and wrapped her arms around herself. She supposed she ought to feel more upset than she actually did. But every time she thought of the first outlaw, with his rank smell and hairy face, Gentleman Niall's face superimposed itself. She remembered how blue his eyes were through the narrow slits of the black mask, how straight his nose above his chiseled lips. He'd lifted her so easily—she remembered how strong his hand had been when it closed around hers. And he'd felt something, too, she knew he had, at least until he'd heard she was connected to Sir Oliver. What could explain his immediate animosity? Could he hate the English that much? The dashing outlaw had quite stolen her heart.

She shook her head and gave a rueful little laugh. At least it would give her something to daydream about when she was married to the Earl. I wonder if there's any way to contact him, she thought. To thank him for saving me. But even as she considered how such a thing could be accomplished, she knew that it was no more likely to happen than she was to fall in love with her intended husband. Besides, the way he'd handed her off to his lieutenant, or assistant, or whatever he called that man Shane, should be enough to tell her that Gentleman Niall would most likely be less than pleased to see or hear from her.

She wondered exactly how early it was, and how Molly and Master Beauchamp were faring. Their ordeal had been as terrifying as her own. But the sunlight was still pale. She slipped out of bed and, barefoot, went to one of the long windows. She pushed aside the lace curtain and gasped. Kilmara lay before her, the wide green lawns sweeping down from the house, the graveled drive lined with oaks. Horses grazed on the lawns and, nearer the house, the gardens, even in autumn, were carefully tended beds where flowers grew. She opened the window, heedless of the hour or the weather, and stepped outside. The stone was cold on her bare feet, but the sun was warm. She wrapped her arms around herself, drinking in the beauty of the land she had come to. No wonder her mother had loved this place. No wonder she had longed to see it again. Elizabeth finally understood why her mother had longed to return here—for the Ireland represented by Kilmara was a land so achingly beautiful, it made her heart stop in her chest. For a moment, she could hardly wait to ride across the wide green fields, exploring. But then she remembered the grim sights of yesterday's journey. She could not forget the haunted eyes in the thin faces of the family huddled beneath the hedgerow, the scrawny bodies so inadequately clothed against the damp chill. How could a land of such lush beauty also harbor such grinding poverty? Were there more families crowded together beneath the hedgerows of Kilmara? Surely it wasn't possible.

She turned back as a chill wind made her shiver, and stepped back inside the high-ceilinged bedroom she'd not had time to properly appreciate last night. A thick flowered carpet, faded to soft pinks and creams and blues, covered the floor, and a long chest stood at the foot of the great bed. Elizabeth opened it, wondering for a moment if it held anything that used to be her mother's. It was empty, and Elizabeth felt a twinge of disappointment. *What were you hoping to discover, you ninny?* she scolded herself just as a soft tap on the door made her look up. "Come in," she called.

"Ah, you're up, miss." The face of an unfamiliar girl peered into the room. "May I bring in your breakfast?"

"Please," said Elizabeth. She rose to her feet, gathering her nightrobe about her shoulders. "Who are you?"

"I'm Sorcha, miss. Your own maid is dead asleep—she's quite worn out, I think, from everything that happened yesterday. Mrs. Gallagher sent me up in her place. I hope it's all right with you?"

"Of course," answered Elizabeth. "Is Molly all right?"

"So far as I know, miss. That was a terrible thing that happened to you both last night," said Sorcha. She appeared to be about Elizabeth's own age, with a wealth of tangled black curls only somewhat confined by the cap she wore. She set a tray with covered silver serving dishes on the table beside the window and bent before the hearth, reaching into the bucket of coal with brass tongs. "I'll build this up a bit, shall I, miss? The room's a bit chilly."

Elizabeth realized that her feet were freezing. She sat down at the table and turned over the silver covers. Savory steam rose from a thick slice of ham and a bowl of the thick porridge from last night. Her mouth watered unexpectedly. Sorcha worked silently while Elizabeth began to eat.

Finally the girl rose to her feet, wiping her hands on her apron. "Is there anything else I can do for you, miss?"

"You can talk to me," replied Elizabeth between bites. "Do you live here at Kilmara?"

"Oh, aye, miss. Ever since I started working here—that will be six years ago at Christmas. They needed an extra hand in the scullery, and Mam needed one less mouth to feed after my da died."

"And tell me please, Sorcha, do you know this earl that I am to marry? Have you ever met him?"

For a moment the girl looked confused. "I've seen him, my lady. Aye."

"Well—does he have a hump? Is it true he wears a mask?"

Sorcha looked uncomfortable. "It's true enough he wears a mask, my lady. The story is that his da threw him in the fire when he was very young."

"Threw him in the fire?" Elizabeth put down the knife she was using to smear the thick jam over the crusty bread.

"That's the story they tell, miss. I've no idea if it's true." Sorcha looked nervously over her shoulder, as though frightened that she might be caught gossiping about her betters.

"But there's no hump?"

"He limps, so that one side of his back looks higher than the other. And he wears a mask—to hide the scars from the burns. I've seen him meself. It's always the same white silk, and . . ." She hesitated as though fearful of saying too much.

"Go on, Sorcha. No one else has told me anything much about him. And my father means me to marry him within the week."

The little maid took a deep breath. "Well, miss. Let me think what I can tell you. He's a tall one—my head would only come up to his chest, I think, and yours to his shoulder, perhaps. His hair is black as pitch, and it's hard to see his face with the mask and all, but he's got a strong chin, if you know what I mean, and a beautiful mouth for a man. His mother, Lady Moira, she was one of the great beauties of her day, Mrs. Gallagher was saying last night. And he might've looked just like her—well, you know, not like her exactly, but enough like her—it's such a shame his father hurt him the way he did."

"But why," Elizabeth asked as she smeared jam onto a slice of the fragrant bread. She licked a spot off her thumb. The jam tasted fresh, as though the berries had been gathered only days before. "Why would anyone do such a terrible thing to a child?"

Sorcha shook her head and shrugged. "I've heard of folk

doing that and worse to their children, miss. Perhaps not among the gentry—" She broke off and shrugged again.

Elizabeth was silent, thinking of the pain and terror the Earl must've suffered as a child. How could any father be so cruel? *Well,* a soft voice spoke in her mind, *look at what your father did to you.* He surely didn't care what sort of man he married her off to—just so long as his debts were clean and he could leave Ireland and start fresh again in London. She thought of her grandmother in the big house in Somerset, dealing with her father all alone, and how she fretted over the antics of her son, saying aloud time and again what would happen to him when she finally died. No, Elizabeth decided, her own father was only marginally better than Lord Neville's had been. She looked up to see Sorcha shifting her weight from foot to foot. "Thank you, Sorcha, I'm fine right now."

Sorcha bobbed a curtsey. "Mrs. Gallagher will be looking for me in the kitchen, miss. And the water for your wash is heating now. I'll start carrying it up directly."

Elizabeth sat for a long time, staring into the fire, her hands cupped around a delicate china teacup. How terrible for Lord Neville. If he was physically deformed, well, at least now she understood why. Still, she shivered at the thought of what he might look like. She reached for the locket, but touched only her throat. Pain lanced through her, pain for the loss of her most precious gift from her mother, pain at the thought of marrying a man she didn't know and couldn't begin to imagine. *Mother, keep me strong,* she thought, as there was another knock on the door. She set down the teacup deliberately and stood up, squaring her shoulders. She would face this day in a way that would make both her mother and her grandmother proud.

The summons from her father came close to noon, while Elizabeth, Sorcha, and Mistress Gallagher were sorting through her trunks. The housekeeper looked up with an exasperated expression on her face. "Trust Sir Oliver to wait until we're all busy," she murmured beneath her breath, but loud enough for Elizabeth to hear. Elizabeth exchanged a glance and a wink with Sorcha. Obviously her father was considered as much an inconvenience in Ireland as he'd always been in England.

He'd been kind last night in an offhand sort of way, patting her uninjured cheek gingerly and declaring he'd have to set up a target tomorrow. Then he'd vanished into his study, and Elizabeth had been too tired and upset to notice.

Now, a bright fire burned in the polished hearth and a small table was laid before it when the housekeeper ushered Elizabeth into the library, where her father waited. "Hello, Father," she said uncertainly, suddenly shy at the prospect of speaking to this man she'd not seen for over a year, and who held such absolute sway over her life.

"Well, well. Feeling better this morning, are we?" Sir Oliver, rounder and more florid than she remembered, rose to his feet as he ran his eyes over her body. Elizabeth felt herself flush under such blatant scrutiny, even as annoyance rose beneath her embarrassment. How dare he look her over like a prize cow? Her own father treated her no better than the ruffian outlaws did. "How you have grown up, m'dear. Lord Neville will be most gratified when he sees you, I'm sure. A title, an estate, and a pretty wife—what more could any young man want?" He chuckled at his own joke. "Come and sit." He gestured to the small table. "You'll wed your bridegroom tomorrow. "

"Tomorrow?" Elizabeth blinked. Surely he jested.

"Aye, tomorrow. I want this matter concluded as quickly as possible, and so does he. We would have had you married today, but I thought in light of last night's circumstances— well, I thought it would be better to postpone the wedding until tomorrow."

"But—but, Father, I've only just arrived. . . ." Elizabeth felt slightly faint. "Grandmother said I'd have some time to get used to—"

"You have a lifetime to get used to the place. I've already had my man book passage on the stage for Dublin on the day after tomorrow, and I mean to be on it. Your bridegroom is just as eager, believe me. We even got a special dispensation from the bishop allowing Mr. Ogilivie—he's the local parson—to marry you here without the banns being called."

"But—but—Father—" Elizabeth began. Her head was beginning to spin.

"Buck up, girl. Here, come and sit and have a bite of lunch. You're a pretty thing, but you need some meat on those bones. If you think about it, Lizzie, you'll see there's no sense in delaying matters. It's a done deal; it only needs a few words before the parson, and then the whole matter can be concluded and I will be back in England before the sheets are dry on your wedding bed." He chuckled. "And who're those interfering dissenters you brought with you? Looks like a lot of Puritans to me—my mother's gone to Puritan toadies, I see."

"They are Master Beauchamp, her solicitor, and Molly, my maid. You didn't think she'd allow me to travel alone, did you?"

Sir Oliver shrugged. "Don't much care to spend any time speculating on what the old lady thinks, m'dear. I knew I'd met that Beauchamp fellow before—I thought I recognized his pinch-faced puss when they carried him off the coach."

"How are Master Beauchamp and Molly? They've been through just as much as I."

Sir Oliver waved an airy hand, "They're fine, I suppose. Still abed, I'm told. After all, what really happened? So a few pence were lost—you know, the same gang attacked me not long ago? 'Twas a disgrace—at least you escaped real injury." He snorted and turned away as an uncomfortable look crossed his face.

"And Mother's locket," Elizabeth said quietly, reaching automatically for her throat.

"Most unfortunate, my girl. But we won't dwell on unpleasantness, shall we—what's gone is gone. No sense weeping over the past, as your grandmother likes to say." He broke off as the door opened, and Mistress Gallagher peered into the room.

Elizabeth glanced down at the silver-covered dishes on the tray. Until she'd learned that tomorrow was to be her wedding day, she'd been hungry. Now she felt slightly sick. She poured herself half a cup of tea with a shaking hand as Sir Oliver frowned at the interruption.

"Well? What is it?"

"Sir William St. Denys and Colonel Melville of the garrison to see you, Sir Oliver," said the housekeeper with a curtsey. "You and the young lady."

"About time they got here. Lizzie, eat your lunch. Sir William and Colonel Melville want to talk to you."

"I don't feel like eating, Father," Elizabeth answered. How foolish she'd been to ever imagine Sir Oliver cared one whit about her welfare. So much for setting up a target and shooting with her father. Right now, she wouldn't trust herself not to shoot at him.

"Well, if you insist, m'dear. Come take this tray and show them in, Mistress." Sir Oliver rose to his feet and threw another log on the fire. "And have Eamon bring in more wood. Can't get the damp of this place from my bones today."

Elizabeth met the housekeeper's disapproving glance. She wasn't surprised to see that Mistress Gallagher shared her low opinion of her father, but it would never do to appear to sympathize with one of the servants. But she had to stifle the urge to giggle when the housekeeper rolled her eyes and winked as she lifted the heavy tray. "Aye, Sir Oliver," was all the woman said.

"Tell them everything you remember, Lizzie," said Sir Oliver. He strode to the door and flung it wide. "Sir William," he boomed. "Colonel Melville. Thank you for coming."

Elizabeth peered around the back of the chair. Two white-wigged men accompanied her father, one short and stout, in a red military uniform bright with braid and ribbons, and the other large and stout, in plain brown riding clothes.

"Sir William, Colonel Melville, may I present my daughter, Elizabeth."

At least he hadn't called her Lizzie. She rose, lowered her eyes demurely, and dropped a curtsey. "Sir William, Colonel Melville."

The men muttered greetings while her father dragged two chairs closer. "Come, sit."

"You must forgive us, Lady Elizabeth," began Sir William as he settled himself in the straight-backed chair.

"But it's imperative you tell us as much as you can about what you remember about the attack. Gentleman Niall is a pernicious—"

"But it wasn't Gentleman Niall," she interrupted. The men stared at each other in surprise.

"The devil you say, Lizzie," swore her father. "I heard you say yourself last night 'twas him—what are you talking about now, miss?"

"'Twas Gentleman Niall who saved me, Father," Elizabeth answered coolly. She turned to Sir William and Colonel Melville. "There was another gang—he said so himself."

"Who said so, my lady?" asked Colonel Melville, chins quivering with interest.

Elizabeth bit back a smile. He reminded her of the fat rooster which strutted around her grandmother's kitchen gardens, terrorizing the gardeners who dared to come too close to the hens. "Gentleman Niall, Colonel. He said there was another gang of outlaws operating in his territory—and they were no gentlemen, believe me."

"Maybe that's who attacked you, Wentworth," said Sir William. He looked over his shoulder at Sir Oliver. "What do you think?"

"It was dark," replied Sir Oliver irritably. "Lizzie, are you quite sure?"

"Begin at the beginning, my lady," said Colonel Melville. "Pray tell me exactly what happened."

Slowly, shuddering, Elizabeth recounted the events of the past night. "But that's when he came along," she said, as she described the whole episode. "I was on the horse—they would've carried me off—but Gentleman Niall and his two men came along—"

"Only two? What were their names?" asked the colonel.

"Shane, the one was. And the third man . . ." Elizabeth wrinkled her brow, trying to remember. "I don't believe anyone ever said."

"Did they mention anything about where they were going, or where they had come from? Did you hear them say anything that might indicate a place?"

Elizabeth hesitated. The bold outlaw who had saved her

had seemed wholly incapable of wrong—a hero like those she'd read about in the romances of King Arthur that she loved. But the men were watching her closely, assessing her hesitation. "They said something about a gathering place," she answered guilelessly. "But they said nothing about where."

Sir William exchanged glances with Colonel Melville then rose to his feet with an exasperated shrug. "They're clever, this lot. They take care to say nothing in front of witnesses, their clothing is dark and always the same, they go about masked so there's no telling one from another. . . ."

"My lady," said Colonel Melville. Elizabeth looked up. His little black eyes, dark and hard as jet, bored into hers and she dared not look away. "Did you notice anything about this self-proclaimed gentleman? Was he a tall man or a short one? Broad or narrow in build? Blue-eyed or brown?"

She swallowed, knowing that every word she spoke felt like a betrayal. "He seemed a well-set-up man to me," she answered slowly. "But I am not well schooled in such things." She lowered her eyes modestly.

"And his voice?"

"It was—" She hesitated. What was she to say? That it had struck her like the taste of custard still warm from the oven? That it was rich and soft and low, the easy consonants and liquid vowels wooing in a cadence that was as comforting as her mother's? "A deep voice," she finished. "Yes, a deep voice. Such as yours, Sir William." She beamed at Sir William, who cleared his throat and looked abashed.

"An English voice, you mean, my lady?" Colonel Melville was watching her closely.

"No, Colonel, not at all. Very Irish—I could scarce understand them when they spoke. I only meant that Gentleman Niall's voice was deep, as Sir William's is." She laced her hands together as she spoke and held them placidly in her lap. "But what about these other outlaws?"

Sir William shrugged. "What about them?"

"Aren't you concerned about catching them, as well? They seem far more dangerous than this Gentleman Niall."

"And so they are, my lady, and we'll be watching for

them at every turn. But you must understand," said Colonel Melville, "that these are garden-variety criminals—petty ruffians not at all clever as a group. 'Twill be relatively easy to apprehend them. This Gentleman Niall is a horse of an entirely other color. Why, he's been robbing the honest people of this district for over two years!"

"Which is precisely why I called Sir Anthony, Colonel," said Sir William. "I know you believe we can capture him without Sir Anthony's assistance, but so far, we've had little luck."

Colonel Melville nearly sneered. "At the moment, Sir Anthony is less than useless."

"I know I've done all I can," put in Sir Oliver. "I've posted guards, organized searches—this one's the very devil for giving us all the slip. It's past time we brought in someone who knows exactly how these outlaws think."

The devil you say, thought Elizabeth. For a moment, she wondered how the men would react if she used that expression. "But the others are the ones who took my locket, Father—the emerald locket Mama gave me. Isn't there some way to get it back?"

Only Sir William acknowledged her question. "My dear Lady Elizabeth, I'm very sorry—it's most likely that the locket is already on its way to Dublin. There's very little chance of ever finding it—"

"Unless Clonmore likes to frequent pawn shops!" Sir Oliver laughed.

Even Colonel Melville regarded her father with something like horror.

"I see," said Elizabeth with a sigh. She remembered how Gentleman Niall had offered to find it for her, but it was highly unlikely he would do it. No wonder he had looked so angry when he heard her father's name. Sir Oliver had clearly accused the outlaw of doing something he wasn't responsible for. But would that be enough? asked a very soft voice in her mind. Surely outlaws get accused of doing many things—

"Can you remember anything else about Gentleman Niall?" asked the colonel.

I remember everything, she thought. But she met his eyes evenly and only said, "No, Colonel. I'm sorry, that's all. If I may inquire, though, sir, how does Sir Anthony?"

"Ah, he'll be laid up for a few days with that wound, but he'll mend," said Sir William. He exchanged a glance with Colonel Melville, who only sniffed and turned away. "Don't you worry, my dear. He'll be up and about in no time, and I will be sure to convey your greetings." He rose to his feet. "Well, Sir Oliver, we'll be in touch—"

"Not with me you won't," Sir Oliver replied. "I'm leaving on the Dublin stage tomorrow—soon as the wedding is concluded. I've had enough of Ireland for one lifetime."

"Ah," said Sir William, as both he and Colonel Melville turned to Elizabeth. "And congratulations, my dear. Lady St. Denys joins me in wishing you much contentment in your marriage."

Elizabeth forced a smile. "Thank you, Sir William, Colonel Melville." She rose and curtseyed as her father escorted the men from the library. For a moment she felt like crying, but what was the use? Even Mr. Beauchamp and Molly believed that marriage to an earl—any earl—was preferable to marriage with anyone else, except of course, perhaps a duke. Automatically she felt at her throat for her locket, before she remembered it was gone. With a deep sigh, she wandered out of the library, feeling lost and alone.

Then she remembered that Mistress Gallagher had said she might speak to Molly after lunch. She glanced out a narrow window beside the front door and saw that her father, Sir William, and Colonel Melville remained deep in conversation. A sniff told her the direction of the kitchens. She started off, eager to see Molly, who now seemed so much more than just a maid. She was the closest connection to her old life that Elizabeth possessed.

Soft gray clouds were massing over the western hills by the time Sir William and Colonel Melville cantered out of Kilmara's long drive and turned on to the road back to Ennis. As soon as they had settled into a fast trot, Sir William turned to the colonel. "Well, sir, what did you think of that?"

The colonel hesitated a moment before replying. "I think the girl's worth watching."

"Ho, sir, indeed!" Sir William laughed. "Who would ever have thought that—"

"I meant regarding the outlaw, Sir William," Colonel Melville said dryly.

Sir William cleared his throat. "Of course, Colonel. But why do you believe that, sir? She sounded as though she had very little real information to give us beyond what I've heard time and again."

The colonel smiled, his eyes fastened on the road. "This is different. He didn't rob her. All the witnesses you've interviewed, Sir William, have all been victims of this man. But not Lady Elizabeth. He didn't rob her. He saved her. And she harbors tender feelings for him—I could see it on her face. It's as though she thinks of him as some knight in shining armor."

"Now, surely, sir, you exaggerate. She seemed quite a congenial young woman. I sincerely doubt she could ever see such a thing in a outlaw like that." Sir William's brow was creased, as if with the effort of trying to imagine such a scenario.

Colonel Melville only nodded with assurance, as he kept his eyes fastened on the hilly horizon. "I think the soon-to-be Countess of Clonmore is quite taken with Gentleman Niall. She might even try to contact him, one way or another."

"How can you even think so, sir?" demanded Sir William. "It would be unheard of—"

"Sir William, no one is so far removed from the circumstances of his environment that it is impossible to make contact with anyone on any level. Lady Elizabeth will decide to contact the outlaw—believe me, I've studied young women like her. That type is highly romantic—she will see it as her duty to thank him for his good deed. That he might turn around and rob her or worse, of course, is not likely to occur to her, even up to the moment he does it." Melville's eyes flickered to Sir William. "But my original point is this: she should be watched, and closely."

"And how are we to accomplish that?"

Colonel Melville turned up his collar as the first fat raindrop stung his cheek. "We must give this some thought, Sir William. It seems we have a clear possibility to lead us to the outlaw. I'm not quite sure yet how to best exploit it." His chins wobbled a little with resolve. "But I'll think of something. Quite soon." *Before Sir Anthony is up and about,* he thought to himself. *It's my turn to snatch an outlaw from under Sir Anthony's long, thin nose.*

Six

Elizabeth opened her eyes to the sunlight streaming through the long window in bright streaks across the flowered carpet and knew at once that it was her wedding day. The thought did not bring the delicious rush of anticipation she had always imagined this day would bring. Today, it brought only dread.

She touched her injured cheek gingerly. It was still swollen and tender, but did her fingers detect that the swelling had diminished? Still, hers was hardly the face of a bride. Well, maybe she should wear a mask, too. They could say it was a real wedding "masque." The pun tickled her fancy and she laughed out loud, and then laughed even harder at the thought of both bride and groom standing masked before the priest. She heard the hysteria rise in her giggles, and she took a deep breath, forcing herself to calm down. No, this certainly wasn't the wedding her mother had imagined with her all those years ago.

She lay in the middle of the white bed, staring up at the canopy. She knew what her mother had hoped for—a good marriage, one with advantages for both bride and groom, of course. But beyond that, she knew her mother had intended her to marry a good man, a man with a keen sense of his responsibility to both his wife and his children. Her mother never intended her daughter to endure the same situation she had found herself in.

But to be fair, she knew less than nothing about the Earl's true character. For all she knew, he could be the kindest man in the world. But would even the kindest be enough to redirect the spark Gentleman Niall had ignited? Her mother had told her long ago what would be expected of her, in terms of the marriage bed. She shut her eyes, deliberately willing away the image of a scarred, twisted form possessing hers.

That image was replaced by the thought of the tall outlaw who had saved her. She remembered the sure but gentle way he'd touched her, even as he'd assured her he meant her no harm. She imagined what the life of the outlaw must be. Did he have some sort of lair to which he returned by day, or did he move from place to place, seldom staying for more than a few days at a time? Either option would seem to preclude any kind of family life. After all, what sort of woman would follow an outlaw like that? What sort of woman could? She rolled onto her side and smiled to herself. She could imagine exactly what sort. She could imagine how horrified her mother would be if she knew what her daughter was thinking. Her grandmother would probably have her locked away. She knew it was an improbable daydream, for the life of an outlaw was far too dirty and dangerous for her. But it was not unpleasant to think about. She rolled flat on her back, clutching her pillow to her chest, imagining how those gentle hands would feel stroking and caressing her body, his soft lips on hers. She took a deep breath as a sudden rush of warmth flooded through her body like an insistent tide.

A gentle tap on the door jolted her out of her daydream. She sat up with a start, as Sorcha peered inside. "Ah, miss, you're awake. Mistress Molly said she'd be up directly and sent me to build up the fire for ye."

Elizabeth nodded, saying nothing as she watched Sorcha work. Life with an outlaw certainly wouldn't include a hot coal fire, or a servant to stoke it. Or more servants to wash her clothes and cook her food, as well as to care for all the day-to-day tasks which made her life so easy. Of course, her grandmother explained the differences between the classes as the preordained Will of God, but Elizabeth was not so sure. But given the chance, would she really want to trade all these comforts for a life with a man she could love?

She was mostly silent while Molly, assisted by both Sorcha and Mistress Gallagher, fussed over every aspect of her toilette, making certain her stockings and garters were fixed just so, that the pad she wore laced on her hips was correctly positioned beneath her voluminous petticoats, that the double layers of lace which fell from her three-quarter-length sleeves draped in an artful fall. Finally Molly stepped back. "Now, let me have a look at you, my lady. Stand up."

Obediently, Elizabeth rose to her feet. With a critical eye and a pursed mouth, Molly made a few adjustments to her pale green satin gown, tugging here, tucking there, until she was satisfied. She stood back and gestured to Sorcha. "Do you see how that was done, girl? If you mean to be a lady's maid, you must pay attention to the details—the fall of the lace, the arrangement of the sash. . . ."

Sorcha nodded, wide-eyed.

"What do you think, Mrs. Gallagher? Do you approve?"

"Oh, aye, Mistress," said Mistress Gallagher through an approving sigh. She clasped her hands together. "She's the picture of a bride."

Elizabeth flushed. To her mind, she looked anything but. Not only was she the unwilling bride of a virtual stranger, but she was bruised and battered as well.

"Now, then," continued Molly, taking up the brush. "Let's see to your hair, my lady."

Elizabeth sank back down on the stool, submitting silently to Molly's ministrations. Outside, she heard the clop of horses' hooves on the driveway, and her pulse began to beat faster. Someone had arrived. "Sorcha," she said quietly, "go look out the window and see who it is."

Sorcha ran to the window and looked out from the balcony. "The parson, miss—I mean, my lady. And—oh, my, that's the earl's chestnut stallion—there's not another horse like it in the county, they say. He must have gone in already."

"Ah!" said Mrs. Gallagher. "I'd best go downstairs and

see to the breakfast, All the best to ye, lass." She bobbed a curtsey and was gone.

Elizabeth bit her lip in frustration. If she could only just have a look at her future husband from a distance, so she could prepare herself. She understood her duty—she'd seen more often than she cared to remember fresh-faced brides married to men old enough to be their fathers, and in some cases grandfathers. But to have to marry someone maimed—someone so scarred he could not show his face in society—she breathed a deep sigh.

At once, Molly patted her shoulder. "There, there, child. It will all work itself out, you'll see. The earl is not known as a cruel man—not one person who's spoken of him says anything bad about his character—"

"They say nothing about his character," Elizabeth burst out. "All anyone talks about is how he looks. How monstrous must that be?"

"Oh, now, miss," said Sorcha, her face soft with sympathy. "'Tis not that bad—I've never heard anyone speak a cold word of the earl. He keeps to himself, mostly, but 'tis understandable. And some years ago—" She broke off. "I shouldn't speak of this, for me mam would have me head, were she to think I even knew the story, but . . ."

"Oh, please tell me, Sorcha," Elizabeth said. "I want to know something of the sort of person I must marry."

"His lordship came back to Ireland when he was a young man—I was perhaps seven or eight. The old lord welcomed him and for a time, they say, all was well. But then one of the maids in the house turned up with child. So the young lord took her away, and never returned until the old lord had been dead nearly a year. But you see, miss, he's not a bad sort at all."

"What happened to the girl—and the child?"

Sorcha shrugged. "I've never heard."

Elizabeth took a deep breath and watched as Molly fussed with her hair, arranging the curls first one way, then another. The story was an old and familiar one, but for the fact that there had obviously been a falling out between father and son. But what had prompted the son to return to a father who'd nearly killed him in childhood? And why had a by-blow engendered another argument, this time driving the son away until the father was a year in his grave? And had he loved this woman—this girl—whom he'd chosen over his father and his wealth? And what had happened to them? Were they still alive somewhere? The man she was to marry was an enigma—each tiny scrap of information she managed to obtain only yielded more questions.

The little clock on the mantel chimed the hour, and Elizabeth jumped.

" 'Tis eleven, miss," Sorcha said.

Molly gave one last pat to a curl here, one last twist to a strand there. She stepped back and smiled. "There."

Elizabeth gazed at herself in the mirror. Her face was pale, her green eyes shadowed, but the thick honey-colored mass of her hair glowed around her face like a halo, the curls falling artfully over one shoulder. Her square-necked bodice revealed the tops of her high, round breasts, while a delicate lace fichu hinted at modesty.

She touched her swollen cheek. It was still puffy and beginning to darken to a deep purple in the center. She didn't feel like a bride. She remembered the mask idea from earlier, and suppressed a sudden giggle. Molly, seeing the fleeting smile, smiled back. "That's right, lamb. There's the spirit. Everything will be fine."

Outside, another set of hooves told her someone else had come. Elizabeth pressed her lips together and closed her eyes, reaching automatically for the locket. But once again, her hand encountered only the soft flesh of her throat. It felt naked and vulnerable. She would have to do this without its reassuring presence. She squared her shoulders. "All right, Molly. I'm ready."

Molly gave her a last pat on her uninjured cheek, then opened the door. Elizabeth rose to her feet. Outside, in the hall, Mr. Beauchamp loitered beneath a portrait. He turned and bowed low as she stepped out of her room. "My dear young lady," he said, his face looking lined and old in the stark morning light. "I thought I would escort you downstairs."

Elizabeth was touched. She'd been angry at the solicitor

when he first reported his findings to her grandmother, but clearly he believed that the decision to marry her to the earl was the best for her. He obviously felt bad that she was so unhappy. But here she was in her mother's childhood home. She glanced up at the portrait of her mother. "Thank you, Mr. Beauchamp," she replied simply.

Together they descended the wide, sweeping stair. The windows there, which rose nearly two stories, overlooked the green park and, in the distance, the shadowy forests. She paused on the landing and looked out. This was her land, after all; was she not bound to it? She raised her chin and gathered her pale green skirts in her hand. She smiled at Mr. Beauchamp. "Lead on, Mr. Beauchamp. I'm ready to meet my groom."

Four men were gathered by the hearth in the room where Elizabeth had eaten the night before—her father, a man in clerical garb, and two others. One man stood beside the chair, his back toward her. He turned to face her as soon as they crossed the threshold, and Elizabeth saw at once he wasn't masked. But the other man was seated in one of the high-backed chairs, one leg stretched out before him. It was encased in a dark brown boot that clung like a glove to the long lines of his thigh.

Mr. Beauchamp paused, and Elizabeth clutched his arm. Her heart was beating hard in her chest. Slowly the man in the chair rose. He was taller than her father and the priest, she noted; indeed, he towered over both. Only Beauchamp and the other stranger came close to his height. From under his white silk mask, his black hair flowed into a neat tail, tied with a wide white ribbon. His linen was simple, but snowy, and his clothes fit him well. Beauchamp started forward, and Elizabeth squared her shoulders and raised her chin. She would not be intimidated by his appearance.

The Earl walked around the chair, and Elizabeth saw that he dragged one leg, and that when he walked, one shoulder appeared slightly higher than the other. She extended her hand and hoped that no one would notice how her fingers shook.

Her father, nudged by the parson, cleared his throat. "Oh!

May I, uh, may I present m'daughter, m'lord? Elizabeth—
Lord Neville Fitzgerald, Earl of Clonmore. And soon-to-be
your husband." Sir Oliver chuckled.

The Earl took her hand in his, bowed correctly from the
waist, and brushed a dry kiss on the back of her hand. "Lady
Elizabeth."

Elizabeth stared at the white silk as he raised his face to
hers. And then she gasped, for she knew the blue eyes behind the mask—eyes which stared back at her as coldly as
twin points of blue ice. She leaned closer, trying to remember the features of the man who had spoken to her so kindly
that her fears had been instantly allayed. Was this the same
voice? Not the accent of course, but the pitch—didn't it
carry the same low, sweet timbre? "I'm very happy to make
your acquaintance, sir," she replied, careful to peek at him
from beneath her lashes. Could it be possible that the outlaw
who'd saved them all—the outlaw everyone called Gentleman Niall—and the man she was to marry were in reality the
same man? She must be mad to even consider the possibility, but her brain screamed out the obvious resemblance.

His cold tone and clipped words surprised and hurt her
for some reason she could not understand. "Are you?" His
voice was as dry as his kiss and as cold as his eyes. He
turned away, although he still held her hand. "Well, Master
Ogilivie, let's get this over with."

The parson straightened up and opened his prayer book.

Involuntarily, her fingers curled around his. The Earl
turned to look at her and their eyes met once more. Recognition flashed like a lightning bolt between them. Elizabeth
felt breathless, hot and cold all at once. It was him. The Earl
of Clonmore *was* Gentleman Naill. There couldn't be any
doubt—he knew her, too. Against all reason, all possible expectation, the man she stood up to marry at this very moment was the outlaw who'd captured her interest so
thoroughly that she could think of little else. He dropped his
eyes and stared fixedly ahead at the parson. He doesn't want
to admit that I know, she thought. How could he? Her father
was his enemy—as surely all Englishmen must be.

Elizabeth glanced desperately at the other men.

Beauchamp's eyes were fastened on the floor, the parson's on his prayer book. Her father yawned and tapped his foot. Only the man who stood so silently beside the high-backed chair met her eyes with silent sympathy. His dark eyes were soft, his mouth was grim. Shocked, Elizabeth recognized him as the man who'd said his name was Shane. He dropped his gaze and turned away, and Elizabeth looked down lest her eyes give them all away. She forced herself to breathe slowly as Mr. Ogilivie began the ceremony in a sonorous voice.

And then she heard the parson say, "By the authority vested in me by almighty God, I now pronounce you man and wife. What God has joined together, let no man put asunder." Before she knew what was happening, the Earl had turned to her with a swift motion, bent, and pressed his firm lips to her mouth with only the barest of pressure. Her breath caught in her throat with a sigh, and he looked down. Their eyes met, and this time she saw his nostrils flare. So he wasn't quite so indifferent as he wanted everyone to think, she thought. He may appear to be a marble statue, but she knew with sudden certainty that beneath the mask, her bridegroom was as much flesh and blood as she.

And then her father was guffawing and shaking hands with both the parson and the earl, and he smacked a wet kiss on her cheek. "Now buck up, Lizzie." He grinned, elbowing the earl. "You look as pale as death—not at all a morsel to tempt a man on his wedding night. Buck up, girl."

"Perhaps Lady Clonmore would care for a glass of wine?" The man she knew to be Shane came forward. He shot Sir Oliver an angry look. "My name is John Harrington, my lady. I serve your new husband as his agent. You can expect to see more of me than you may care to." He bowed.

Elizabeth glanced away, lest anyone notice her reaction. Let them all think she was a shy bride overcome with the vapors. "Thank you, Harrington," said the earl. "By all means, fetch the bride a glass of wine." She was acutely aware of the warm pressure of his hand beneath her forearm.

"Shall we go in to breakfast?" Sir Oliver asked, taking the parson by the arm. "Quite well done, Mr. Ogilivie." He winked at the parson, and Elizabeth saw something round and gold pass from her father's hand to the parson's.

Elizabeth sat beside her new husband, who seemed to be intent upon pretending that he'd forgotten she was there. From time to time, she stole a glance at him from beneath her lashes. She listened as both Neville—which was the name she assumed he went by—and Harrington questioned her father extensively on the state of Kilmara's wide holdings. She glanced at Harrington once or twice, as well, but he was genuinely absorbed in the conversation. Well, she supposed if he really were the Earl's agent, he had to be. She nibbled on her food and sipped the wine. The wine helped somewhat, but she was still startled when her father rose to his feet and threw his napkin on the table. "Well, gentlemen, shall we finish this?"

"Where are you going?" Elizabeth asked.

Beauchamp started. "Let me fetch my legal case, Sir Oliver." He got to his feet and left the room.

"Harrington, escort the countess to the gardens," the earl said.

At once Harrington got to his feet. "Will you come with me, my lady?"

Elizabeth looked from Harrington to her father to her husband and back. "What is it?"

"There are documents which must be signed, my lady," Harrington answered gently. "Normally such matters would've already been concluded. Will you come?"

"Such matters don't concern me?" Elizabeth asked with bitter irony. For a moment, she was reminded of her position as little more than part of the fulfillment of a debt of honor. She rose to her feet and swept out of the room ahead of Harrington. She did not see the look which passed between the earl and his agent.

Harrington caught up to her in the garden. She sat on a bench beside a fountain built in the French fashion. It splashed merrily in the bright October light. Already the beds had been carefully mulched in preparation for the winter, but a few bright daisies lingered.

He hesitated before approaching her. She appeared so dainty, so vulnerable, and yet he sensed a certain strength within her, a strength he'd sensed when she'd remained calm despite her near kidnapping. And her beauty had taken him off guard—he'd seen two nights ago that she was beautiful, but in the full early afternoon light, only the swollen bruise marred the flawlessness of her face. The delicate nose turned up at the tip, the soft, full mouth such a kissable shade of peach, and the eyes—pale and huge and green, fringed by long, curling lashes. Neville hadn't said much about it, but Harrington knew he'd find it far more difficult than he'd first believed to keep his bride at arm's distance.

He paused a few paces from where she sat, her head high, her shoulders squared, but when she turned to look at him, he saw her eyes were sad. "Forgive me if I intrude, Lady Clonmore. Would you rather be alone?"

At that she gave a short, bitter laugh. "Alone? I am quite alone, sir. I'm in a strange place, surrounded by strange people, given in marriage to a man who's quite a stranger to me."

Harrington drew a deep breath. Her face, for all its beauty, was achingly young. How old was she, he wondered—surely no more than twenty? It was never in his nature to be anything less than courteous to women. He was very conscious of her position. There should've been a woman here, he thought suddenly. Neville was wrong not to have insisted that Lady Moira come. "I'm sorry, Lady Clonmore. I understand this must be very difficult for you."

She shrugged and turned away, fingering the base of her throat, but not before he saw that her eyes filled with tears. "You must forgive me, Mr. Harrington."

He reached into the pocket of his waistcoat and withdrew a large linen handkerchief. Awkwardly he held it out, and she took it with long slender fingers, turning away once more with a little shake of her head. "I—I understand that your journey here was harrowing," he said.

There was a long pause, and for a moment he was afraid he'd said something that had upset her more. But her next words shocked him into silence. "You're Shane, aren't you?"

He knew the blood drained from his face. She'd recognized them. It was unthinkable. "I—I don't know what you're talking about, my lady." He managed to speak with the barest composure.

"You were with him. The two of you rescued me. You said your name was Shane. You took me back to the coach when *he*"—she looked back over her shoulder in the direction of the house—"told you to. And you saw us all safely into Ennis." Her green gaze seemed to penetrate his thoughts.

He gave a little laugh. *Admit nothing,* he told himself. She had no proof, only what she remembered. Beauchamp had shown no sign at all of recognizing them. He wondered how soon he could talk to Neville. He sat down on the far end of the stone bench and placed his hands deliberately on his knees. "My lady, I assure you, two evenings ago I was on my way from Clonmore Castle to Ennis—quite the opposite direction, as you'll come to know. As much as I would like to take the credit, I'm afraid I had nothing to do with your rescue. Speaking for myself, of course."

Her clear green eyes, framed by long dark lashes, did not waver. "You don't want to admit it. You don't know if you can trust me yet, and the Earl is the one who makes the decisions, right?" She paused momentarily, and when he only stared back at her, she went on. "But assure him of this—I have no reason to betray either of you. You saved my life, as well as my honor. I owe you both a great debt. And furthermore, I am now his wife. If he's convicted, his estates would be forfeit, including Kilmara now. So I have many reasons to be loyal." She held his eyes a moment longer, and then turned away.

Harrington sat stunned. It had never occurred to either of them that she might recognize them. No one else ever had. But then, the circumstances were different, weren't they? The robberies went quickly—the men moved constantly with carefully choreographed efficiency and, most often, the victims were frightened and quite willing to do as they were told. He opened his mouth to speak, thought better of it, and shut it again. This new development was completely unexpected. A hundred possible outcomes swirled through his brain like the eddies of a swiftly moving stream. "My lady," he began.

"We need not speak of it any more, Master Harrington. I can see I've upset you now." She glanced down at the handkerchief in her hands and smiled ruefully. "I didn't mean to do that. Perhaps I should've spoken to the earl first. But he—he scarcely wants to look at me."

"The Earl is a very difficult man to get to know," Harrington said slowly. "He's a very kind man, really, but his defenses are . . ."

"Impenetrable," she finished. "Unless he decides to allow you in."

Harrington met her eyes and smiled. "Exactly." He hesitated, thinking of what to say next, when a discreet cough made him look in the direction of the garden gate. A liveried footman stood just inside the garden.

Elizabeth raised her head and saw the man at the same time. "Yes?"

"Lady Clonmore, there is a woman here with an urgent message for his lordship."

"For the Earl?" Harrington narrowed his eyes. "What's her name?"

"She says her name is Emma, sir," replied the footman.

Harrington stiffened. A message from Lady Moira? "I'll take the message. Where is the woman?"

"Waiting by the servants' entrance near the kitchen, sir."

"Thank you, footman." Harrington turned back to Elizabeth. "I must leave you, lady. This message is . . . from someone who cannot be disregarded."

"Do as you must, Mr. Harrington."

"I shall tell the Earl you're here?"

But Elizabeth had risen to her feet. "No. If you should see his lordship, please tell him I've gone inside to rest. I was up early." Their eyes met once more. Again he was tempted to speak, but thought better of it. What could he say, without Neville's permission? He bowed, then turned on his heel and followed the footman into the house. He knew Elizabeth watched them as they disappeared around the garden wall.

The footman led him to an entrance on the other side of the house, where he found Emma sitting on a bench just inside the door. Her thick shawl was clutched close around her shoulders, and her gray hair was escaping in little wisps from beneath her bonnet. She rose to her feet as soon as she saw him, a look of relief on her face.

"Emma, what is it?" He reached for her hand and felt it tremble.

She glanced beyond him at the footman, who stood loitering a few paces away.

Harrington turned to the footman. "That will be all," he said. He waited until the man had disappeared, then bent his head to Emma once more. "What is it?" He spoke softly, in case anyone had decided to eavesdrop.

Emma glanced around. "Have you met the young lady?" she breathed. "We hear she's lovely." Evidently Lady Moira had coaxed a full description of her new daughter-in-law out of Neville.

"Yes, of course, and she is," Harrington answered shortly. "But what's wrong? You walked all this way? Is Lady Moira ill?"

"Ah, no. I hitched a ride with the baker's boy." Emma shook her head as though remembering. She reached for his hand and placed a slip of sealed parchment in his palm. "'Tis a message Turlough brought. From a friend in a very high place." She raised an eyebrow. Her lips twitched as though she wanted to say more but dared not.

"Ah." Harrington stepped back and looked over his shoulder. He glanced at the seal and was startled to recognize the crest of the Duke of Desmond. He peered at it more closely to be sure. Yes, it was indeed Desmond's seal. So something was afoot. What could Desmond want of Gentleman Niall? As a Catholic, any involvement in politics on his part was dangerous, but it went without saying that Desmond stood to lose much if he allied himself in any way with the outlaws. It was urgent that Harrington speak to

Neville alone as soon as possible. "Have you a way back to Lady Moira's?"

"I hoped you'd take me, sir."

"I can surely do that, Emma. When did this message come?" Harrington turned the sealed message over in his fingers, calculating the urgency. He had to speak to Neville before Neville talked to Elizabeth, at any rate.

"Turlough brought it this morning, sir. Just after dawn. He said his lordship should have it at once."

"All right, Emma. Wait here. I'll take you with me, but first I must see Neville. I'm sure he'll come as quickly as he can, but you understand—he has other matters he must attend to at the moment." Harrington looked over her shoulder to the narrow hallway which led to the main part of the house.

"I understand perfectly, sir." Emma seated herself once more on the bench, while Harrington found a scullery maid to point him back to the dining room. He crossed the hall and knocked on the dining room door. The door opened almost at once.

"Come in, Harrington, come in," said Sir Oliver, looking even more jovial than he had before. Documents lay on the table, and an inkwell and pen lay before Neville. Neville looked up as Harrington entered.

Harrington bowed. "Forgive the intrusion, gentlemen."

"Everything all right with that girl of mine?" asked Sir Oliver. "She's not giving you any trouble, is she?"

"No, Sir Oliver, none at all," answered Harrington. It took every ounce of control he possessed to remember that the knight was older and still injured. How could he be so uncaring of his own daughter's feelings? No wonder the mother's locket had meant so much to the girl. "Lady Clonmore has gone upstairs to rest. When you're finished here, my lord," he continued, looking at Neville, "I've a message for you."

"A message?" Neville rose to his feet. "We're finished here, aren't we, Beauchamp?"

"Quite so, my lord. I shall have copies of the documents drawn up and conveyed to you as quickly as I possibly can."

"Yes, that's fine." Neville crossed the room and took Harrington by the arm. He led him from the room and across the hall, then paused just inside the library. "What's wrong?"

Harrington cocked his head toward the door. "A message, my lord." He slipped the paper into Neville's palm. "Turlough brought it to your mother early this morning, and Emma carried it here."

The two men's eyes met. Neville looked down at the message and examined the seal. "This is from the Duke of Desmond." He broke the wax and opened the message. His mouth tightened into a thin line as he read the few urgent lines. "Apparently although we foiled the attack on my bride, our rivals found other prey. Desmond's son's been kidnapped. He's begging to meet us."

"Meet us? You mean . . . but why?"

Neville gave a soft snort. "Can't you guess? He's going to ask us to get the boy back."

"Will you do it, Neville?" Harrington drew back and glanced over his shoulder at the door across the hall. It was still closed.

Neville shrugged. "We'll have to think about it. It could kill two birds with one stone, if you see my meaning. But in the meantime"—he raised his eyes to the ceiling—"I've other matters to deal with. You take Emma back to the dower house, and have Turlough take a message back to Desmond. Tell him the gentleman will meet him at eight o'clock. But we must take all precautions. I suppose this could be a trap. Then meet me at Clonmore."

Harrington grabbed Neville's arm. "I've got to tell you— the girl knows."

Neville's lips thinned once more. "I know she knows. I could see it in her face the moment she saw me." He looked at Harrington and his eyes were hard.

"She says we can trust her."

Neville frowned. "You didn't admit to anything, did you?"

Harrington shook his head. "I admitted nothing, but there was no gainsaying her. She was far too certain. She said we can trust her—that she's grateful to us for saving her honor and her—"

"Spare me the details, Harrington. Apparently she sang a different song yesterday in front of her father, Sir William, and Colonel Melville. Even inquired sweetly into the state of that blackguard Addams's health. Sir Oliver wants to see Gentleman Niall swing, and who knows what game she's playing at?" He shook his head and drew a deep breath. "What have I told you time and again, Harrington? Trust no one. We've taken too many risks already as it is."

"What will you tell the duke?"

"I'm not sure. We'll talk about it back at Clonmore. But for now, take Emma back. I'll say my good-byes here and be on my way."

"You won't bring Elizabeth to Clonmore?"

Neville gave a short laugh. "Hardly. Leave her to me, Harrington. We've enough to deal with now that Sir William's brought in this bounty hunter. It's lucky that Sir Anthony is laid up for a while—Sir Oliver gave me a complete report of his health. But Elizabeth is my problem now."

"As you say, my lord." Harrington bowed, although his expression was dubious.

Neville walked back into the dining room, where Beauchamp and Sir Oliver sat chatting. "I would speak with my wife, Sir Oliver. Would you be so kind as to tell me where she might be resting?"

"In her room, most like," replied Sir Oliver with a wink. "Right at the top of the stairs, beside the portrait of her mother."

Neville pressed his mouth into a thin line to stifle the sharp retort which rose to his lips, bowed to both men, and slowly walked out of the room. The heavy heel on the altered boot dragged slightly, reminding him to exaggerate his limp. So much of his disguise depended upon the perception that he was less than agile. A woman servant, stout and florid, in a spotless white apron, passed him. The housekeeper, he remembered. "Ah, Mistress Gallagher," he began.

"Aye, my lord?" She bobbed a curtsey and looked down, careful to keep her eyes anywhere but on his masked face.

He sighed inwardly. "Would you be so kind as to point me in the direction of my lady's room?"

The woman pointed up. "Straight up the stairs, me lord. First door in front of you. You can't miss it." She bobbed another curtsey and continued on her way.

At the top of the staircase, his eye was caught by a portrait hanging on the wall. A dark blonde girl gazed down at him, a replica of her daughter. Her face was a smooth oval, her hair arranged in the ringlets of thirty years ago, and her eyes—her eyes were Elizabeth's eyes, large and green and soft. At her throat she wore a green heart-shaped locket. The emerald locket, he thought, remembering Elizabeth's plea. So it had been her mother's. He thought of this delicate beauty married to the boorish Sir Oliver, and an unexpected pang of pity went through him.

He mounted the steps slowly, thinking of how to confront her. He could not deny that his heart had leapt at the look he'd seen in her eyes when she'd recognized him as her rescuer. For one bright, fleeting moment, he'd thought it might be possible that they could have some sort of relationship together—but then he'd heard in great detail from Sir Oliver how she'd relished telling Sir William and Colonel Melville all she could remember. He thought of the look in her clear green eyes, eyes as clear a green as the water which tumbled over the wet rocks in the hillside streams above Kilmara. He remembered how small and white her hand had appeared in his black gloved palm. What sort of loyalty could he expect from the daughter of Sir Oliver Wentworth? Even if she were as different from her father as night from day, she was the product of an upper-class English upbringing. She'd been bred to believe that the Irish were an inferior race. It simply wasn't possible that he could trust her. No, for the near term, at least, the best thing would be to keep her at Kilmara. She was a stranger here, and after her near abduction, she would be reluctant to venture too far afield. And of course, now that they were married, neither Sir William nor Colonel Melville would attempt to interview her without notifying him. Not to mention the fact that for at least a month, he could plead the honeymoon.

And then after the bishop's tithe money had been safely redirected, as he liked to think of it, he would see where matters stood. Momentarily, an image of her face flitted through his mind, and he suppressed it, feeling irritable. The fact that she was a beautiful woman only made it more imperative to keep her at a distance. He dared not risk being lured into a trap. Reaching the top of the steps, he touched the white silk scarf, making certain the upper half of his face was decently covered. He paused on the landing, looking right and left. A gilt-framed portrait of a young woman wearing a lavishly embroidered gown of the English Restoration caught his eye. Beside it was a closed door. He took a deep breath and knocked gently on the door.

"Come in." Elizabeth turned away from the balcony, staring in astonishment as the earl stopped into the room in response to her summons. "My—my lord."

"You may call me Neville," he said stiffly. "My first name is Edmund, but my mother and all who know me address me as Neville."

"All right," she answered. "Neville." Her heart was pounding in her chest.

"I am aware that this marriage was not of your desire." He spoke quickly, his voice clipped, as though eager to be gone.

She stared at the man before her, desperately wishing she could think of something to say that would convince him she meant him no harm. Despite the mask, the nose and lips and chin were as finely molded as though they were chiseled out of marble, but his face was expressionless beneath the mask, his shoulders rigid. She inclined her head and spoke softly. "I am prepared to do my duty, my lord. My mother, and my grandmother, taught me well."

"I have no doubt." His voice was a slow drawl, and the uncertain expression he'd worn at first was replaced by a cold stare. She looked up at him, startled. What had she said that displeased him? He fastened his eyes on some point above her head and began to speak. "I've come to explain to you our living arrangements for the foreseeable future. I don't expect to live with you as man and wife. I shall continue to reside at Clonmore Castle; you shall remain here at Kilmara. My agent, Harrington, whom you met downstairs, will begin to make a thorough assessment of this property starting tomorrow. He'll be here quite regularly and will report to me at once if there's anything that you require." He paused, then continued to speak over her head. "Your father, as you know, intends to leave this afternoon—I believe his coach has already arrived." He nodded toward the window, and Elizabeth turned to look. Sure enough, a coach had been brought to the front of the house, and great trunks were being loaded onto it. "I shall return in maybe a week's time—perhaps less, perhaps more. You may familiarize yourself with the household and if there are any changes you would like to make, you may discuss them with Harrington. You will not find me unreasonable. And I have instructed the housekeeper and the butler to provide you with any assistance in that regard you require." He paused. His eyes flicked over her, and then slid away.

She wet her lips, scarcely believing what she heard. She knew this man felt something for her—even across the room, she could feel the tension surging beneath the rigid barrier he'd erected between them. And here he was calmly informing her that they were to live in virtually total separation. She might reasonably expect to see a neighbor more.

When she said nothing, he went on, and this time he seemed distinctly uncomfortable. "I would suggest that for your own safety, you limit your travels about the property to the immediate vicinity of the house, unless you are escorted by at least two of the footmen or the grooms, and for God's sake, do not go out after dark. Even late afternoon can be dangerous—as soon as the sun begins to set, I suggest you stay safe inside."

Elizabeth watched him, wide-eyed, listening intently. There was nothing in the clipped speech that sounded like his alter ego, but his voice had that same dark timbre that made her bones weak. She tried to seek out his eyes behind the white mask. "Neville," she said faintly.

"Yes?"

She gathered up all the courage she could summon and plunged ahead. "I know—"

"You know nothing, madam." The savagery with which he cut her off felt like a blow. "I suggest you keep your speculations on matters of which you know nothing entirely to yourself, or you may find your own life has taken a decidedly unpleasant turn." He gave her the briefest of bows, turned on his heel with nearly military precision, and shut the door firmly behind him as he left.

For a moment, she was tempted to go after him, but she turned instead to the window, where the bright midday sun was giving way to gathering gray clouds. Her father's coach was fully loaded, and as she watched he strode from the house, crop in hand, to his horse, ready and saddled beside the coach. The coachman cracked the whip and the team leapt forward, trundling down the drive. She opened the door and stepped out onto the balcony, where a wild wind whipped at her skirts. Her father looked up.

"Be a good girl, now, Lizzie," he called up. He blew her a kiss as she stared down, expressionless. This was the man who had so cavalierly turned her over to a stranger. He swung into the saddle with more grace than she would ever have thought possible, just as Neville himself emerged. A stable boy was leading a sleek chestnut stallion toward the front door. "Good-bye, my lord. Best wishes and felicitations!" With another chuckle, Sir Oliver tugged at the reins and his horse galloped after the coach.

As Elizabeth watched, Neville shook his head and put his hand on the horse's bridle. The stallion whickered at the familiar touch, and Neville swung himself into the saddle. As he moved, Elizabeth noticed that one of his boot heels appeared thicker than the other. Could that account for his limp? Or was that an attempt to ameliorate it? A cold raindrop splashed on her cheek as Neville cantered down the drive after her father. She shivered as the wind gusted through her thin dress.

So this was her wedding day . . . and all but for the sun setting, it was over. There was to be no party, no giggling friends, no blushing best wishes. And this was scarcely the wedding night she'd envisioned for herself, At the thought of Neville in her bed, she felt that same sudden rush of heat, despite the chilly air. But it wasn't to be. This man who made her tingle and her heart and her body grow so warm— her new husband, whose right to her body was absolute— was as cold to her as the chill wind sweeping across Kilmara.

She wrapped her arms around herself and gazed at the wide green meadows, at the lawns, at the low brick out-buildings. Kilmara was hers. For the first time in her life, she was truly the mistress. For at least a week, she could do exactly as she pleased. The thought of freedom, heady and sweet, rushed through her like a drug. She would deal with the reality of Neville when he returned. For the moment, she would enjoy her first taste of real freedom. She stepped back inside her room with a heart unexpectedly lighter than she'd had in days.

Seven

The sickle moon hung silver in the autumn night, a thin crescent that curved just above the thin stand of trees on the low hills on the opposite side of the narrow valley. Water gushed over the rocks and ran down the hillside in the thin stream that ran past the cave's entrance. To the rear of the cave, the horses whickered at their tethers as a gust of wind made the leaves swirl about their ankles. Neville looked back over his shoulder and spoke softly. "Easy, there, easy. Easy, now," he murmured. He glanced at Harrington and nodded at the moon. "Nearly time. They should be here any moment."

Harrington nodded, and, as if on cue, there was the crunch of footsteps on the path below. Bobbing points of light coalesced into a small group of five men, with two carrying lanterns.

Both Harrington and Neville leapt to their feet as the five dark shapes emerged from the shadows. They drew their pistols and held them cocked and ready. As the small group of men came closer, they saw that the middle two men wore blindfolds and each man's hands were loosely bound together and resting on the shoulders of a man who carried a lantern. The fifth man led the two horses.

"All right, McMahon," said Neville addressing the first

escort, as they stepped into the circle of wavering orange firelight. "Untie His Grace and his attendant, and take their blindfolds off."

With a curt nod, the man complied, and the Duke of Desmond stepped forward, squinting and rubbing his wrists. The other men formed a loose circle around the two. "Gentleman Niall?" he asked, looking at each masked face in turn.

"Aye, that's me," replied Neville, his speech falling into a thick brogue. He was careful to remain well out of the low circle of light. "My lord of Desmond?"

"Aye," said the Duke. "That's me." He squinted into the shadows, trying to make eye contact, but Neville stayed back.

"What can I do for you, Your Grace? It seems odd to me that a nobleman such as yourself would come to an outlaw such as me for help."

"I thank you for trusting me enough to allow me to come here and talk to you, sir." The shorter man drew a deep breath and he glanced at each outlaw around the circle in turn. "I've come to you for help because I doubt there's anyone else who can help me."

"We can make you no promises tonight, Your Grace. But come and sit and we'll talk." He gestured to the hard ground, and the outlaws settled themselves, crosslegged but alert. "What's the trouble?" asked Neville gently. Curiosity had gotten the better of all the men, and they were crowding close, listening intently.

"It's my son," said the Duke. "Last night he was kidnapped."

"Kidnapped?" echoed Neville. "By whom?"

"By a group of outlaws led by someone who calls himself Declan McCrory. They attacked him on his way from Dublin last night—" The Duke broke off, his face grim. "I knew I should never have allowed him to travel at night, but he was so eager to come home—"

"That must be the gang we encountered, Niall," Harrington said quietly. "Shortly after dusk, was it?"

"Jonathan was waylaid sometime around eight."

Desmond's voice broke. "He's only ten—not a very strong boy—his mother is beside herself—"

"Why haven't you gone to Sir William, Your Grace?" asked Neville. The other men were muttering to themselves, and he caught snippets of their remarks, mostly muttered curses.

"Sir William?" Desmond shrugged. "Jonathan is my only son and my heir. I cannot trust his life to a pack of bumbling incompetents."

Low snickers and guffaws greeted that remark, and Neville quelled them with a look. "I hear that Sir William's brought in a bounty hunter, Your Grace. He may not be such a bumbling incompetent."

At that, the Duke leaned forward. "This is my son, sir. He means the world to me—my wife can bear no more. Jonathan is a good lad, but sickly—he'll not survive for long in the wild such as this. Surely you see that? I come to you because I know there's not much time. And I'll pay, sir. I'll pay well."

Neville met Desmond's eyes. In the firelight, he saw the desperation etched on the man's face, the stricken look in his eyes. And Desmond was right. The boy, for he knew him well, was indeed sickly. There was little doubt that he would sicken easily in the cold, damp autumn air. From the looks of the outlaws they'd encountered two nights ago, it was doubtful their hideout was any snugger than this cave. And even if they'd managed to hide him in a "safe house," as the houses of farmers sympathetic to the rapparees were called, there was little chance that the boy would have access to the kind of care he was used to.

Desmond looked around the ring and nodded at his servant. "All right. You know you'll have my favor forever if you get him back safe for me."

Neville shrugged. He heard the desperation in Desmond's voice, but as much as he would like to say yes, there were too many other factors to consider. Whether it could be done, for one thing. "Then why not just pay the ransom? After all, what makes you think we'd agree to work for less?" He chuckled softly.

The Duke leaned forward again. His voice was hoarse with emotion. "Because I haven't the sum they demand. I could raise it, but it would take time—more time than I believe my son has." He glanced at each man in turn. "I can pay—I will pay—and you will not find me forgetful should the day come when you need a friend with some influence. And you will one day, Gentleman Niall, I think you all know that." He stared steadily at each man once more in turn.

"We realize the advantages of helping you," Neville said as gently as he dared. "But we could offer you no guarantees—it's not as simple as attacking a rival gang. To get someone out alive—well, that will take some planning, and more than a bit of luck. I promise you we will discuss it tonight and give you our answer in the morning. But I can give you no more than that." He rocked back on his heels and rose to his feet. "All right, Your Grace. Padraig here will lead you to your horse. I'm afraid we must blindfold you again—we can take no chances, you understand? But I promise you will hear from me tomorrow."

Desmond rose to his feet slowly and extended his hand. "If you can bring my son back to me alive, Gentleman Niall, you will find in me the truest friend you could ever have in all of Ireland."

"I believe you, Your Grace," replied Neville. He reached across the fire and shook Desmond's hand, and this time he allowed their eyes to meet. But no spark of recognition flared in Desmond's face, and Neville knew that even a man he regarded as a close friend could not see his crippled alter ego in the masked outlaw.

The other men crowded even more closely when the duke and his attendant had disappeared down the path, each with a hand on Padraig's shoulder.

"Do you really mean to do this, Niall?" asked Liam Malley, Seamus's brother and a tenant of Neville's.

Neville shrugged. "We need to get rid of McCrory and his band, Liam. And now's the time to do it, while Sir Anthony Addams is still laid up. For 'twill be far more difficult once we must contend with him."

"Aye, what about the bounty hunter?" asked Derry Ryan. "Why not let him flush out McCrory?"

"He's been hired to flush us out," answered Neville. "Once he's up and about, it'll be even more difficult than it already is for us to move about. We're going to have to lie very low, if we hope to have any chance at all to get the tithe money. And it seems to me we have a score or two to settle of our own with these dogs." He shifted his position beside the fire once more and nodded to Harrington. "Break out the provisions." Harrington moved to the back of the cave, and Neville beckoned the man to come in. "Would you give that up, Derry? Seamus is your brother-in-law, too, isn't he? And that rent money from Knockamurra—we could have redistributed that to everyone's satisfaction, wouldn't you say? Not to mention all the other times he's stolen from us."

"You sound like you want to do it, sir," said Liam.

"What do you think, Liam?"

The burly farmer hesitated. He rubbed a huge hand across his face and stared into the fire. "I admit it's tempting. Wipe out the rivals and get the lad back—question is, can we? There're fewer of us than them."

"We don't know how many there are now," Neville said softly. "We killed three at least two nights ago. I've sent Eamon and Rory out to scout—let's hear what they come back with."

"I'd do it," said Liam. He looked up at Harrington as he placed five sacks filled with provisions in a pile by the fire. "What do you say, Shane?"

"I've nothing to do with the sons of the gentry, but I'd like to put a bullet in the one who got Seamus." Harrington handed Liam one of the sacks.

Liam rose to his feet as he slung it over his shoulder. "Put that way, I suppose I must say yes." He looked at Neville. "You're right. We do have a score or two to settle, and I'd like to see it done myself, not by a troop of redcoats. Count me as a yes." He nodded, grim-faced, and sighed. "Well, I'm off. Will you come with me, Derry?"

"And what do you say, Derry? Do you want to wait for

the others?" Neville asked as the fair-haired Derry got to his feet, his own sack hanging across his back.

Derry looked at Liam. "I agree we have far less to lose now than if we wait. Hell," he continued with a chuckle, "I've no mind to share a gallows with the likes of them. We make a powerful friend and lose an enemy we don't need right now, especially just before the bishop's tithe train." He shrugged. "Let's give Sir Anthony something more to chew on while he lies abed."

"Fair enough," said Neville. He waited while the men murmured quiet good nights and disappeared down the path, carrying their lanterns. When they were alone, Harrington squatted down beside Neville. "An entirely unexpected development, wouldn't you say?"

At that, Neville laughed shortly. "I can see that by rescuing Elizabeth I saved myself the expense of paying her ransom, which I'm quite sure Sir Oliver would insist I pay. And as far as Desmond goes, from his point of view it does make better sense to come to us. McCrory's gang has to be holed up somewhere—and it's more likely that we'd know before the garrison does." He sat back. "This is going to take some thought to execute." He glanced up at the night sky. "Eamon and Rory should be here soon." He pulled a long clay pipe from his coat and lit it with a piece of burning peat. White smoke filled the air, and he sighed softly as he settled back to wait. "It's been a long day full of interesting developments, wouldn't you say, Harrington?"

Harrington chuckled softly. "Indeed, my lord, I couldn't agree more."

"Can't you see it?" Sir Anthony hissed with impatience. He reached across the bed and pounded on the parchment map with an emphatic finger. "Look, it's plain as the noses on your faces!"

Sir William coughed. He wondered why it had never occurred to him to plot out the places of the attacks on a map. It certainly seemed to make sense, but he failed to see the pattern Sir Anthony so obviously discerned. "Well, Sir Anthony, to be quite frank—"

"The attacks occur in a circle?" asked Melville, peering down with a squint. He remembered this particular step from the last time he'd worked with Sir Anthony. "Is that what you mean, Addams?" He'd be damned if he called Sir Anthony "sir" ever again, after the way the man had repeatedly gone out of his way to set him up as a laughing-stock to both the public and his own men.

Sir Anthony gave a frustrated sigh. "Look again. Where is the center of the circle?"

"Well," said Sir William, frowning down, "just east of Kilmara, I'd say. On the Dublin road—not far from the house."

"Ah." Sir Anthony lay back with a sigh. "Which most likely means the outlaws have some sort of base of operations nearby—"

"We've searched the hills above Kilmara day after day," interrupted the colonel. "And we've found nothing but a few shepherds and their miserable sheep."

"Did I suggest in any way it was in the hills?"

"But—but the lands around Kilmara are all cleared—" began Sir William.

Sir Anthony sighed. "For two years this outlaw has robbed the travelers of this district. He seems to have the magical ability to show up when the rents are due, when money is being transported, when there's a ball in the area or a meeting of some sort. Uncanny at times, wouldn't you say?" He folded his arms across his chest above the bed-clothes. "There's more than one victim who says that. So what would that suggest, do you suppose?"

"Gentleman Niall has a very good spy network throughout the tenants?" asked Sir William.

"Perhaps," Sir Anthony conceded. "Or what if he's one of the tenants himself?"

Sir William glanced at Colonel Melville. The idea had, in fact, occurred to him, but Colonel Melville had dismissed the idea as preposterous and refused to consider it.

"Or even yet, one of the landowners?"

"Come, come, Addams, you go too far," said Colonel Melville. "On what would you base such a preposterous allegation? Why, the gentry have been the most cooperative I've ever encountered—to a man they desire this dog put down."

Sir Anthony leaned back against his pillows. "And what say you, Sir William? Does the idea seem as preposterous to you?"

Sir William hesitated. He had no wish to feed the obvious animosity between the two men. "The thought has crossed my mind a time or two," he said at last.

"And why?"

Sir William shrugged. "The way this chap seems to disappear off the face of the earth, for one reason. He doesn't so much escape as melt away. One moment he's there, and the next, he's just gone. Oh, I don't mean he vanishes—people see him ride away. But he escapes so effortlessly without a trace . . ." He shook his head. "If I were a superstitious man, I might believe it was the work of the devil."

"But you are not a superstitious man and you know damned well that this 'gentleman' is going to ground in a very human fashion. So. We must consider every remaining possibility that has not been considered up to this point, no matter how preposterous it may seem." He glanced at Colonel Melville, who stood rigid beside the map, chins quivering in indignation. "If we are to flush out the quarry that has so effectively eluded us heretofore, we must approach it from every angle possible." He shifted his injured leg on its pillows with a wince.

"Why, you make him sound like an animal," declared Sir William with a chuckle.

"And so he is," snapped Sir Anthony. The pain made him peevish. Suddenly he wanted nothing more than for the two of them to be gone, and for more of the poppy juice that dulled his senses and sent him spiraling into lurid dreams. The ones last night had featured Elizabeth in quite compromising positions.

"And there's always the girl," put in Colonel Melville. "If we can somehow spy on her—"

"Melville, you id—" Sir Anthony stopped himself just in time. "The girl's a witness, perhaps, not a suspect."

"You think I'm stupid." Colonel Melville's jaw jutted forward. "That girl was moonstruck by that cad—any fool could see it." He stopped short, abruptly aware he'd nearly referred to himself as a fool.

Sir Anthony shot him a look. "Are you sure of this, Melville?"

"I saw it myself, sir," put in Sir William. "I'd agree the miss was quite taken with him."

"Hm." Sir Anthony lay back against the pillows. "Perhaps there is a way to exploit this weakness. I should like to speak to the young lady myself. Perhaps there's a way to bait the trap—she is quite lovely, isn't she?" He flashed his teeth in a predatory grin.

Sir William coughed. "Personally, I say we bait the trap with something we know he's going to go for. Say, the bishop's tithe money—he'll move that to London in another month or so."

"Hm," said Sir Anthony, considering. "Interesting. How does he get it there?"

"It's a different route every year. He'll be calling on you soon, Colonel. You might want to give some thought to planning it—he likes to have something presented to him because he likes to wait till the last possible moment. After all, you never know how much pence you can squeeze out till you try." Sir William chuckled.

"Yes, don't wait. This year, Colonel Melville, we'll call upon the bishop, and the sooner the better." Sir Anthony winced with the effort of moving to a more comfortable position. "It's the perfect opportunity to lay a trap for this bastard—and possibly to use the luscious Lady Elizabeth as a pawn. Say we start a rumor, perhaps that this year there's so much it can't be hauled overland. It's got to be taken downriver all the way to Dublin, or some such tale. Then we can either send the real money by another route or let it wait for another day. And in the meantime, we should perhaps talk to a few of the landowners about Kilmara. We know it's not Sir Oliver—he's gone. But we've got to speak to the bishop—he should be part of this from the beginning."

"I agree, sir." Sir William nodded. "And I think under

the circumstances that I shall send the invitation to the
bishop, Colonel. But what about these other outlaws, Sir
Anthony? What's to be done with them?"

Sir Anthony shrugged. "Melville, that's your bailiwick.
Surely you can find a passel of ordinary ruffians."

Colonel Melville looked stung. "Indeed, sir." He met Sir
William's eyes. "The garrison has begun to scour the country, sir. Just today I sent out ten patrols."

"Did they come up with anything?" barked Sir Anthony.
When Melville did not immediately reply, Sir Anthony
waved an impatient hand. "Then tomorrow send twenty.
These rogues are like dog packs—like jackals. Scoundrels
like that shouldn't be difficult at all to find—unless, of
course, there's gross incompetence or collusion."

Colonel Melville's eyes blazed with not very well con-
cealed dislike, but he said nothing more. He picked up his
hat and bowed slightly from the waist. "Gentlemen, I bid
you a pleasant evening. And may you continue to improve,
Addams." He bowed once more and was gone.

"Blast this leg," said Sir Anthony through clenched
teeth. "I'd like to throttle with my bare hands that dog that
shot me."

"You'll be up and about in no time, Sir Anthony." Sir
William reached for his own hat. "And I'm sure you'll have
ample opportunities to do all the throttling you want—I'm
counting on you to bring us Gentleman Niall, although I
hope you'll confine your throttling to outlaws, and leave
Colonel Melville out of it."

"Come, Sir William, be honest with me a moment, and
think about it. Melville's done little enough in the last
weeks to improve things," replied Sir Anthony. "He speaks
through a silver trumpet, but I've seen little evidence of real
action on his part. But he always finds a way to take some
credit at the end."

Sir William blinked. Any antagonism between the two
men he counted on to end his thorniest problem was the last
thing he wanted to have anything to do with. Best to ignore
it, he decided. Addams is simply fretful with the pain. He

cleared his throat. "The hour grows late, Sir Anthony. I'll leave you to your rest."

"I want to talk to the bishop myself, Sir William, so the meeting must be here." Sir Anthony lay back against his pillows with a groan. "Now find that woman with the poppy juice—I've had enough of this pain."

Eight

The days following her wedding were fair and cool, and Elizabeth found herself bounding out of bed in better and better spirits each morning. The effects of her near kidnapping and the hasty marriage receded as the days passed in the pleasant pursuit of exploring her new home. Like clockwork, the great house ran on a precise schedule, overseen, to her great surprise, from a distance by her grandmother.

She inspected the kitchens and found them amply provisioned for the winter. Clearly Mistress Gallagher ruled as her grandmother's representative with an iron hand. Everything from laundry washing to mattress airing, from window cleaning to jelly making, was subject to her direct supervision. In her, Elizabeth thought with a smile, her grandmother had found a truly kindred spirit.

Elizabeth spent a whole day in the gardens, taking stock of both pleasure and kitchen gardens. Her especial interest, of course, was the herb garden, which she found to be adequate, but not at all as elaborate as her mother had described. She realized that it had been scaled back since her mother's day, and made a note to discuss enlarging it with Master Harrington. The idea that here, in her own domain, she could grow what she liked, and do largely what she pleased, filled her with a heady pleasure, tempered only by unsettling thoughts of Neville. She thought of him whenever she glanced at her left hand and saw the thick gold wedding band on her finger. They were married, whether he liked it or not. Sooner or later he would have to deal with that, and when he did—she was determined to understand the enigma who was her husband. She knew he felt something for her. And she had a lifetime to crack his shell. It was simply a question of determining how.

Now she sat in the butler's office off the kitchen, inspecting the household account books, realizing the extent of Lady Frances's involvement with Kilmara. Carefully itemized lists of plans and expenditures were initialed by Lady Frances or accompanied by letters sometimes signed by Beauchamp, but most often by Lady Frances herself. Elizabeth marveled at how carefully her grandmother had managed her dowry, painstakingly ensuring that the property would remain unscathed by her father's greedy demands. Elizabeth turned page after page in the great journal, skimming the details, but her eye was caught by a discrepancy in one sum.

"Flynn," she said, wrinkling her brow and pointing, "there seems to be an error in the arithmetic here. The rent due from Ballyveen—here it says five pounds and, why, in the next column it says rent received is eight pounds . . . and all the way down through the year. . . . And here, the rent for Dunaine—five pounds a quarter—and yet, received nine—" She broke off and looked up at the butler, who was standing just to her right, with hands crossed behind his back.

She glanced at Beauchamp. He was due to return to England the next day, and she knew she would miss his quiet humor, his fastidious ways, and his gentle good sense. But her grandmother relied so heavily upon him. "Let me see, my lady." She pushed the heavy book toward him, and he peered at the pages, brow wrinkled. He scanned the crabbed writing more quickly than she, running his gaze up and down the columns. He turned the pages back and forth, and finally looked up. "Did you know this was going on, Flynn?" He looked at the butler.

"Sir Oliver wouldn't let me write to ye, Master Beauchamp. He told me to keep the books, and that it was none of my business."

"What's going on?" asked Elizabeth.

"I think we've discovered how Sir Oliver was able to maintain his habits while he was here, my lady, although even these sums were not sufficient, apparently. He raised the rents unbeknownst to your grandmother, which he had every right to do, although at these amounts, I imagine the tenants are struggling."

"More than struggling, sir." Flynn met Beauchamp's eyes directly.

Elizabeth glanced from one man to the other. "My father was taking money he wasn't entitled to?"

Beauchamp shrugged. "Your father took money he was entitled to take, my lady. But whether or not the tenants can sustain these levels, I would question. This is a matter that must be made known to Lord Clonmore. We shall speak to Master Harrington as soon as he arrives this morning."

"Master Harrington has arrived," said Master Harrington from the doorway. "How may I be of service?"

Elizabeth jumped. "Why, Master Harrington, it appears that my father's raised the rents of the entire estate in the last two years—nearly doubling most!"

Harrington raised an eyebrow. "This is something I shall have to look into in closer detail, my lady. But I'd intended to ride to Dunaine today—that's the village farthest from Kilmara."

"Oh, let me come with you." Elizabeth rose to her feet, pushing away the ledgers. "I'm eager to see the country— will you come, Master Beauchamp?"

"I think I would prefer to stay and look through the ledgers myself, my lady. Perhaps I could prepare an accounting, or at least make a start? This is something that Lady Frances should hear of—her son's antics are a great trial to her, but she never shirks from the facts."

"But—but, my lady," began Harrington, "my lord—"

"My lord said that I should not venture out unless accompanied, Master Harrington. And since you're riding out, with whom could I be safer?" She met his eyes squarely and smiled meaningfully. Harrington blanched and swallowed visibly. She knew he was defeated. "I'll just go change into my riding clothes. Flynn, will you have a horse saddled and brought round? That little gray mare I noticed in the stables yesterday—she seemed to have a pleasant temper."

"As my lady wishes." The butler bowed and left.

"I'll be down directly, Master Harrington." She swept from the room as Harrington exchanged a glance with an amused Beauchamp.

"My lady very often has her way, Master Harrington," remarked Beauchamp mildly when she had gone.

"I can see that," Harrington replied. "I must be sure to warn his lordship."

"I'm afraid, Master Harrington," Beauchamp said wistfully, "that is something every man must discover for himself."

In her room, she found Sorcha making the bed. "Why, Sorcha," Elizabeth said, when she saw that the girl's eyes were wet and her nose was red. "Sorcha, are you all right? Are you ill?"

Sorcha shook her head hard and wiped her eyes with the corner of her apron. "No, my lady, not I. I'm fine. But I'd a message from me mam this morning. There's fever in the cottages, my lady. My sister's little Tam's been taken sick, and me da, too. Me mam's sent for the hedgemaster, but there's little enough he can do."

"Oh, Sorcha, I'm so sorry." Elizabeth held out her hand and squeezed Sorcha's when she took it. "Please don't worry. I'm sure it can't be too serious. I'll tell you what. I know a little about tonics and such—when I return from my ride, I'll see what's in the stillroom. And there must be herbs in the kitchen gardens—if there's nothing already made, I'll see what I can make. We'll put together a basket and you can take it to your sister later. Please don't be upset."

Sorcha raised her head and looked at her with something close to bewilderment. "That would be very kind of you, my lady." Elizabeth saw something in Sorcha's eyes, something she didn't understand. Why did the girl look at her as if she'd grown two heads? She cocked her head. "A hedge-master—he's a healer too?"

Sorcha bit her lip. "Lord, I shouldn't have said anything about him, my lady. Please—please don't go saying—"

"Saying what to who? To his lordship? His lordship clearly wants little enough to do with me—you've no fear on that score. And besides, I've no wish to see anyone punished—I saw a hedgemaster in Dublin publicly whipped."

"He's not a bad man, at all, my lady—it's true he teaches the children the old stories, but he's a doctor, too, of sorts—he can set bones and knows all the old ways and—" She threw herself on the floor at Elizabeth's feet. "Please, my lady, you must understand that you can't say anything to anyone about him. They hanged the hedgemaster at Dunbarda last January, and a fearsome thing it was. Now those poor people have no one to turn to at all."

Elizabeth patted Sorcha's shoulder, feeling helpless and confused. The more she learned about Ireland, the more confusing it seemed. She made a silent resolution to ask John Harrington to explain the plight of these people. But today she would see for herself what conditions were like at Kilmara. "Come, Sorcha," she said gently. "I won't say anything to anyone. But you must help me change my clothes. I'm riding out this morning—I'm riding all the way to Dunaine with Master Harrington. I want to see Kilmara for myself."

The little maid got to her feet. "Oh, my lady—that's where the fever is! You must stay away—if you take the fever, the Earl will be sure to have the heads of all who live there!"

I doubt that, thought Elizabeth with a wry twist to her mouth. But she said nothing more than "I'll be careful," to Sorcha, as she helped her change from her pink muslin morning gown into her riding costume of dark green wool. She set the little cap at a jaunty angle on her head and picked up her skirts. She turned back to Sorcha one last time before she left the room. "Don't forget, now, Sorcha. When I return, I'll put a basket together for you. Don't fret now. Do your work like a good girl. All right?"

"Yes, my lady, thank you, my lady," said Sorcha with a curtsey that was more of a bob.

With a troubled heart, Elizabeth made her way to the hall, where she found Beauchamp and Harrington deep in conversation. Both men looked up and smiled when they saw her on the stairs. She smiled back. "I'm ready."

"The horses are just being brought around," said Harrington. "Are you certain, Lady Clonmore? The roads can be most unpleasant—"

"Why, Master Harrington, I almost think you don't want my company," Elizabeth teased lightly. She was rewarded to see him flush. Neville might be a closed book, but his agent was as transparent as they came, she thought, and susceptible to her flirtation.

"Do be careful, my lady, and don't take any risks," said Beauchamp.

"Oh, you go back to your books, Master Beauchamp," Elizabeth said with a toss of her head. "I'll be very safe with Master Harrington."

Harrington's lips tightened, but he said nothing more than a low, "Shall we go, my lady?"

"Indeed, let's be off." Elizabeth smiled gaily and swept out the door, where a stable boy waited with Elizabeth's gray mare and Harrington's chestnut gelding. Neville could ignore her all he pleased, but she was determined to make a home for herself in this new place. Harrington was silent as they trotted down the long drive.

She glanced sideways at him several times from beneath the brim of her hat. He was her most tangible link to Neville, her only real conduit for gleaning any kind of knowledge of the man she'd married. She had a thousand questions she wanted to ask, but she knew Harrington was bound to deny all knowledge of Neville's outlaw activities. Unless and until she could convince Neville that she was to be trusted, she had to dance as lightly around the subject as she could. But she felt that information about his past, his childhood, and his relationship with his parents should be fair game, and she intended to milk Harrington, bit by bit. "Where was the earl raised, if not in Ireland?" she asked.

Harrington glanced at her, clearly startled. "In London, my lady. His mother took him there as a child when he was quite small and they remained there until my lord returned to Ireland to claim his title."

"I heard my lord came back here when he was in his teens."

"Well, that's true. My lord did return alone, to attempt a reconciliation with his father. It ultimately failed, and my lord returned to England."

"I see." Elizabeth nodded as she stared off into the distance. They reached the end of the drive, and Harrington indicated they should turn to the left. They trotted down the road at an easy pace. Here, the hedgerows were lower, and Elizabeth could see the rolling meadows where flocks of sheep grazed in quiet contentment. The late morning light was warm on her face, and the October breeze soft against her skin. She drew a deep breath, and her nostrils were filled with the grassy scent of the lush meadow fields. They crossed a narrow bridge over a gurgling brook. The water foamed over half-submerged stones, round and flat as stepping stones. The rolling Irish hills stretched to the horizon, green as emeralds beneath the sun.

"Well, Lady Clonmore," asked Harrington, when they had ridden a little further in silence, "what do you think of your new home?"

"The countryside is beautiful," Elizabeth replied thoughtfully, "but there's a kind of brutality about this country I didn't expect."

"What do you mean, my lady?" Harrington sounded surprised.

"I saw a man being whipped in Dublin, and a family huddled under a hedgerow for shelter. And those outlaws—the ones who attacked the coach and killed poor Jack Whittaker—well, they seemed like such desperate men. There were more of them, and they took us by surprise, but they weren't strong men. Even Molly was able to fight them off for a while—if we'd had one more man with a gun, I think we could have fought them off." She shook her head and sighed. "I don't understand."

"Ireland is an occupied country, my lady," said Harrington quietly. "Henry Plantagenet set his sights on Ireland for his youngest son, and the English haven't been able to take their eyes off this island since."

Elizabeth laughed shortly. "I'm afraid I have little head for history, Master Harrington. I only know I've seen more suffering here in Ireland than I ever did in twenty-one years in England."

Twenty-one, he thought with a sigh. There was a healthy resiliency about Elizabeth that he had glimpsed the first night he'd met her, but she would need more than resiliency and spirit to get through to Neville. She would need patience, and perseverance, until such time as she'd proved her loyalty. Her next question took him once again off guard.

"Why does he do it?"

"Why does who do what, my lady?" Harrington cursed himself for sounding like a fool. There was something about this woman he found damned unsettling. Maybe Neville was right to keep her at arm's length until the matter of the tithe money was concluded.

"You know what I mean. Why does Neville—why does Neville pretend—"

Harrington cut her off with a cough. He nodded up ahead. The road disappeared around a bend, but a wisp of smoke behind the rise in the road told him they were approaching one of Kilmara's tenant villages. He wasn't even sure what the name of this hamlet might be. "My lady." He pointed to the smoke. "I think if you will have patience for some five more minutes, you will see the answer for yourself."

Elizabeth shot him a curious look, but only flicked the reins to make the mare trot a little faster. They rounded the rise and came to the top of the hill. Below, in a slight impression too shallow to be called a valley, huddled some four or five cottages of the most miserable degree. Mournful chickens scratched in the dust, and scrawny children crouched in the sunny side of the cottages, as though hugging the walls for warmth. Elizabeth gasped softly as they rode slowly down the middle of the miserable square, if such it could be called. She wet her lips and looked around, as the women, clad in dirty smocks of rough-spun linen, looked up from their housekeeping and stared at her with empty eyes.

"These people are starving," she whispered, more to herself than to Harrington. She looked at him. "But—this morning—there were eggs and bread and bacon and jam— there is no lack of food—"

"This is what comes of your father nearly doubling their rents, my lady. He has driven these people to this." Harrington gazed around. Neville would not be pleased to hear of this, although it was hardly something he could blame Elizabeth for.

Elizabeth gazed around, distress plain on her face. "But—Master Harrington—something must be done—"

"Something will be done, my lady. Fear not. Come, it's getting on to noon, and I must be back at Clonmore by four."

They trotted on, Elizabeth suppressing a shudder. At last they came to a fork in the road and they paused to rest the horses briefly. "That's what you do with the money, Master Harrington?"

Harrington met her eyes. "We do what we can." He pointed to the left fork, and they rode on in silence.

At last they came to the village listed on the rent-rolls as Dunaine. Perhaps a dozen turf-topped cottages clustered around an open green. The streets were empty, with only a lanky dog or two slinking listlessly in the shadows. They slowed once more to a walk while Harrington looked around, frowning, and Elizabeth stared in horror at the eerie, silent village.

Then a door swung open with a sudden shriek of rusted hinges and the edge scraped over the uneven ground. A man staggered out, drops of sweat shimmering on his brow. "Away, away wi' ye," he gasped. "The fever is here—away wi' ye!"

"Is everyone here sick?" called Harrington.

"Aye, mostly all—the two or three left standing are tending to the rest. Are ye from Sir Oliver?"

"No," answered Elizabeth, amazed at her own presumption. "Do you know Sorcha who works at Kilmara?"

The man turned fevered eyes on her. "Sorcha—m'niece. M'brother's daughter. She's not sick, is she? Good—tell her to stay away."

"But we can bring you medicines—"

Elizabeth made as if to dismount, and Harrington cried, "No, my lady! You must not risk contagion!"

She looked at Harrington. "These people need help."

"And so they do, my lady." Another voice spoke from the dark doorway of a cottage roofed in squares of peat.

Harrington turned to the new speaker, a gray-bearded man of middle height, in surprise. "Turlough! How long have you been here?"

Turlough wiped his hands on an unbleached linen towel. "Young Tom, the baker's boy, brought word to me last night. I'm doing all I can, Master Harrington. It would help greatly if the lady means to keep her word." His level eyes met Elizabeth's. For a moment she bristled, wondering how this ragged little man dared to question her intentions, but then she calmed. Doubtless these people had heard many empty promises over the years. "There's little enough I can do."

Elizabeth drew herself straighter in the saddle. There was a kind of nobility in Turlough's carriage, and he looked at her as if he were her equal. "Have you tried willow bark?" Elizabeth asked, wrinkling her brow, mentally taking stock of her supplies.

"Aye, my lady, willow bark tea would serve greatly, but there's no willows here to take the bark from."

"I know there's some at Kilmara. I'll have it sent down as soon as I return." Elizabeth looked around, then gathered the reins. "Come, Master Harrington, there's nothing we can do here right now."

"Where—where are we going?" asked Harrington, spurring his horse after hers.

"Why, to Neville, of course. He must know the state of things here—and I intend to tell him myself."

"But—but, my lady—"

"Yes?" Elizabeth asked. "I won't hear any objections."

"We're riding the wrong way."

Elizabeth pulled up short on the reins and the mare stopped. She looked at Harrington and burst into a giggle. "Oh." She stifled another short laugh. "Well, lead on, then, Master Harrington."

A stir in the hall below brought Neville to the balcony to see exactly what was happening. He rose from his desk, where he'd been examining his maps of the county, and made certain that his white silk mask was tied securely in place. Then he strode out of his study and leaned over the balcony, where he was shocked to see Elizabeth standing in the middle of the hall, Harrington by her side.

At that moment, Mistress Aislinn, who'd been his father's housekeeper for years, looked up. One look at her shocked and incredulous face told him what he had to do. He leaned over the ancient stone railing and spoke as quietly as he could. "It's all right, Aislinn. Bring her up here, Harrington." He turned on his heel and strode back into his office, where he sank down behind the desk. His heart was pounding in his chest. What the devil was the woman doing here? And why on earth had Harrington agreed to bring her?

He forced himself to remain composed as the swish and rustle of her skirts announced her imminent arrival. He looked up at Harrington as Elizabeth strode into the room, eyes flashing.

He rose to his feet. "My lady." He bowed shortly. "Why did you bring her here, Harrington?"

"I brought him, my lord," snapped Elizabeth. "He was kind enough to allow me to accompany him on an inspection of several of the villages at Kilmara. And to say that I am appalled by the conditions I find there is an understatement. Something must be done at once—people are sick, children are starving. I won't tolerate the people—my people—being mistreated like that. And I was not about to leave such matters to Master Harrington. He may have other priorities."

Neville glanced at Harrington, who had paused just inside the door. "Thank you, Harrington. I'll just be a mo-

ment." Harrington shot him a warning look as he took the
hint and left, shutting the door as he did so. The ghost of a
scowl flitted across Neville's face. He knew what Harrington's look meant. But he had no intention of mistreating the
girl. What did Harrington take him for? This was the last
thing he'd ever have expected from Sir Oliver's daughter.
Who would've thought that she would notice the plight of
the people, let alone care? He gestured to the chair on the
other side of his desk, regarding her with more speculative
interest than he ever would've thought possible. "Please, my
lady. Sit."

Elizabeth did as she was told. She sat stiffly in the
wooden chair, chin high, shoulders squared.

Unexpectedly, Neville felt a warmth for her. She looked
so determined, so intent. Her cheeks were flushed a delicate
peach, and a little pulse pounded in her long white throat. He
looked at the curve of her cheek and the hollow of her
throat, and forced himself to suppress the desire to take her
in his arms and plant kisses along the line which curved
from cheek to jaw to neck. He shifted in his chair, uncomfortably aware that his body resisted any such control. "You
should've sent Harrington with any requests." He spoke far
more shortly than he'd intended and a momentary hurt flickered through her green eyes.

But her voice was steady as she replied, "I thought it was
more efficient to discuss it with you myself."

"What if I'd been away?"

"Master Harrington would've told me."

"Ah." He regarded her over the tips of his fingers pressed
together. "The short answer to your request is of course. You
may do what you please to alleviate whatever suffering you
find at Kilmara, but I'm a very busy man and I don't expect
you to come barging in here again."

She looked him squarely in the eyes as though refusing
to acknowledge his rebuff. "There are certain medicines
they must have as well—"

At that Neville sighed. "Look around you, my lady." He
waved his hand around the shabby room. His desk was old
and battered, his chair, although high-backed and thickly

padded, dated back two generations or more, and the rich fabric was faded and badly frayed, worn bare in many spots. "Clonmore Castle is not half so grand as Kilmara, my lady. And I would caution you that the finances at Kilmara are in some disarray—Harrington's initial assessment of the books with Master Beauchamp would suggest—"

"I'm not talking about spending money, Neville," interrupted Elizabeth. "I brought certain items with me, and there are herbs growing at Kilmara, and more around the countryside. I can make much of what's needed myself."

He stared at her. Her concern seemed to be genuine. "You may of course make what you wish, my lady. I'm sure the people—your people—will appreciate it."

"Thank you." She met his eyes and he saw a certain pleading in them. "Neville, I—"

He held up his hand. "Not now, my lady." He swallowed hard, tempted by the intensity he saw within the clear green depths. Her determination was clearly stamped across her dainty features, and he was sharply reminded once more of the night he rescued her. He had not expected such mettle in his bride. But he did not dare allow himself to be distracted. There were far more important matters at stake than Elizabeth's feelings. Or his own, for that matter. "I am in the midst of some rather pressing business." He did not look away. "Perhaps you and I may meet and—and discuss our mutual interests upon its completion." He cursed the stilted phrases, but knew he did not dare relax. Any carelessness could cost him, his men, and the Duke of Desmond's heir their lives. He rose, acutely aware of her presence. "I shall send you back to Kilmara with two of my grooms. They are strong, stout fellows. No harm will come to you."

She stood up. "Thank you."

"For agreeing that the tenants of Kilmara should not live like animals? What do you take me for, my lady?"

"No," she answered coolly. "For agreeing that we might discuss our mutual interests. When your business is concluded, of course."

Their eyes met, and Neville felt a surge of desire for her as acute as what he'd felt on their first meeting. "Of course," he echoed faintly, and stared after her as, without further words, she swept from the room.

Harrington rushed in at almost the exact moment her footsteps faded down the stairs. "Neville, you have to understand—I agreed to bring her with me—"

Neville looked at Harrington and shook his head. "It's all right. It doesn't matter." For a moment he gazed into space thinking of the firm set of her shoulders as she marched out of the room. He smiled involuntarily. Lady Moira was sure to approve, even while the county dowagers raised eyebrows, of a daughter-in-law possessed of not only a social conscience, but the energy to put her ideas into action. It was not the first time thoughts of Elizabeth had made him smile, he realized with a start. He shook himself mentally and turned back to Harrington. "Really. It doesn't matter. Come, shut the door and sit down. I want to show you what I've worked out for tomorrow night."

"You've decided tomorrow for sure?"

"Aye." Neville nodded and indicated the map. "From everything the men have told me, I think it's clear that they've got the boy holed up here—in this hollow. Tomorrow night the moon will be close to full—and they've been quiet ever since they took the lad. I think they'll make a move for the Galway stage just before it comes into Ennis for the night. You take the boy—the rest of us will wait for the outlaws to get back. They like attacking the coaches—they're easy marks."

Harrington nodded. "All right." He hesitated. "I do apologize for allowing Eliz—"

Neville airily waved a hand, but his eyes softened momentarily as he thought of her. "I told you, Harrington, think nothing of it. We've much more important matters at hand than whether or not my wife wishes to speak to me."

Elizabeth rode silently between the two grooms, her mind a tangled jumble of herbal recipes, instructions for tinctures and decoctions, baskets of bread and broth, blankets and balms. And Neville. All the rest was merely an attempt to distract herself from thinking about him. He seemed subtly different from the last time she saw him—the *last* time she saw him, she laughed to herself. She'd been in his company exactly twice before. And only once, for fifteen minutes, alone.

But surely he'd been different—less indifferent, certainly, even if she suspected that he'd have accommodated almost any request, if only to get her to leave. Though really, if he did give away all the money he stole—and it didn't look as though he were keeping much of it for himself, judging from the shabby state of Clonmore Castle—how could he have refused her?

She glanced up to see the roof of Kilmara just visible over the trees, and smiled. She knew with sudden certainty that Neville had a heart. It was merely a matter of finding the way to it.

Nine

Frantic pounding pulled Moira from a sound sleep. She sat up in bed, not even registering the chilly air through her thick wool night shift, and reached for her robe. Emma called out from the next room, but Moira did not answer. She pounded down the steps as quickly as her bones would allow and peered out the door. A lone figure stood there.

She fiddled with the latch. "Who's there?"

"'Tis John Harrington, my lady."

She ripped open the door. "What's amiss?"

"'Tis Neville."

"I'll get my bag." She turned around to see a white-faced Emma peering over the rail. "My bag, Emma." She looked at Harrington. "Has he been shot?"

"Aye. Shot in the leg. And shot through the shoulder. That's where it's bad."

Moira bit back a curse. "Will we need the physician?"

"Neville refuses to send for him."

"Damn that son of mine!" she swore before she could stop herself. Even Emma looked shocked. "All right. I'll just be a moment. Come, Emma."

She was dressed and bundled in her warmest cloak in no time. Harrington helped her onto the horse, then swung up into the saddle behind her. Emma bolted the door shut as they trotted off in the moonlight.

"What happened?" she asked.

"They surprised us—soldiers were chasing them—we got the duke's boy out, but Neville was caught in the cross fire." Harrington spoke quickly, softly, as though he feared every tree harbored a spy.

Moira shut her eyes and murmured silent prayers to every deity she could think of that her son be all right. At last they arrived at Clonmore. She rushed up to his bedroom, where Neville lay breathing shallowly on the great bed. A bloody bandage was wrapped around his leg, and another around his shoulder. "Hello, Mother," he said when she hurried over to his side.

She met his eyes. The mask was off, and his face, pale and clammy, was laced with sweat, little rivulets beaded in the thick ridges of scar tissue above his right eye. She touched the burned side of his face in one fleeting caress then pursed her lips. "Neville, what have you done?"

"It wasn't me, Mother." He grinned at her through his pain.

Moira sighed. "Have you any whiskey, Master Harrington?"

"There's some right here." Harrington held up a clay goblet.

"Good. Let's get some of that into him, and then we'll see how bad it really is."

An hour later, Moira shut the bedroom door. Neville lay in a drunken, pain-fogged stupor. She wiped her hands on her apron and looked at Harrington, who was leaning against the stone railing that looked over the great hall. "I've done all I can do."

"Will he live?"

Moira shrugged. "My son has the devil's own luck. Neither bullet was lodged inside the wound—both went clean through. If there's no infection—well, I'd say he has a good chance. But there's always fever, and there's fever in the cottages."

"Yes." Harrington sighed. "I know." He looked out over the hall. "Two men were killed tonight. Rory O'Connell and Derry Ryan."

Moira closed her eyes and whispered a brief prayer for the repose of their souls. "What about their families?"

"We'll do what we can."

Moira shook her head. "And will you feed the whole of Ireland? Can't you see, you and Neville, that what you're doing is only a stopgap? It doesn't help anything in the long run. And one of these days, it'll be you or Neville—or both of you—that's carried home hung over the back of a horse." She shook her head and threw up her hands, forestalling any further discussion. "I'm going to rest. And you should, as well. There's nothing more you can do now. We'll see how Neville is in a few hours." She shook her head again and left him still staring moodily into space.

Mist swirled across the surface of the lake, and the black rocks rose from the dark water like stunted fingers of some giant hand, grasping for the air. The ground squelched beneath her feet and Elizabeth looked around. Something was out there—something that searched for her in the mist, hunted her scent. She listened, every sense strained to its limit. Was that a grunt behind her? She whirled and saw a dark shape, a cloaked and hatted man, standing there. Neville, she thought with a sigh, and the figure raised its head . . . to reveal a bloody skull's face. She screamed.

Elizabeth sat straight up in bed, her heart racing, sweat trickling down her back. She looked around the dark room. Moonlight streamed through the lace curtains, and in the shadowy light she could see her mother's portrait over the fireplace. She'd had it moved from the bottom of the staircase to a place where she could see it more frequently. A deep sense of foreboding filled her. She got out of bed and peered out one of the long windows, hugging herself in her nightgown. But nothing stirred beneath the trees, and the wide lawns were empty beneath the clear sky. She went back to bed and lay staring up at the canopy. Was it Master Beauchamp's departure that day that upset her? No, she decided. Master Beauchamp was a pleasant guest, but she had no real need to keep him here. And nothing else had happened that day. She tossed and turned until nearly dawn, wondering why she felt as though something were deeply amiss.

She had her answer when Harrington did not come the next day, as she'd expected him to, and was late the following day. He found her in the stillroom, where she was carefully working a mixture of mint and beeswax into a balm. She looked up, surprised to see him.

"My lady, will you come with me, please?"

She put the pestle down, uncertain that she'd heard him correctly. "Where?"

"You're needed—Neville needs you—at Clonmore."

"Neville needs me?" she repeated, incredulous. "What for?"

Harrington glanced over his shoulder. They were alone in the stillroom, but still he shut the door before answering. "Two nights ago we rescued the Duke of Desmond's son from the same outlaws who tried to take you. But we were taken off guard—the garrison soldiers were in pursuit of them, and Neville got caught in the cross fire."

"He's hurt?"

"Shot twice. The leg and the shoulder. Lady Moira—his mother—is with him and is doing all she can, but she lacks certain ingredients. Turlough told her about the things you've sent to the cottages, and she begs you to come and help her."

"So Lady Moira sent for me?" Elizabeth asked slowly, eyeing the small pots of salves and vials of oils on her workbench. She glanced up at the herbs hanging in bunches to dry from hooks in the ceiling.

"Will you come, my lady? I realize Neville means nothing to you, and that the circumstances of your marriage have been less than ideal, but out of human decency—"

"Of course I'll come, Master Harrington." Elizabeth placed a gentle hand on his arm. "I told you before I feel I owe Neville and you both my life. Just let me think what to bring. And summon my maid, Molly, would you please? Ask her to pack a small bag for me—I expect I will stay at least a day or so?"

Harrington nodded. "I know Neville will thank you."

Elizabeth glanced up and bit back the retort that rose to her lips. She had the distinct feeling that Neville knew nothing of her being summoned to care for him. He'd probably believe she was capable of poisoning him. Didn't he see that her fate was closely linked with his? What would be the point of betrayal? She reached for a large and small basket. "Will there be room for all my things?"

"I asked to have the coach brought round, my lady," said Harrington. "Is there anything I can do to help?"

"Not yet, Master Harrington, but come back in fifteen or twenty minutes. I think I have all I need here." She frowned at the worktable, quickly assessing her inventory. "What exactly is wrong?"

Harrington sighed. "The leg wound is healing nicely. But the arm—the shoulder—the wound will not close. It seeps pus."

"There is an infection deep within the tissue then," Elizabeth declared. "Let me see—basil, pennyroyal, and thyme to cleanse the tissue, and certainly oil of clove to lessen the pain. Sage and tansy for the fever—and does he suffer from chills or sweating, Master Harrington?"

"Both, I believe, my lady. His mother is quite worried."

"Well, sage will help lower the fever and assist the bleeding to stop. . . ." Her nimble fingers skipped over the small glass jars filled with dried herbs from her grandmother's gardens. She could be sure that those gathered under Mistress Maddy's supervision were at the height of their power. She turned to Harrington. " 'Twill only take me a few moments. Please go ask my maid to pack."

When Harrington was gone, she filled both baskets with as much as she thought she could possibly need. She picked them up, testing their weight. She could certainly manage both. She took a last look around the stillroom, then went to find Harrington.

In the entrance hall, she found Molly hovering over a

small satchel. "Are you sure you don't want me to come with you, my lamb?" asked Molly.

"I'll be fine, Molly," said Elizabeth, as she kissed the older woman's cheek. "There's too much work for you to do here, and besides, I can always send for you if need be." Somehow, she knew that the last thing Neville would want was another unfamiliar face in his household. And while she knew that Molly was fiercely loyal, she wasn't quite sure how Molly would react if she discovered that her dearest lamb was married to a secret outlaw.

"You will do that, won't you?" Molly searched her face anxiously.

"Of course." Elizabeth followed Harrington outside, where he stowed her baskets and her satchel beneath the seat of the small two-person coach. He took the reins himself, and Elizabeth peered out the window and waved good-bye to Molly. She was still stunned by Harrington's request. She hoped she had the skill to be of real use to Neville.

They arrived at Clonmore Castle shortly before noon. Harrington hastened Elizabeth inside. Footsteps sounded on the balcony above and Elizabeth looked up. A woman, her gray hair covered by a white housecap, and her dress by a large white apron, stood in nearly the very same spot as Neville had when she'd barged in two days ago. "Oh, my dear," the woman breathed, and hurried down the staircase. She held out her hands to Elizabeth. "Thank you for coming. I'm Moira, Neville's mother."

Elizabeth bobbed a curtsey, but Lady Moira stopped her. "We'll have none of that between us, my dear. If half of what I've already heard about you is true, we shall be good friends. Now, would you care for some refreshment? Or would you care to rest from your journey?"

"I'd prefer to see Neville," she replied, feeling shy suddenly.

A worried smile broke out across Moira's lined face. "All right, my dear. He's sleeping at last, but we'll take a peek. What have you brought there, in your baskets?"

"Something for the fever, of course, and a concoction of

basil, thyme, and pennyroyal to take the infection from the tissues—"

"Ah, pennyroyal." Lady Moira's eyes widened. "I never heard of that one. But I'm no healer, you see, only used to bandaging up my son's scrapes. Come, this way." She gathered her voluminous skirts of gray wool and started up the steps, Elizabeth trailing in her wake. Halfway up, she turned and spoke to Harrington. "Have someone take Lady Elizabeth's satchel to the room next to mine—and bring those baskets up to Neville's office—I've turned that into a sort of supply closet, you see, my dear"—here she addressed Elizabeth. "And tell Cook not to let the lamb boil—a stew boiled is a stew spoiled, don't you think, my dear?"

Elizabeth blinked. She knew only a little of the art of cooking, and much of that secondhand. But she had a feeling that Lady Moira was not quite like any other lady she was ever likely to meet. She followed her obediently up the steps and into Neville's office, where the door on the far wall, which had been closed when she'd been in the room before, stood partially open. Lady Moira gestured. "There. Have a look at him, if you like."

Elizabeth peeked in. He lay propped up by pillows, covered from the waist down by quilts, a nightshirt of unbleached linen tied loosely on his chest. She could see the dark hair which curled so tightly on the pale skin. The silk mask was tied across his face, and for a moment, she was tempted to ask Lady Moira what terror it hid that he refused to take it off, even wounded and asleep. She sighed softly. An odor came from the sickroom, the odor of infection, of pus and sweat and dried blood.

"When he wakes, we'll have a look at his wound. Have you ever treated wounds, or do you simply know the properties of the herbs?"

"My mother cared for the sick and the wounded on our estate in Somerset, my lady," Elizabeth answered.

"No, child, don't call me that. I'm no one's lady, not anymore. Harrington calls me that because he can't stop himself, but that's not what I am." Moira smiled. "Come. We'll have a cup of tea together and you can tell me all about the herbs you've brought."

When they were settled in front of a fire in Neville's office, with teacups and a plate of sweet cakes before them, and a basket of linen for folding between them, Moira smiled at Elizabeth. "I must confess I was curious to meet you. Turlough told me how kind you were, and how much your medicines have helped, not to mention the food and blankets and such you sent down to the tenants. That was very kind of you, you know." Moira's eyes, nearly the exact shade as Neville's, twinkled over her teacup.

Elizabeth picked up her cup and sipped. The cup and saucer were mismatched. What sort of a household did Neville keep? "You—you don't live here, do you?"

"No, child." Moira shook her head. "I had enough of grand houses years ago. My cottage in the wood is enough for me. It pleases Neville to call it a dower house, but it's not much more than a grand version of a cottage. It's enough for me and it suits me well. You must come and visit me someday."

"I will be glad to do that," answered Elizabeth, wondering how she could possibly begin to ask all the questions which were racing through her mind.

Moira smiled, and, as if reading her thoughts, said gently, "Tell me about yourself, Elizabeth. I know Sir Oliver is your father—what of your mother? Where did you grow up?"

Haltingly at first, but coaxed by Moira, Elizabeth told the story of how she'd been raised on the great estate in Somerset, close by her grandmother's home, and how they had divided their time between London and the country. She spoke of her mother's love of herbs, and all green growing things, and her father's gambling, which had caused her mother so much grief. "He continues to be a trial to my grandmother," Elizabeth finished. "I have no idea what he's up to now, but I'm sure Grandmother is quite peeved. She's cut him off several times—refused to have anything to do with him. But he always finds a way back."

"Ah," Moira said, as she bent and folded the linen with an easy rhythm, "how well I know that old story, child.

Gambling has been the ruin of more than one noble house. I wish all who would try their luck at games of chance would be forced to limit what they lose to what they win—and leave the poor wives and children and families out of it. But I suppose it will never be that way, hm?"

Elizabeth sat back and drank the rest of her tea. So the stories about Neville's father were true—or at least true enough that Moira understood what it was like to deal with someone like Sir Oliver.

"And so now you find yourself here, and I'll warrant you wonder what you ever did to deserve such a fate." Moira chuckled softly. Her smile faded as she met Elizabeth's eyes. "I always wanted someone very special for my son. I have a good feeling about you, my dear. But you must have a thousand questions." She gestured for Elizabeth to hand her the teacup. "More? Ask away, my dear."

Elizabeth glanced at the door which led to the bedroom. She could hear Neville muttering in his sleep. Moira followed her eyes and listened. "I think he'll sleep a bit more. I'm sure there's time for at least one or two questions."

Elizabeth felt herself flush. "How did he come to wear a mask?"

Instantly she regretted her words, for a visible shadow fell across Moira's fine-boned face. "He was three. His father came in early one night, much earlier than was his custom, and found Neville still awake. He'd lost a great deal of money that day—more than I ever knew we had to lose, in fact. He picked Neville up. And dropped him into the fire."

"Deliberately?" Elizabeth gasped.

Moira sighed. "At the time I thought so. Now? I'm not so certain Edmund truly understood what he did. But he was a very angry man—he could never accept any sort of blame for his own actions. I think that's why he continued to gamble, even when there was nothing left to lose. *He* couldn't possibly be a loser, do you see? He had to keep gambling until he won." Moira smoothed a linen pillowcase on her lap and stared thoughtfully into the fire. "But in the end, he lost everything, and everyone. Even Neville." She shook her face, her eyes soft with regret.

"Was Neville—was Neville terribly hurt?"

"For a time I doubted he'd live. But he was lucky. He was young and strong and healthy otherwise. And the burns were clean. The scars were worse when he was younger. That's when he started to wear the mask. He was ten when he went to school for the first time. And the children made such fun of him, he refused to be seen without it. It was very hard for him."

"How—how does he look now?"

Moira's lips twitched. "When he trusts you, he'll show you. It's the part of his face above his right eye that's particularly scarred. He doesn't have much hair on his right temple, but really, I think he could manage to show his face in public and not scare small children. But he prefers to wear the mask and who am I to tell him not to?"

"But you left Ireland? When he was still quite small? Where did Neville go to school?"

"In London." Moira's mouth twisted and, momentarily, she looked bitter and sad. She looked up at Elizabeth, the expression in her eyes almost pleading. "I left his father, as soon as Neville could travel. First I brought him to Dublin, but there it was clear that I would have no recourse, no possible hope of ever attaining a divorce, so I went to—"

"You tried to get a divorce?" Elizabeth stared at Moira in amazement. She'd never met anyone, let alone a woman, who'd attempted to get a divorce.

"I couldn't live with a man who would jeopardize the life of his own son." Even across the years, Elizabeth sensed the depths of Moira's frustrated rage and overwhelming instincts to protect her child. "So I went to England and petitioned Parliament—yes, it takes an act of Parliament to grant a woman a divorce, did you know that?" She gazed off into the distance, her eyes bitter. "I never got the divorce. Neville and I—well, we lived the best way we could. His father refused to send me any money, of course. There were a few lean years, especially in the beginning, and then things got better." She paused, and looked as though she might say more, then shook her head as though deciding better of it.

"What gave him the idea to . . ."

"Play Robin Hood?" Again the comers of Moira's mouth lifted in a fleeting smile. "Neville was a very romantic child, I suppose you could say. He had an amazing imagination—he was always playing at one thing or another. When he came back here after his father's death, and assumed the title, he was shocked to see how poorly the tenants were treated. And he knew what it was like to be cold and hungry and not certain where the next meal might come from. So he decided to do what he could." Moira placed the folded pillowcase neatly in the basket and picked up a towel. "There was almost nothing left here—what you see now is what's left after everything was mortgaged and sold—" She broke off and shook her head. "When I came to Clonmore as a bride, it wasn't half so shabby as this."

"But—but it's so dangerous—"

"I know it is, and that's why I want you to help me convince Neville he must stop."

"Me?" Elizabeth stared at her mother-in-law wide-eyed. She was still having trouble absorbing the fact that her husband's childhood had obviously been far less comfortable than hers, and if she thought that her father's problem with gambling had made her childhood difficult—well, she obviously had never really considered how much worse things could have been. Suddenly she understood just how strong Lady Frances was. Without her influence, acting as a bulwark between Sir Oliver and the family money, Elizabeth and her family could just as easily have ended up on the streets of London as well. But the possibility of that happening had never before occurred to her. And now, Lady Moira was suggesting that she could somehow convince Neville to give up his masquerade? "He won't even live under the same roof with me. He's spoken to me three times in all of our acquaintance—how can you think I could ever have any influ—"

"Because I can see you're different. You're kind and care about something other than the color of your next ball gown. You recognized him right away—do you realize in over two years, no one else ever has? I've tried to warn Neville that it was bound to happen sooner or later and he's always put me off—but you picked him right out, didn't you? You could see behind the mask. And Neville knows he cannot continue to live like this indefinitely. Every day it grows more dangerous. He must find another way to work for a better Ireland."

"I'm not sure I'm at all the right person for your son," Elizabeth said slowly. "I was raised to do my duty—"

"Ah, Elizabeth, how many ladies of your station have ever ridden out to the outlying villages? How many ladies spend time pounding out salves and distilling tinctures for their tenants? Turlough told me the extent of your work. There are too many good Christians in this land who think their duty is dispensed every Sunday with a prayer or two for the repose of the souls of the newly departed poor. I think you understand what I mean."

Elizabeth smiled dubiously. She liked this woman, who was as frank and forthright in her own way as Lady Frances. "I'm still not sure what influence I can have on Neville."

"Stay here. Help me nurse him back to health. You're beautiful and knowledgeable about herbs and healing. We'll show him you can be trusted. And he's a good man, truly he is. I know an absurd set of circumstances brought you together. But all things happen for a reason, don't you think? Are we not all players in God's grand game?"

Elizabeth opened her mouth to reply when a long groan issued from the bedroom. She looked at Moira expectantly.

"He's awake." Moira got to her feet. "I'll go in to see him first, and then bring you in when it's time to change the dressings. A new nurse might do him some good." She winked at Elizabeth. "Come, come, my lass. No man, no matter how formidable, is ever a match for two women. And I think it's time Lord Neville learned his lesson."

Ten

"*I cannot believe* you brought her here, Mother." Neville glared at his mother as she bent to remove the dressing from his leg wound. He began to fold his arms across his chest, but stopped in midmotion as pain lanced through his shoulder and down his arm. He bit back a curse beneath his breath.

"I need some assistance," Moira replied coolly. She gently trickled some of Elizabeth's herbal distillation over the wound. "Emma and I are not that young any more, Neville. She's very knowledgeable about healing. And she's your wife." Moira smiled as she expertly bound a clean bandage around Neville's leg. "Lucky for you that was just a flesh wound. Now, let's see that shoulder."

With a groan, Neville allowed her to undo the bandages. The flesh around the wound was puffy and red, and Moira frowned as she bent closer. "What's wrong?" he asked.

"I don't like the looks of this." She pressed her lips together and carefully dribbled more of the herbal mixture onto the wound.

Neville winced. "What's that?"

"An infusion, I think she said. Or maybe a tincture. I'm not quite sure." Moira peeked at her son sideways. His eyes were closed and his skin was pale. She touched his cheek with the back of her hand, and then his neck. "You've got a touch of fever." She rebandaged the wound with a fresh dressing, then picked up a glass bottle full of Elizabeth's concoctions. "Here." She poured it into a glass. "Drink some."

Neville opened his eyes and glared. "How do you know it's not poison?"

"Neville." Moira shook her head. "Then she's poisoning all the tenants, too." Neville did not reply, but obediently drank the entire glass with a grimace. "I understand why you feel the need to keep her at arm's length until you get to know her better. But she's not going away. From what she's told me, you've been downright rude. Why?"

Neville looked up at her. His eyes had that glassy, bright quality which so often accompanied fever. "What if she goes to Sir William? Offers to turn me in for, say, the deed to Kilmara? She walks away free, while I go to the block."

"You can't believe she would—"

"Trust no one, Mother. God knows in the last few weeks I feel as though I've risked far too much as it is."

"I should say so." Moira tapped his injured leg gently with the tip of one finger. "I don't think you're being fair to Elizabeth. It's not her fault that she recognized you—I've told you over and over again that was bound to happen sooner or later. Don't you think that if she really wanted to turn you in she could have done so by now? Instead, what's she done but taken an interest in the people of Kilmara?"

"It's foolish to trust her until I know her."

"Well, then, my dear son, look at this as an opportunity to learn to know your wife." Moira patted his rough cheek and picked up the basket of dirty bandages, and was gone before he could respond. Neville stared at the closed door. He lay back against the pillows and shook his head. All that mattered now was that he get better. The bishop would be sending the tithe money to London in a little over a month now. He moved his injured shoulder cautiously and pain shot down his arm. He closed his eyes, willing his arm to heal. Much as he hated to admit it, he knew his mother was right. One more robbery—one more spectacular robbery—

and then Gentleman Niall could retire, at least for a while.
And the boy was safe. An image of the boy's face when he
realized he was going home drifted before Neville's closed
eyelids. He'd done what he'd set out to do then. Pray God,
just once more, he thought, as he drifted toward sleep. Just
once more.

The basket of mending seemed never-ending, thought Elizabeth as she reached for yet another shirt. Where did all this
clothing come from? The quality of it ranged from items she
might have worn herself, to the cheapest and flimsiest of
cotton shirts and shifts. The shirt she held up for inspection
had a broad band of embroidery at neck and cuffs, and a
long rent in the seam of the collar. Elizabeth threaded her
needle and began to work, keeping one eye on her patient.
Neville slept in the huge bed that dominated the entire room.
The fire snapped and hissed gently and raindrops tapped
against the leaded panes of the small window.

She drew a deep breath and let it out slowly. She wished
she felt as peaceful as the small room appeared. Her talks
with Lady Moira were giving her a great deal of insight into
her husband's character, but she was not at all sure she
would in any way be able to break through the hard shell
Neville wore like a shield. A subtle movement made her
look up.

He was awake and watching her, those piercing blue eyes
fastened on her with an intensity that took her breath away.
She started. "You're awake."

His lips lifted in the hint of a grin. "Don't worry, I'll be
asleep again soon. I'm weak as a new kitten."

"That's the fever." She set the shirt aside and walked to
his bedside. She placed her hand gingerly against his face.
His cheek was rough with stubble, but his skin was hot and
dry and still pale. "How do you feel?"

"Like someone shot me," he returned.

Their eyes met and she laughed. "That's not what I
meant."

He dropped his gaze and shrugged. "Leg's feeling as
though it's starting to get better. Wish I could say the same

for the shoulder." Suddenly he lay back against the pillows and shut his eyes.

"Are you all right?"

"I feel sick all over." He shifted his head on the pillow, and the silk mask slid smoothly across the unbleached linen pillowcase. "My mother thinks you can help me. Do you?"

"I know something about herbs and their uses—mostly how to heal with them."

He turned his head to look at her, and once more, she felt drawn to the force in his blue eyes. She thought for a moment he was going to say something biting, but instead he only looked at her with a hint of a sad smile on his lips. "Do you, now?" he asked softly.

He spoke with a lilting trace of Gentleman Niall's brogue, and Elizabeth swallowed hard as the memory of that night flared through her mind, sending the ghost of a shiver down her spine. His tone was nearly tender, his eyes almost soft. His next words surprised her even more.

"I've been rude, Elizabeth. It was not my intention. You took me off guard, you see, when you so clearly recognized me—"

"The feeling was mutual, believe me." Their eyes locked once more and this time he chuckled.

"Well. Now I see I must trust you with my life—" He nodded at the bottles and jars which now lined the small table beside the bed. "After all, you could poison me—I'm at your mercy, my lady."

She opened her mouth to protest, met his eyes, and saw that he was teasing her. To her horror, she felt herself flush. What was it about this man that so unsettled her, that drew her to him like a moth to a flame? He was so totally unlike anyone—let alone any man—she had ever met in her life. She dropped her eyes and turned away. "Why should I poison you, my lord? A lifetime spent as a murderess is not one to my liking."

"Ah, but the murderess of Gentleman Niall—the cunning outlaw—why, you'd be celebrated throughout the length of Ireland." He spoke lightly, teasingly, but there was the slightest edge in his tone that told her he was testing her.

She raised her head and met his eyes. "That never occurred to me."

His face relaxed momentarily into the most genuine smile she'd ever seen. "I know, my lady. I know."

"I'll fetch you some broth." She turned to leave, but he stopped her with a question.

"Why should you care for me? I mean nothing to you."

"You saved my life," she answered coolly. "What did I mean to you then?" She smiled briefly and left him lying silent against his pillows.

Three days passed, quiet days which settled into a pleasant routine determined by Neville's needs. By the third day at Clonmore, despite its shabby appearance and lack of Kilmara's comforts, Elizabeth nevertheless felt more at ease than she had since leaving England. Meals were taken in the great hall, at a battered table that had clearly seen better days, but the food was hearty and Lady Moira regaled her with stories of her own Irish girlhood that made Elizabeth feel as though she'd had a chance to connect with a part of her mother she otherwise would've missed.

The breakfast dishes had just been cleared, and Elizabeth was sorting through her supplies, when Mistress Aislinn, the housekeeper, entered the hall with a worried look on her face. "Is my lady about?" she asked Elizabeth in a low voice that made Elizabeth wonder what was wrong.

"I believe she's gone to the kitchens, Aislinn, to see about dinner. Why? What's wrong?"

Aislinn wet her lips and glanced over her shoulder. "Sir William St. Denys just rode through the gates—he's looking for the master."

Elizabeth blanched. "Sir William? What on earth is he doing here?"

Aislinn shook her head and looked even more nervous. "That I wouldn't know, my lady, but he's here to see the master."

"Well—well—offer him something to eat, Aislinn—" Elizabeth glanced up at the balcony, then to the doorway which led to the kitchens. Clonmore Castle was medieval in layout—the kitchens were in a separate outbuilding. It would be faster to run up and speak to Neville himself. She gathered her skirts and dashed up the steps, just as the outer door opened and Sir William stepped into the hall.

She did not pause to look over her shoulder, but she heard a nervous Aislinn clear her throat. "Welcome, Sir William, my lady's gone to fetch the master."

She darted into Neville's office and knocked on his door. Lady Moira had brought him his breakfast an hour ago. She opened the door after his muffled summons, and paused. Neville was standing on the other side of the bed. He wore a pair of breeches, and his chest was bare save for his bandaged shoulder. She stared at the sight of his broad shoulders, the wide planes of his chest covered with dark, close curling hair. "For-forgive me, my lord."

"Elizabeth. I thought you were Harrington. Is he here?"

"N-no," she managed to stammer. "Sir William is."

"Sir William?" Neville swore beneath his breath. "What the devil is he doing here?"

She shook her head, eyes averted. The limited time she'd spent in his company in the last few days had not been unpleasant, and now the sight of his nearly naked body made her uncomfortably warm. She swallowed hard.

"Well, don't just stand there—help me dress."

She hoped he did not notice how her hands trembled when she handed him his shirt or how she nearly tripped over the low stool by the fire when she brought him his boots. He moved slowly, gingerly. His leg wound was well on the way to recovery, but the shoulder wound was slower to heal. Fortunately, Elizabeth's remedies coupled with Lady Moira's diligent nursing were proving effective.

Finally he sat back, and adjusted the mask over his face. She saw the beads of sweat which beaded his upper lip. "Are you—are you quite sure you can manage, Neville? I could speak to him in your place—"

"No," he said sharply. He saw at once the look which crossed her face. "Sir William is my problem," he added gently. "I'll deal with him."

"But—but what will you say? How will you explain—"

He grinned at her. "There's fever in the cottages, isn't there? I've picked up a touch of that."

"You'll frighten him," she said with a little laugh.

"That's the point." He winked. "Now, my lady, would you be so kind as to assist me down the stairs? I don't think falling down the stairs would make much of an impression on Sir William. Not to mention what I'd have to listen to from my mother. I can count on you to play dutiful, concerned wife, can't I?"

She bit back a giggle. "Of course. Let me help you." Awkwardly, she held out her arm. It looked daintily insignificant beside his.

He looked down at her dubiously. "On second thought . . ."

"What's wrong?"

He smiled shortly. "Nothing, my dear. Lead on."

My dear, she thought, as she helped him limp across the room, his weight pressing against her shoulder. She was acutely aware of his closeness. A scent rose from his body, sharp and tangy and warm as an herb garden beneath a summer sun. He faltered on the first step and his hand brushed the back of her head. It lingered for a moment on her hair, as though caressing her thick, soft curls, which she'd only bundled loosely into a net. "Are you all right?" she breathed.

"I'm fine," he muttered. "Go slowly."

Sir William noticed them when they were halfway down the staircase. "My God, Clonmore, what ails you, man?"

Neville smiled weakly. "A touch of fever, Sir William. There's fever in the cottages, didn't you know?"

"Aye," answered Sir William, looking uncertain. He shifted his weight from one foot to the other, and Elizabeth had the distinct impression he'd rather be gone.

"But we're delighted to see you, are we not, my lady?" He patted Elizabeth's back, even as he clung to the banister with the other hand. "We hope to call on your lovely wife soon, Sir William."

Sir William coughed. "I'm sure she'd be delighted, Clonmore. But the reason why I've come—I don't suppose you heard about the other night?"

"My lord came down with the fever five nights ago," blurted Elizabeth. Neville shot a warning glance down at her.

"No—no, Sir William, as my wife says, I was indisposed. Tell me, what about the other night?"

"The damnedest thing, sir. That pack of rascals who attacked your father, my lady, and you as well, took the bait we set—a patrol from the garrison chased them all the way back to their hideout and got every last man. There's to be a meeting of the landowners on Wednesday next—" He paused and nodded. "Er, that's two days away."

Neville spread his hands. "I will send my agent in my stead, Sir William. This is too important to miss, of course— I presume Colonel Melville will share with us at last his plan to capture Gentleman Niall?"

Sir William nodded. "Aye, at last. We've a plan worked out we think can't fail."

Neville smiled mildly. "Indeed, sir. Let's hope at last."

Sir William glanced longingly out the door. "Well, Clonmore, I won't keep you. I can see you're still quite ill. Good day to you, my lady. Better get back to bed, Clonmore. A touch of the fever can kill a man, especially when he least expects it."

Without saying any more, Sir William nearly bolted for the door, Before it slammed shut, they heard him calling, "Boy! Boy! Bring that horse here!"

Elizabeth glanced up at Neville. Behind the silk mask, his eyes glinted with humor. Then his face paled, and he sagged against the balcony. At the same moment, Lady Moira emerged from the door to the kitchens, accompanied by Harrington.

"Neville!" she cried when she saw her son leaning so heavily against the stair rail. "What on earth are you doing out of bed?"

"Fending off Sir William, Mother," he managed. Beads of sweat gathered on his upper lip and, beneath the silk mask, Elizabeth saw splotched stains appear on his pale cheeks.

"Master Harrington," she cried just as Neville sank to the steps.

Harrington and Moira rushed forward. "Easy, man," Harrington said, and he wrapped an arm around Neville's body.

Moira, meanwhile, had rushed to the door. In response to her summons, a groom rushed in, wiping his hands on a rag. "Hold on there now, me lord." The little man hurried across the scuffed wooden floor. Although he was not much larger than Elizabeth, he was obviously very strong, for he wrapped his arm around Neville's waist, and together he and Harrington carried Neville up the stairs and back to bed, Elizabeth and Moira hastening behind.

They got Neville settled on the bed. Moira carefully peeked beneath the shoulder bandage. "If you've opened that up again . . ." she began. But the wound was undamaged by his exertions. "I'll get you something to drink." She left the room, shaking her head.

The little groom tugged at his forelock. "Take care, me lord." He bowed awkwardly to Elizabeth and to Harrington, and backed out of the room.

Neville opened his eyes with a deep sigh. His gaze fell on Elizabeth where she stood beside the bed. "I'm sorry. Perhaps we shouldn't have done that."

"Perhaps?" said Harrington. "What made you get up?"

"Sir William came calling," Elizabeth answered. "It was my fault."

"Don't be ridiculous," said Neville. He turned his head restlessly on the pillow, plucking at the silk mask. "It was as well I went down and let Sir William see me. Now it will be all over the county that I've taken the fever, and there is fever in the cottages, so it's a perfect alibi, and it certainly got rid of Sir William quickly. But you must go to Ennis, Harrington, on Wednesday. There's to be another meeting of the landowners."

"Another meeting?" Harrington laughed. "What's this— the third? Colonel Melville is more interested in talking than he is in finding the dread outlaw."

"Melville may not be much more than a strutting cock," said Neville, lying back against the pillows. He stared up at the ceiling. "When I met Sir Anthony in Dublin that time, two years ago it was, I'll never forget it. There aren't many men who frighten me, Harrington, but Sir Anthony was one of them. I remember he had a trick of looking straight into your eyes, as if he could see all the way to the bottom of your soul. And when you looked back, you weren't sure he had one." Neville paused.

Elizabeth crossed her arms around herself and shivered. Harrington stared silently at his master. "He frightened me in the coach," Elizabeth said. "I didn't like the way he looked at me at all."

Neville looked at her, an unreadable expression playing across his face. "No, my lady, I don't imagine you would. They're going to announce a plan," he said to Harrington. "I think Sir Anthony's finally about to make some sort of move."

"Hm," said Harrington. "I don't believe I should miss this."

"Nor do I," said Neville. "They'll never say exactly what they intend to do."

"Let me go," breathed Elizabeth.

"You, my lady?" asked Neville.

Harrington shrugged. "Why not, Neville? Lady Clonmore is, after all, your wife. Kilmara's her dowry. And if everyone's agog with Lady Clonmore, I will be much freer to move behind the scenes and find out what I can."

Neville looked at Elizabeth. Their eyes locked. *Trust me,* she wanted to say. *Truly. I have no wish to hurt you. I'd love you if you let me.* That thought made her drop her eyes and blush. She heard the sharp intake of his breath.

"Very well, my lady. If Harrington thinks your presence would be helpful, well, so be it, then. And you might enjoy the society of the other ladies—the last meeting was nearly the social event of the season, wouldn't you say, Harrington?"

Harrington shrugged with a wry grin. "You could say that."

"Say what?" asked Moira, as she carried in a tray with a

pitcher and a goblet. "Now what are you plotting, Neville? Haven't you learned your lesson yet?"

Neville smiled grimly. "Not yet, Mother. Gentleman Niall has one more job to do before he retires. And I mean to do it."

Moira set the tray down with a thump and glared at her son. "Well, let's hope Gentleman Niall doesn't find himself permanently retired, courtesy of Her Majesty's soldiers." She held the goblet in one hand and helped Neville sit up far enough to drink with the other.

"Faugh, Mother," he grimaced. "What's in that?"

"Whiskey. The water of life. Diluted with a bit of real water."

"Christ, how could you do that to good whiskey?" He rolled back down and closed his eyes.

"All right, we'll leave you—" Moira began.

"No," Neville interrupted. "Elizabeth, please stay."

Elizabeth flushed at the look Harrington and Moira exchanged. She stepped outside to allow Harrington to go by, then waited with clasped hands as he shut the door, leaving her alone with Neville.

"I have something to say to you." He sounded abrupt. "Please look at me."

Scarcely daring to breathe, she raised her eyes and was surprised to see him glance away.

"I said to you the day we were married that I understood that this marriage was not of your choosing. Well, it wasn't of mine, either." He gave her a crooked smile. "But I found myself in the position of having saved your life. And now I see that you've saved mine."

Elizabeth shook her head. "Oh, I wouldn't go that far—"

"Hush," he said. "I would. I've seen what can happen when a wound goes bad." He paused, then reached beneath his pillow. "When I met you that night, you told me the thieves had robbed you of something very precious. And I very foolishly, very rashly, promised you I'd get it back." He beckoned her forward with his uninjured arm and gave her another rueful grin. "I think this is what you lost." He held out his hand.

Shocked into silence, Elizabeth held out her own hand. Her palm quivered as, with a quick flash of green and a shower of gold, Neville poured the locket on the chain into her hand. She closed her fist around it, feeling her heart begin to pound. She opened her palm. There, in the middle of her hand, lay her mother's locket. She shut her eyes against a sudden rush of tears. "How—how did you get this?"

"I, uh, I took the time to look around and see what was there," Neville said.

"Is that how you came to be wounded?"

"No," he answered.

"I never expected to see this again." She smiled as she blinked back the tears. "I—l don't know how to thank you."

"No thanks are necessary, my lady." He smiled, and this time, it reached his eyes. He winked, and spoke in Gentleman Niall's brogue. "After all, a gentleman always keeps his promises."

Gratitude rushed through her like a tide, gratitude and something more. The scars he bore went deeper than the ones the mask hid. But beneath his gruff exterior, she sensed a gentle and kind man, who adhered religiously to his own code of right. Impulsively she took his hand and pressed a kiss onto the back of it. "Thank you," she whispered, blinking back tears.

His long fingers curled around hers, and he did not shake her away. As she swallowed hard, he tugged gently on her hand, drawing her close. She stepped to the very edge of the bed. He raised his hand and slowly traced the line from her cheek down her jaw to her throat with the tip of one finger. She gasped as a burst of heat suffused her body as though she'd been engulfed in a flame. "You are so very beautiful," he whispered.

Her lips parted, and her mouth felt puffy, warm, and moist.

He reached around her waist and drew her close. She gave a little sigh as his arm closed around her and their mouths met. His lips were warm and firm, the skin amazingly soft. She opened her mouth to his of her own volition, and he delicately traced the very edge of the warm interior of her mouth with the tip of his tongue. She moaned softly and leaned into him.

With a little cry of pain, he jerked back.

"Forgive me," she cried, as her hands flew to her hot cheeks. Her body tingled all over, and between her legs she felt the trickle of moist heat.

"Forgive me, my lady." He straightened up, leaning back against his pillows. "You scarcely know me—I should not take such liberties." He touched his mask, adjusting it with little tugs, and Elizabeth felt her heart melt.

It doesn't matter to me what you look like, she wanted to cry. But he'd never believe her. He barely trusted her as it was. She would have to prove herself to him somehow. She squared her shoulders and drew a deep breath, forcing herself to be composed. "If my lord will excuse me, I must see to my wardrobe. I may need to send to Kilmara for something suitable to wear."

"Whatever you require, my lady, it shall be done." He lay back and closed his eyes.

Elizabeth hesitated, but his mouth was pressed in a tight, thin line, so different from the soft pressure of his kiss. "Thank you, my lord." She pressed a kiss into her fist that held the locket and tiptoed out of the room.

Eleven

"Beastly cruel," declared Lady Jane, leaning closer to Lady Susannah. "Why, it was beastly cruel, if you ask me. Can you imagine that man expecting his daughter to be married the day after she arrived—the day after she was nearly kidnapped—kidnapped, can you believe?—and not even a woman to comfort her? A woman to stand with her at her wedding? You should have gone, Susannah, you should have insisted Sir William take you."

"But I didn't know!" protested Lady Susannah. She stared round-eyed and open-mouthed at Lady Jane. "Why, Sir William didn't even tell me he'd spoken to the girl till the next day—for all I know she could've been being married at that very moment. Surely, I've never heard of such a thing."

"They had to get a special dispensation from the bishop," put in Mrs. Hayes. She looked around the crowded hall. The weak November sun streamed through the clear panes of glass in the high windows of the sheriff s mansion.

"Well, some woman should've been there with her. It's not Christian!" Lady Jane thumped her cane on the floor and her cheeks quivered.

"What about his mother?" asked Mrs. Hayes. "Wasn't she there?"

"From what I heard from Master Ogilivie, there were four men—Sir Oliver, Lord Neville and his agent, that nice Master Harrington, and himself. And poor Lady Elizabeth was the only woman there." Lady Susannah sighed. "You are right, Jane, but I didn't know. What could I do?"

Lady Jane, having made her point, sat back in a satisfied huff.

"Do you suppose she'll come today?" asked Mistress Hayes.

"Well, I wouldn't think so," answered Lady Susannah. "Why, it's not even been a month—"

"Tush, Susannah," said Lady Jane. "'Twould do the poor girl good to get out and meet her neighbors. Why, you should host a reception for her, Susannah. Welcome her to the county, introduce her to everyone."

Lady Susannah clasped her hands in her lap. "Jane, I'd be more than happy to do just that—but it's unthinkable right now. You know that. Why, who would come? No one will travel after dark as it is. It will have to wait until all this non-sense is settled."

"Indeed, indeed," tittered Mistress Hayes. "These out-laws are becoming unbelievably bold! Why, just the other day there was a robbery on the Dublin road—and did you hear that a hedgemaster was taken just a few miles away?"

"Where?" demanded Lady Jane. "So at least all this car-rying on has led to something."

Lady Susannah looked troubled. "There's bound to be a public trial—I told Sir William I can't bear the thought — there's too much of that sort of thing—I just wish we'd have some peace."

"There'll be no peace," declared Lady Jane, "until every last idolater and insurrectionist is run out of Ireland or hanged."

Lady Susannah sighed. "I'm sure you're right, Jane." She gazed over her shoulder with a troubled frown. "I wish Sir William would start the meeting. No one will want to travel after dark." She beckoned to a passing footman. "Go and find Sir William, please. And tell him he'd better start the meeting. He won't have an audience if he doesn't."

"At once, my lady." The footman bowed and threaded his way through the throng.

Lady Jane settled back on the sofa with a sigh. "Oh, he'll have an audience, all right, my dear. It's you that will have a passel of overnight guests!"

"What have you there, Sir Anthony?" asked Sir William as he put the final touches to his speech. He looked up as the knight limped slowly into the room, leaning heavily on his cane, a sheaf of parchment tucked under his arm. Sir William blew on the ink to dry it and rose to his feet. "Are you ready, man? Are you sure you're up to this?"

"Quite sure," answered Sir Anthony. "I wouldn't miss it for the world. Where's our friend Melville?"

"He's gone to escort the bishop here. What have you got there?" Sir William nodded at the parchments Sir Anthony carried.

"This is a compilation of all the descriptions of Gentleman Niall I could gather. If what I suspect to be true is in fact the case, we should at least be able to narrow the playing field considerably, if you will indulge me."

Sir William shook sand over his notes and frowned at Sir Anthony with a doubtful look. "I can't have you making any enemies, Sir Anthony. The landowners here have been most helpful—"

Sir Anthony drew himself up. "My dear Sir William, we've been over this a dozen times. Indulge an injured man if you will. I promise to be discreet."

"Hm." Sir William shook off the sand. "All right, let's go." Walking slowly to accommodate Sir Anthony, the two men started off down the corridor in the direction of the reception hall. "What exactly are you looking for?"

"Well, for example, it's generally agreed by all that Gentleman Niall is a man of above average height—well above it, I might add, although I discount the reports that he's a 'veritable giant.' That alone will shorten the list of suspects."

"Hm." Sir William clasped his hands behind his back. "But Gentleman Niall is always masked—"

"As is every other member of his band. But we know Gentleman Niall is clean-shaven—all the reports agree that he has no facial hair at all." Sir Anthony met Sir William's eyes and smiled. His cane tapped an odd counterrhythm to his halting gait on the parquet floor.

They reached the entrance of the reception hall, and found it in a state of near chaos. Landowners, some from as far away as Belfast and Dublin, who possessed property in the area, crowded into the large room, which was packed to overflowing. Sir William tapped a footman on the shoulder. "Clear us a way to the front," he said. "Sir Anthony here mustn't be jostled."

The servant bowed an assent, and together, the three men started forward. "Well," asked Sir William, when they were perhaps a third of the way through the crowd, "Do you see any uncommonly tall men? Who happen to be clean-shaven?"

Sir Anthony did not immediately reply. He was scanning the crowd, navigating slowly in the wake of the young footman, who did his best to clear a path. "There's Lord Trevaine . . . and Sir Harry Rosslyn . . . and that gentleman, Sir William—yes, the tall one in the dark russet coat—who is he?"

"Ah, that's Donal MacMurray. He's here to represent the interests of his father, the MacMurray of Skye. Now there's a possible suspect for you. The Scots are as thieving a race as the Irish." Sir William exchanged a meaningful glance with Sir Anthony.

"Hm. Where is the MacMurray's property?"

"Ah, mostly in Ulster, I believe. You very seldom see . . ." Sir William's voice trailed off.

"Well, perhaps not, then," Sir Anthony said briskly. "Ulster is, after all, some leagues away." He was silent as he peered over the heads of those who pressed closely about them. "I don't see Clonmore, Sir William."

Sir William started. "I wouldn't expect to see him. I told you he was down with the fever when I stopped at Clonmore."

"Ah, yes, you did mention that. How sick did he look to you?"

"Extremely sick, man. I told you—he was leaning on that sweet little wife of his for dear life—" Sir William stopped short. "Surely you don't suspect *him*?"

"Sh," cautioned Sir Anthony, a finger against his lips. "Not so loudly, Sir William." They had reached the corner of the dais by this time, and Sir William swung around to confront Sir Anthony. He drew him behind the dais, where a row of soldiers stared woodenly out over the crowd.

"You truly think it could be Clonmore?"

"How well do you know Lord Clonmore?" Sir Anthony asked.

Sir William stared. "For more than two years, I suppose—he and I arrived at about the same time."

"And he's a sociable sort? Attends all the parties? A real favorite with the ladies? He's very dashing with that mask, don't you think?"

"Why, no, as a matter of fact," Sir William said. "Just the opposite. Clonmore keeps very much to himself—I believe he travels frequently on business."

"And what sort of business is this? Horses?"

"I believe so, yes. Why don't you ask him yourself?"

Sir Anthony smiled blandly. "I believe I will, Sir William. That's another distinguishing characteristic I've been able to glean from these notes." He raised the sheaf of notes in his hand like a trophy. "Gentleman Niall's horses are of remarkable quality. I observed that for myself."

Sir William said nothing. A footman rushed up, wig askew. "Beg pardon, m'lord, m'lord, but her ladyship bid me ask you to best start the meeting. She says there'll be no one left as soon as the sun turns in the sky!"

Sir William sighed. "Tell her ladyship that as soon as the bishop arrives, I'll get the meeting started." He hooked his thumbs in his belt and stared at Sir Anthony, mouth pressed tight. "I'm not sure what to think."

"I understand, Sir William. Leave it to me. It's how I earn my keep, after all."

Sir William found it difficult to dismiss the chill which

sped down his back like a bullet at the look in Sir Anthony's cold gray eyes.

"Ah," fretted Lady Susannah, "I don't know what ails my husband—surely he can see that everyone's growing restless." She picked up her fan and batted the air vigorously.

"So true, Susannah, so true," said Mistress Hayes. She had only just that day first called Lady Susannah by her Christian name, and now was using every opportunity to repeat it.

"Who's that coming in now?" asked Lady Jane, fanning equally hard. "See, there, someone's coming in."

"My goodness," answered Lady Susannah. "As I live and breathe. It's that nice Master Harrington now, with a young lady on his arm."

"Lady Clonmore?" Mrs. Hayes craned her neck. "Oh, where, Susannah?"

"Sit down, Mrs. Hayes, you look like a rooster stretching your neck that way." Lady Jane raised her cane and pointed through the press of bodies. "Over there, by the door. Do you see them, Susann—why, where on earth did she go?"

"She went that way," answered Mrs. Hayes. "She's just about to greet them now."

"Ah, we've been spotted." Harrington raised his head just as their lavishly dressed hostess bore down upon them with the force of a gale-driven ship.

Elizabeth followed his gaze through the shifting mass and managed a smile as a middle-aged woman in dark green silk rushed up to them.

"Master Harrington, Master Harrington, how lovely of you to come. Why, Sir William told me the earl was down with a fever—" She broke off and turned to Elizabeth, beaming. "And you, my dear, must be the new Lady Clonmore? Sir Oliver's daughter?" She planted a warm kiss on Elizabeth's cheek. "I'm so glad to know you, dear. I'm sure we'll be great friends."

Elizabeth stared at the woman, as Harrington cleared his throat. "Ah, Lady Clonmore, may I present Lady Susannah

St. Denys, wife of Sir William, whom you've already met twice now?"

"And for shame on Sir William for not bringing me to Clonmore Castle sooner, my dear. I've been dying to meet you—everyone has, of course. Come with me and meet some of your new neighbors. You don't mind, Master Harrington?"

"Lady St. Denys—" Elizabeth began, taken off guard by this verbal barrage. She glanced helplessly at Harrington, but it was clear her presence was having just the effect Neville had predicted.

He winked in response, then said, "Oh, please, my lady. My lord expressly wished that you have an opportunity to meet some of the neighboring ladies—and if you will excuse me, I see Master Hayes—I have a matter of some urgency to discuss with him." With a correct little bow, Harrington melted into the throng of people who were beginning to crowd the reception hall.

"You come with me, my dear," declared Lady Susannah. She gripped Elizabeth firmly by the arm and steered her with a forceful purpose toward a low couch where a black-clad woman about her grandmother's age waited with a scrawny woman the same age as Lady Susannah. "Come, sit and talk to us, Lady Clonmore. May I present Lady Jane Fitzbarth, widow of the late Sir Roland Fitzbarth, and Mistress Addison Hayes?"

"My lady," murmured Elizabeth with a slight bow. "Mistress Hayes." She smiled carefully at the group who stared at her with such avid interest. "I'm very glad to meet you all."

"And we you, my dear," said Lady Jane. "I knew your mother when she was a girl. Lovely young woman, and I see you're very like her."

"Oh," Elizabeth flushed. "Thank you. I miss her very much."

Lady Jane fixed her with a keen eye. "I'm sure you do. Now do sit down, please. We've a thousand questions for you."

Amused by the old lady's bluntness, Elizabeth sank down

on a couch to the left. Lady Susannah signaled to a footman. "You may tell Sir William he must start—the hour is growing late. He forgets that the days are shortening. And everyone must be well on their way home by dark."

The footman bowed and withdrew, and Lady Susannah turned to Elizabeth. "We've all hesitated, you know, my dear, not that we didn't want to meet you, but because— well, we wanted you to be comfortable here. Given the circumstances of everything, you know."

"But now that you've come out," cried Mistress Hayes, "you must join us on every opportunity. For example, there's to be a trial of a hedgemaster within the next weeks—you simply must come to that!"

"A trial?" Elizabeth stared blankly at Mistress Hayes, her mind reeling. She had felt so determined when she'd first walked in, so sure that she would make Neville proud in some way she wasn't sure she could even define. But now she felt sick and faint, first by the press of bodies, and now by the all-consuming interest of these women who so clearly meant to be friendly.

"Of a hedgemaster, my dear," said Lady Jane, leaning forward to shout. "Dreadful men. Simply dreadful. They foment rebellion among the natives at every turn."

Elizabeth looked down at her hands knotted in her lap. How was it possible that these women, who obviously considered themselves good Christians, had no idea of the suffering all around them? Were they ignorant? Or merely oblivious? "I cannot believe they are so dreadful, Mistress Hayes," she said. "The hedgemaster at Kilmara has worked endlessly to help the people who are sick with the fever without any care at all for his own health."

"There's a hedgemaster at Kilmara?" Mistress Hayes stared back at her, clearly shocked.

Elizabeth gave a soft gasp. Had she said something wrong? She saw Lady Susannah exchange a glance with Lady Jane, and then Lady Susannah leaned forward and patted her hand once more. "Now, now, my dear, I'm sure you've only seen one side of him."

Before Elizabeth could reply, there was a stir at the entrance of the hall. Lady Susannah rose to her feet and stood on tiptoe, craning to see who had come in. "Well, glory be," she said with a deep sigh. "It's the bishop, at last. Now William will start the meeting."

Elizabeth looked up, but it was impossible to see over the heads of the people who were pressing close. The hall grew even more crowded as those who'd been waiting outside filtered in after the bishop. She finally got a look at him when he joined Sir William on the dais.

"Well, there's nothing I can do," said Lady Susannah. "I'm not about to fight my way through this crowd." She plopped down beside Elizabeth. "Just wait until these people begin to leave, my dear. I'll be sure to introduce you."

Elizabeth smiled and nodded, murmuring something perfunctory. Had she made some terrible mistake by alluding to Turlough? She had seen the startled look which passed between Lady Jane and Lady Susannah. None of them had ever met a hedgemaster, that much was clear. She thought of Turlough, his gentle voice, his patient touch, his deep caring for the people of the district, whom no one else cared much about. How could they be so sure about something they knew nothing about? She looked up as Sir William rapped on the table with a gavel. Suddenly she longed for the fresh air and the open road. She peered into the crowd, searching for a glimpse of Master Harrington, but the press of bodies was so tight, it was impossible to see him.

"Attention! Attention, everyone," cried Sir William. "We've asked you all to come because we wanted to inform you of our latest efforts to apprehend the outlaws." He paused and glanced around the room, smiling jovially. "And we are most pleased to tell you that we have already captured nearly a dozen and slain nearly that many more."

They did not, Elizabeth thought. Neville did!

"What about Gentleman Niall?" shouted one man from the back of the room. He spoke in a thick Scottish burr, and Elizabeth had to strain to understand him. "Have ye caught him yet?"

Sir William cleared his throat. "Ah—"

"And what about our money?"

"What about our jewels?" The cries came from various corners of the room.

"How do you plan to catch him?"

"Hanging's too good for him!"

Sir William wet his lips and held up his hands. "Good people—"

"Sir William, if I may?" Sir Anthony Addams limped heavily on his cane to Sir William's side. Elizabeth noticed that though he appeared pale and drawn, he looked out over the crowd with cool assurance. "Allow me to introduce myself. My name is Sir Anthony Addams. Some of you may have heard of me—I make it my business to hunt down outlaws such as this so-called gentleman and bring them to justice. Those of you who've heard of me know that I've never failed in the pursuit of a quarry, for I accept no failure. Gentleman Niall will be caught, as will the rest of his gang, and I promise you—you have my solemn oath on it—I'll carry his head to Dublin personally on a pike and put it on the city gate for all to see." His voice, like the expression on his face, was dry and cold, and the sound of it reminded Elizabeth of dead leaves blown across barren ground. His pale eyes roamed across the crowd from face to face, as if daring anyone to challenge him. Elizabeth swallowed hard, and even though the room was hot and airless, she felt cold as his gaze swept over her, unseeing.

"Rest assured, good people," Sir Anthony continued, "that we have redoubled our efforts and our redcoats are scouring the countryside, under my direction, even as we speak."

"We've heard that story before," muttered someone standing close by Elizabeth.

"So what are ye going to do differently?" asked the Scotsman. "We've a' heard that promise. And there've been pitifu' few results."

Despite Sir Anthony's cold compelling stare, the low whispers swelled once more into a chorus of complaints. Sir William glanced at Sir Anthony, desperation in his eyes.

"Ahem." Sir Anthony raised his cane and thumped hard on the dais, effectively cutting through the rising voices. The crowd fell silent, and Elizabeth saw how they eyed Sir Anthony with sullen expectation. "I understand your frustration. For two years, this outlaw has preyed upon you all, without constraint. Our work has already borne fruit, as Sir William just said. Almost a dozen ruffians languish in the jail, and a hedgemaster was flushed out as well. You have my personal guarantee that I shall not rest until this outlaw is found. For I believe I know exactly where our 'gentleman' is." He paused dramatically, and the crowd pressed in closer. Elizabeth held her breath, feeling a cold sweat break out down her back. "I have every reason to believe that Gentleman Niall is something more than simply just an outlaw."

"What do you mean, man?" The tall Scot pushed his way through the crowd.

Sir Anthony smiled calmly as he raised his portfolio. "I have reason to believe that Gentleman Niall may be living among us right beneath our noses." There was a collective intake of breath, and Elizabeth felt her blood freeze. "All the evidence would seem to point to someone local—someone perhaps whom others do not recognize. Gentleman Niall is, after all, always masked."

Elizabeth felt sweat trickle from her armpits. She swallowed hard and glanced sideways at the other ladies. They were listening to Sir Anthony wide-eyed and open-mouthed.

"You mean it's one of *us,* sir?" called a speaker whom Elizabeth could not see.

"That's exactly what I mean," replied Sir Anthony, with that cunning-fox face that chilled Elizabeth to her marrow. She swore he turned to look in her direction, and she shrank instinctively closer to Lady Susannah. "Maybe someone here, now, someone within this very room—someone who's pretending to be other than who he really is." He paused, looking out over the crowd, as heads turned back and forth, as everyone looked at their neighbors, suspicion and skepticism warring across their faces. "Or perhaps one of your tenants—someone who's close to the ground, so to speak, but could surface quickly before he's missed."

There was a short pause, and then an excited babble broke out.

Elizabeth felt sick and faint. Where was John Harrington? Suddenly she longed for the safe comfort of Clonmore or Kilmara. She remembered the strength in Neville's arm when he'd kissed her. They had to get back—Neville had to know immediately that from this moment on, even the gentry were under suspicion. She twisted her hands in her lap, feeling the palms grow wet, as Sir Anthony answered a few more questions. She heard the word "tithe," and glanced up in time to see a man of middle height step up beside Sir William.

"That's the Reverend Nicholas Carey, bishop of Clare," Lady Susannah whispered, just as the bishop nodded and raised his right hand in a gesture both blessing and greeting. "He's a most devout man."

Elizabeth pressed her hands against her temples, muttering something she hoped was appropriate. Sir Anthony addressed the crowd once more. "I promise you this, good people. We'll every man—and woman—of us watch Gentleman Niall swing!"

This time, she thought, there could be no doubt. He did look in her direction. The room tilted and spun, and Elizabeth saw Lady Susannah turn to her with a startled look, before the world went dark.

"I see Lord Clonmore could not attend." Sir Anthony Addams leaned heavily upon his cane and smiled at Harrington with the look of a cat sniffing out a mouse, as the crowd began to disperse all around them.

Harrington returned the predatory look with one of complete equanimity. "A touch of the fever, Sir Anthony. I'm sure Sir William mentioned it?"

Sir Anthony's lips quivered. "Most unfortunate. I had a few questions I'd have liked to ask him."

Harrington bowed. "I'm his agent, Sir Anthony. May I be of assistance?"

"Perhaps, Master Harrington. Would you be so kind as to step aside for a moment, sir? I would speak with you in private"—he paused to glare at one of the mingling throng that jostled his injured leg—"and I would fain sit down."

"Of course, Sir Anthony. Shall we?" Harrington gestured toward the side room where Neville had won the card game with Sir Oliver, and pushed the door open to allow Sir Anthony to limp past.

Sir Anthony sank down heavily on a straight-backed chair. He planted his cane between his legs and looked up at Harrington. "It occurred to me, when looking at a map of the area with the sites of all the attacks plotted out, that the area encompassing both Kilmara and Clonmore is an area of very significant outlaw activity."

"Indeed, Sir Anthony?" Harrington leaned forward. "I cannot say I've noticed a rash of robber—"

"I'm not talking about robberies, man. I'm talking activity—witnesses, sightings, that sort of thing. And the caves in the hills above Kilmara House offer the best sort of shelter of that kind around—Sir Oliver complained of it bitterly, or so I've heard. You've just ridden over the property, haven't you? Surely that's the first thing Lord Clonmore would direct you to do? Perhaps you've noticed something? Even as Sir Oliver did?" Sir Anthony's eyes were fastened on Harrington's face.

"That is very true," Harrington conceded. "Sir Oliver was most vociferous in his complaints."

"Well, Master Harrington? Are you aware of any activity? Have you witnessed anything?"

Harrington forced himself not to flinch. "Not personally, Sir Anthony, no."

"But you've heard of things?"

Harrington shrugged and spread his hands. "Who has not, Sir Anthony? Gentleman Niall is the talk of three counties. I scarcely think my version is any different from any other."

"Hm," said Sir Anthony. He hesitated, as though he wanted to say more, and then seemed to change his mind. "Perhaps. What about your farmers on Clonmore? Any evidence of outlaw activity among them?"

Harrington hesitated and decided to give Sir Anthony a quizzical look. Plead ignorance, he decided. "Not that I have personally noticed, Sir Anthony."

"And what about Lord Clonmore?" asked Sir Anthony. "Has he mentioned any evidence of activity to you? Or have you not personally noticed?"

Harrington forced a chuckle, but a cold chill had gone down his back. We must stop, he thought. Neville has to stop. It was true that the tithe money was an enormous sum, but it was hardly worth their lives. "Sir Anthony, when Lord Clonmore is well again, I shall suggest he ride to see you. I'm sure you would prefer to interview him personally. Or you are always welcome at Clonmore Castle."

Sir Anthony opened his mouth to speak, but in that moment, a footman rushed up. "Master Harrington—you're Master Harrington, are you not? Lady Susannah bid me find you—Lady Clonmore has fainted."

"Oh, good God," Harrington said, silently blessing Elizabeth, even though he was alarmed. "Excuse me, Sir Anthony. Take me to her at once, man." He followed the footman through the crowd, aware of an acute sense of relief. Addams suspects Neville, he thought. Or it's only a matter of time until he does.

The footman led him into a room off the hall, where Elizabeth was propped on a sofa, Lady Susannah fluttering around her with a wine goblet. "It's so dreadfully warm, William," she was saying. "And you waited so long to begin."

"Had to wait for the bishop, m'dear," he answered. "Ah, here's Harrington." Sir William looked relieved. "Will you take our young bride home?"

"At once, Sir William. Lady Clonmore, are you all right?"

"I'm fine," Elizabeth answered, but her face was very pale, and she looked up at him with enormous green eyes in which he could clearly read fear. She thinks the same as I, he thought. We must speak to Neville immediately. "If someone could fetch our carriage, Sir William?"

"I'll summon a groom myself," said Sir William, obviously happy to escape.

"It was so dreadfully warm in there," Lady Susannah

said. "Elizabeth, my dear, are you sure you're quite all right?"

"I think I just need some air, Lady Susannah," Elizabeth answered.

"Well, have a bit more of this—'twill fortify you for the journey home." She thrust the goblet into Elizabeth's hands. "I'll go see to your wrap, my dear."

When they were alone, Elizabeth raised her eyes to Harrington once more, and glanced out the open door. No one lingered, and they were alone. "They think it's Neville," she whispered, so softly he had to bend down to hear her.

"Sh," he whispered back. He dropped down beside her on the couch and took her hand. "They don't know anything for sure. I'm not sure they've pinned it to Neville—it's Addams who suspects someone local—don't fret. We'll speak to Neville the moment we get home."

"You must convince him to stop."

Harrington drew a deep breath and let it out in a short sigh. "That, unfortunately, my lady, is easier said than done. I've known him for more than twelve years and in all that time, I don't believe I've ever managed to convince him of anything he didn't want to do." He patted her hand. "But perhaps between the two of us . . ."

Elizabeth flushed. "Why would he listen to me?"

Harrington paused before answering. She turned to him and searched his face, her eyes full of questions. "Because whether Neville knows it or not, my lady," he answered as lightly as possible, "you aren't like any woman he's ever met outside his own mother, and in all the years I've known him, she's the only one who's ever had any influence at all over him. So I think there's a strong possibility that you may have the same effect." He patted her hand again. "Now, we'll say nothing more, until we're well away from here. All right?"

Elizabeth smiled a little doubtfully and sank back against the cushions. Harrington glanced at her profile. Yes, he thought, whether Neville wants to admit it or not, Lady Elizabeth has already made quite an impression.

•　•　•

"I'm not an invalid, Mother," Neville was saying as they entered. He was sitting at his desk, Moira fussing over him with a cup of tea. His shirt was open at the throat, and Elizabeth could see the strong cords of his throat, the muscled planes of his chest, and the dark hair which curled on it. His arm was bound across his chest in a loose sling. He glanced at Elizabeth and their eyes met. Automatically, she touched the locket she wore once more at her throat.

She saw his nostrils quiver and the motion in his throat as he swallowed. He shifted in his seat and his eyes behind the white silk mask slid over to Harrington. "Ah, Harrington, you're home."

Elizabeth glanced from Neville to Moira. "Hello, Neville. Moira."

"Well, well, my dear, you survived your first introduction to county society. And I must say, you look a bit worn out." Moira exchanged a glance with Neville, then beckoned to Elizabeth. "Come with me, my dear. We'll have a cup of tea and you can tell me all about it. Was that dreadful Lady Jane there?"

Harrington waited until the women had gone. He shut the door and sat down in the chair opposite Neville's beside the fire. He rubbed his hands together near the flames. "It's getting cold."

Neville nodded. "Well? What news?"

Harrington ran a hand over his chin and shook his head. "They suspect us, Neville. Well, not us, precisely, yet, but Addams announced that he believes that Gentleman Niall is either a tenant farmer or one of the landowners in the district. This man's intelligent, Neville, and we mustn't underestimate him. I had a lengthy conversation with Master Hayes, Sir William's agent. Apparently Addams has a score to settle with Colonel Melville, who Addams believes got more of the credit for apprehending the outlaw in Cork than he did. He's put more together in the last few weeks than Sir William has in two years."

"What makes you think they suspect us?"

"Addams made a point of accosting me right after the meeting. If Elizabeth hadn't fainted—"

"Elizabeth fainted? Is she all right?"

Harrington shrugged. "It was hotter than an oven in there. She was fine the moment I got her into the air. But I don't think I've ever seen so many people in one place even on market day. Neville, the county's up in arms. We've got to stop. It's far too dangerous—even a sum as great as the tithe money isn't worth it. And the bishop was there. I think it's likely they're going to try and lay a trap for us—flush us out. Surely you see that no sum of money is worth our lives."

Neville pressed his lips together. "What did Addams want with you?"

"He's had the presence of mind to plot out the robberies on a map. And it's fairly clear that the bulk of the activity is centered around Clonmore and Kilmara. I saw the map myself. They had it on display." Harrington met Neville's eyes through the mask. "Neville, I really think we ought to stop."

"And not take the tithe money?"

Harrington shrugged. "There's always next year. Sir Anthony questioned me about your absence, and about what we might have heard or seen at Clonmore."

"What did you tell him?"

"That I couldn't speak for you. And that I couldn't recall anything untoward, either. He mentioned the horses."

"What about the horses?"

"Addams put together a list of what people have said regarding Gentleman Niall. He may have been laid up in the last weeks, but he's been busy. He's got a description—tall, clean-shaven—Neville, it's not much, but eventually it could point to you. And then there're the horses—I overheard some men talking about the fact that Gentleman Niall's band rides excellent horses. That alone makes you a suspect."

The two men stared at each other. Finally Neville nodded. "I'll think about it. It sticks in my craw—all that money going to Canterbury—but I know for a fact it will make my mother very happy."

"It will make Elizabeth very happy, too."

"What does Elizabeth have to do with this?"

"I don't think she fainted from the heat, Neville. I think she's worried about you. She is, after all, your wife."

Neville's mouth twitched. "Harrington, you're as much a romantic as my mother."

"Maybe so, my lord. But she perceives that it's not in her self-interest to betray you. Surely you don't believe that she would?" Harrington shook his head. "She helped save your life—and certainly you owe the use of that arm to her. What more must she do to convince you we can trust her?" He shrugged.

"It's not just a question of trust," Neville said softly.

The men's eyes met. Harrington shook his head once more. "I don't know, Neville. I've seen the way she looks at you." He grinned. "But have it your way. I'll get word to our men to be doubly careful. They've already increased patrols—they're going door to door across three counties."

"But in the meantime warn everyone that everyone is a suspect."

"There's something else—they've captured the hedge-master in Dungannon."

"No!" Neville closed his eyes. "Old Sean is nearly seventy—what have they done with him?"

"I wasn't really able to find out. There was some talk of his being sent on to Dublin."

"He won't survive the trip."

"He's an old man. I doubt he will."

Neville leaned back in his chair and a shadow of pain flickered across his face. "But right now—" He shook his head, as a look of futility washed across his face. "Our hands are tied—"

"Neville, just get better. You can't take the weight of the world on you. Sean knows the risks as well as anyone. But if I can think of something, I'll let you know."

"All right. I know you're right, Harrington. What about Elizabeth?"

Harrington gave a short laugh. "Lady Susannah fastened herself to her side and wouldn't let the poor girl out of her sight. And there was a steady parade of the curious. No one paid me much mind, except Sir Anthony. But that was enough."

"How's his health?"

Harrington shrugged. "He's about on par with you, I'd say. His leg wound was much more serious. He's hobbling about on a cane. I think that's the only reason things haven't happened more quickly. He looked as though he was champing at the bit to get started personally. He seems to have some rivalry with Colonel Melville. They dislike each other intensely. Hayes was telling me it's because Melville finagled all the credit for the Black Mike affair."

"Hm." Neville stroked his chin. "Well, that's only going to make him more rabid. Get the word out—lie low, say nothing, trust no one. At least until Sir Anthony is gone, we're in the business of breeding horses, and nothing else."

"I'll get started tonight—"

"Tonight, Harrington?" Neville raised an eyebrow.

"There's a housemaid at Kilmara—her family lives in Dunaine—I thought I'd escort her!"

"Ah." Neville grinned. "Of course. By all means, then. Get started tonight." He winked at his friend, then stared moodily into the fire. "Oh, Harrington?"

"Yes?" He paused with his hand on the door.

"Send Elizabeth in to me, will you?" Neville spoke lightly—almost too lightly.

Harrington hid his own grin. "Of course, my lord. At once."

He was still sitting by the fire when Elizabeth peered hesitantly around the door in response to his "Come in!"

"Master Harrington said you wanted to speak to me?" She felt her face grow warm. He looked like a cross between a Greek god and a pirate, sitting there in his open shirt and breeches, the white sling stark against the tanned chest, his face expressionless beneath the white silk mask. The tails of the scarf hung down his neck. All he needed was an earring, she thought, and a knife between his teeth. She thought of how he'd fought her attacker so ferociously, and then had treated her with such kindness. She inhaled sharply at the memory, and felt her cheeks grow warm.

"Please, come and sit." Neville gestured to the opposite chair. "I'd like to hear what you thought of the good women of the county. Were all the good matrons there?"

Elizabeth rolled her eyes. "I think all the good matrons of *every* county were there—and all the men, too. I never saw so many people crowded together in one place in my life." She paused a moment to gather her thoughts. "Those who I met—Lady Susannah, Lady Jane Fitzbarth, and Mistress Hayes, I think her name was—although she looked more like *straw*—" A smile tugged at the corners of her lips. "They seemed quite nice."

He raised a skeptical brow. "Oh, really? Your face suggests otherwise."

She met his eyes. "I suppose I found them puzzling, my lord."

"In what way?" His voice was soft and he watched her face closely.

She glanced into the fire. "They were all—" She broke off, searching for the words. "They were all quite obviously *good* women, of birth and breeding, such as I've met in Bruton or London or Bath. But I cannot understand—" She hesitated and shook her head, and turned to meet his eyes behind the mask. "They seem so—so oblivious to the lot of the tenants of their land. How can they call themselves good Christian people and know that children starve not a mile from where they sit?"

His face grew grim, but he spoke lightly. "Such has it ever been, my lady. Don't you think that children starve in London, not a mile from the palaces of the Queen?"

Elizabeth shrugged and looked away, confusion on her face. "I suppose that's so, my lord. But I've never seen such—"

He leaned forward. "You've never seen such sights, my lady, because you've never looked. The difference is that here in Ireland, the people's lot is worse than in England. Here they are conquered and deliberately kept down, by laws purposefully passed for no other reason than to force them into submission."

"What makes you different?" she whispered, emboldened by the passion she heard in his voice. "Why do you risk your life for them?"

He rubbed his chin, and it was his turn to stare moodily into the fire. "Because I know what it is to be hungry and cold, to have less than a roof over my head." For a moment his face darkened and he looked almost angry. "I've seen such things, my lady—things that such as you cannot even imagine—nor would you care to."

"But—but what—" she began.

"Don't ask." He cut her off with a brutal tone. "I've no wish to revisit such unpleasant memories. I only do what I can to alleviate them in the only way that seems to work."

"So that's why you masquerade as Gentleman Niall?" She chose her words with care, lest she slam the door he'd just begun to open.

He shrugged. "I know my mother thinks I'm mad. And doubtless you do as well."

"But I don't." She touched the locket at her throat. "I think it's quite brave."

"Do you, now?" he asked thoughtfully. He shook his head once more. "You're very naive, my lady. I'm a murderer and a thief, and a traitor to my class and my title. They'd send me to the block for treason, if they knew. And I would deserve it, for the things I've done aren't pretty. There's more to playing Robin Hood than you think." He spoke with a sudden savagery that made her pulse pound, but she gripped the arms of the chair and refused to be intimidated. "You know nothing about me, my lady, and I doubt you would care to know me at all if you did."

She raised her chin. "You're right, Neville." She saw something like surprise in his eyes. "I am naive. But whatever you've done, I don't think it's any worse than anything the landowners do every day. Tell me that they don't commit murder? Or rob the people? Oh, it's a slow death, I grant you, and I suppose that many of them manage to survive, but one thing that was made clear to me today was that at least you're not a hypocrite." She rose to go, but his gaze was fastened on the flames. "I'm sure Master Harrington told you, but today Sir Anthony announced to all that they suspect that Gentleman Niall could be someone in disguise. And Lady Susannah mentioned that they're relying on me to be a witness."

"You? Why?"

"Because they believe that I got a better look at Gentleman Niall than anyone else ever has. After all, you rescued me; you didn't rob me."

Neville swept her up and down, as though measuring. "I see." He gazed into the fire, then roused himself from his reverie to look back at her. "Harrington told me only that they suspected someone in the district."

"I didn't tell him. I was too upset."

He closed his eyes momentarily as if tired, then nodded. "I understand. You look as if you're worried, Elizabeth." His voice was gentle.

"Of course I'm worried. You're my husband, after all."

"A husband who was foisted on you," he replied. "One scarred and crippled—one who regularly breaks the law—"

"One who breaks the law for a very good reason," she responded. "If there's nothing else, my lord, I will see if Lady Moira requires any assistance."

"My mother requires very little assistance from anyone." He chuckled.

She dropped a quick curtsey and turned once more to go.

"Elizabeth."

"Yes?"

"I mean to ride out tomorrow. I'm sick of being confined. It occurs to me that you've seen much of Ireland's misery and little of her beauty. Would you care to come with me?"

She swallowed hard and spoke slowly so he wouldn't hear the sudden quaver of excitement in her voice. "It would give me great pleasure to accompany you, my lord. I would like that very much."

He nodded a dismissal and turned away to stare at the map above the hearth, chin cupped on one hand, his mouth a thin line. "Tomorrow, then. After breakfast. Around nine or so."

"Very well." She dropped another brief curtsey and escaped before her voice could betray how her pulses raced.

Twelve

The following day dawned gray and overcast, and Elizabeth's heart sank when she woke and saw the clouds. Surely there'd be no riding out today. But she was surprised when she went down to the hall for breakfast, for not only was Neville up and dressed, but he was eating with a heartier appetite than she'd yet seen, while Moira fussed over him like a hen with a wayward chick.

"But you can't be serious, Neville," she was saying, as Elizabeth walked down the stairs. "It looks as if it's likely to rain at any moment."

"This is Ireland, Mother," Neville replied with a wink. "It's always likely to rain at any moment."

"But it's getting cold out, Neville—what if you take the fever?"

Neville shrugged and spoke in the same teasing tone. "Then you'll not have to worry about my dying on the road, will you?"

Moira threw up her hands with an exasperated sigh. "You will be the death of me yet, my boy. Is there no talking sense into that thick skull?"

"None, Mother." He munched on a bite of toast and caught sight of Elizabeth. He smiled at her, and she felt the breath stop in her chest.

Dear God and the devil, she thought, as one of her father's favorite oaths ran unbidden through her brain. What was it about this man that so unsettled her? She smoothed her skirts and smiled at them both. "Good morning. So, you still intend to ride this morning, Neville? It's threatening rain."

"Oh, come, you won't gang up on me, will you, Elizabeth? My mother doesn't think we should ride today."

"You're scarcely out of your sickbed," put in Moira.

Elizabeth slipped into her place at the long table and settled down on the bench. "Perhaps we should wait, then," she said, though disappointment washed over her like a shroud.

"I'm going," Neville declared gently but firmly. "I don't care what either of you say." He looked at Elizabeth and smiled. "It's going to clear—the sky's fair in the south."

For a moment, her heart felt as though it had leapt in her chest. Their eyes met, and in his she could read an unmistakable invitation.

Elizabeth glanced at Moira, who only looked from her son to Elizabeth and back again. She paused and smiled, as if amused. "Ah. I'm glad to see you're feeling so much better, Neville. Only don't do anything foolish."

"Why, Mother." He looked at her and laughed. "I have no intention of doing anything foolish."

As Neville said, the clouds had begun to break and spots of blue sky showed through the gray by the time they were well into the hills. At the base of one, Neville leapt lightly off his saddle and tied his horse swiftly to a tree, as Elizabeth brought hers to a stop. He reached up and wrapped his hands around her waist. She covered his hands with her gloved ones, and she felt the passion flare between them. "What is this place?" she asked. "Why are we stopping?"

"Come," he answered. "I want to show you something— and it's best reached on foot."

He lifted her off the horse and set her down on the grass. For a moment, she thought he might kiss her, but he turned his back abruptly and started off up the barely discernible path. The rough track wound up the long hill, and Elizabeth found herself breathing hard as she struggled to keep up with his long-legged stride. "Neville," she cried, struggling to hold up the hem of her riding dress, "have mercy!"

He looked back over his shoulder, and his lips curved in that same sweet smile that had taken her breath away at breakfast. "Come, my high-born lady." He held out his hand, and she took it, gripping it hard as she nearly stumbled over a lichen-covered boulder half camouflaged in the ground. "See," he said, gesturing with the other, which was still in the loose sling, "the yellow is the gorse, and the purple—that's heather. The hawthorn's the white—have a mind for the prickles," he said. "They'll stick in your stockings."

"Where are you taking me?"

"To the top." He gestured with his head. "Don't worry about the horses. They're as happy to eat the grass down there."

"What's at the top?"

He looked down at her and smiled again. "You'll see." He tucked her arm under his, and they walked in silence the rest of the way, Elizabeth quite certain that her heartbeat was audible. They reached the summit and Neville pointed. "Look."

The late morning sun peeked through the puffy gray-white clouds, and long shafts of light fell over the rolling hills. Elizabeth gasped at the serene beauty of the land that lay before her, a patchwork of greens and browns, golds and lavenders. A sudden wind blew cloud shadows over the ground, and Elizabeth shivered as a wisp of hair escaped its pins. She was conscious of Neville's arm beneath her gloved hand, and of the long length of his body beside her, and she knew that if they turned to face each other, they would be standing close enough to kiss. She shut her eyes briefly as the memory of the physical sensations his kiss had roused swept once more through her.

"What do you think?" Neville asked.

"I think I liked it very much," she answered, scarcely aware she'd spoken aloud.

He laughed and looked at her quizzically. "Liked it?" His

lips quirked up in the hint of a grin. "What were you thinking just now? I was talking about the view." j

She blushed to the tips of her ears. She pulled away and
walked away, confused by the depth of her own emotions.
She had never experienced anything like this—ever. Her
brief crushes on the London dandies hadn't felt anything
like this.

"Elizabeth?" His voice was soft and gentle, easy with
that hint of brogue. Even the way he said her name sent a little thrill through her.

She turned back and smiled. "I'm sorry. The view—the
view is quite lovely."

He ran his eyes over her. "Do I discomfit you in some
way, my lady?" There was a touch of bitterness in his question, and she realized that, for him, that possibility must
have been a reality more than once.

"No," she whispered. "Not in the way you mean—not because of your mask."

"Oh?" He took two steps closer. "In what way, then?"

She wet her lips with the tip of her tongue and lowered
her eyes. "I've told you before I don't care what you look
like. From the first time I met you, you . . ."

"Yes?" he prompted. He took another two steps nearer,
until they were standing less than an arm's length apart.

"You've made me feel things I've never felt—"

"Ah, the dashing outlaw," he said, mockingly.

"No." She shook her head. "Not that—"

"Not that?" He looked at her blankly, feigned disappointment on his face.

She laughed in spite of herself. "Neville," she said, "I can
only tell you what is true. I've never met another man like
you. And I want to know you better."

His lips gave that little quirk, and he stepped forward and
gathered her in his arms. Another gust of wind blew the
scent of the heather to her as he bent his head and brought
his mouth to hers.

Her arms went around him and she opened her mouth beneath the pressure of his lips. His tongue slid along the inner
edges of her lips, and she met it with her own, amazed at her

own boldness. He twined his tongue around hers, gently sucking on each lip in turn. She moaned.

He raised his head and smiled. "Is that what you liked?"

She pressed her lips together and nodded, clinging to him as the world seemed to settle into focus once again.

"Ah. Well, then, what do you think of the view?"

She forced herself to gain some semblance of composure. She broke away from his embrace and smoothed her riding skirt. "I think the view is quite amazing." She walked a few paces toward the edge of the hill and gazed out over the land once more. "What is this place? Why did you bring me here?"

He shrugged. "I think it's one of the prettiest places on Clonmore. It's the highest spot for miles around. And I told you yesterday—you've seen enough of Ireland's ugliness. I wanted you to see her beauty, too." He looked out across the land. "I fell in love with Ireland when I came here at sixteen. I climbed this hill the first time I argued with my father." His voice dropped, and when he went on, it was as if he'd forgotten she was there. "I'd been here just a month. Everything was fine at first. My father greeted me with open arms—the true prodigal's return. He was very careful to show me only his charming side. And then one day, he lost his temper. And I found out for myself that what my mother tried to tell me all those years was true. Poverty *was* better than life with him." He kicked at a loose pebble with the toe of his boot. "Ireland wasn't much different then than it is now. But I knew someday, when he was dead and I was earl, I would do what I could. It seemed an easy thing to rob the others—they were so complacent—so unseeing."

"But, why not found a beneficial society?" she asked. "What made you think of robbery?"

He looked at her with a sheepish grin. "I suppose my mother filled my head when I was young with all the stories of Robin Hood and his Merry Men. And hunger makes for desperate hopes and dreams. Perhaps you've never known anyone who grew up ever truly hungry?"

She was silent for a long moment. "No, I suppose I never have. But didn't your mother—"

"My mother did what she had to do to keep us both." He met her eyes levelly and smiled sadly at the confusion on her face. "My mother didn't tell you that part when you were sharing confidences with her, did she? No, I thought not."

"Neville, I don't understand."

"I know," he answered softly. "My father refused to send us money. My mother had no funds of her own. At first she tried genteel pursuits—sewing, painting, that sort of thing. Even tutoring young girls. But there was simply no way she could earn enough to feed us both like that, although God knows she tried. So one day when a wealthy merchant happened to meet her—well, let's say he was very generous to both of us. But before that, and in between that first one and the next, and then the next, there were quite a few hungry days, and some very cold nights."

"Had you no friends?"

"My father was a very powerful man. Clonmore—but for the fact that he nearly bankrupted it with his excesses—was very wealthy. And he wasn't afraid to spend his money in the punishment of my mother. He didn't want me back, you see. He was happier trying to destroy my mother."

"He sounds like a monster," Elizabeth said.

"He was," Neville replied. "I learned that myself, when I came here for the first time when I was sixteen. But what about you? Sir Oliver didn't strike me as a particularly loving parent."

"Well," Elizabeth answered slowly, "I wouldn't call him a monster—but he was certainly very difficult. My poor grandmother has always had her hands full with him, but I think I understand why she's always tried to keep him reined in—if he'd had his way, he'd've gambled it all away."

"Your grandmother is a wise woman," Neville said.

Elizabeth nodded and looked over the summit. "Neville—what are those stones on that hill over there?"

"Ah—they call those Finn's Gathering. It's said to commemorate a gathering by Finn MacCuill and his Fianna."

"His what?"

"Finn MacCuill was the founder of the Fianna, an elite

group of warriors charged with keeping invaders from the shores of Ireland."

"What happened to them?"

Neville shrugged. "They disappeared. Into the past, into the mists of history. Like King Arthur and Lancelot—like Robin Hood and Little John—where do you suppose all the heroes go, Elizabeth?"

She gave a little laugh, not knowing how to answer. "Why is it so difficult here for the Irish?"

Neville thrust his hands into the pockets of his coat and stared out over the landscape. "It's the laws, Elizabeth. A Catholic is forbidden to carry a weapon, to teach in school, and may not lease or purchase land. The English think that with these laws they can keep the people down, but what they don't see is that we could govern this land—we could do it fairly, so that there would be no threat of rebellion. But the English lords won't allow it. And so all of us born Irish—Protestant or Catholic alike—are oppressed by the yoke England imposes. This is not an easy country, Elizabeth, and I'm not an easy man to deal with." The teasing tone was gone completely, and his voice was as sober as his face. "I told you on our wedding day that I recognized that this marriage was not of your choosing. If I had not believed that I needed Kilmara, I wouldn't have done what I did."

"What do you mean?"

Neville drew a deep breath. "If we are to go forward together as man and wife, in any sense of those words, I want to be honest with you. It was not an accident that I won Kilmara, Elizabeth. I set out to win Kilmara from your father deliberately. The Kilmara lands are valuable because of the way the roads and the river converge. I had no idea you were a part of it."

Elizabeth could not help but stare back at him, not quite believing what she heard. "You mean you wanted Kilmara? And when you won it, my father told you about me?"

"Yes." Neville paused a moment, then shook his head. "Elizabeth, if you wanted an annulment, I'd understand. Marriage was the last thing I'd planned. It was never my intention to inflict this way of life on any woman, even though

I thought I'd keep whoever it turned out to be at arm's length. I see now I was mistaken. You're not at all what I was expecting, either."

She flushed and lowered her head. "What were you expecting?"

"Some silly society miss, I suppose. Someone who cared for nothing but where her next dancing dress was coming from. You were quite a surprise, Elizabeth."

She bit back a smile. "Then I suppose that makes us even." She reached for his uninjured arm. "No, I don't want an annulment. Do you?" He dropped his eyes and in that moment, she sensed something of his vulnerability. Empowered by that knowledge, she drew closer. She slid her hand down his arm and curled her fingers around his.

"It was never my intention to interfere in your life, my lady."

"I don't think you've interfered. I think you've given me a whole new way to see the world. So no, I don't want an annulment at all."

He pulled her closer to him. "As you wish, my lady." He raised her chin with the tip of one finger and gently kissed her upturned lips. "But if we go forward from here together, it may be impossible for you to extricate yourself, if the worst should happen."

"I don't care," she answered. *Oh, Neville, I'm going to teach you to trust me,* she thought, as his mouth came down on hers. *If it's the last thing I do, I'm going to teach you to trust me.* And then, maybe, just maybe, she thought, as his kiss deepened and her fingers reached up and twined in the thick dark hair at his neck, maybe then we'll fall in love.

They stood there a long time, and at last he raised his head. A bitter wind whipped at her skirts. He looked up at the sky. Purple clouds were massing over the western hills. "I think we better go," he said. "I think it might rain."

He wrapped her hand in his, and together they half-ran, half-stumbled down the steep slope to where the horses were tethered. He helped her onto her mare, then swung up into his own saddle. They had scarcely gone a few hundred yards when the first drops of rain stung her cheek. She looked up and saw that the sky was black with heavy clouds that swirled in the air currents. Another icy raindrop stung her cheek.

"I'm sorry, Elizabeth," he called over the rising wind. "I suppose we lingered too long up there—I think we'd better take shelter until this passes."

She nodded, gripping her reins with one hand and clutching her jacket to her throat. The cold wind blew right through her heavy riding suit.

"Follow me," he cried.

He turned off the road and led them across a narrow track, back toward the hills. As the rain began to fall in earnest, he led her into a low cave with an overhanging ridge that partially obscured the opening. He looped the horses' reins around a knotted mass of roots, and helped her out of the saddle. He drew her into the cave as the sky opened, and the rain came down in sheets.

She looked up at him. The white silk mask was spotted with water, and rain drooped his normally downy linen. For once he looked more bedraggled than dashing. She bit back a giggle.

"I'm glad you see the humor, lady." He drew her close and they stood for a moment, watching the rain fall. "Are you cold?" he asked when she shivered.

"No—not really." She looked back over her shoulder. The cave seemed dry, although it was shallow, no more than an impression in the hillside. "How do you know of this place?"

"I know of all sorts of little nooks and crannies where one might duck out of sight," he answered. "This is not the largest, but it was the closest." He drew her away from the entrance and nodded at the piles of hay along the wall. "I can make a fire if you're cold—there's kindling beneath the hay."

"No, I'm all right," she said, stripping off her gloves. "Is this—is this one of the places you hide?" She looked around the shallow cave, wide-eyed.

"Not often," he answered. "It's too close to home."

He settled down on the hay and reached for her. "The

storm should blow over soon. But until then . . ." He wrapped his arms around her and kissed her once more. This time, he pressed her back against the hay, and she lay cradled in his embrace. His hand crept up to cup her breast, and she arched her back as his thumb rubbed her nipple through the fabric of her gown.

She covered his hand with hers, straining against him. A rushing need flooded through her blood like a river at spring thaw. He rolled on her, and she felt the hard muscles of his thighs beneath his tight breeches.

"Here now, what're you two about?" The rough male voice cut through the haze of passion like a knife through cheese.

Breathless, she lay gasping softly as Neville pulled away. He leapt to his feet, and she slowly sat up, feeling dazed and somewhat dizzy. Six redcoats peered into the little cave, their uniforms sodden. "May I help you, Sergeant?" Neville's voice was cold and clipped, without a trace of the liquid Irish brogue she loved.

"Who're ye, and what do ye think ye're doing?" the soldier demanded, the others crowding close beneath the overhang.

"My name is Neville Fitzgerald. I'm the Earl of Clonmore, and this is my lady. We sought shelter from the storm."

"How'd ye know this place was here?"

"These are my lands," Neville shot back. "Would you care to explore the cave, Sergeant? It seems that the weather is easing. My lady and I will be on our way."

"Not so fast." The sergeant made a motion and Elizabeth gasped as the others raised their bayonets, pointing them at Neville.

Neville didn't flinch. He pinned the sergeant with a cold stare and his lip curled in a sneer. "Are these your orders, Sergeant? To threaten a peer of the realm at knifepoint? In front of his lady? Is this a new policy of Her Majesty's army I must discuss with Colonel Melville? Or should I go directly to the lord lieutenant in Dublin?"

The sergeant coughed. "The lads is on edge, m'lord. Everyone is a suspect, is our orders."

Neville drew a long slow breath and took one step forward. "Order your men to drop their weapons, or you'll not have to worry about who's suspect and who's not. If you wish, you may escort us to Clonmore Castle, where my agent and my servants will be more than happy to confirm my identity to you while I pen a message of complaint to Sir William."

The sergeant waved to the men. "Stand down, men. These two are all right." He glanced at Elizabeth, and she felt herself flush as he raked her with his eyes. "Let's go, lads."

Neville waited a long moment until the tramp of heavy feet across the muddy ground had faded. His face was shuttered behind his mask when he reached down to help her stand. "Let's go, Elizabeth."

He was silent and brooding on the way back. The rutted roads were muddy puddles and the wind was cold and damp, but at least the rain had stopped. Elizabeth glanced at him more than once out of the corner of her eye, wishing she could think of something to say to him. But he seemed to have completely withdrawn from her—the glimpse of the lover replaced by some darker aspect of his personality.

When they reached Clonmore, Neville tossed the reins to the stable boy who came running up to greet them, then strode away toward the stables, with a curt nod at Elizabeth. Faintly stung, she allowed the boy to help her off the saddle and walked into the hall to find it deserted. A fire burned in one of the huge hearths which lined the walls, and she walked over to it, feeling let down and suddenly lonely. She stripped off her gloves and held her hands out over the fire. Neville was right about one thing—he was indeed a difficult man to know. But obviously he'd built those defenses for good reasons. It would take some patience to breach them, but she believed it was possible.

"Would ye care for a cup of cider, m'lady?" Mistress Aislinn startled her out of her reverie.

She looked over her shoulder at the kindly woman. "Not right now, Aislinn. Where's Lady Moira?"

"She's gone back to the dower house."

"What? She's not here?"

"No, m'lady. She said her work here was done." Aislinn peered more closely at Elizabeth. "Is there aught you need, m'lady? You look a bit peaked—you're not feeling poorly, are you?"

"No." Elizabeth shook her head. "Would it be too much trouble to have a bath, Aislinn?" Suddenly she longed to immerse herself in warm water and lie back. So Moira had gone back to her own home. Was it time for her to return to Kilmara? Where did she stand with Neville? Her sense that they'd reached some sort of understanding between them evaporated like the afternoon mist around a fire.

"I'll tell them to start heating the water at once, m'lady." Aislinn gave her another close look. "Are ye sure there's naught ailing ye?"

"No, Aislinn," Elizabeth said gently. "I'm just tired from the day."

"Ah, the air will do that to ye, m'lady. Best to have a care." The housekeeper turned to leave, muttering, and Elizabeth drew a deep breath. She missed Molly, missed Kilmara, missed Sorcha and her bright dancing eyes, although she knew that the two of them had taken charge of seeing that the tenants were adequately fed and clothed and supplied with medicines. She glanced at the door. Where had Neville gone? Well, she would have her bath, and her dinner in her room, and then tomorrow she would speak to Neville about where matters stood between them. Today she'd allowed the sun and the hills and the sky and the heather to fill her head with romantic notions. And his kisses, of course— had it only been the sudden appearance of the soldiers that had made him turn so cold?

She made her way to her room slowly and found a huge wooden tub already set before the fire, and Mistress Aislinn laying out towels and soap on a low stool. "I'll help ye as best I can, m'lady—'tis a long time since I assisted Emma with m'lady."

Elizabeth smiled sadly. She missed Molly—her easy ban-
ter, her comforting familiarity. "That's fine, Aislinn. Just
help me out of my dress—I can manage well enough on my
own."

"Are ye sure? 'Tis no trouble—"

Elizabeth held up her hand. "Not in the least."

Aislinn unfastened the lacings of her bodice and said,
"Will you be coming down, m'lady?"

"For dinner? No—I'm tired. Would it be too much to
send up a tray?"

"Oh, m'lady, ye're not feeling poorly, are ye? Ye overdid
it with his lordship today, I can see it."

"Perhaps you're right. Will you tell his lordship, when he
comes in, I'm resting?"

"Of course, m'lady." Aislinn gathered a basket of linen
together. "If that's all then—"

Elizabeth nodded and allowed her chemise to fall to the
floor. She stepped into the hot water and relaxed with a sigh
against the back of the tub. She picked up the soap and a
small square of linen and soaped herself from toe to head.
She ducked beneath the water and came up, water streaming
down her face. She wiped her face with the linen and lay
back against the tub once more.

Steam drifted over the surface, fragrant with the scent of
the herbs in the small muslin bag floating in the water. The
peat fire flickered, and she heard the first hard pelting rain
as the wind whistled around the ancient towers. She looked
down at her body in the dark water. Her waist was narrow,
her hips lushly curved. Could it be he found her displeasing?
She touched the tips of her rosy nipples. A slight tingle ran
through her, similar to the reaction to Neville's kisses. She
remembered how she'd felt the heat of his hand through the
fabric of her riding gown as he'd cupped her breast, and how
her nipples had hardened at his touch. The taste of his mouth
on hers, slightly sweet, and minty, and very warm, flooded
through her memory. She sank further down in the water and
heard the door open and close. Thinking it was Aislinn, she
called, "Just put the tray by the fire, thanks."

She heard the click of booted heels cross the antechamber and stop just inside the entrance. The heavy footsteps didn't sound like Aislinn's, and she turned to see Neville standing in the doorway, leaning against the frame. "And does my lady require anything else?" he asked, as she gasped.

"Neville—you—you—"

"Frightened you. I know. I'm sorry." He straightened. "And I'm sorry if I confused you this afternoon. I wasn't expecting to run into half a dozen redcoats. If you'd prefer I leave, I shall."

She hesitated. "No," she said at last. "Stay."

"Are you sure?" His eyes sought hers across the space that separated them.

She nodded slowly, unable to speak, and gripped the edge of the tub with wet fingers. Moisture trickled down her neck, and between her breasts, and between her legs she felt a slow throb.

"Good," he said. "Because I would like so very much to kiss you."

"I think I would like that very much," she answered softly.

Swiftly he shut the inner door of her bedroom. With three long strides, he was beside the tub, wrapping his arms around her, heedless of his shirt. He gathered her wet, naked body in his arms, and her head fell back against him. Their eyes locked. Elizabeth inhaled sharply, her lips parted. He lowered his head slowly. Her eyelids closed as their mouths met in a slow, gentle kiss. At last he raised his head, and she realized he wasn't wearing his sling. "What about your arm? Where's the sling?"

"I think I can manage without it." He smiled. "I'd lift you up, but I don't think I can quite do that yet." He reached for one of the towels and held it out. "Would m'lady care to dry off?"

She sat up, taking the towel he offered, and held it up against her breasts as she stood, acutely self-conscious. He turned his back while she patted herself dry and wrapped the towel around herself, tucking it securely beneath her arms. It fell to just below her knees, but when he looked at her over his shoulder, she felt as naked as she would've without the towel.

"Elizabeth." He whispered the name as if it were a caress. "You are so very very beautiful." His damp shirt clung to his arms. He held out his hand. "Will you come?" He glanced at the bed, then smiled at her.

She swallowed and took a single step closer, and he took her hand once more. She shut her eyes as he kissed her again. This time, though, he bent her back, his mouth roaming over her face and throat, as one hand gently cupped her breast.

Her body seemed to swell, to ripen with every touch. He drew her closer and she felt the hard pressure of his thighs against hers, and something else, something thick and rigid between them. Of their own volition, her legs ached to part.

He raised his head at last when she moaned against his mouth. "Come."

His eyes behind the mask were dark blue. He drew her to the bed and gently pulled her down beside him. He stretched out, and she rolled onto her back. He gently sucked on her earlobe, parting the long wet strands of her hair. She wrapped her arms around him, her hands roaming down his back and across the span of his shoulders. He slipped off the bed, and tore off his shirt. Then, deliberately, he straightened and would've turned away to unlace his breeches, but she stopped him. "No," she said. "Please. I want to know what you look like." Her eyes flicked up to his face, and his mouth curved in a softly bitter smile.

"Perhaps, my lady." He pulled off his boots and stockings and straightened once more. She watched as he undid the lacings, and stepped out of his breeches and small clothes. She gazed in fascination as he stood before her, allowing her eyes to roam over his body, over the fading red of his latest wounds, and the ridges of scars which puckered the skin of his chest, to his erection which rose from a nest of dark curls at the base of his taut abdomen.

He smiled and settled into bed beside her. She lay back as he reached for her once more. He plucked at the towel. "Fair's fair," he whispered.

She let him pull the towel away, and lowered her eyes as she felt his gaze sweep over her as she lay naked before him for the first time. She heard him sigh as he touched the curve of her breast. "So sweet," he breathed.

He moved over her and she lay back against the pillows, drawing him close, cradling him with her body, marveling at how easily it seemed they fit. And then she felt the hard length of him push against her inner lips and she felt her wet flesh part of its own accord and she sighed against his ear. He raised his head and kissed her. "Not yet."

He eased down the length of her body, kissing her breasts, sucking at her nipples, delving into the tiny impression of her navel. He spread her legs and settled between her thighs, kissing each leg in turn, dragging his tongue along the soft white flesh. He looked up at her, and slowly lowered his head to the nest of blonde curls between her legs. She gasped as she felt his mouth on her most private parts, and lay back, her fingers clawing at the sheet. She gasped as her blood seemed to flow in heated waves, and the most exquisite tension built in the pit of her belly, radiating like a flame through every fiber. She gasped as his lips suckled gently, driving her into a sudden burst of ecstasy that shook her to the core. She lay breathing deeply, feeling the waves of pleasure pulsate through her flesh. He lifted his head and smiled. He rose up and crawled toward her, and she saw the newly healed wound on his shoulder. "Be careful—"

"Sh," he whispered. He gathered her mouth to his once more, and settled down beside her. She felt the hard length of him press against her hip. "I don't want to hurt you, Elizabeth." His breath was hot on her ear.

She moved her hips, seeking some release, needing something that she'd never before wanted. "Please," she breathed.

He rolled above her, settling on her body, and she felt the tip of him press into her flesh. He thrust forward gently, then eased back as he encountered resistance. It seemed to take forever and she moaned against his shoulder, as he took his time, thrusting gently, then easing back, until she thought she'd go mad with desire to feel the length of him within her. "Please," she begged.

"I don't want to hurt you, Elizabeth," he replied, his breath a hot whisper against her ear that sent a sharp thrill down her spine. But he raised up and with two sharp, quick thrusts, he was inside her, even as he lifted her shoulders and cradled her close to his chest, as she cried out at the unexpected pain. "I'm sorry," he whispered, not moving. She turned her head, and his mouth found her once more. He moved his hips gently, just a bit, and she lay still, not sure what he wanted. "Let me show you," he said.

She closed her eyes, feeling him settle into an easy, yet forceful rhythm that swept through her like the reverberation of a drum. She spread her thighs a little more, and wrapped her arms around him, feeling him swell. He stiffened, then relaxed, body spasming. She held him close.

She looked up at him through the mask. Their eyes met and he smiled. He fell to one side and gathered her close once more. He kissed her forehead, and she nestled against him. "I didn't know it was like that," she whispered after a while.

"Like what?" he prompted.

"Like that—like this—as if two puzzle pieces have been put together."

"Oh," he said, smiling, his voice soft. "Neither did I, Elizabeth." He lifted her chin to his mouth and kissed her once more. "Neither did I." And then, they said very little for a very long time.

She woke to see him sitting in the chair beside the fire, clad only in his breeches and the mask. Outside, she could hear the wind howl around the towers and the rain spatter against the window. She sat up, pulling the blanket around her shoulders. "Neville?"

"You should be asleep. It's late."

She shrugged. "I woke up."

"I see that." He smiled at her across the room. "Are you hungry? You never did get your dinner—Aislinn left a tray for us both outside the door." He got to his feet and made as if to get it, but she shook her head.

"No, I'm not hungry." She cocked her head. "What was wrong this afternoon? When we came back—you scarcely spoke to me—"

"Ah." He spread his hands. "I told you I wasn't an easy man to get along with. This—this husband thing—is new to me. Can you be patient?"

"New to you?" She glanced down at herself and looked back at him, a grin playing at the corners of her mouth. "You seemed to know what to do."

He laughed. "That's not what I was referring to, my lady, and well you know it."

"Will you come back to bed?"

He hesitated and for moment she thought he might refuse her. Then his face softened. "All right." He stripped off his breeches and slipped beneath the covers. "Come here," he said, pulling her close against his chest. They lay side by side curled like two spoons, and he kissed her shoulder.

"Did you mean what you said before?" she asked.

"I usually mean most of what I say, my lady," he replied lightly.

"About puzzle pieces?" She looked at him over her shoulder.

A quizzical expression came into his eyes, one which puzzled her. "I meant it then," he said, and he dropped a quick kiss on her shoulder. "I mean it now." He rolled over on his back and lay staring up at the canopy. "I have the feeling we're to discover much in the next few days, my lady." It was the last thing she remembered as she drifted off to sleep.

Some time later, frantic knocking roused Elizabeth from a sound sleep. She turned over to see Neville rolling out of bed, adjusting his mask, reaching for his breeches. He pulled them on quickly and flung wide the antechamber door. She heard him throw open the outer door and slam it shut, pulling whoever it was into the room with him. "What's wrong?" she heard him say.

"Dear God, Neville—" It was Harrington's voice, but the exact words were unintelligible.

She slid out of bed and reached for her robe. She tiptoed across the floor and peered out into the antechamber. Harrington stood there, face pale, water dripping down his face. "What's wrong?" she asked, unconsciously echoing Neville.

Harrington broke off in midsentence and looked beyond Neville to where she stood clutching the door frame. "Turlough, my lady. Turlough's been taken."

"Oh, my God," she whispered, her own words echoing at once in her mind. *The hedgemaster at Kilmara*— damn herself for a witless fool. She remembered how she'd spoken so unthinkingly to Lady Susannah and the other women, and the look they'd all exchanged. She shut her eyes and pressed her lips together, scarcely hearing Neville's clipped conversation. Turlough had been taken. And she was afraid it was her fault.

Thirteen

"*'Twas terrible, m'lady*, terrible," Sorcha said, sobbing. She wiped her eyes on a grimy scrap of linen that bore evidence of many tears.

"Sorcha, I'm so sorry." Elizabeth offered her own white handkerchief as another pang went through her. She thought of the kind old man in the hands of the soldiers. What would Neville say if she told him it was her fault? Would he believe it was an accident—that she'd never have deliberately mentioned the hedgemaster, if she'd been more circumspect? Or would he immediately believe that she had laid a trap for them if she tried to explain it all? Because of her folly, an innocent man's life was at stake. She raised her eyes to the balcony above the hall. Neville had been closeted since daybreak in his office, joined only an hour ago by Harrington, who'd collapsed on Neville's own bed in exhaustion after his predawn appearance. She sat back with a sigh as Sorcha dabbed at her eyes. "What happened last night?"

"The soldiers came through Dunaine just as we were settling down to have a bite of the dinner I brought from the house. They rode in like thunder and tore sick people from their beds—they had me uncle against a wall—and said if he didn't tell them where the hedgemaster was, they'd smash the children's heads in one by one. But Master Turlough came out of the wood and went with them." She looked at Elizabeth. "I hope I didn't do wrong to come here—"

"No, no, not at all, Sorcha. I understand—we'll make it all right with Mistress Gallagher. And now that you're here, you must take a note back to Molly for me. I've been quite remiss in not sending for her."

"Will you—will you be living here, then, m'lady?"

Elizabeth felt herself flush. She touched her locket. "I'm not quite sure what our plans are, Sorcha. But if you'll wait, I'll write a note for Molly. Why don't you have some tea?"

"That'd be kind of ye, m'lady."

"Then go find Mistress Aislinn in the kitchens—she'll see to your tea." Elizabeth smiled and rose, but her heart was pounding and her stomach was clenched with tension. She walked slowly up the steps and paused outside Neville's door. What would he say if he knew? She twisted her hands in her dress, thinking she had better tell him before anyone else did—what if they expected her to be a witness against Turlough as well? She shut her eyes against a sudden flood of tears. Surely whatever softness he'd felt for her last night would vanish like spring snow in the heat of his anger. He'd never trust her. She raised her hand to knock, but her resolve failed. Maybe she should wait until she was certain they would be alone.

She walked on to her room. Better to write the note to Molly while Sorcha waited. She would speak to Neville later, when John Harrington was gone.

Neville paused in midsentence as the footsteps stopped just outside the door. He glanced up, half-expecting to hear a knock, but the footsteps continued past. It was probably Elizabeth, he thought. He knew she was worried, but there was no time to address her fears right now. They had to think of a way to rescue Turlough. He rubbed his hand across his chin and stared at the door, frowning. "We don't have any choice in this, Harrington. You know that. If we don't get him out, Turlough's a dead man. We owe him more than that."

Harrington nodded slowly. "When I go to town today, I'll

try to find out what I can. It may be they're holding him in the garrison, not the jail. And if that's the case, it'll be doubly hard to get him out."

"Maybe I should come with you. Two of us could gather twice as much information."

Harrington hesitated. "I'm not sure that would be wise. I know you're tired of staying in and doing nothing, but under the circumstances, I think it's better if everyone, including Sir Anthony, thinks you're still recuperating. It's the perfect alibi."

Neville said nothing for a long moment. Finally he nodded. "I agree. I'll stay here, then, and try to come up with some sort of plan. What we really need to know is if he's being held in the garrison or in the jail. And I don't think we have too much time to plan. I don't put it past Sir Anthony to torture him if he thinks there's information to be got. But I need to get a message to Liam—and without Turlough, if you're gone to town—"

"There may be a way. His niece, Sorcha, is in service at Kilmara. She's been helping Turlough with the sick. No one would think it odd if she goes to see her uncle."

"So how do we get to her at Kilmara?"

"Well, she's not at Kilmara at the moment. She's here—she was there last night when the soldiers took Turlough, and brought me the news. That's how I found out."

Neville pressed his fingertips together. "Can she be trusted?"

"She's Liam's niece—Seamus's, too. They're her people, Neville. I know we can trust her."

"I just don't like the idea of getting someone else involved right now. Things are already difficult enough, and one more person involved is one more who might suffer if we're all taken. But all right. I suppose it can't be helped. You go to town. Find out what you can. I'll think of the message for the girl to take to Liam. The sooner we act the better."

Harrington rose. "All right. I'll tell Sorcha to wait. I'll be back by nightfall."

Neville nodded a dismissal then turned his attention to

the crude map of Ennis he'd drawn earlier, trying furiously to think of a plan. There had to be a way, he thought, clenching his pen tightly. And if it wasn't possible, he'd just have to find a way to do the impossible.

Harrington descended the stairs to the empty hall. He walked down the corridor which led to the kitchens and there found Sorcha huddled by the fire, her hands cupped around a thick mug of tea. She leapt to her feet when she saw him. He smiled despite his exhaustion. Her crisp dark curls tumbled about her face, and her blue eyes were as clear as the autumn skies. "I'm glad you waited," he said.

"My lady asked me to take a note back to Kilmara for her maid," Sorcha replied, her cheeks pink.

"Ah," he began.

"Master Harrington." Mistress Aislinn spoke from the door which led back to the hall. "Do ye know if his lordship's busy?"

Harrington turned in surprise. "My lord is about his own affairs, I believe. Why?"

"Sir Anthony Addams is here." Mistress Aislinn jerked her head over her shoulder. "I told him to wait in the hall."

"Addams? What does he want? Never mind—I've had enough conversations with Sir Anthony. I think his lordship would want you to disturb him," Harrington replied. Sir Anthony's presence augured only trouble. He took Sorcha's hand in both his own as Mistress Aislinn's footsteps faded down the hall. "Listen, Sorcha. I want you to take a message to your uncle Liam. It won't be written down—you'll have to remember it. Can you do that?"

"What sort of message?" She frowned.

"A message—a message about Turlough."

"I'm sure he's heard by now."

"I'm sure he has," he replied.

Sorcha cocked her head and frowned up at him. "Then what does it have to do with Turlough?"

Harrington hesitated. He wanted to tell her all of it, for ever since he'd noticed her that first day at Kilmara, he'd known his feelings for her were deeper than anything he'd ever felt for any other woman. But now was not the time or place. They could trust her with the message, for she returned his feelings. But Neville was right. To tell her the whole story now would only jeopardize her. "Sorcha, can you trust me?"

"Of course." She raised her chin. "You know I do."

"Good." He touched the tip of her nose and smiled. "I promise to tell you everything as soon as I possibly can. But right now, it's safer for you if you just take the message to your uncle Liam. All right?"

"As you wish, Master Harrington," she replied, her eyes beginning to dance despite the situation, "I'm sure my uncle Liam will be very happy to see his dear niece."

Sir Anthony Addams shifted on the hard wooden bench. Clonmore Castle was certainly not at all the grand residence he'd imagined. The furnishings were sparse, and those obviously extremely old. Why, the bench he was sitting on was blackened with age, and smooth with that patina created only through many years of use. The walls soared sixty feet or more, bare and smudged gray with the soot of centuries. There were lighter spots on the walls. In places they seemed to make a kind of pattern, and as he frowned at it, cocking his head one way and then the other, he realized what they were. They were the places where medieval weapons had hung in times of peace. Or between battles, he thought, gazing around the great hall, envisioning savage Celts dressed in skins shouting for whiskey, pounding their cups on the tables, while their pipers played one of their eerie, unearthly songs. If Clonmore really were Gentleman Niall, as he strongly suspected, the Earl certainly wasn't using the proceeds to refurbish his home. Or maybe, he thought, as a sudden movement above caught his eye, maybe he likes it this way.

The idea of an English lord preferring to live in decrepit medieval splendor was so foreign that he tried to dismiss it out of hand. And yet, he thought as he watched Elizabeth descend the wide stone steps from the second floor, this had to be a clue as well.

Elizabeth was obviously lost in thought, but the pensive expression was replaced by one of surprise when she saw him sitting on the bench beside one of the hearths. Was it only surprise, he wondered, or was there a hint of fear in her face as well? He regarded her with close interest, and noticed at once the little parchment packet she held in her hand.

"Good morning, Lady Clonmore." He struggled to his feet and bowed. "Forgive the intrusion."

"No intrusion, Sir Anthony," Elizabeth replied lightly. "Please, do sit. I'm surprised to see you out and about. What brings you to Clonmore?"

"May I say you're looking quite lovely. Marriage agrees with you, my lady." He smiled, and his gaze took in the dark circles beneath her eyes and slight purple bruise beneath her chin. And the locket she wore about her neck—the green emerald locket—wasn't that the very one the outlaw had ripped off her throat? And which loss she'd lamented all the way to Ennis that very first night?

He peered at it more closely as she fingered it automatically. There was that same gesture he remembered from their first meeting. "Allow me to extend my congratulations, my dear. I'm sorry I didn't have a chance to speak to you personally the other day—I saw you in the crowd, of course. I must say, I thought it was quite civic-minded of you to leave your husband's sickbed and come to the meeting."

"He wanted me to meet our neighbors, Sir Anthony," Elizabeth replied coolly.

"I see you've a message there, my lady?"

"For my maid. You remember her, I'm sure, Sir Anthony? Mistress Molly?"

"Ah, yes, of course. How is she?" Sir Anthony's gaze flicked down to the locket and Elizabeth touched it again.

"She's quite well. And I'm very glad to see that you're recovering, Sir Anthony."

Sir Anthony bowed. "As you see, my lady. I do hope I haven't come at a bad time. I trust Lord Clonmore's health continues to improve?"

"Indeed it does, sir." Neville spoke from the top of the

stairs, and they both looked up. "How happy I am to meet you at last, Sir Anthony. My agent, Harrington, has told me so much of your great plans to apprehend our local villain."

Sir Anthony narrowed his eyes. The masked earl limped down the steps, his face unreadable, his appearance little changed from their one meeting in Dublin so long ago. "Indeed, my lord. I had the honor of making your acquaintance some time ago. I doubt you would recall it."

"But of course I do," answered Neville. "And stories of your exploits have kept us entertained and hopeful all the while we've been victimized. But I wish you would take a message to Sir William for me, sir."

It was Sir Anthony's turn to look surprised. If the little wife were fearful, the earl himself was totally at ease. Perhaps he'd misread the situation completely. And yet, he thought, glancing at the locket she fingered so desperately, what could explain its reappearance? Was it possible that it wasn't the same one? If that's what she claimed, he thought, it should be easy enough to see who'd made it. Something identical would have to have been commissioned. "Of course, my lord. What can I tell him?"

"Yesterday my lady and I were forced to seek shelter from a rainstorm in one of the shallow caves in the hills. And six redcoats accosted us at bayonet point. It was most off-putting, as you might well imagine, and frightened my lady for no reason."

"Ah, but surely your lady understands the need to find this outlaw?" Sir Anthony made a little bow toward Elizabeth. "The soldiers were acting under orders from me, my lord, although I apologize if they frightened you, my lady. It's completely possible that they may have been a little overzealous."

Neville sniffed. "I don't expect such a thing to happen again. There's no reason to accuse decent people."

"Ah." Sir Anthony raised his eyebrow. "As soon as Gentleman Niall has been flushed out of hiding, there will be no need."

"So to what do we owe this visit?" Neville limped past

Elizabeth and settled down on one of the long benches.
"Will you sit, Sir Anthony? Care for some refreshment?"

"I thought to come and speak with you, Clonmore, because you were unable to come to the meeting the other day.
Is there a place where we can talk alone?"

"You may speak freely in front of my wife," Neville
replied, even as Elizabeth glanced at him.

Sir Anthony narrowed his eyes. The wife was clearly
nervous, but the husband was hard to read. There was that
damnable mask, of course, which hid his face so effectively.
A mask very much like the sort described by witnesses as
worn by Gentleman Niall. Suddenly Sir Anthony wondered
what the mask really hid. Had anyone actually ever seen the
Earl unmasked? "It partially concerns your wife, my lord."

"Oh?" Neville cocked his head and gazed at Sir Anthony
coolly.

"She's our best witness, we believe. We hope you will
allow her to testify in court if necessary."

Neville's lips turned up in a tight smile, even as he
thought Elizabeth paled. "My lady will of course cooperate
in every way with whatever the law requires of her."

"And I was wondering, my lord, if—" Sir Anthony
paused.

"Yes?"

"If you've ever had a problem with horse thieves? The
general consensus from all the reports I can gather is that
Gentleman Niall rides a stallion of superior breeding, and I
can attest that in my own brief encounter with him he was
well saddled. And since you're known to breed the best
horses in the county—in several counties, in fact—I wondered if you'd ever had a problem."

Neville shrugged. "Ever? Of course. Lately? No." He
met Sir Anthony's eyes as if daring the man to question him
further.

Sir Anthony spread his hands. "It is part of the mystery,
of course. Such men are lucky usually to own the meanest
of beasts—and yet, here's an outlaw band not only well
horsed, but able to hide them so effectively a trace can't be
found."

Neville shrugged. "I think you've only not looked in the right place, Sir Anthony."

"And sometimes the right place is right under one's very nose." Sir Anthony smiled. "They flushed out another hedgemaster last night, my lord. And this one on your lands—did you know it?"

Neville nodded his head slowly. "My agent brought me word this morning. 'Tis a hard thing to understand, I think, Sir Anthony, the tenacity with which these people cling to their heathen ways, wouldn't you say?" His eyes, dark behind the mask, met Sir Anthony's and held them.

It was Sir Anthony who broke the stare. "Well, my lord, I won't disturb you further. May I offer my congratulations to you on your marriage?"

"Of course. Thank you."

"And may I ask where you managed to find Lady Clonmore's locket? I remember how sad she was to have lost it to the robbers the night of her arrival."

Elizabeth gasped, but Neville smiled smoothly. "Of course. My agent was able to locate it in a pawn shop in Dublin. I instructed him to keep his eye out for it—and of course as it was Elizabeth's mother's it appears in a portrait at Kilmara. He knew exactly what to look for, which made it much easier to find."

"How fortuitous." Sir Anthony bowed. "Good day, my lord. My lady." With another brief bow, he turned on his heel and limped slowly out of the hall.

Neville was silent until the great door had swung shut behind Sir Anthony. Elizabeth clutched the locket. "Neville, he suspects—"

"Sh," he admonished gently. "I know. It was probably a mistake that he saw the locket, but what can we do? It's done now."

"What did Sir Anthony want, Neville?" Harrington walked across the hall, accompanied by Sorcha, who was staring up at him with rosy cheeks and starry eyes.

Why, the girl's in love with him, Elizabeth thought.

"A social call, you might say," Neville replied. He looked down at Elizabeth. "I want Harrington to take you back to

Kilmara on his way into town. It—" He hesitated. "It would be safer for you there, I think."

"But, Neville—"

"No, Elizabeth. Don't argue. I'll take you back to Kilmara myself—gather what you have here that you will need."

Elizabeth bit her lip. She wanted to say more, but Harrington's presence, as well as Sorcha's, deterred her. "All right, my lord. As you will."

As she walked up the steps, she saw Neville beckon to Sorcha. "This is what you must tell your uncle," she heard him say.

Her cheeks burned. She couldn't be angry with him that he trusted Sorcha. After all, Sorcha had access to places that she, Elizabeth, could not. But how should she tell him that Turlough's arrest was her fault?

She was sorting through her clothes when he knocked on her door. "Come in," she called. He stepped into the antechamber and hesitated at the door of the bedroom. For a moment, she remembered last night, how the smooth skin gave way to ridges of puckered scars, how his long limbs had wrapped around her and brought her to the point of ecstasy again and again. She flushed and looked down.

"Elizabeth," he said. He crossed the space between them and took her in his arms. "You must understand why it's best for you to go. If anything happens—if the worst happens— you'll be able to say you knew nothing about this. You'll be able to keep Kilmara, although I'm afraid Clonmore will be forfeit to the crown."

"Neville, why are you talking like this? Is it absolutely necessary for you to do this? Isn't there some other way to rescue Turlough? Some legal way?"

"How can you think that?" he asked softly. "Can it be you don't understand? There is no justice in the English courts for men like Turlough. And given the situation, they'll torture him if they believe he might know anything. And believe me, they do." He reached out and caressed her hair. "It won't be long, I promise. We can't afford to let him linger there. Harrington's going to Ennis to see what he can learn. We'll make our move tomorrow night, or the next at the latest."

Torn by conflicting emotions, she stared helplessly up at him. Her mind screamed the words silently. *Tell him, tell him.* It was the only honest thing to do. Or maybe—maybe there was another way. Maybe the time to tell him was afterward. *What if there is no afterward?* a small voice spoke silently from deep within. *No*, she thought firmly, pushing the little voice deeper down, where it couldn't be heard. When Turlough was safe, then she'd tell Neville. And in the meantime, perhaps there was something she could do to help. What it was, she wasn't sure. But she'd speak to Sorcha, see what role he'd found for her to play. And maybe to Moira. There had to be something she could do. She knew it. Resolved, she smiled and nodded up at him. "All right. I understand. But you must promise me you will be careful. It wouldn't be fair—" She broke off and glanced at the bed, where they'd shared such bliss only a few short hours ago. It seemed like another lifetime ago.

His eyes twinkled behind the mask. "And believe me, my lady, I have every intention of returning to your side, and to your bed, as soon as possible."

Oh, Neville, she thought silently as he gathered her in his arms and pressed a slow kiss on her mouth, so that her whole body tingled. *Let that intention become a reality,* she prayed. *Let that intention be a reality, and I swear, I'll do everything in my power to save Turlough myself.*

"Sir Anthony." Master Hayes looked up in surprise when the knight limped into his office. He pushed his chair back from the desk and stood up. "We didn't expect you back so early, sir. Are you all right?"

"Quite all right, Hayes." Sir Anthony waved away assistance and sank down in the only other chair the dusty office held. He planted his cane between his knees and nodded at Hayes's chair. "Have a seat. There's a few things I wanted to ask you."

"Me, sir?"

"You've been here how long, Master Hayes? Did you come with Sir William?"

"No, sir. I've been here all my life. Not here, exactly; I was born and raised in Belfast."

"Ah." Sir Anthony sat back. "And had you ever met the Earl of Clonmore before he arrived here to take up residence in Clonmore Castle?"

"No, sir, not I. There won't be many around these parts that really remember him at all, before. He came here as a young man of sixteen or seventeen, I think, when this part of the country was being settled then by newcomers. The only one who might have met him then was Lady Jane Fitzbarth. She and her husband, the late Sir Roland, go way back in this county."

"And he's always seen masked?"

"Always so far as I know. I hear he's a monster under that mask."

"So do we all, Master Hayes." Sir Anthony caressed the top of the cane as though it were a lover's hand. "Thank you."

"Is that all?" Master Hayes asked, genuine concern on his broad, honest face.

"Is Sir William about?"

"I believe he's dining with the bishop this afternoon, sir."

"Hayes, if I wanted it spread about that the money and the hedgemaster were being moved to Dublin, how would I do that?"

"You mean, so that other people knew but thought it was a secret?"

"Ah, I see why Sir William is so pleased with you, Hayes."

Hayes sat up a little straighter, and the action reminded Sir Anthony for a split second of Colonel Melville. "Why, I suppose I'd see it was dropped at the Jug 'n' Fiddle in the square. That's where all the men stop, eventually."

Sir Anthony shook his head. "'Tis too far for me."

"Well, you couldn't do it, anyways, sir. Someone hearing it from your mouth would think it a trap."

Sir Anthony smiled. He withdrew a guinea from his

money belt and set it on the desk in front of Hayes. "It's nearly the dinner hour, isn't it, Master Hayes? I hear the Jug serves rare roast beef beyond compare."

Hayes's eyes widened at the sight of the coin. "True enough, Sir Anthony, but my mistress expects me home. She's promised me Yorkshire pudding."

"My favorite," Sir Anthony said with a wistful sigh.

"Why—perhaps you could go in my place, Sir Anthony!"

"Would it upset your mistress, Master Hayes? I would never want to discomfit a lady."

"Well, she might be taken aback a bit at first, but she'll come round if you explain you sent me on an errand." Hayes's broad face was wistful as he fingered the coin.

Sir Anthony leaned forward and spoke softly. "The nature of the errand you must not share with her, you understand?"

"Of course not, Sir Anthony. What do you take me for?"

Sir Anthony smiled again. "Then we're agreed."

"But what about Sir William?" Master Hayes looked perplexed. "Does he know of this? Has he agreed?"

"Oh, yes," Sir Anthony replied, inspecting his fingernails for dirt. It was difficult to hide his pleasure that his small manipulation had worked so easily. "Of course Sir William has agreed." *He just doesn't know it yet,* he finished silently.

Fourteen

They were mostly silent on the way to Kilmara, both lost in their own thoughts. Elizabeth glanced sideways at Neville several times, but he was too absorbed to notice. Finally, as the cluster of brick-red chimneys rose over the golden oaks, Elizabeth reached over and touched the hand which lay slack upon his thigh. "Neville?"

He turned his head slowly, as though dragged from some deep place. "My lady?"

Her heart quailed. As much as she wanted to, she couldn't quite bring herself to tell him. She swallowed hard and smiled. "How will I know—?"

"It's better that you don't know, Elizabeth."

They reached the gates and turned up the drive. The gate-keeper stuck his head out of his cottage and gave a startled wave. Elizabeth responded with a nod and a forced smile. "But—but, Neville, what if the worst happens?"

"Then, believe me, my dear, you'll know all too soon." He gave her a crooked grin.

She bit her lip. The less willing he seemed to trust her, the more difficult it became to imagine ever telling him the truth. Sorcha, she thought, she'd have to rely on Sorcha to bring her the news. She returned his grin with a hesitant smile. He obviously only thought her concerned. What would he say if he knew she was responsible for the entire situation? "Isn't there something I can do?"

He looked at her in surprise. "Do?"

"To help—I want to—"

He reached over and patted her hand. "Elizabeth, believe me when I say that right now, staying out of the way at Kilmara is the best way for you to help."

She stifled a little sigh. At least she'd asked, she thought. She said nothing more as they rode down the tree-lined drive. She wondered fleetingly what Neville would say if he knew she could shoot a gun. He'd probably lock up the guns, she thought glumly. Especially after she told him about her part in Turlough's capture—he'd lock her out of his life.

Oak leaves lay in drifts at the bases of the great trees, and the afternoon sun sparkled on the wide windows. The gravel crunched beneath their feet. Suddenly Elizabeth wanted Molly desperately. Molly would understand. Molly would listen. And Molly would keep the secret—she knew she could trust Molly. As they approached the doors, a stable boy ran up to take their reins. The front door opened, and Molly dashed out. "My lamb! Oh, my lamb, I'm so happy to have you back here with me."

Elizabeth waited until Neville helped her out of the saddle, then rushed to the older woman. Molly hugged her tight, and for a moment, tears filled her eyes. It was so good to feel the familiar arms around her. Molly hugged her once more, as if to reassure herself that Elizabeth was real. "I was beginning to think you had no more use for old Molly."

"Oh, Molly, how could you think so?" Elizabeth pulled back. Unexpected tears filled her eyes. Molly was her link to home and her grandmother and everything about her old life. "You're being silly, you know that? Oh!" she cried when she saw the twinkle in the old woman's eye. "You're teasing me!" She wiped at her eyes.

"Are you all right, my lady?" Molly's voice was soft, and she glanced past Elizabeth to Neville, who stood directing the removal of Elizabeth's small trunk.

"I'm fine, Molly, really. I'm just so glad to see you." She

gave Molly's hand a little squeeze and leaned closer. "We'll talk later, all right?"

Molly curtseyed as Neville walked up. "Shall we go in, my lady?" He nodded to Molly and offered his arm to Elizabeth. He escorted her into the house. Molly bobbed another curtsey and went up the steps, leaving the two of them alone in the hall.

Neville took her by the arms and gazed down at her, his eyes compelling and blue. She caught her breath. "Try not to worry."

She gave a little laugh and felt as though she wanted to cry. "How can I not worry?"

"I suppose you're right. Just—just think of me as away for business. I promise I will come home."

"All right." She nodded, and felt her bones begin to melt as he drew her closer.

"Then you must kiss me good-bye," he murmured, as his mouth came down on hers. She sighed as delight spread like a wave through her body, and he drew back, eyes twinkling. "Why, I do believe I've awakened a wanton in my lady." His voice was soft and wooing.

She smiled tremulously and pushed away. "Have a good trip, my lord. Fare well, and travel safely."

"Fare well, my lady." He drew the tip of one finger down the line of her cheek, bowed, and was gone.

She went to the door and watched him ride away, eyeing the easy motion of the muscles in his long thighs. She murmured another silent prayer, and turned to see Molly watching her from the step.

"How—how does it stand with his lordship?" Molly's eyes spoke volumes behind the simple question.

Elizabeth sighed sadly. "Let's go upstairs and talk." She picked up the train of her riding gown and followed Molly up the steps. Once inside her room, she gazed up at the portrait of her mother. *I know, I know,* she thought. *I know I should've told him. But how could I risk losing something before it's ever really mine?* She gave another deep sigh, then stripped off her gloves and handed them to Molly. "How does it stand? Well, as you can see, his lordship is almost completely well. And I believe we might find a way to get along together—as married people—but—" She broke off, and turned her head away as tears flooded her eyes.

"Why, lamb, what is it? He's not been cruel to you, has he?"

"No, oh, no, Molly," Elizabeth said, her eyes shut against the memory of his touch, his smell, his taste. Her body burned at the thought of his mouth on hers, the long length of him nestled in the cradle of her thighs. "No, he's—he's a gentleman—" She broke off again, and faced Molly. She took both the maid's hands in hers and pressed them together. "Molly, you must swear to me, upon pain of death, that what I will tell you, you will reveal to no one, no one at all, do you understand?"

"Why, my lady." Molly drew back a little, her hands stiff in Elizabeth's grasp. "He's not forced you to some unspeakable act, has he?"

"No!" said Elizabeth. "Molly, you must promise—it's nothing bad—but you must promise—"

"All right, all right, my lamb." Molly's hands softened and she squeezed Elizabeth's gently. "I promise. What's the secret?"

"Neville—my husband—Molly, you may not believe this. But I know who Gentleman Niall is. He's Neville."

Molly's hands jerked in Elizabeth's and her eyes flew wide. "My lady!" Her voice was a hushed whisper, and she glanced fearfully over her shoulder, as if to reassure herself that the bedroom door was indeed closed.

"It's true, Molly, and now that I've told you, you must tell no one."

"But—but, my lady—what does he do with the money?"

Elizabeth looked at Molly in disbelief. "Why, that's the point, Molly. He helps his people. The people of Clonmore are better taken care of than those of Kilmara, believe me. And Clonmore Castle itself is nearly a ruin compared to this." She looked around the room, at the delicate lace curtains and heavy velvet drapes, at the embroidered hangings on the ornately carved bed. "Why do you think it's been so easy for me to get the supplies we've needed?"

Molly shook her head slowly. "I've never heard of such a thing, my lady. I scarce know what to think!"

Elizabeth bit her lip. "Molly—you mustn't say anything, do you understand? Please?"

"My lady, of course I won't say anything." Molly caressed her cheek with a gentle hand. "He saved you, didn't he? He didn't even know who you were, and he went after you when I told him they had taken you. How could I ever betray the man who did that?"

Elizabeth pressed a kiss on the back of Molly's work-roughened hand. "Thank you, Molly." She gave a deep sigh.

"Feel better now, my lady?"

Elizabeth shrugged. "Molly, I think I've done something terrible."

Molly stared. "My lamb, surely not—"

"No, listen. You must. The reason I came back—Neville sent me here because he believed I'd be safer here—"

"Safer? What's he about?"

"He intends to rescue someone, Molly. Someone who's in prison because of me." Elizabeth pressed her lips together. She was determined to maintain her composure. Nothing was to be gained by crying. She could almost hear her grandmother's crisp voice echoing in her ear.

"Oh, my lady. I can't believe that. But tell me all of it. Why do you think you're to blame?"

Haltingly at first, and then more fluently, Elizabeth told how she'd inadvertently come to mention Turlough to Lady Susannah and Lady Jane. "So you see," she finished miserably, "it's all my fault."

"My lady, it could be just a coincidence, you know. These things happen. You said yourself there'd been a lot of soldiers about—why, we've seen them here, tramping through. Don't blame yourself, my dear. I'm sure it wasn't you." Molly rose to her feet and patted Elizabeth on the shoulder. "I'll bring up a nice hot cup of tea and something for you to eat, how's that?"

"All right, Molly." Elizabeth waited until the woman had closed the bedroom door behind herself, then rose and walked over to one of the long windows. She gazed out over the still-green lawn. Golden leaves still clung to the oaks which lined the drive, and the long rays of the afternoon sun lay in bright shafts across the leaf-strewn grass. What other reaction could she have expected from Molly? But now she was here—here, out of the way, with no way to find out anything. She understood why Neville wanted her to be safe. But now she chafed at the idea that she'd have to wait to learn what was happening. She wished that Sorcha would return. There had to be a way to find out.

Elizabeth was in the stillroom when Sorcha slipped quietly into the room. Her cheeks were pink from the cold, and she still wore her cloak. The room was golden in the glow of the late afternoon light, and Elizabeth looked up and smiled with relief. "Sorcha, I'm glad you're back."

"My-my uncle's babe is sickening—" Sorcha began uncertainly.

Elizabeth beckoned. "Sorcha, it's all right. I know Neville sent you with a message."

"Can you tell me why he sent me, my lady?" Sorcha's eyes were troubled. "I asked John—Master Harrington—he wouldn't tell me. But the message—my uncle seemed to be expecting it."

"What was the message?"

"Some nonsense—moonrise tomorrow at midnight. But the moon doesn't rise at midnight—"

"No, but maybe that's when they plan to meet." Elizabeth gazed out the windows as the shadows fell across the lawn.

"They, my lady? Who?" Sorcha edged forward, a fearful expression on her face as if she dreaded the answer.

"Have you not guessed, Sorcha?" Elizabeth asked softly. She paused, but Sorcha only stared at her blankly.

Then a light seemed to dawn in her eyes, and she started. "Blessed Mary, you don't mean that my John is involved with Gentleman Niall? And his lordship knows?"

"Sorcha, his lordship *is* Gentleman Niall, and your John is his lieutenant. They mean to rescue Turlough."

"Blessed Mary," breathed Sorcha. "I wondered—when I told John—Master Harrington—last night—and he went right to his lordship—I knew he'd be concerned, but the way he bolted from the room—"

"But you didn't think they'd react quite the way they did?"

"It was not what I expected, my lady. You understand."

Elizabeth nodded, then smiled. "And when did Master Harrington become 'John' to you?"

"Oh, my lady, we mean no offense—he's an honorable gentleman—"

"Sorcha, I think he's a fine man, too."

"We came to know each other these last few weeks, my lady, nursing the farmers. Master Harrington was so very kind and helpful—" Sorcha ducked her head and blushed. "It seemed we'd known each other forever when we spoke."

Elizabeth smiled sadly. Not for her the easy path of love at first sight. "I'm happy for you, Sorcha. I hope you will be happy together."

Sorcha shrugged. " 'Tis hard to believe that so fine a gentleman would care for me, my lady. We'll see what happens."

"But in the meanwhile—in the meanwhile, you must be our ears, Sorcha. My lord sent me here to keep me safe, but now I've no way to know what's happening. You must visit your uncle tomorrow and find out. Otherwise—" Elizabeth broke off. She didn't even like to shape the unthinkable into a coherent thought.

"I understand, my lady." Sorcha came forward hesitantly, and impulsively, Elizabeth hugged her. "I'll be your eyes and your ears, my lady."

"For both of us," Elizabeth murmured fiercely. "For us both."

A thin line of light shone beneath Neville's door as Harrington walked down the wide stone corridor. He knocked on the thick-paneled door.

"Enter!"

He swung the door open. Neville sat before the fire, and even beneath the mask, Harrington could see his eyes were red with weariness. He pulled the door shut. "They mean to take him to Dublin. With the money."

"No!" Neville leapt to his feet. "That's got to be a trap."

Harrington shrugged. "Aye, I agree. The tale I heard made a rough kind of sense, though—Sir William doesn't want to wait any longer—the winter's coming on early and the seas are getting rough." He rubbed his hands together and held them out over the fire. "It has been cold."

"Sweet Jesus," Neville swore beneath his breath. "We have no choice. When do they leave?"

"Two days."

"Then I say we have to get him out tomorrow night, when the element of surprise is with us, and we have a chance of knowing where he is. Where are they holding him?"

"In the garrison. This isn't going to be easy. In fact, I'd say it's the most difficult thing we've ever risked. Even your father wouldn't take these odds. Are you sure you want to try this?"

"What choice do we have? They'll torture Turlough to death, those bastards will, and you know it, John." Neville's use of his Christian name made Harrington look up. "That business with the tithe money and moving him to Dublin—that smells like a trap of Sir Anthony's to me. He's trying to draw us out. It's more than likely that poor Turlough won't even be there."

Harrington sank down into the chair opposite Neville's. "My lord, I don't disagree, but how do you propose to do this?"

"I've been thinking all day." He strode to his desk, and held out several large sheets of parchment. "See?"

Harrington surveyed each in turn, then looked at the first again. "If it works, it's a great idea." He grinned.

"And you mean to say that if it doesn't, it's not?" Neville laughed.

"That would seem to be so self-evident that any statement to that effect would be an overstatement of the obvious."

"I want you to go over that plan tomorrow when you're

rested. Go over it with as close an eye as you can. Any mistakes will mean our lives."

Harrington nodded. He took the plans and tucked them under his arm. He hesitated, then looked Neville in the eye. "Will this be Gentleman Niall's last caper?"

"No question, my friend." Neville extended his hand. "You have my word—the word of a gentleman." He winked.

Fifteen

Sorcha had no word to give her the following day. Elizabeth worked in the stillroom, inspecting the herbs that Molly and Mistress Gallagher had harvested in her absence, assessing her supplies, and making notes as to what needed replenishing the most. Each time footsteps rang out on the path, or a shadow crossed the window, she looked up, half-eager, half-afraid of what she might hear. Finally, the door of the stillroom opened, and Sorcha slipped inside, her face flushed from the cold wind.

"What news, Sorcha?" asked Elizabeth, envious of the other girl's ability to travel at will across the country.

Sorcha shook her head. "My uncle will say nothing to me." She spread her hands. "Perhaps we should wait, my lady."

Elizabeth wiped her hands on her smock. "There's one more person he trusts." Sorcha looked puzzled. "Lady Moira, my husband's mother." She reached behind her back and untied her smock. "Do you know where Clonmore's dower house is?"

Sorcha raised her eyebrows. "I—I know it, my lady, but they say Lady Moira is a witch—I'd not want to go near her house—"

"Sorcha, don't be ridiculous." To her horror, Elizabeth

heard herself speak in her grandmother's no-nonsense tone. "Lady Moira's not a witch," she said more kindly. "She nursed Lord Neville back to health—she's a kind woman."

"Of course she'd be nursing her son back to health, my lady," replied Sorcha. "Begging your pardon, my lady. I don't mean to sound saucy. And we shouldn't go now—there's a storm coming up—" She nodded to the window, where the afternoon light had darkened considerably.

Elizabeth squared her shoulders. "Well. I'm going to visit my mother-in-law. If you won't come with me, Sorcha, one of the grooms shall."

"But—but, my lady, what if there's talk about you rushing off like—"

"I need to consult with her regarding my herbs."

Sorcha hesitated, and Elizabeth went to her side and took the other girl's work-roughened hand in hers. "Sorcha, don't you want to know what's happening? Maybe there's something we can do—maybe we can help them in some way—"

Behind the doubt, hope flared in Sorcha's eyes. She gathered her cloak closer to her throat and nodded. "All right, my lady. But—but the storm—" She looked once more to the window, where a cold blast blew leaves against the panes.

"We'll ride. It's not raining yet, is it?"

"Not yet."

"Good. Tell the grooms we want two horses—and to hurry. I'll be right down."

Sorcha bobbed a curtsey and Elizabeth dashed out of the stillroom. She wouldn't bother with changing, she decided. She grabbed her cloak and went down the stairs to the front, where Sorcha waited with one of the stable boys and two horses. "Let's go."

The stable boy helped her into the saddle. Sorcha swung herself up with more practiced ease than Elizabeth would've thought. She gathered the reins capably in her hands and looked at Elizabeth. "Come, my lady."

The wind was rising and the first drops of rain stung her cheeks by the time they reached Moira's cottage. Elizabeth halted before the small stone structure in surprise. "This is the dower house, Sorcha? Are you sure?"

As if in answer the front door opened and Lady Moira stepped out, a red shawl around her shoulders, her eyes wide in surprise. "Elizabeth! What are you doing here?"

Elizabeth slipped out of the saddle, while Sorcha tied the horses to a low-hanging branch in the small stone-fenced yard. "We came to see you, my lady. I hope this isn't an intrusion?"

"Of course not," Moira answered, stepping aside and beckoning. "But come in at once—the storm's about to break. And girl, take those horses round to the back—there's a place by the kitchen to shelter them."

Elizabeth stepped through the front door and paused on the threshold. The little house was snug and warm and very clean. The smell of something rich and beefy filled the air. A gray cat was curled on the red hearth rug, and a basket of knitting lay spilling beside one of the high-backed chairs by the fire. "This—this is lovely."

Moira smiled over her shoulder as she shut and bolted the door. "Come and sit, my dear, and tell me what's wrong?"

Elizabeth sank into the chair opposite Moira's. "I'm worried about Neville."

Moira picked up her knitting needles and smiled ruefully. "Well, at least now there's two of us."

"What do you mean?"

"My dear, sometimes I think my entire adult life has been one long worry about Neville." She shrugged. "He was always so set in his own way of doing things. And the trouble of it is that very often, he gets it right, and things work out to his advantage—but when they don't—" She paused and shook her head. "He's always taken risks. I try and tell myself that's his father in him, you see—his father was such a gambler, and at least Neville doesn't gamble in coins."

"No," Elizabeth said slowly. "He just risks his life." The eyes of the two women met in perfect understanding.

Moira's mouth quirked in that same little gesture as Neville's and Elizabeth's heart twisted in her chest. "I know what you came to ask me. It's tonight. They're going after Turlough tonight."

As she spoke, the storm broke. A sheet of rain fell from the heavens like a thunderclap and a few drops of water dripped onto the fire, so sudden and so fierce was the onslaught. The fire rose in a sudden shower of sparks and the cat sprang to its feet with a yowl. Moira touched the cat with the tip of her slipper. "Now, now. 'Tis only the rain. And the wind." She looked up as a gust shrieked through the trees.

Sorcha peered around the doorway, accompanied by an older woman about Moira's age who carried four bowls and spoons. "Come, girl, 'tis only the rain—there's no sending you back in this, so we might as well eat." She spoke over her shoulder to Sorcha, as she placed the dishes on the table.

Moira looked up with a smile. "Elizabeth, my dear, this is Emma. She began as my maid nearly forty years ago, and she's become my mother in the process."

"Tush, my lady," Emma said, but she looked pleased. She set the dishes down on the scrubbed wooden table and bobbed a curtsey. "Honored to meet you, m'lady. We'll fetch the rest, m'lady."

Elizabeth turned to Moira when they had gone back to the kitchen. "You think they mean to do it in this weather?"

Moira shrugged. "Who knows, my dear?"

"How—how do they mean—"

"I don't know the plan." She smiled sadly. "Neville never tells me."

As Emma and Sorcha carried in a bubbling iron kettle, steaming with beef and herbs, Elizabeth walked to the window and peered out. The rain was a sheer gray curtain in the black night. "Even in this?"

Moira shook her head. "I'd like to say no, my dear. But knowing Neville . . ."

The two women looked at each other in the warm, fragrant haven of the room. "He always takes the risk," Elizabeth finished softly. Moira came to stand beside her. She slipped her arm around Elizabeth and drew her close, and for a long moment, they stood there, while the rain lashed at the window, and the fire snapped and hissed.

•   •   •

The rain ended long before midnight, but the wind turned cold and a thin crust of ice lay over the cobblestones as Neville, Harrington, and three other black-garbed men led a black horse with rag-wrapped hooves down the narrow street between the courthouse and the massive pile of medieval stone which served as the garrison headquarters. A silver sickle of moon hung high in the dark sky, and in the quiet night, the only sound was a fitful drip off the roofs above their heads. Behind the courthouse lay the cattleyards, where livestock were kept when brought to market, and in the cattleyards, a byre led down to the cellar of the courthouse. The courthouse windows on the upper story overlooked the garrison. Neville peered out and around. "All right," he hissed. "Let's go."

They slipped into the courthouse, and Harrington lit a torch. The cellar smelled of animals and moldy hay. They slipped up the stairs and proceeded to the upper floors. It was an easy matter to open the windows and shimmy down a rope onto the roof of the garrison. They lay for a moment, flat against the icy slope of the roof. Neville eased forward and peered over the edge. The drop was perhaps eight to ten feet. He beckoned to the others, and silently, one by one, they slipped over the edge, onto the perimeter of the walls. They flattened back against the walls as the slow tramp of booted feet echoed in the still night.

A weary redcoat yawned as he turned the corner, his paces slow. Neville stepped forward, and the guard stared in shocked surprise. Liam knocked him on the head and he crumpled, still wearing the startled expression. Neville motioned them down the way the man had been heading.

On the far side of the courthouse, the clock struck the hour. "Let's go," Neville whispered beneath the gongs. As quickly as they dared, they set off toward the guardhouse where Turlough was being held. Harrington had only just late that afternoon confirmed where the old man was being kept. Below, in the courtyard, came the tramp of feet. "Right on schedule," Neville breathed.

At the changing of the guard, the upper story was left unguarded but for the jailer. They stole into the room, where the jailer snored, head against the back of the chair, legs stretched out on a rickety table. Harrington seized the keys as McMahon smashed the jailer on the head. He crumpled to the floor, and Harrington fitted the keys in the cell door. It swung open smoothly on well-oiled hinges.

"Turlough!" he cried, his voice a harsh whisper. From the pitch darkness of the cell came the low moan of an animal in pain. "Give me a light." He peered into the darkness as Neville handed him a candle. Harrington raised it high. The yellow light shone on the still figure lying on the low cot. He uttered another harsh moan. "My God," said Harrington. "What's this?"

Neville stepped around Harrington and crossed quickly to Turlough. He gently raised the sheet which covered him. "Sweet Jesus, just as I feared," he muttered. "We'll have to carry him. Get Liam." He spoke over his shoulder, then turned back to the wounded man. "Turlough, we're taking you out of here. Just try to hang on."

"Is he alive?" Liam asked as he pushed into the room.

"Barely," Neville said. "There were no plans to take him to Dublin. Let's go."

Liam stepped over to the narrow cot and picked up Turlough. He swung the old man over his shoulder. Turlough only groaned. Harrington peered at him closely. "I hope he survives."

"No time to assess now," Neville said, motioning them forward. He paused at the door. "The watch should have been replaced. Come on, let's go."

They left the room and ventured once more out on the parapet. Neville peered around the comer then motioned the rest forward. They made their way as quickly as possible across the wet stones. Below, they could hear the slow paces of weary feet as the new squadron of the guard marched to their posts. They had just reached the most exposed point on their way back when a single soldier shouted from the direction of the jail: "Sound the alarm! The prisoner's escaped!"

From below, there was a sudden pounding, and a cry

went up, spreading throughout the garrison. Lights flared in dim windows.

"Run," hissed Neville.

They took off down the narrow parapet, and came at last to the place where the rope still dangled off the roof. With great effort, they managed to hand Turlough up to Liam and McMahon. Neville glanced over his shoulder. "Now you, Harrington," he said as the sound of running footsteps came closer.

"You first," Harrington said. "You've not the strength to pull yourself up."

Twelve redcoats burst around the comer and Neville did not hesitate. He leapt up into Harrington's cupped hands as one soldier shouted, "Get them! There!" McMahon hoisted him over the edge of the roof. He twisted like a cat and leaned down as far over the edge of the roof as he dared. "Come on, John."

Harrington gripped the rope and kicked against the walls for purchase, but his leather soles slipped against the icy stones. The redcoats rushed up, reaching for him with eager arms. He looked up at Neville. "Go!" he cried as he was pulled backward into the punishing embrace.

A rough hand shook her from the dream. Elizabeth opened her eyes and gasped to see the black-masked man leaning over her. She gasped, then realized it was Neville. She turned her eyes away from the light of the candle he held above her. "Elizabeth," he said, "what are you doing here?"

She sat up slowly, blinking away sleep. Beside her, Moira shifted on the mattress and bolted upright. "Neville! Are you all right?"

"I'm all right, Mother. It's Turlough. Can you come and look at him?"

"Of course. Where is he? Downstairs?"

"Aye, Emma let us in. She said she was expecting us."

"So was I," Moira said dryly as she shuffled from the bed. She wrapped a robe around herself, and walked heavily down the stairs, the steps creaking beneath her weight.

Elizabeth looked up at Neville. In the candlelight, his

eyes shone dark behind the black mask. It was the first time she'd seen him dressed as Gentleman Niall since their first meeting and suddenly she felt shy.

"What are you doing here?" he asked again, his voice soft.

"I was worried about you. I knew your mother would probably know your plans. So I came here, and we were caught in the storm. She said we might as well sleep here. What happened tonight?"

Neville sat down on the bed with a sigh. "We got Turlough. We lost Harrington."

"What?" She clutched at her locket. "Master Harrington's dead?"

Neville shook his head. "Worse. The soldiers have him."

"Oh, Neville." She put her hand on his arm.

"I suppose my mother was right. I should've stopped this long ago—before anyone got seriously hurt."

A nagging suspicion took hold and she shook his arm. "Neville, you aren't thinking of turning yourself in, are you?"

He hesitated. "I don't want to do that, no." He gazed into the flame. "But you should see what they did to Turlough—he's barely alive. I can't imagine what they'll do to John."

"Surely there's another way?"

Neville drew a deep breath. "Right now I want to think so. But first, I want to find out what Mother thinks of Turlough—will you come down?"

"Neville, Sorcha's here."

"Ah—Liam's niece."

"She's in love with John Harrington."

Neville sighed. "I know." He rose to his feet. "I'll go down and tell her."

"I'll come." She slipped out of bed, shoved her feet into the slippers Moira had insisted she use, and reached for the voluminous robe Moira had laid out for her. Silently she followed Neville down the stairs.

Three men were clustered disconsolately by the table, while Sorcha, Emma and Moira knelt by the hedgemaster's side. Turlough lay on the pile of quilts Emma had made up for herself by the hearth. She looked up when Neville and Elizabeth appeared.

"Sorcha," said Elizabeth. "Come with me?"

The eager expression changed to wariness as Sorcha got to her feet, but she waited until they were in the kitchens to face them with a raised chin and arms crossed over her chest. "Don't be telling me John Harrington is dead?"

Neville shook his head. "I don't think so, Sorcha. But he was captured."

Sorcha closed her eyes and covered her face with her hands. "Blessed Mary and all the saints."

"We'll do all we can, Sorcha." Elizabeth enfolded the girl in a hug, thinking furiously. There had to be some way to save Harrington. Neville would think of something.

The morning light was just beginning to brighten the room when Turlough gave one last sigh and lay still. Moira looked up as she passed her hand over the eyelids. "I'm sorry, Neville. I did all I could."

Neville gazed down at the slight, battered body. His mouth was a grim line, and deep lines ran from beneath the mask down the sides of his cheeks. "I know, Mother." He let his breath out in a long sigh.

Elizabeth got to her feet. She had taken Sorcha's place in the effort to save Turlough, when the little maid had been sent upstairs to Emma's bed to cry herself to sleep in peace. She wiped her hands on a linen towel, but before she could speak, Neville opened the door and strode out of the cottage. "Nev—" she began, but Moira stopped her with a gentle hand.

"Leave him for a few moments," she said gently.

"I'll see to some of this, shall I, m'lady?" asked Emma.

Moira nodded wearily. "Aye. And we must send for the priest. We cannot bury poor Turlough unshriven, although I suppose technically, it's too late." She stood up heavily. "I'm too old for this, I think."

Elizabeth darted to the window. Neville stood in the yard, leaning against a chestnut tree. His back was to her, and he faced the sunrise. Quietly, she lifted the latch and stole out into the chilly morning. She went to stand beside him.

"I've never told you how I came to know Harrington. It was in the navy—after I'd met my father and gone back to England. I saved his life, by accident, as it happened. A barrel had fallen off a ship—it came crashing to the ground and Harrington was under it—we were in the middle of a fist-fight on the deck below." He smiled ruefully at the memory.

"But why? Master Harrington is such a gentleman—why on earth would you—"

"Another lady thought so, too." Neville grinned. "We were young—a couple of young bucks showing off for women—I don't even think she was very pretty, now that I think of it." He broke off. The sun was higher now, and bright rays of gold light flooded through the trees. The air was cold but very still. "I don't know what to do, Elizabeth." His voice was low. "I can't let Harrington die in my place."

For a moment, another cold fear that he would confess his identity stabbed through her heart. She reached for his hand and gripped it. He looked at her, and she saw the deep lines of fatigue etched along his mouth and nose. A dark haze of beard covered his chin, and his eyes were red behind the tattered mask. "Neville, you're exhausted. You should rest—"

"I'll rest at Clonmore." Their eyes met. "Come back with me, Elizabeth."

For answer, she twined her hand in his. He raised it to his lips and pressed a kiss on the back. "I don't know what to do, Elizabeth. But perhaps you'll help me think of something." And for once, there wasn't a trace of his usual teasing tone.

Sixteen

Gently, Elizabeth eased herself away from Neville. He slept heavily, sprawled across the bed. He'd kissed her tenderly as her body had stopped quivering, and held her in the warm afterglow, then had rolled to his side and fallen suddenly and completely asleep. His lovemaking had stunned her with its intensity, leaving her feeling breathless and bruised, but not weary. She quickly dressed and went down to the deserted hall. She found Aislinn in the kitchens. "Ah, you're awake, my lady! And his lordship?"

"Still asleep, I'm afraid."

"Tired from his journey, no doubt?" Aislinn spoke archly.

"No doubt." Elizabeth forced a smile. "Is there—is there any mending to be done? It seems I was in the middle of quite a lot—"

"Mary love you, lady, there's a basket here that needs doing." Aislinn nodded at the all-too-familiar basket.

Elizabeth picked it up with a sigh. It was the last thing she felt like doing, but it would keep her hands occupied. "And a bite of breakfast, perhaps?"

"It's closer to dinner, but I'll make you something light, if you wish."

"All right, Aislinn." Elizabeth found she had little appetite. "I'll be in the hall."

"I'll send in young Terence to light the fire for you, my lady."

"Thank you."

She settled down beside the fire in the hall and threaded her needle. She picked up the first shirt and spread it out on her lap. The whole affair was becoming worse and worse. Turlough's rescue had not only failed to save the old man's life, but now Harrington was in mortal danger, too. And she knew that Neville, unless he could think of some way to rescue Harrington, was most likely to come forward to save his friend. Harrington was doomed either way, of course. Neville's stepping forward wouldn't save Harrington's life—he had to see that. And there had to be a way to rescue Harrington.

The hall door opened and closed with a bang and Elizabeth jumped so abruptly, she stabbed her thumb with the needle. "Ow!" she cried involuntarily, as she rose to her feet at the sight of the stranger who paused just inside the threshold, hesitating.

He was a short man of less than average height, but powerfully built in the chest and shoulders. His cheeks were red, and his immaculately powdered hair was drawn back in a long queue at his neck. He wore dark green riding clothes. "Lady Clonmore?" he asked, and his voice was cultured and deep.

"I'm she." Elizabeth drew herself up. "Who are you, sir?"

"My name is Hugh O'Neill, my lady. Forgive this intrusion in your day, my lady. I'm the Duke of Desmond, I thought we might speak privately?"

Elizabeth glanced around. No one was about. "Certainly, Your Grace. No one will disturb us here." She gestured to the wooden armchair opposite hers. "Please, do sit." What on earth could have prompted the highest-ranking peer in the district to come calling at this hour?

He sat and spread his hands before the fire. "I'm not sure

how to begin, my lady. My agent brought me word this morning that Gentleman Niall has been captured."

Elizabeth raised one eyebrow. "Has he, indeed?"

"You've heard, then?" The duke was looking at her closely.

Elizabeth cast a quick eye to the stairs. "Well, yes, I have." She wet her lips and glanced once more above. "Thank you for bringing the news, though; it was very kind of you to think of us. Clonmore is somewhat isolated, I think." She heard herself chatter, but she could scarcely stop.

"Lady Clonmore." Desmond leaned forward in his chair. "My concern is for your husband—"

"Your concern is appreciated, but unwarranted, Desmond." Neville spoke from the balcony above. "You've heard I was down with the fever?" He started down the steps as the duke rose to his feet.

"Clonmore! I didn't expect—"

Neville said nothing until he stood before the Duke. "Didn't expect what, Desmond? Didn't expect me to be here?" He stared down at the little man.

Elizabeth's hand flew to her throat.

"A man's eyes are always the same, Neville, no matter what color mask he wears," Desmond answered softly. He took a single step toward Neville. "You saved my son's life. I knew you'd need my help someday. I came to try and pay back the debt I owe."

There was a long moment of silence. Then Neville said, "I always thought I could trust you if I had to."

Desmond smiled. "I'm not sure that's a compliment. But no matter—I came to see if there was anything to be done to save you—who, then, is it?"

"Harrington."

"And he's claiming to be Gentleman Niall."

Neville swore softly beneath his breath. "No."

Desmond nodded slowly. "That's why I came, Neville. The word is out, up and down the county, that Gentleman Niall's been caught."

"Oh, my God." Neville sat down heavily on the long wooden bench. "I knew it. He's lied to protect me."

"Look, Neville, that's why I've come. I'm here to help. I'm sure between the two of us we can think of something."

Neville leaned back, staring into the flames. "Aye, Desmond. I'm sure you're right. I hadn't even thought—" He broke off and shook his head. "It makes sense, though. Otherwise they'd be here—I'm surprised they're not here already."

Elizabeth glanced from Neville to the duke. "Would you want me to leave, Neville?"

"I want you to stay." Neville gripped her hand. "Please." Flushed, she sat down and picked up the mending. He looked at the duke. "Well. At this point, I'm not sure what to do."

"What happened last night?" Desmond asked.

Neville cocked his head. "Bad timing, I suppose. We were trying to get Turlough O'Donal out of the garrison. He's worked as our messenger. I knew they'd try to torture something out of him. We got him out but we were too late. He died at my mother's house this morning."

"Hm." Desmond sat back in his chair, considering. "You tried to get him out of the jail?"

Neville nodded. "Aye. And it almost worked. Hadn't counted on the cold and the wet—that slowed us down, too."

"But perhaps it would be better to attempt a rescue in the open air, Neville. That's really Gentleman Niall's turf."

"I would agree. But there was a rumor put round that Turlough would be taken to Dublin, and that was obviously a lie. I can't depend that they'll move Harrington."

"I'm not so sure," Desmond replied. "The bishop wants the money moved."

"Indeed?"

"And I think it likely they will move Gentleman Niall to Dublin. This is too sensational. The word's spreading even as we speak. And believe me, the bishop has already called on Sir William, if I know him at all."

"Hm. If only there were some way to ensure they do it

quickly." Neville looked at Elizabeth. "Would you do me a kindness, my lady, and fetch me some breakfast? I'm hungry."

Elizabeth rose to her feet but hesitated. "Neville, remember how Sir Anthony told us that he was relying on me to be a witness? What if you took me there today—so that I can identify Gentleman Niall. Then, once Master Harrington is identified, they'll have no reason not to move him, and if they don't—well, they'll think they have the real Gentleman Niall—"

"That would give Sir William some added pressure to conclude this quickly," the duke added. "And I would think Sir Anthony would want to see it moved to Dublin, as well. If they hold the execution here, Colonel Melville is sure to capture the credit. That's what happened in Cork, you know."

Neville stroked his chin as he looked up at Elizabeth. "Well, my lady. Would you fancy a drive to town today?"

Elizabeth bobbed a quick curtsey. "Indeed, my lord. I think the air would do us good."

"And I say he's lying." Sir Anthony leaned over Sir William's desk, his mouth tense, his shoulders rigid.

"Oh, come now, Sir Anthony." Colonel Melville spoke from the comfortable chair beside the fire, as he inspected his fingernails. "I think you're angry because it was my soldiers who brought him in."

"Brought him in? It was my idea to hold the hedgemaster in the garrison—if they'd been in that medieval gatehouse of a jail, they'd have gotten away scot-free."

"No one's ever escaped from our jail before," Sir William put in.

"That's not the issue here," Sir Anthony said. He glared at Sir William. "I tell you, sir, John Harrington is not Gentleman Niall, and if you persist in believing him—"

"But it makes perfect sense, Sir Anthony," Sir William replied. "Harrington's tall and clean-shaven, he has access to some of the best horseflesh in the county, knows the area like the back of his hand—why, even in his position as

Clonmore's agent, he has an excuse to ride wide and far. Not to mention to come to town and hear all the latest gossip—why, I think it's self-evident, based on your own analysis. You should be proud."

"I know I am." Colonel Melville stretched his short legs out and raised his glass. "I ordered extra rations for the men—they've been working very hard the last few weeks."

"I'm telling you, you're making a mistake," snapped Sir Anthony. He stalked to the window.

"Come, man—you've done well. You've earned every penny of your fee—"

"He's not the right man."

Sir William sighed. "Sir Anthony, Harrington admits it. He knew times, dates, places. He fits your own profile— tall, locally based, clean-shaven, access to horses, reason to know the area quite well—"

"Harrington's a man of business—what do you suppose he's doing with money? Buying shares in the East India Company? He's not the sort to steal, I tell you. Clonmore is the thief, and Harrington's protecting his master."

"Then he's protecting him to the grave," Colonel Melville put in. "He knows he's to die."

"He knew he was to die anyway. What difference does a name make, unless of course, it keeps the blame off the real culprit? And he's counting on being rescued—Gentleman Niall is still at large."

"Addams, get a hold of yourself, man. There's no reason to fret like this. Harrington certainly convinced me. And now," continued Sir William, "we can inform the bishop that the tithe money can proceed to Dublin without further ado—we'll be able to ship it across the sea before the winter storms worsen."

"You can't be serious." Sir Anthony stared.

"Well, of course I'm serious," Sir William said.

"What reason is there to wait, Sir Anthony?" asked the colonel. "We send both Harrington and the money to Dublin. Kill two birds with one stone, so to speak." He chuckled at his own cleverness.

A knock on the door made all the men look up. "Come in," cried Sir William.

A liveried footman peered into the room. "Lady Jane Fitzbarth is here to see you, Sir William."

Sir William raised his bushy white brows. "Lady Jane? What the devil does the woman want with me?"

"I sent for her," answered Sir Anthony. "She's the only person I could find who was here when Clonmore was here as a boy."

"What's that got to do with anything now?" demanded Sir William. "I do believe——"

"And I do believe that Master Harrington is lying to protect his master," Sir Anthony replied. "No one has ever seen these terrible scars that Lord Clonmore is supposed to bear. No one's ever seen him unmasked. And no one seems to know whether or not he wore a mask when he was here as a boy of sixteen. Everyone assumes he's telling the truth— but what if he isn't? What if it's merely a ruse to throw you all off the scent of Gentleman Niall?"

"That's a fairly elaborate ruse," said Melville, as he crossed and uncrossed his legs. He folded his hands over his belly. "Well, let's ask the woman, shall we? If she says he's scarred, will that satisfy you, Addams?"

Sir Anthony's lip curled as he replied, "Yes. If Clonmore can be proven to be scarred, I'll believe that Harrington is really Gentleman Niall. Although I'm quite sure he's not."

"Damn, man, I appreciate your zeal, but, surely you're going overboard? He admits it, sir. What more proof do you need? He knows he'll hang." Sir William threw up his hands, as the footman coughed discreetly. "Well, show her in, I suppose." He looked at Sir Anthony. "Really, man. I don't know what more you expect."

Sir Anthony only shrugged. "Let's see what she has to say."

The door swung wide, and the footman bowed, as Lady Jane paused expectantly on the threshold. "Lady Jane Fitzbarth, Sir William."

Colonel rose and Sir William bowed. "My lady. How kind of you to come."

Lady Jane surveyed each man in turn and looked questioningly at Sir William. "Is something wrong with Susannah?" she asked without further greeting.

"Why—why, no," said Sir William. He walked forward and bowed over Lady Jane's hand. "What on earth gave you that idea?"

"I didn't know what to think." Lady Jane looked at Sir Anthony. "His note only said you wished to consult with me on a matter of great urgency. What else could it be?"

Sir William shot Sir Anthony an exasperated look. "No, no, my dear lady, nothing ails Susannah. It's actually Sir Anthony who wishes to consult with you." He held out a chair. "Do sit." He waited until Lady Jane was settled then sat behind his desk. "Well, Addams?"

Sir Anthony smiled at Lady Jane as he roused himself from his perch by the window. "Forgive me, madam, if my awkward sentences gave you any grief."

"Nothing awkward about your sentences, young man, and well you know it." Lady Jane cocked a jaundiced eye at Sir Anthony. "What do you want with me? I heard you captured Gentleman Niall last night. You'll be leaving us soon enough, won't you?"

The corners of Sir Anthony's mouth folded up in an approximation of a smile. "Soon enough, my lady. But now, tell me, you've lived in these parts how long?"

"Over twenty years. Sir Roland brought me here."

"And you've always found the area congenial? Pleasant neighbors and such?"

"For the most part." Lady Jane sat back. "Pray get to the point, Sir Anthony. I'm not a young woman and I fear I shall be in my grave before you give me the chance to tell you what you obviously want to know."

Sir Anthony gave a short chuckle. "You were here when Clonmore came here as a boy of sixteen? To reacquaint himself with his father?"

A shadow crossed Lady Jane's face. "Yes, we were. I was nursing my youngest through measles—they took him, you know."

Sir Anthony had the grace to look sad. "I didn't know,

Lady Jane. Forgive me, and my deepest condolences. But you were here at the time?"

"Aye," said Lady Jane softly, staring into some place the men could not see. "We were here."

"And you met young Clonmore?"

Lady Jane hesitated. "Yes, I believe so."

"You believe so? Or you did?" Sir Anthony gave her a penetrating stare, and Lady Jane's expression changed from sad to startled.

"What is this all about? Is Clonmore in some sort of trouble?"

Sir William leaned forward. "You've heard that Gentleman Niall was captured last night?"

"The whole county's heard it. You should see the crowd gathering at the courthouse now. 'Tis all the soldiers can do to keep order." She looked at Colonel Melville as though she held him personally responsible.

"Have you heard who it turned out to be?"

At that Lady Jane blinked. "No, I haven't."

"It's Clonmore's agent, Master John Harrington."

"Master Harrington? That nice Master Harrington Susannah was so fond of? Surely not!" Lady Jane looked to Sir William, as if pleading with him to tell her it was false.

Sir William sighed. "I'm afraid so, my lady. He's confessed."

"No!" Lady Jane's jaw dropped. "What did Susannah say?"

"That's immaterial right now, Lady Jane." Sir Anthony leaned down. "Did you at any time see Lord Clonmore unmasked as a young man?"

Lady Jane blinked and Sir William rose to his feet. "No—no, Sir Anthony, I don't believe I ever did."

"You always saw him with his mask?"

Lady Jane looked confused. "Everyone's seen him with his mask—"

"Lady Jane," said Sir William gently, with a chiding look at Sir Anthony, "when Clonmore was young, did you meet him? Did you know him then?"

Lady Jane hesitated. "I-I knew him—"

Sir Anthony opened his mouth, but Sir William spoke quickly. "Lady Jane, if you've told my wife, or some of the other ladies, certain—exaggerations, shall we say, it will remain here privately with us. Can you confirm, as a witness, that Clonmore always wore a mask?"

Lady Jane gave a little shrug and a little shake of her head. She pursed her lips. "I can't. No. I never actually met him then."

Sir Anthony slowly straightened as Sir William let out a long breath. There was another knock on the door. "Come in," barked Sir William.

The footman peered around the door. "Lord and Lady Clonmore to see you, Sir William."

"The devil you say," said Sir William. "What are they doing here?"

Sir Anthony nodded at Colonel Melville. "He called for them."

"Well, you've made such a point that Lady Clonmore is your prime witness, Addams." Melville got to his feet in a huff. "I summoned them. Show them in, if you please."

Lady Jane rose to her feet. "If you don't mind, Sir William, I would like to see Susannah. I'm quite spent from this—this interrogation." She glared at Sir Anthony and swept out of the room. She grasped the startled footman's arm. "Take me to Lady St. Denys."

As her heavy footsteps faded down the hall, Sir William sighed and shook his head. "I don't know what you think that proved, Addams." He would've said more, but the double doors opened wider and Lord and Lady Clonmore stood on the threshold, accompanied by a second footman. "Ah, Clonmore. Lady Clonmore. How kind of you to come so quickly." He reached out for Neville's hand and was satisfied that his grip was as firm as ever. If Harrington was lying, and Clonmore really was Gentleman Niall, he seemed as cool and collected as ever. He bowed to Elizabeth. She looked tired, for the pale skin beneath her eyes was smudged with dark circles. But there was most likely nothing to that. After all, she was a young bride, and if Clonmore were keeping her up at nights, well, that was perfectly understandable. Maybe he even had her breeding already. "And how are you, my lady?"

"Quite well," she replied in a pleasant voice. "We heard you've captured Gentleman Niall, Colonel?"

The little colonel puffed visibly. "Indeed, Lady Clonmore, indeed, just last night—"

"We're relying on you to identify him," interrupted Sir Anthony.

"I thought he confessed?" asked Neville.

"We would like Lady Clonmore's confirmation," said Sir William. "If that's acceptable to you, Clonmore, of course."

Neville looked down at Elizabeth. "As long as it's acceptable to my lady. However, this Gentleman Niall—a ruffian—I wouldn't want—"

Melville coughed. "No one's told you, my lord."

"Told me what?" Neville cocked his head. There was an awkward pause. "Well?" Neville demanded.

"If you don't mind, my lord." Colonel Melville took Neville's arm and led him some distance away from Elizabeth. He spoke softly so that Neville had to lean down to hear him, "We'd rather not prejudice your lady in any way, my lord. If you understand my meaning."

Neville straightened and glanced over his shoulder. "All right, Colonel, as you say."

The colonel gave a little nod. "If you'll excuse me, Sir William, my lady, my lord, I'll have the prisoner brought in."

"He's here?" Sir Anthony's face was red.

Colonel Melville ignored Sir Anthony.

"By God, St. Denys," began Sir Anthony.

"Now, now, Addams, no harm's been done." Sir William shook his head and looked disgusted.

Elizabeth glanced at Neville. His shoulders were rigid with tension, but he wore a careless expression. How could he be so carefree, she wondered, with his closest friend about to take his place? She closed her eyes.

"Come and sit, Lady Clonmore," said Sir William quickly.

Elizabeth looked at the older man gratefully. She knew that Neville disliked him, but she thought him courtly and old-fashioned. There was a long silence, and then the door swung open. Elizabeth hesitated, bracing herself for the sight. She turned around. John Harrington, clad in black from head to toe, and masked with a black silk mask similar to Neville's white one, stood in the doorway, wrists chained together, flanked by four soldiers. For a moment, she remembered the first time she'd seen him—when he was Shane, the outlaw who rode by Gentleman Niall's side.

She pressed her lips together and rose slowly.

"Now, my lady," Sir William said and took her arm to support her, as though he feared she might faint, "take a good look and tell us, as you swear on your immortal soul, is this man Gentleman Niall?"

Elizabeth glanced at Neville. His face was as blank as a stone, but she could read the suppressed tension in every rigid line of his body. Harrington looked her squarely in the eyes, and she flinched. *Forgive me, Master Harrington,* she thought. *I pray that you see this for what it is.* "Yes," she said, almost with defiance. "Yes. There can be no doubt. This is Gentleman Niall—no question."

Sir William sighed audibly, and Colonel Melville beamed. Sir Anthony stepped forward, looking down at her closely. "Are you quite certain, my lady? Take a very good look at him. Are you sure you know this man? Are you sure this is the very man who saved you from a fate admittedly worse than death for someone like you?"

Elizabeth stared up at him. His cold eyes were boring into hers, and for a moment she faltered. *He knows,* she thought. *He knows.*

Then Neville was stepping closer, taking her other arm, and drawing her closer protectively. "Enough, sir, my wife is quite upset enough as it is. Surely you can see that."

"Indeed, sir, enough," said Sir William. "Take the prisoner back to the guardhouse, Sergeant. Take him back and chain him to the walls. There's to be no chance for this one to escape."

Elizabeth swallowed hard and leaned against Neville's

chest. She could hear the rapid beating of his heart as it thumped beneath her ear. Despite his outward calm, he was as anxious as she. She closed her eyes as the room began to spin. Pray God, Neville's plans with Desmond worked. She'd just condemned a good man to die if they didn't.

Seventeen

"They'll come to the bridge at Croissagh's Point by noon." Neville tapped the map with one long finger. He shifted on his heels as the other men leaned in closer to see.

Liam looked up at Neville. "'Twill be the first time we've shown ourselves to the light of day. Are you sure you want to risk that?"

Neville paused. "That's true. But if we trap them on the bridge, they won't be able to maneuver so well." There was a pause as the other men surveyed the map, faces grim in the firelight. The wind whipped the fire into long orange tails, and Neville's horse whickered and stirred. "The boat will be waiting here," Neville went on. "Once I've got him, I'll take him into the water."

Red-haired Rory O'Connell looked up. "Why you?"

"I can swim."

"Ah." Rory nodded.

"What about the money?" Francis McMahon leaned back on his haunches and stroked his chin, his eyes eager in his rough-shaven face.

Neville hesitated. "If—and I do mean if—it should happen that you can get to the money, take it. But you're not to risk yourselves, do you understand? I'm not risking my neck again to save your ugly face, Fran." The others chuckled softly. Neville looked around the circle, from Liam to Rory, then Fran. "Any questions?"

"We are but four," said Liam. "There'll be at least a dozen of them, and in the broad light of day. These are long odds. And where will ye be getting the boat?"

Neville hesitated. He'd struggled with whether or not to tell the other men of their new ally. Well, why not, he thought. If anyone could keep a secret, it was they. "We won't be four, Liam. Remember the Duke of Desmond? He'll provide men who'll cover the other side of the bridge—keep them from turning and running—and the boat. Croissagh's bridge will be surrounded."

"Ah," said Liam, sitting back, while Rory whistled softly. "Now I see. It didn't take long to call in the favor, eh?"

"Not half so long as I would've liked." Neville shook his head. He met Liam's eyes squarely. "The boat will take him to another boat—this one bound for America."

"America?" Rory leaned forward once more. "He's going to America?"

"He can't stay in Ireland any longer," answered Neville, his voice low in his throat.

Liam nodded slowly. "I see that." He reached over and clapped a firm hand on Neville's shoulder. "Count on us."

"I do, Liam." Neville smiled grimly.

"When do we leave?" asked Fran.

"Dawn. Get some rest. Stay here—they're combing the countryside for Gentleman Niall's men."

"You don't have the right man," Sir Anthony snapped.

Sir William leaned back in his chair. The weather made his bones ache. Blasted Irish damp, he thought, as he stretched his legs before the fire. He downed another gulp of whiskey and sighed as warmth rolled through his body. "My dear Sir Anthony. Harrington's confessed. Lady Clonmore confirmed his identity. The bishop is pleased. The lord lieutenant is pleased. Everyone in the county is pleased. You've gotten your money. You should be pleased." Sir William chuckled a little at his own cleverness. "We'll round up the stragglers over the next few weeks and the affair will be done."

Sir Anthony shook his head in disgust. "It's not about the money. That fool Melville is strutting like a cock because his soldiers captured Gentleman Niall. Well, they didn't capture him at all. And you won't let me prove it."

Sir William stared at Sir Anthony. "No, you're quite right, sir. I won't allow you to attempt to prove the unthinkable by insulting a peer of the realm. No one would like that—not me, not the county, and most especially not the lord lieutenant. No one's been robbed for weeks. Take your money, Sir Anthony. And go."

Sir Anthony drew himself up. "I shall do just that, Sir William. You are a very foolish man, sir."

Sir William bolted upright. "That's quite enough, sir." His red face darkened to crimson. "What exactly would you have me do?"

Sir Anthony cocked his head. "I predict there will be some sort of rescue effort tomorrow evening when the troop sets up its camp. The gang hasn't been rounded up, and Gentleman Niall remains at large. And I predict that if you and I go to pay a call on the Earl tomorrow, he'll be absent. And that pretty little wife of his will give us a big-eyed story about how he was suddenly called away on 'business.'" He leaned back and folded his arms across his chest.

Sir William stared at Sir Anthony. "And what if he has?"

"Then we wait, and when he comes home, we take him aside and have him remove the mask. And I'd be willing to wager twice my fee that his face is no more scarred than mine."

Sir William hesitated, thinking furiously. "This could be very ugly, Addams."

Sir Anthony shrugged. "That's a risk I'm willing to take."

"Ah, but you'll be gone in a day or a week or a month. And I'll be left here, sweeping up the pieces." Sir William sighed heavily. "All right. Tomorrow we'll ride out to Clonmore."

"Good." Sir Anthony stood up. "I'm off to bed. Do your

lady the favor, St. Denys, and tell her you won't be home for dinner."

The full moon rose above the trees as Elizabeth stared out over the dark landscape. Behind her, she heard Sorcha moving about the room, stoking the fire, turning down the bedclothes. Neville had agreed that she could stay at Clonmore, and Sorcha had begged to stay with her. Now Neville was out God only knew where, making his plans. The duke had agreed to provide whatever help was necessary.

Elizabeth fingered her locket as Sorcha came to stand beside her. "It's a pretty night, m'lady."

"It is, Sorcha. I think the weather will hold fair."

"I hope so," Sorcha said, with a little catch in her throat. "I don't like to think of him in the jail with nothing warm. I saw what they did to Master Turlough. I don't even want to think about what they will do to him." The two women glanced at each other and Elizabeth saw the tears in the other girl's eyes.

"Don't worry, Sorcha." Even as she said the words, a pang of anxiety shivered through Elizabeth. But she put an arm around the girl and hugged her. "It will be all right, I'm sure of it. My lord will make sure everything turns out all right."

There was a short tap on the bedroom door, but even as Elizabeth answered, "Enter," the door opened and an exhausted-looking Neville stepped into the room. "Good evening, my lady. I hope I don't intrude?"

"Never, my lord," Elizabeth answered, as Sorcha bobbed a curtsey.

"Oh, my lord, beg yer pardon, but is there any word— any news?"

Neville sighed gently. "They leave tomorrow for Dublin, Sorcha."

Sorcha paled, but raised her chin. "And what will happen to him there?"

Neville hesitated. He glanced at Elizabeth. "We won't let him get that far."

Sorcha's face lit up. "You really think there's a way to save him?"

Neville nodded. "I do, Sorcha. I really do. Would you be a good girl and fetch me some supper? Bread, cheese—whatever's in the larder." He sank down into a chair by the fire and closed his eyes.

"At once, my lord." When she had gone, Elizabeth knelt beside Neville and took his hand.

"Neville?"

He opened his eyes and smiled at her. "Forgive me. This is nothing like you've ever imagined it would be, is it?" His eyes twinkled gently behind the mask and his fingers curled around hers.

She laughed and shrugged. "Not at all. Not one moment of it, really. So far." She tugged at his hand. "Will you tell me what you plan?"

"Tomorrow, when they leave, they'll come to a long narrow bridge at a place called Croissagh's Point. We'll attack in the middle of the bridge from both sides—there'll be a boat waiting beneath the bridge to take Harrington downriver. Not far from there, there's a landing just below a place called Ardagh. A coach will take him overland to Cork, where he'll take another ship to America."

"America?" Elizabeth sank back on her knees and stared up at Neville. "But—"

"Elizabeth, he can't stay here," Neville said sadly. "No one will miss him more than I, but—"

"But what about Sorcha?" Elizabeth asked. "She loves him—we can't let him go—"

Neville sighed. "This is the only way. And a great deal of money has been spent to arrange all this—it's far more complicated than you know. Harrington can't stay in Ireland, and to add Sorcha—" He shook his head sadly and ran a finger down the tip of her nose. "I'm not a rich man, Elizabeth."

"What about Kilmara?"

He smiled. "Ah, Kilmara is an asset, there's no denying that. But most of its worth isn't what the bankers call liquid. We could borrow against it, but that might raise questions right now. And without Harrington—" He gave a deep sigh. "We'll think of something, Elizabeth."

There was a knock on the door and Elizabeth rose to her feet and went to open it. She saw Sorcha's eager, hopeful face, and she couldn't bear the thought of breaking the girl's heart. If only there were some way she could help. "Thank you, Sorcha." She took the tray, and saw the questions in Sorcha's eyes. "We'll talk tomorrow, all right?"

Sorcha nodded eagerly. "Then God send you a good rest, my lady. And to my lord."

"Thank you, Sorcha." Elizabeth shut the door gently and turned with a sigh. "'Twill break her heart, you know."

Neville shook his head. He rubbed his eyes through the mask as Elizabeth set the tray down on a low stool beside the chair. He plucked an apple off the tray and bit into it savagely. "What would you have me do, Elizabeth?"

She shrugged, then settled down on the opposite chair and watched him devour the apple to its core. "I just wish there were some way—"

"There will be a way, someday. All right? Not yet. Not now." He flung the core into the fire and tore a piece off the small brown loaf of bread and offered it to her. "No? Don't worry, Elizabeth."

She fingered her locket and sighed, remembering how Molly had tried to comfort her the day she'd found out she had to marry Neville. *It will be all right,* the old woman had said, rocking her back and forth. *It will all turn out.* Molly had been right about Neville after all. And one way or another Elizabeth knew that this would, too.

Neville was gone before the red sun rose. Elizabeth struggled out of a sound steep long enough to feel his harsh kiss on her mouth. By the time she bolted upright, realizing he had left, he was long gone. Sorcha tapped on the door shortly after dawn, still wearing her nightrobe. "Forgive me, my lady, his lordship left so early, and I just had to know where's he gone—is it today—?"

"I believe so, Sorcha." Elizabeth looked away. She had to tell Sorcha about Harrington. It simply wasn't fair. She patted the edge of the bed. "Sorcha, come and sit. There's something I must tell you."

Sorcha perched on the edge of the bed, looking puzzled. "Is there something wrong, my lady?"

Elizabeth started to shake her head, then stopped. Something was about to be very wrong for Sorcha. "Sorcha, I know you love John Harrington. But there's something you have to know. He's going to America. He can't come back here."

Sorcha drew back, staring as if wondering if she'd heard correctly. "America? That's so very far."

Elizabeth sighed. "I know—and I asked Neville, but—Sorcha, it's been very difficult to arrange all this—"

"I hadn't thought, you see." Sorcha's face was sad. "I suppose I thought he'd move to another place in Ireland—but to America?"

"I'm sorry, Sorcha."

"I never thought I wouldn't see him again." She knit her fingers over her belly and flushed. "My lady," she whispered, "I bear his child."

"Oh, my." Elizabeth sank back against the pillows. "Oh, Sorcha. Then we must find a way. Are you sure you want to go with him? You must leave your family—are you sure you want to do that?"

"I'd follow him forever, my lady." Sorcha's tears spilled down her cheeks. "But even if he doesn't want me to go, please, at least help me see him once more—he must know that his child is coming."

Elizabeth sat up. She pressed the locket in her palm, and suddenly remembered her grandmother's voice as she'd said good-bye. *Buy yourself a trinket.* "The sovereign!" she whispered. She sat up. "Sorcha, I've just remembered. The day I left my grandmother's house in England, she gave me a gold sovereign. I'm sure that has to be almost enough—at least. Come, get dressed, and get packed. Neville told me where the boat was coming ashore—some little town called—" she paused. "Artha —Arta—"

"Ardagh?" Sorcha asked.

"Do you know where it is?"

"I've heard the name—it can't be too far—"

"Well, we'll find someone to take us there. Let's hurry—we don't know what time they expect to be there."

Sorcha leapt off the bed and seized Elizabeth's hands in hers. "Oh, my lady, I'll send back the sovereign, I swear, but I'll never be able to repay your kindness."

"I'm not expecting to be paid back, Sorcha. Now go, hurry." Hurry, she thought as she fumbled into her clothes. For first they'd have to go to Kilmara, just to retrieve the sovereign.

She'd managed to make herself barely presentable, when Sorcha knocked once more. She eased the door open with a tray in both hands. "I brought us some breakfast, my lady."

"Sorcha, you're quite sure about this?"

"Never surer. I wrote a letter to me mam—would you see that she gets it, my lady? And that she knows I love her?"

"Of course I will," Elizabeth said quickly. She gulped a quick swallow of tea to cover the surge of her emotions. "Did you tell the grooms to saddle us two horses?"

Sorcha nodded. "And I talked to m'brother, the one who works in the gardens. He knows the way to Ardagh. He'll take us there—but I had to promise him you'd give him a sugar cake every day for a month."

Elizabeth laughed. "He can have sugar cakes all year, if he wishes."

They finished eating, and Elizabeth took a last look around. "All right, let's go."

Elizabeth paused at Neville's office door. "Wait a moment, Sorcha." She pushed open the door and went to his desk. She knew he had several pairs of pistols. Was it possible he'd left at least one pair behind?

She opened the gun cabinet and smiled. "Come here, Sorcha," she called.

"Aye, m'lady?"

"Here, Sorcha, take one. Something makes me think we might be wise to have these."

"Do you—do you know how to use it, my lady?"

Elizabeth smiled grimly. "It's the one useful thing my father ever tried to teach me."

• • •

Rory was the lookout. He raised his arm and beckoned to the others. "They're coming."

Neville craned his neck and saw the line of bobbing heads as the soldiers marched in loose formation. In the center of the double column, a rough wagon jounced between the ruts. Harrington sat in the back, a soldier beside him, with two more in the front. He nodded at the other men. "All right, men. You know your places. Let's go."

Neville spurred his mount forward. He trotted down the embankment, and waited behind the hedgerows just before the bridge. He peered down into the river. The boatman waved and nodded to his partner. The two began to row into the middle of the river.

The soldiers began to cross the bridge, and Neville looked over his shoulder. "All right," he said. "Fire on my word." The men drew their guns and aimed carefully. Neville waited until the first two soldiers in the column were nearly halfway across the bridge. "Be careful of Harrington."

"Let's hope he's the sense to get down," said Liam.

Neville nodded a quick assent, then aimed once more. "All right, men. Ready. Aim. Now!"

Ragged gunshots rang out. Two of the soldiers buckled in their tracks. The others reacted, some freezing where they stood, some aiming their muskets. From the other side of the bridge, more shots rang out, and three more soldiers collapsed. Neville drew his other pistol and spurred his horse into view. "Stand!" he cried at the top of his lungs, as he pulled on the reins until the stallion reared and wheeled. "Stand and deliver!"

The sergeant shouted for order, as more shots rang out from the opposite side of the bridge. The soldiers scattered, seeking to use the wagon for cover, and Neville galloped forward. He aimed the pistol and fired at a soldier who began to aim, and the man fell back, screaming as the bullet pierced his hand. Neville drew another pistol. Behind him, the other three galloped, riding hard in his wake. He charged up to the wagon, where most of the soldiers lay dead or

wounded. He reached into the wagon and dragged Harrington up. "Hello, John," he said, firing at a soldier who lunged
forward with his bayonet. The man fell back as more shots
rang out near their heads. "Time for us to go." He helped
Harrington out of the wagon and, with Liam, helped him toward the rail.

"Niall," cried Harrington. "I was starting to think you
weren't coming."

Neville grinned and held on to him as they plunged into
the water.

Elizabeth reined her horse as they entered the town of
Ardagh. Unlike so many others, it was more than just a col-
lection of cottages on a central square. It boasted a church
on one perimeter, and a small tavern on the opposite side.
Two more streets branched off from the main square, one
heading to the right, the other forking off to the left. A few
empty stalls stood on the square, testimony to a market day,
and opposite the church, a smithy rang with a blacksmith's
hammer. Another street ran past the blacksmith's. The
church was shuttered and barred, to be sure, but the weathered walls still stood, and Elizabeth felt certain that it was
secretly used for its original purpose.

Sorcha's brother, Tim, looked over his shoulder expectantly. "Where to now, m'lady?"

Elizabeth nodded in the direction of the tavern. "Let's go
there. We'll go inside and perhaps someone can tell us
where the landings are."

"Aye, m'lady." Tim tugged his forelock, and the three
slowly walked their horses across the square. Women
paused in their sweeping or scrubbing and looked at them
quizzically, but no one challenged their presence.

Elizabeth slid out of her saddle and swept into the tavern,
followed by Sorcha and Tim. She looked around and, to her
surprise, saw the Duke of Desmond sitting in one corner. He
rose to his feet.

"Lady Clonmore," he said, his voice low, but clearly
taken aback. "You're the last person I expected to see."

Elizabeth extended her hand. "I'm so glad to see you, Your Grace. I need your help."

Desmond glanced at Tim and Sorcha. He drew Elizabeth a little way apart and peered at her anxiously. "Are you all right, my lady?"

Elizabeth nodded. "It's Sorcha. She must go with John Harrington. Neville told me he was meeting the coach here to take him to Cork—please, Your Grace, Sorcha must see him before they leave."

Desmond looked at Sorcha. "Why?"

Elizabeth lowered her voice. "She bears his child. And if possible, she should go with him."

Desmond started. "My lady—"

"She has money for her passage."

"That's well, but what if Harrington—"

"Master Harrington is an honorable man, sir, and I believe he loves her. If he chooses to behave like a cad there's nothing we can do, perhaps, but he should know his child is in the world, don't you think?"

Desmond chuckled softly. "I do indeed, my dear. Well, so be it. You caught me just in time—I was about to go to the dock now."

"But l thought you said—"

"In the stable behind the tavern, my lady. One moment."

Elizabeth walked over to where Tim and Sorcha waited. "It's all right. He'll take us to the dock."

Sorcha closed her eyes. "Pray God they get there safely."

"Wishing won't make it happen," Tim muttered. "Come on, let's go."

They stood outside and from around the side, two coaches rolled out. The duke stuck his head out of the first one. "Follow me," he called.

The strange procession followed the road behind the edge of the village and took a left fork in the road. Another turn brought them to a landing. Elizabeth dismounted and walked to the edge of the dock. The river meandered past her feet, the water brackish and brown. "When do you expect them?" she asked the duke as he walked up to stand beside her.

"Any time now."

Elizabeth glanced at Sorcha. The girl was pale in the afternoon light. "Would it be all right if we waited in the coach?"

"Of course," the duke said. "Let the lad keep the watch." He nodded at Tim, who slid off his horse and tugged his forelock.

It seemed that no sooner had they settled themselves into the coach than Tim's voice rang out. "They're coming—I see them, m'lord, m'lady. I see them!"

Desmond started, and Elizabeth pushed open the door. The heavy weight of the pistol fell against her leg, and, unconsciously, she gripped the butt of the pistol.

She got out, fingering the locket with the other hand. A gunshot rang out.

Sorcha stifled a scream, and Elizabeth jumped. Desmond glanced around frantically. "Get back inside, ladies. Now."

Sorcha immediately ducked, and Tim flew back for cover. The horses whickered as another shot rang out, closely followed by three more.

Elizabeth drew the pistol. A boat bearing Neville and Harrington came into sight, with two other men rowing frantically. A horseman pounded down the opposite shore, loading a pistol. The horseman paused. The boat reached the dock, and Neville shouted, "We've no bullets—"

Horrified, Elizabeth saw the horseman take aim. Elizabeth raised the gun and pointed the pistol, remembering her father's voice. "Aim in the middle, Lizzie, and you can't go much wrong." She pulled the trigger, and the horseman toppled over, even as one last shot rang out.

Sorcha cried out, and Neville looked up, staring at Elizabeth in amazement, as Sorcha ran forward, arms wide, to embrace Harrington. He struggled out of the boat, and Elizabeth saw that his hands were chained in front of him.

Neville hopped out of the boat nimbly. Elizabeth waited. Desmond held out his hand. "Well done, Clonmore."

"Thanks to you, Desmond." The two men shook hands, and the Duke turned to Harrington.

"We'll see to those irons, Master Harrington."

Harrington looked up from Sorcha's embrace. "That won't be too fast for me."

Neville walked over to the coach where Elizabeth waited. "That was quite a shot, my lady."

Elizabeth flushed and looked down. "My—my father. It's the only useful thing he ever taught me."

"And damn useful for me that he did."

She looked up and saw that he was smiling. "You aren't—you aren't angry?"

He laughed and shook his head. "How could I be angry? You saved my life—Harrington's life. That damn soldier on horseback—he was the only one who got away somehow and I was out of bullets. 'Twas naught we could do but lie low." He took her hand and bowed as he kissed the back of it. "No, my lady, I see that you are ever full of surprises." He glanced at Sorcha and Harrington, who were standing a little apart, speaking softly. "I should've known."

Desmond coughed. "Come, we must be off, Master Harrington. I'm handing you off to the stage at Enniscarthy. Time's a-wasting." He looked at Neville. "I'll be in touch."

Neville nodded, still holding Elizabeth's hand. "Aye." Together they walked to Harrington and Sorcha. Her face was radiant, and Elizabeth knew at once that Harrington had said all the right things. "Take care of yourself, man. And the girl." He held out his hand to Harrington, and he took it, shook it hard, and then the two men embraced.

Sorcha looked at Elizabeth, "I'll send the sovereign back, m'lady."

Elizabeth smiled. "Be happy, Sorcha."

"And you, m'lady." She glanced at Neville and the two women smiled at each other and embraced.

Desmond coughed discreetly once more.

"All right," said Neville. "We'll look to meet again."

And then Desmond handed Sorcha into the coach and Harrington climbed in behind her. The coachman took up the reins, and they waved.

Neville looked at Tim. "Take the horses back to Clonmore, boy. Can you find the way?"

"I found my way here," Tim answered. He wiped a tear from his cheek, and Elizabeth felt sorry for him.

"Tim, your sister loves Master Harrington," Elizabeth said.

"I know, ma'am. 'Tis just—we'll all miss her."

"Yes," Elizabeth said sadly. "We will."

"Come, my lady." Neville bowed toward the waiting coach as the boatman leapt aboard on top. "Your carriage awaits."

He handed her into the coach and shut the door firmly. He placed his head back against the cushioned seat and sighed. "You continue to amaze me, Elizabeth."

Elizabeth smiled, knitting her hands together in her lap. "As do you, my lord."

He grinned, then stuck his head out the window. "Take us to that inn in Ardagh, driver. I've a wicked thirst." He poked his head back into the coach and grinned at her. "And a wicked hunger as well."

They reached the inn, and Neville ordered a room and a bath. He led her upstairs to the room and pulled her inside as two maids struggled up the stairs with steaming buckets of water. Suddenly she was shy with him. She drew away to the window as he stripped off his jacket and shirt and came to stand beside her in just his breeches and boots.

"What is it?" he whispered. The black silk of his mask tickled her cheek as he leaned close to kiss her.

She drew a deep breath. The time had come to tell him. He'd seen her shoot a man to save him. Surely he'd believe her now. "Neville."

"What's wrong?" He drew back a little, frowning down at her.

"There's something I have to tell you." She broke away from him and went to stand beside the hearth. "This whole affair—everything—it's all my fault."

"Your fault?" he repeated as if puzzled. "How?"

"It was at the landowners' meeting. I was talking to Lady Jane and Lady Susannah—I mentioned there was a hedge-master at Kilmara. They looked at each other and I know they told someone—for the very next night, Turlough was taken."

"I see," he said quietly. "Why didn't you tell me before?" He sat down heavily on the window seat, and her heart twisted in sympathy at the way the muscles rippled beneath the scarred skin.

"I meant to—I wanted to. But I was so afraid you'd think I'd betray you—and I didn't mean to betray Turlough—"

"Turlough wasn't taken at Kilmara," Neville said softly. "They found him on Clonmore lands. There is no hedge-master at Kilmara. And hasn't been for a long time."

She twisted her hands together.

"Elizabeth, look at me." She raised her eyes to his hesitantly as he continued. "I agree, 'twas an indiscretion. But no harm was caused of it. Turlough knew the risks of what he did. As do we all. Whether it was your words or not—the soldiers were combing through the district. Turlough wasn't the only one they found." Neville sighed heavily. "None of this was anyone's fault but mine."

"Yours?" Elizabeth stared at him, confused.

"I'm Gentleman Niall, after all. We used Turlough as a go-between. Harrington was my second in command. If I hadn't had the idea three years ago, well, none of this would've happened." He spread his hands. "What's done is done, Elizabeth. There's no going back. When I won Kilmara, I knew I was taking a risk. But so far, I'd say it's paid off well. What do you say?" He opened his arms and pulled her against him. She opened her mouth to reply, but his lips came down on hers, and her answer was forgotten in the wave of need that flooded through her like a tide.

It was much, much later when they arrived at Clonmore. Torches burned in the ancient brackets on the great arching tower which opened into the cobbled courtyard. As the coach drew up, the head groom dashed from the direction of the stables. Neville peered out, concern on his face. "What's wrong?"

The groom opened the door as the coachman came to a stop. "'Tis Sir William and Sir Anthony awaiting for you, m'lord. They been here since nigh on noon, and refuse to budge until you come."

Elizabeth gave a soft gasp, and Neville hissed sharply. "What in God's name—" he began, then bit off a curse. "Forgive me, my lady. Come, we might as well face the music."

"But what can they want, Neville?" she asked as he handed her down from the coach.

"I can't begin to imagine," he answered grimly. "And there's only one way to know." Together, they walked into the hall, where they found Sir William sprawled in one of the armchairs and Sir Anthony pacing beside the leaping fire. "To what do I owe this pleasure, gentlemen?" Neville drawled.

Sir William leapt to his feet. "Clonmore. You're back."

"I live here, after all." Neville looked Sir William up and down. "Well, sir? The hour grows late, and my groom informs me you've been here since noon. What do you want of me?"

Sir Anthony gave Neville an icy stare. "We're here to ask you to take off your mask, sir."

Neville gasped softly. "I will not."

Sir William spread his hands. "Come, Clonmore. We'll say nothing—we're not a couple of gossiping hens. But Sir Anthony has it in his head that—well, that *you* are Gentleman Niall—not Harrington as he confessed—and he wants to prove that you wear the mask of necessity and not of deceit. Come, sir, will you show us?"

Elizabeth looked up at Neville. For the first time since she'd known him, his eyes reminded her of a hunted animal. "Go on," she said gently. "I'll leave, if you wish."

His eyes seemed to penetrate to her core. "Do you want to see?"

Elizabeth nodded mutely. He was offering something of himself, she knew, something terribly vulnerable. It was an act of absolute trust.

He looked at Sir Anthony. "Then I will, sir. Not because you demand it. But because my lady wishes it." He raised his hands and untied the mask. The silk slithered through his hands and he raised his head. For a moment, Elizabeth gazed at his profile. His face was clear, unmarked, the chiseled line as proud as a Roman statue carved from marble. She gasped, and then he turned his head. Sir Anthony began to speak, a note of triumph in his voice, but the words died in his throat as the firelight fell upon Neville's face.

Elizabeth bit down on her lip. Knotted rows of twisted scar tissue ran from his temple to just above his ear, the top of which was a lumpen, misshapen mass. Small tufts of black hair grew between the scars, and where his eyebrow should be was a puckered, cratered ridge. He turned away. "So you see?" His voice was low.

"Let's go, Addams," Sir William said angrily. "My lady, forgive this intrusion. My lord, you have my word."

"But—" Sir Anthony began.

"I've had enough, sir." Without further ado, Sir William seized Sir Anthony's arm and practically dragged him out of the hall. The door echoed as it swung shut.

Neville retied the silk around his face and turned to face her. "So now you know."

Elizabeth nodded. "Yes. Now I do."

"Well?"

Elizabeth cocked her head. "Are you expecting me to leave?"

He shrugged. "Do you want to leave?"

She smiled then. "You asked me back at the inn this afternoon what I thought of your winning Kilmara." She spread her arms wide and they came together with a little sigh. Elizabeth clung to him with all her strength, and she felt his long body relax against hers. "May I say, sir, that it's turned into the finest hand my father ever lost?"

SEDUCTION ROMANCE

*Prepare to be seduced...by the sexy
new romance series from Jove!*

**Brand-new, full-length, one-night-stand-alone
novels featuring the most seductive heroes in the
history of love....**

❏ **A HINT OF HEATHER**
by Rebecca Hagan Lee   0-515-12905-4

❏ **A ROGUE'S PLEASURE**
by Hope Tarr   0-515-12951-8

❏ **MY LORD PIRATE**
by Laura Renken   0-515-12984-4

All books $5.99